ONLY A BREATH AWAY

Sarah's hands braced on his chest. Wide, lavender-blue eyes stared at him as her rose petal mouth parted slightly and her tongue flicked across her bottom lip.

All at once it ceased to be a game. His desire flared. Blood pumped urgently, bringing life to his loins. Nate wanted to explore every inch of her exquisite body, to see into her mind, to touch her soul.

With her mouth only a breath away, he whispered, "Sarah—"

The train gave a lurch, toppling her onto him. She gave a soft gasp and leaped up. He reached for her hand, but she backed away. After one last astounded glance, she gathered up her skirts and fled.

He started to rush after her, but she slipped into the berth and closed the curtains behind her. A slamming door could not have been clearer. Nate turned around and threw himself onto his bunk.

Damn, he'd rushed her. He'd been thinking with the wrong part of his body this time and let his desire for her override his judgment. Now he'd driven her away . . .

Other Books by Caroline Clemmons

BE MY GUEST

THE MOST UNSUITABLE WIFE

Published by Kensington Publishing Corporation

THE MOST UNSUITABLE HUSBAND

Caroline Clemmons

ZEBRA BOOKS
Kensington Publishing Corp.
http://www.kensingtonbooks.com

Thanks to my real-life hero, my loving husband, for his continued encouragement, and to my family and friends.

ACKNOWLEDGMENTS

Special gratitude is offered to George Deeming, Curator of the Pennsylvania Railroad Museum, for his in-depth assistance with railroad history.

Sincere thanks to my exceptional critique partners Mary Adair, Sandra Tucker Crowley, and Jeanmarie Hamilton. Thanks also to the Raven Mavens for their guidance: Tricia Allen, Liz Scott, Earl Staggs, Dee Stuart, and Mark Troy.

ONE

January 15, 1885
Lone Pine, Arkansas

Sonofabitch! The bastards are burying me!

Nate Bartholomew braced against the coffin sides and grappled the terror that pumped through him. The wooden box dropped for long, heart-stopping seconds, then bounced hard. Supreme willpower prevented his outcry. Dirt thunked onto the pine a few inches above his head while dust sifted inside the case. He bit back a cough.

Total darkness enshrouded him. The complete absence of light accelerated his panic. Stifling heat pressed in on him despite the bitter wind he'd heard above ground.

What happened to Monk? His friend had promised to get the coffin on the next train to anywhere. Out of this crazy town. Away from the angry mob before anyone discovered he hadn't died from gunshots at the saloon.

All sounds ceased. Senses sharpened. He smelled copper.

Good God Almighty, help me!

His wounds had reopened, and his life seeped from him. Would he bleed to death before he suffocated? He tasted dust on his tongue, felt grains of dirt on his face. Each breath choked him.

Mustn't cough, uses too much air.

Terror surged again. How much time had passed? Had the

gravediggers left? He bent his legs a few inches, then shoved hard against the flimsy pine. Again. Again.

Watch out, you bastards. Hell hasn't got me yet.

February 1, 1885
St. Louis, Missouri

"Sarah Rochelle Kincaid! As if it's not bad enough, a Kincaid inheriting a bordello. You stop acting like one of the trollops right now. Quit gawking at the other mourners and try to look like the respectable lady you are."

Sarah winced at Aunt Lily's terse whisper and bowed her head for the funeral ceremony. Some ceremony. The few pitiful words her mother's remains received from a hasty minister who probably wouldn't have spoken to a live Rochelle Jorgensen hardly qualified. Poor Mama. Not even forty years old and nothing to show for her life but a saloon, a few motley friends, and consumption.

Sarah peeked from under her lashes at the other mourners. Her adopted Aunt Lily stood ramrod straight, face puckered like a sour lemon. Sarah regretted bringing Aunt Lily to the cemetery, but it wasn't proper to come alone. In fact, she regretted having brought Aunt Lily with her on the trip from Texas. She had wanted to hire a pleasant companion, one who would sympathize with her poor mother's plight and make the trip interesting instead of an ordeal.

Three saloon girls sobbed into their handkerchiefs, their bright satin dresses as gaudy and tawdry in the daylight as their brilliantly dyed tresses. Sarah had wondered why the girls wore such gaudy saloon clothes to the funeral instead of daytime dresses, but Ruby explained these were the last dresses Mama had given them. With the breeze came the smell of the cheap perfume worn by the girls. Those three, the bartender, and the man who stood guard at the saloon door were the only other mourners at the cemetery. Five lost souls from her mother's short life.

It won't be like this for me. I won't let it.

She wanted friends and family, a stable home, to be respected in the community. When she died, plenty of people would mourn her loss. She intended to leave a legacy of good works—and children, grandchildren, friends who would celebrate all she had accomplished on this earth.

And she wanted to accomplish a lot. To serve others in need as her half sister, Pearl, had served her and their half brother, Storm. To make a change in the lives of others as Pearl did with her healing. To set a good example.

The minister droned on about repentance and the life hereafter. Sarah's gaze roamed the cemetery. Not far away, a lone man stood staring at her little group. Perhaps he had lost someone, too. No, he stared directly at her. My stars, glared would be more like it.

Sun streaking through tree limbs over his head shot his light brown hair with gold. Dressed in a black suit and gray patterned vest, he wore a fancy white shirt and a black string tie. In his hand he held a flat crowned black hat with a wide brim. Could he be some gambler who had known her mother?

A handsome man, she thought, if only he would smile. He braced one shoulder against the tree trunk. She wondered if grief brought him here. He looked angry, not sad.

"Sarah," Lily's harsh whisper caught her attention. "I declare, are you staring at that man during your very own mama's funeral?"

She felt herself flush before she whispered back, "He keeps watching us. I wondered if he knew Mama."

"Half the men in town *knew* your mama. And I do mean in the Biblical sense. Now pay attention and quit embarrassing me."

One more time, Sarah wondered why she let herself be bullied into bringing Lily as chaperone. And why did she let Lily talk to her so rudely? She sighed and admitted she always let others dominate her. What kind of good works could she accomplish if she couldn't stand up for herself?

At first she had wondered why Lily agreed to act as escort, but now she knew the answer. Lily used any opportunity to her own advantage. Her old beau, Harold Vermillion—now an eligible widower—lived near their host and hostess, Harold's brother Walter and sister-in-law Margaret. Wild horses couldn't have prevented Lily visiting St. Louis once she learned Harold would welcome her consoling presence.

The minister ceased his admonitions and mourners filed past to offer condolences. Poor little Faye cried so much the kohl around her eyes smeared into a raccoon mask. Her hair escaped its headdress and tumbled in an iridescent yellow spill down her puce satin gown.

"You know Roxie was the best person in the world. I would have starved if it wasn't for her. She helped me when no one else would."

"Thank you for telling me." Sarah felt as if someone else spoke the trite phrase. "And thank you for coming."

Ruby's orange hair belied her name, but Sarah liked her best of the girls. Lollie and Ruby approached together.

"She's better off," Ruby said, smoothing a crease in the black lace of her red dress. "But don't ever forget she thought of you every day, and was so proud of you."

"That's right," Lollie said. "Kept your little portrait with her all the time."

Though she deeply mourned her mother's death—and life—Sarah had thought herself cried dry. Now she fought tears as she repeated the same phrase, "Thank you for telling me. Thank you both for coming."

The bouncer nodded to her. "Sorry 'bout your ma. She gave me a job when I was awful hungry. Trusted me like I was somebody. I won't never forget her."

"Thank you. That would make her proud."

Bowler hat in his beefy hands, the bartender stopped in front of her. "Reckon we'll be finishin' up our business tomorrow?"

Sarah nodded. "Yes, Mr. Fykes. I'll come to the saloon to clear out the rest of Mama's things. The attorney will meet us there at two, then The Lucky Times Palace will belong to you."

"Been waitin' a long time to have my own place. Still and all, I'm right sorry it come about from Roxie's passing on."

"Thank you. I'll see you tomorrow."

When the last of the mourners had offered condolences, Sarah stood by the open grave. Workmen arrived and shoveled dirt onto the casket holding Mama's remains. Sarah's heart broke for all the pain her mother had suffered. She wanted to stop the workmen, to urge them to let her have more time to say goodbye, but couldn't speak.

She jumped when she felt a firm grip on her arm.

"Come along." Lily pulled at her. "Margaret expects us for dinner and Harold is stopping by later. Thank goodness this debacle is over."

Sarah pushed down the goose-egg sized lump in her throat to defend her mother. "Mama was a good person, Lily."

Lily's nose tipped up. "I suppose everyone thinks his or her own mother is a good person."

"In this case I'm right. She helped a lot of people. Didn't you listen to the people who worked for her?"

Her aunt stopped and shot her a frown, her mouth open in surprise. "No, I did not listen to that riffraff. Surely I hardly need remind you of how your mama earned her living?"

Sarah walked ahead with her head high. Though she felt a blush spread, her heavy veil hid it from Lily. "I know she let the girls take customers upstairs if they chose to, but she didn't do, um . . . that and didn't encourage them to. Cal and Mama were married as well as being professional partners until he died. Mama ran a saloon, a successful business, not a brothel as you said."

Surprised at her own long speech, she wished she had the gumption to remind her holier-than-thou aunt of Lily's own checkered past, but the words wouldn't come.

"Well, it's a sordid business at best. Thank goodness you're selling that awful place immediately."

"Mama had the sale all arranged. Besides, I couldn't very well run a St. Louis saloon from Texas. Mama was proud I have my teaching at home."

"Your teaching? I declare I do not understand why you insist on teaching those low class children in your very own school. If their parents don't want to teach the children English so they can go to school in town, why should you?"

Refusing to be drawn into an old argument with her snobbish aunt, Sarah fell silent. She hated confrontation, and conversations with Lily brought nothing else.

The Vermillion's driver helped them into the buggy as if they were rare porcelain. Lily arranged her skirts carefully. Sarah caught herself imitating her aunt's actions automatically and sighed again. Sometimes she felt invisible, just an imitation of her aunt or her sister Pearl. Not that she minded being like Pearl, but she wanted to be her own person.

That man in black stood watching as they drove past. Lily pointed her nose in the air as if he were unworthy of notice. From beneath her veil Sarah turned her head and returned his stare. What a handsome man—if only he would smile.

Nate watched the two women leave the cemetery in a fancy carriage before dizziness reclaimed him. He held onto a low tree limb and looked for a place to sit before he fell.

"Thought that was you. We heard you was dead. Sorry about your pa, Lucky."

He pivoted toward the voice to face Fykes. "Don't call me that. Lucky Bartholomew is officially dead and so are Nathaniel Madison Bartholomew, Ace Bartholomew, and all the other names I've used in the past ten years. I hope you'll not say differently to anyone."

"Depends on your plans. You staking your claim to The

Lucky Times Palace?" The man carried his bowler in his hands, twirling the brim this way and that.

"Heard you and Roxie's daughter talking. I've no mind to upset your plans. No, you're welcome to it."

He sank onto a stone bench beside a crypt and watched the bartender's eyes narrow in speculation.

"You don't mean you're giving up The Lucky, like that?"

"I'm giving up nothing, just changing sources. That little skirt will share with me whether she wants to or not."

"We had a wire from some sheriff in Arkansas. Came after Cal died. Said you was dead and buried."

"I was, so to speak, even hid out in a coffin. The bastards buried me before Monk could get the coffin out of town on the train. Had to start digging my way out before he got there. Like to have died."

"Monk here, too?" Fykes looked nervous, fidgeting with his hat and frowning.

"On his way. Had some business in Poplar Bluff." Nate didn't want the bartender running to the law with news of his miraculous survival and sought to reassure the other man.

"Look, you got no reason to worry about me. I have to stay officially dead to stay out of jail, so I can't be claiming my share of The Lucky Times Palace. I can't even be seen around town."

Fykes's shoulders relaxed. "Too bad about Cal."

Nate nodded. "Damn right, it's too bad. He always tried to run a clean game. What happened?"

"Breaking up a fight over a poker game. One of the men was a sore loser, claimed the other fella cheated. Cal caught the bullet meant for one of the card players."

"He sent for me. With Roxie sick and all, he wanted Monk and me to take a hand in running The Lucky." Bitterness roiled in Nate's gut. Once again, fate had dealt him a losing hand. No. This time he would make it work, one way or the other.

Fykes said, "After the wire, Roxie thought everything belonged to her. She knew she didn't have long left and started arranging her business. Sent for her daughter."

"What's the girl like?"

Fykes brightened and a smile split his round face. "Right sweet. You know, gentle and refined-like. Got here five days 'fore Roxie died. Roxie must of been just aholdin' on 'til she come. She was a blessing to Roxie at the end, I can tell you. And purty. Lordy, she's a purty little thing."

"Little? She looked to be taller than you."

"Oh, she's a tall woman, all right, mebbe three or four inches under six feet. It's how she acts, you see, real dainty-like. Makes you think she'll break if you don't take special care."

"Couldn't tell much with that veil she wore," Nate said.

"Her hair's darker than Roxie's, more like ale than champagne. Her eyes are blue and turn purple when the light's just right, kinda the color of them wine bottles from Germany you used to favor. And her skin, Lordy, you ain't never seen skin as purty and soft lookin' as hers." Fykes flushed red as a bandana, as if embarrassed spouting such soft phrases.

"Seem to remember years ago the daughter was adopted by some rich family in Texas. You hear about that?" Nate asked.

Fykes scratched his balding head and donned his hat. "Kind of a crazy mixed-up family, I'd say. Half sister's husband adopted her, rich folks I heard. Don't that beat all? Never heard the likes of such before, a man adoptin' his sister-in-law. Hurt Roxie and made her happy all at the same time."

"Well, no rich family adopted me. She's got my money and my mother's jewelry. I need them, she doesn't. No matter how beautiful she is, I'll be relieving her of both. Soon. I refuse to be cheated out of what's mine."

"What you gonna do?"

"Soon as I get what's coming to me, I'll be heading to New Orleans and open my own Lucky Times Palace there." He shivered, and a chill swept through him even as beads of sweat gathered on his brow.

"That's right nice, Nate. Must've been a shock, comin' back to find your pa and Roxie both gone."

"You bet it was. Pa sent for me. I thought I was comin'

home to make things up with them, help with Cal's share of the business. Thought things were finally going right. When I got here, he was dead, Roxie was dead, and this slip of a girl had everything." Another shiver racked Nate's body and he fought to remain seated upright on the bench.

Fykes took a step toward him. "Say, you okay? You look pale as a corpse yourself."

Nate clutched his side. "A gift from the citizens of Lone Pine, Arkansas, two weeks ago. Wounds are infected, but I don't dare go to the doctor."

"You put on your hat. Pull the brim low. Duck your head and come on over to The Lucky. Go round back. Can you make it up the stairs?"

"I reckon." He hoped he could. "The door unlocked?"

Fykes nodded. "Your old room's vacant. All the girls are new since you was here before, so they won't have any idee who you are."

"A safe place to rest would sure be welcome." The thought of a place to sleep, a familiar place with reasonably clean sheets and a lock on the door gave him hope.

"You can hole up at The Lucky 'til you can travel. I owe that much to Cal and Roxie. Still and all, you keep out of sight if'n you want to stay dead to old john law."

"Thanks." Nate set his hat firmly on his head, brim pulled low. "That won't help these festerin' wounds, though."

"I'll send Ruby up to look after you. She's good at patchin' people up."

Nate pushed himself off the bench. "Yeah? Hope she does better with me than she must have with Cal and Roxie."

The morning after the funeral, Sarah opened her eyes to Margaret Vermillion waving a folded paper in her face.

"Wake up, Sarah," she insisted. "Wake up. They've run away."

Sarah sat up in bed and rubbed sleep from her eyes. She

tried to focus on what her hostess said while the woman paced back and forth waving her arms in distress.

Margaret said, "I can't imagine what got into Harold. He's usually so dependable. Of course, Lily always was impetuous. That's what happened to her the first time when she married Wes Stephens instead of Harold."

"Who's run away where?" Sarah asked around a yawn.

"Lily, that's who." Margaret stamped her foot and waved the paper. "Will you listen, Sarah? Lily and Harold have eloped. They left us this letter, but they're on their way to Boston to be married."

"What? That can't be." Sarah slid from the bed, grabbed her wrapper, and stepped into slippers.

"Read for yourself." Margaret thrust the letter at her.

She took the sheet of paper and read.

> *Dear Margaret, Walter, and Sarah,*
>   *I can't let love pass me by a second time. Please try to understand. Harold and I belong together. After our two-week honeymoon, we'll live in St. Louis near his children. I'm sorry to leave you on your own, Sarah, but I'm sure Margaret and Walter will find an escort home for you. Give my love to our family and be happy for me,*
>   *Lily*

Sarah sat on the edge of the bed, her mind reeling. "My stars, it's true. Who would have thought Lily would ever do something so unconventional?"

"Selfish as usual, you mean." Margaret flushed and waved a hand of dismissal. "I know she's your adopted aunt and one of my oldest and dearest friends, but you have to admit she's totally self-centered. Always has been."

"I'm glad she's found happiness after all these years. She waited so long."

Though she sought to remain calm in the face of Lily's surprising news, Sarah's mind whirled with reactions.

Relief flooded her. No more constant censure from Lily. No more reminders of her lowly beginnings and shortcomings.

Panic gripped her. Who would act as her companion on the trip home? What would Grandpa and Drake and Pearl think? Surely they wouldn't blame her. What would she tell them?

Oh, what did it matter, anyway? Now she was free to hire a pleasant traveling companion and enjoy her trip back to Texas.

"You're a lovely girl to take this so well." Margaret pursed her lips in thought. "The Welborns are leaving next week to visit their daughter in Houston. Perhaps you could travel with them."

Sarah remembered the Welborns from a dinner party and suppressed a shudder. Mr. Welborn's sly glances made her skin crawl. "No." She caught herself and added, "Please, don't trouble yourself. It's not necessary. I'll hire a companion. There are always advertisements in the newspaper for women who want to make a journey West."

Margaret patted Sarah on the arm. "Now, don't you worry your pretty head a bit. You go on about settling your business and Walter will make all the arrangements. Are you certain you don't need him to go with you today?"

"No." She spoke too quickly again and the word sounded harsh. She sought to soothe the effect. "Mama had all the details arranged. Her solicitor is meeting me to make certain everything is in order. It's just a formality before I turn over the deed to Mr. Fykes."

"Well, I'll send Jonathan with you when you get your mother's things, just in case."

Sarah sighed. She hated having Margaret's son tagging after her all day. Jonathan Vermillion was about as useful as a parasol in a hurricane, but she wouldn't insult her hostess. Oh, why couldn't she stand up for herself and insist on making her own arrangements?

* * *

The paddleboat glided along the current toward Memphis. Compared to her train ride from Texas, the slower pace of the water vessel allowed Sarah time to speculate on the lives of people in the houses dotting the shoreline and fueled her active imagination. She pulled her new black shawl around her shoulders and wished for her thick cape against the cool night air. At least her black bombazine traveling suit had long sleeves to ward off the chill.

A light breeze carried a blend of odors from the big paddle wheeler and the Mississippi River it cruised. The almost tangible fishy scent of the water and the mud and weeds along the shore blended with the smells of the boat. Her tongue tasted the moisture in the air, but she didn't know if this meant a promise of rain or came from being on the water.

Living near the Pedernales River in Texas had not prepared her for navigating the great Mississippi River. The steady movement of the paddle wheeler plowing through the water lulled her. She lost track of how long she stood at the rail, and started when Mr. Welborn brushed against her.

"Enjoying the trip?" he asked.

She stepped away. He smelled of cigar smoke and whiskey. She liked neither. In spite of their travel together, she still felt an uneasiness toward Mr. Welborn. "Yes. This is a lovely way to travel."

"It could be even nicer." He edged near. "You slip me into your stateroom tonight when I tap on your door and I'll make it plumb delightful." His arm brushed against her breast as he leaned forward.

She moved away again. "You insult me, sir, and your wife." Sarah looked around, hoping other passengers were near. Hatred rose like bile in Sarah's throat. Her instincts about him had proved correct.

He pressed forward. "Now, now, I know all about your mother. Been to Roxie's place a few times, had me some fun with her girls there."

Sarah stepped toward the nearest door, the one which led

to the dining salon, but he grabbed her arm. She tried to pull from his grasp. "My mother ran a business. I'm sorry she had to deal with men like you, but it has nothing to do with me."

"Don't play the outraged virgin, missy. The apple doesn't fall far from the tree." He jerked her toward him.

"Why, you odious man. How would you like it if I told your wife about this?" She tried to pull free, but he held tight.

"She knows about your mother and wouldn't believe the likes of you. You cooperate with me, or I'll tell the captain you propositioned me." His foul breath fanned her face.

"Tell him whatever you wish. I wouldn't *cooperate* with you if I had to swim home." Sarah tried once more to pull away.

Timid she might be, but she was far from defenseless. Her brother, Storm, had taught her to protect herself against unwanted advances. She stamped hard on Mr. Welborn's foot and elbowed him in his considerable gut, kicked him in his other shin, and rushed away. He was lucky she didn't take time to disable him completely. She heard muttered curses as she stepped into the light of the large salon and pulled the door closed behind her.

On deck, Nate stepped from the shadows. When Welborn turned to follow Sarah, Nate stepped in front of him.

"Far too nice a night to go inside, don't you agree?"

"Get out of my way. I'll fix that brassy little chit. I'll call her out to the captain in front of everyone." Welborn put out a hand to shove Nate's arm.

Nate stood firm. "I think not." At Welborn's surprised glare, he added, "Not unless you want to swim the rest of the way with a grappling hook tied to your neck."

"Say, who do you think you are?" Welborn's weasel-like eyes widened and he stepped back.

Nate advanced a step. "I'm no one. No one at all. But I'll be watching that young woman. If anything happens to her, you will be blamed. And I will personally see that you regret it—and that your wife knows what I just saw and heard. I can assure you, she will believe me." He leaned forward, towering over the portly older man. "Treat Miss Kincaid with respect and courtesy or join the fish. You understand?"

"Y—yes." Welborn nodded, his eyes wide with fear. "No need to get upset."

"See you remember." Nate turned and entered the salon.

Now what possessed him to defend the woman in possession of the inheritance rightfully due him? From what he'd seen, she could take care of herself. He credited disdain for Welborn and his type for his actions against the man.

He saw Miss Pure-And-Simple Sarah Kincaid across the room standing next to Mrs. Welborn. She twisted a handkerchief in her hands and looked the prim wallflower. Bright spots of color still decorated her cheeks, but otherwise her pale skin against black clothing emphasized the impact of her encounter with Welborn. She looked ready to pass out now the crisis had passed.

Deliberately controlling his pace to an amble, he stopped a couple of feet from where she stood. He ignored her and spoke to her companion. "Isn't there a musicale tonight?"

"What? Oh, yes," Mrs. Welborn said. "It will begin in a few moments."

Too much rode on this to take any chances. He feared using his true last name. Sarah, as he had come to think of her, might connect the last name with Cal and find it more than a coincidence. In fact, he figured he'd better come up with a name he'd never used. He smiled, hoping inspiration would strike. As always, deception came easy.

"I'm Nathaniel Barton. Perhaps you and your sister will allow me to find seats for you."

The woman preened at his timeworn flattery. "This is our traveling companion, Miss Kincaid. I'm Mrs. Welborn."

"Let's take these seats right over here, ladies." As he stepped behind them, he put a hand at the waist of each woman. Sarah wore a money belt, just as he'd thought. Her jacket almost hid the tell-tale bulge above her small waistline.

Mrs. Welborn fluttered her eyelashes at him. "Oh, we must

save a seat for my husband. He stepped out on deck for a bit of air."

Nate watched Sarah's face harden into a mask. Her fingers worked harder at the black-bordered white linen square. She would reduce her handkerchief to shreds before evening's end if she continued twisting it.

He maneuvered the ladies so Sarah sat between him and Mrs. Welborn with the empty seat on the other side of Mrs. Welborn. "How are you finding the journey, Miss Kincaid?"

She looked straight ahead rather than at him, but answered, "It's been . . . eventful."

She turned her face to his. The full impact of her large lavender-blue eyes hit him. Good Lord. If she'd smiled at the same time, he would have melted like a pool of wax at her feet. On second thought, part of him was growing, not melting. He adjusted his posture to conceal the front of his britches.

Welborn's face when he saw Nate sitting with the two women was worth the price of several boat tickets. The man almost stumbled, but regained his composure and pasted a false smile on his lips.

"Well, well, I see I'm back in time for the show."

"Clyde, this is Mr. Barton. Mr. Barton, my husband."

Nate pushed down a laugh and smiled his brightest. This was the most fun he'd had in a month. Damned if he wasn't enjoying himself.

Nate spoke to Mrs. Welborn, "Mr. Welborn and I met earlier in the evening. You folks going far?" Mrs. Welborn said, "We're going to Houston, Texas, to visit our daughter and her family."

The lights dimmed and the musicians launched into the evening's program. He flashed a warning glare to Welborn before he nodded at Mrs. Welborn. "I wish you a *safe* journey."

TWO

When the music was over, Welborn stood. "Say, Barton, several of us have a card game scheduled. Care to join in?"

"Let me see the ladies safely to their cabins first. I'll be back in time for the second hand."

"There's no need, Mr. Barton." Sarah stiffened her spine.

As far as he could tell, most times it needed a little starch in it. Her creamy satin skin, on the other hand, needed only his touch.

"Nonsense, Miss Kincaid. I would never forgive myself if you encountered any unpleasantness because I had been remiss in my duties as a gentleman."

Mrs. Welborn leaned on his arm. "It's very kind of you. We're through here on the next deck."

To avoid any suspicion of impropriety, he deposited Sarah first, then her traveling companion. But now he knew in which space Sarah stayed, where his money and jewelry were kept.

Damned if she wasn't wearing *his* mother's ring on the trip. It was all he could do not to say something when she took off her gloves at intermission and he saw the rubies on her hand. That very ring was the reason he and his father had the fight that parted them. Cal gave it to Roxie against Nate's protests when the two decided to wed.

His mother had been a genteel lady. The fact that her family disowned her for marrying a gambler didn't change that. The ring should have stayed in the family. He vowed the ring was coming back to him with his share of the money from the sale of The Lucky Times Palace. And his mother's other jewelry as well.

Words he'd said about Roxie to his father haunted him. She had always treated him square. Maybe Roxie wasn't born a lady, but she tried to act as much like one as her job and life allowed. He wished again he could have told her he was sorry, could have told his father the same.

Too bad Roxie got consumption.

Too bad Cal got shot.

Too bad Nate got left out in the cold—again.

But this time he would get his own back. This time he wouldn't let anyone stand in his way, no matter how tempting the morsel. And Miss Butter-Wouldn't-Melt-In-Her-Mouth Sarah Kincaid was as tempting a morsel as he'd ever met.

Sarah hurried up the hotel stairs behind the porter, happy to escape while the Welborns still sorted their bags and complained about the trip, their room, and the crowds. How Sarah would love to be rid of the couple forever. Mr. Welborn had made no further advances toward her on the trip, hardly spoke to her, which was fine with her. When he did speak, his face pinched up as if he smelled something foul.

Mrs. Welborn prattled on and on in the most tedious way. Her endless stories of past social events centered around herself, except for her occasional remarks intended to insult Sarah and her mother. Sarah turned to look down the stairs to see if she had truly escaped the tiresome couple and gasped.

That man in black—he'd introduced himself as Nathaniel Barton—had been at the cemetery. He was always around on the boat, too, and now he was here in their hotel in Memphis. He trailed behind her as if he hadn't a care in the world. Surely it was coincidence. Lots of people traveled from St. Louis to Memphis every day.

The porter stopped in front of a room and opened the door.

He stood back for her to enter, but not before she saw Mr. Barton at the next door. He even glanced her way and smiled as he nodded his head in greeting.

My stars, he's staying in the very next room to mine.

What kind of hotel would allow a single man on the same floor as a single woman? She fought down panic as she dealt with the porter, then locked the door behind him and slid the bolt. Alone in her room, her imagination ran its course as she paced. Had she strayed into a den of iniquity?

No, that couldn't be. Mrs. Welborn assured her this was a family hotel suitable for a young woman. After all, the Welborns registered here, too. How did Mr. Barton come to be in the room next to her? It wasn't proper. What would people think? What would they say?

She caught herself. The Welborns were the only people here she knew, and she hardly cared what they thought other than their reports back to the Vermillions and Aunt Lily. Even they could hardly blame her for the hotel's room assignments.

This Mr. Barton could not mean her harm. There'd been ample opportunity on the paddle wheeler had he intended to hurt her. They'd never had a conversation on a personal level. His comments had centered on the trip and the weather, not a hint of anything improper and always with others nearby. Perhaps his constant presence was a coincidence. Just the same, he made her nervous. She felt like a rabbit waiting for the wolf to pounce whenever Mr. Barton was near.

In the midst of her concern, she admitted his presence offered reassurance that she was protected from others. Surely he would rush to her aid if she needed assistance. Her instincts proved right regarding Mr. Welborn. Perhaps she should rely on intuition in this instance. She wished she were more decisive, not a victim of warring emotions.

She raised her skirt and checked the little double-shot derringer given her by her brother, Storm. Best to be prepared. The little gun still rested securely in its garter holster on her thigh. Storm had insisted she practice until she was a fair shot. Would she have the courage to use the weapon against a human? She doubted it, but its weight reassured her.

Sarah spied the door connecting her room with the one in which Mr. Barton resided. Rushing to check the lock, she stopped. She must not let him know she suspected him of following her. Very slowly she turned the knob of the connecting door. Locked. She released a heavy sigh.

Curiosity nudged her. Kneeling, she peered through the keyhole. The opening framed him as he pulled a fresh shirt from an open valise on the bed. Shucking his jacket and waistcoat, he took a pistol from his waistband and placed it on the bed beside the satchel. He unbuttoned his shirt.

She knew she should move away but couldn't. Oh, my stars! He might dress like a riverboat dandy, but this gorgeous man was no weakling. Trouser fabric pulled taut against trim hip muscles when he turned and bent over the things on the bed.

Her mouth went dry as a Texas dust storm. She watched him turn back to face her. He removed his shirt and tossed it behind him on the bed. Then she saw the bandage across his shoulder and another at his waist. She wondered which side of the law he was on when he got those, but thought she knew. The wrong side, of course.

He picked up a fresh shirt and she caught the ripple of muscles across his chest as he slipped the shirt on. His movements were swift and powerful, not the sluggish ambling she had witnessed in public.

Occasionally in summer she had caught glimpses of her brother, her brother-in-law, and the hands at the ranch with their shirts off. Unlike their tanned torsos, Mr. Barton's pale skin made her fingers tingle to touch the brown chest hair that converged in a vee at his belt. She wondered how far below his waist the pelt descended. A pool of warmth gathered at the base of her stomach.

My stars, what disgraceful thoughts.

Where did they come from? They weren't proper. No, not

at all suitable. Being away from home must be having a poor effect on her.

Never before had such scandalous ideas entered her head about any man. She didn't have these thoughts about Peter Dorfmeyer, and everyone expected her to marry Peter. Mr. Barton was the most attractive man she'd ever seen, but she must get her wayward thoughts under control.

Buttoning his shirt, Mr. Barton stepped from her view. When he returned and glared at the keyhole, she froze. Surely he couldn't know she watched him. She sank further to the floor and sat with her back against the door.

Sarah pressed her hands to heated cheeks, shocked at her own behavior. She was no better than a window peeper. What on earth had come over her?

A sudden thought assailed her. What if he planned to look through the keyhole as she had? Taking a hanky from her cuff, she draped it over the doorknob so it hung across the tiny opening. No, that wouldn't do. It kept sliding off. She rose and opened her traveling bag and took out a shirtwaist. Hanging it on the knob, she stepped back. Perfect. It looked as if she used the handle for a hook.

She crossed to the vanity. Not taking time to change from her traveling suit into a dress, she contented herself with pushing stray hair back into her chignon and grabbing her shawl. With any luck, she could purchase her train ticket while her neighbor had his dinner.

Sarah walked briskly to the train station. A line greeted her at the ticket window. Oh, well, she loved watching people, so she wouldn't mind the wait. Taking her place in the row, she surveyed the other prospective passengers wandering to and fro. She studied the clothes of other women, compared them to her own black clothing. In her head she made up stories of who they were and where they might be headed.

A young boy bumped with a wham into the man in front of her. The child's hand darted into the man's pocket and out with a flash and secured the lifted wallet under his shirt. Probably no more than seven or eight, the lad wore the dirtiest clothes Sarah had ever seen. His hair might have been blond at one time, but it and his skin had gone a long time without touching soap and water.

"Oh, excuse me, sir." The boy's large blue eyes were the picture of innocence when he gazed up at the man.

Sarah gasped. What should she do? She couldn't bring herself to cause a scene by screaming, but neither could she stand by and let the child rob this man.

"Steady, you little ragamuffin." The victim placed a hand on the boy's shoulder. "Slow down and see you're more careful next time."

"Yes, sir, sorry. I will, sir." The boy moved swiftly away into the crowd.

Sarah took off after the little thief. He looked over his shoulder and she motioned to him. His eyes widened in alarm and he ran. She gathered her skirts and rushed after him, weaving around groups of people.

When she had almost caught up with the light-fingered boy, she thudded against a solid wall of chest.Mr. Barton grunted and clutched Sarah's shoulders, then dropped his hands and made a slight bow. "Why, I believe it's Miss Kincaid, is it not? Are you in some sort of distress?"

"No, it was nothing." She peered over his shoulder but the thief was nowhere in sight. "I thought I saw someone I knew, but I was mistaken." She felt her cheeks flush again with guilt. Their collision must have jarred his injured chest, but she couldn't ask him about it. How could she explain that knowledge?

"Your traveling companions—Welwoods or Welworths—are they with you?"

"No. The Welborns were tired and planned to have dinner sent to their room." She thanked heavens for that. Eating with the odious Mr. Welborn soured her stomach. But now this man who, for all appearances, followed her everywhere had neatly trapped her. A shiver of apprehension skittered down her spine, but she stood mesmerized by his tawny eyes.

As if he sensed her fear, he offered a crooked smile and proffered his` arm. "May I escort you back to the hotel?"

"I was . . ." she stopped. Her nerves jangled with alarm, but she strove to appear calm. She preferred buying her ticket in private. If he hadn't yet learned where she headed, she didn't want him to know her exact destination. "That would be very kind, um, Mr. Barton."

"Bit cool this evening, isn't it?"

My stars, didn't the man ever talk about anything but the weather? Maybe he was one of those gorgeous physical specimens with the brain of a rock.

She sighed and answered, "Yes, there's a chill in the air. I suppose we're in for more winter."

What should she do? Panic turned her stomach in knots. She should send him on his way, but didn't know what to say or do. Hating herself for her timidity, she once more flowed with the easiest course and allowed herself to be escorted back to the hotel.

In the lobby, he patted her hand where it rested on his arm. "Would you be kind enough to join me for dinner?"

"Thank you, but I have several things left to do before I retire. Good evening."

She slowly climbed the stairs. From the landing, she watched him enter the dining room. She counted to ten, then descended the stairs and crossed the lobby. Only when she safely stepped outside the hotel did she slow her walk.

The breeze rose and turned icy. She'd forgotten her warm serge cape, but dared not take time to fetch it now.

Before she reached the depot, she heard a hiss from between two buildings.

"Ssst, Lady."

She stopped and searched for the origin of the sound. From the shadows a child beckoned to her. It was the little thief. "You!" What nerve he had accosting her in public!

"Please don't yell or nothin', lady. I need your help."

"Why? To help yourself to my money as you did that poor man's?"

"No. I'm sorry I had to take his money, but he looked awful well-heeled. I'll bet a swell like him has so much he won't even miss it, and we need it real bad."

"We? So you have accomplices."

"I don't know what that means. What I got is a little sister who's real sick. Since you're a lady and all, and you didn't turn me over to the coppers, I thought maybe you'd help her."

Indecision tore at Sarah. This might be a trick, a trap to lure her into danger. On the other hand, a sick child struck a most sympathetic chord. Still she hesitated. Ladies didn't go off down dark alleys. What should she do?

She asked, "How do I know you're telling me the truth? You could have friends waiting to cosh me on the head—or worse." If there really was a sick child, she couldn't turn her back.

"Honest," he pleaded, "my sister needs your help bad."

"Who are you, and what's wrong with your sister?" She stalled for time to make her decision.

"My name's Luke, hers is Cindy. She's not breathin' right, and it scares me. I done ever' thing I know, but she's gettin' worse."

She was hooked, and she knew it. "Where is Cindy?"

"She's back down this alley. It's only a short way. Please, lady, you gotta help her."

Sarah peered behind the boy, but only shadows and darkness greeted her. She darted a look over her shoulder to see if anyone else witnessed the exchange in case she needed to cry for help.

Oh, no. There came Nate Barton ambling along as if he hadn't a care in the world. Strolling as if he had no particular destination in mind, he headed straight for her. She touched her skirt where the little derringer rested on her leg and nodded to the boy.

"All right. Take me to your sister."

"You'll have to be careful where you step," Luke cautioned. "There's traps and shit everywhere. Just follow me real close."

Sarah wondered what traps he meant, and if he meant the foul word literally. From the acrid smell, she suspected he meant exactly that.

He stopped at a shack where half the roof had caved in. It looked like a death trap. Sarah had seen packing crates constructed more sturdily than this shanty.

The boy knocked three times, paused, and knocked twice more. She heard the sounds of scraping from inside before the door opened a crack. She wondered who opened the door, almost decided to turn and run herself.

Luke stepped in and held the door open for her. She took a deep breath and forced herself to enter the sad excuse for a shelter. The boy closed the door and placed a wooden barrel against it.

The chill of outside was nothing compared to the frigid room. A small fire burned in a large bucket. With the steady draft whistling through, she wondered how smoke survived to hang in a heavy haze over the room. Nearby, a single lantern on an upended wooden barrel furnished light for the place. On a ragged pallet, a tiny girl coughed and gasped for air.

Sarah took stock of the room. For the first time, she saw the other boy in the corner shadows. Older, maybe nine or ten, he stood with his hands at his sides. His dark hair and clothing blended with the dim recesses of the room, at first making his pale face appear to float in the dark. In one hand he held a large board with a huge nail in the end.

"That's Joe. He don't never talk, but he helps me take care of Cindy."

Luke rushed to his sister's side. "Cindy, this here's a real lady. She's come to help you."

"Are you an angel?" The little girl gasped out the words in a whisper, her blue eyes wide with wonder.

Sarah knelt beside the child and pressed a hand to her forehead. Cindy's skin burned with fever. "No, dear. I met your brother outside, and he thought I might be able to help."

Blond hair wet with the exertion of breathing clung to her head. A rack of coughing left the girl limp. She turned her face to the side and closed her eyes.

Sarah met Luke's worried gaze. "How long has she been like this?"

Luke shrugged. "I don't know, maybe a week. We kinda lost track of time since we been here."

"We have to get her out of here." She paused to plan her words. No point in lying to him. "She won't ever get well unless we get her to a clean, warm place where she can rest and see a doctor right away."

Tears ran down the boy's cheeks. He leaned near Sarah's ear and whispered. "Is she gonna die?"

"Not if we get her help. I'll take her to my hotel room and then send for a doctor. You and Joe gather up all your stuff and come with me. I'll carry Cindy."

"We cain't both leave." Luke looked at Joe, then back at Sarah. "We take turns leavin' so nobody won't steal our place here."

"I'll find you a new place. Think how scared Cindy would be without you."

Sarah bent and picked up the little girl. "Wrap that blanket around her."

Luke helped tuck the blanket around his sister. Though Cindy was slight, her dead weight for the three blocks to the hotel and up the stairs worried Sarah. What if her arms gave way and she dropped her? Her mind struggled for a solution. She didn't want to involve the authorities and that left only one choice.

"There's a man outside near where you found me tonight. Maybe you saw me bump into him earlier when I was chasing you." Luke nodded his head, so Sarah continued, "His name's Mr. Barton. Find him and ask him to come here with you. Tell him Miss Kincaid needs his help. He can carry Cindy."

Reluctantly, Luke left the shack. Sarah motioned the other boy over. "Joe, if you have a trunk or valise, please put your things in and help gather up Luke's and Cindy's belongings."

Joe hesitated, but moved to a small trunk. With one hand he raised the lid and added a soiled pink dress and scuffed pair of brown shoes from the floor. He stepped back and stared at her defiantly, his jaw set and eyes hostile, the board still in his grip.

Deciding the trunk belonged to Cindy, Sarah asked, "Does Cindy have a coat?"

Joe nodded. He laid down his weapon and rummaged through the clothes until he pulled out a bright blue coat. Sarah let the blanket drop and Joe placed Cindy's arms in the sleeves and gently slid the coat on her shoulders. Then, he retrieved the blanket and tucked it carefully around the little girl.

"I'll let her lie back down until her brother returns." Sarah knelt and smoothed Cindy's small frame on the pallet.

When Luke's coded knock sounded, Joe grabbed the board, scooted the barrel away from the door and took his armed stance in the corner. The door flew open and Nate stepped in with gun drawn and his other arm raised to ward off a blow.

"Good Lord, woman. I thought you'd been shanghaied." He looked like a man ready for any challenge, a man used to danger.

"The same thought occurred to me but, as you can see, three homeless children hardly pose a threat."

He glanced to his right at the boy in the shadows. "The nail on the end of that club could do a lot of damage."

"Luke summoned you so we could ask your help getting Cindy and their things to my hotel room." She'd forgotten his injuries. Would he be able to carry the child?

He stuffed the gun into his waistband. "What's wrong with the kid?"

"I don't know, probably pneumonia, but she can't stay here."

Looking from one child to another, he crossed his arms. "You think the hotel people will let you bring this lot in?"

My stars, they would look a fright to others, wouldn't they? It couldn't be helped. She had to save these children.

"Of course, they will. I'm quite willing to pay extra, so why would they care? I can't carry her that far, though. I hoped you'd carry Cindy while the boys and I bring their belongings."

He looked around the shabby room, his disgust apparent. "Probably all have fleas. Who knows what else?"

"Mr. Barton, please. The fact that they are children does not mean they are deaf. Show some sensibility. Will you help us or not?"

"Okay, okay. What do I know about kids?" He knelt and picked up the little girl.

In spite of his hard words, he held her gently, placing her head on his shoulder and patting her back softly. Cindy slid her small arms around his neck. His tenderness touched Sarah.

Luke and Joe helped Sarah add more things to the trunk. When Sarah would have added a small box, Joe stopped her and shook his head.

"You want to leave this here?"

He nodded. She set the box aside.

"Aren't you afraid someone will take it?"

He shook his head and wielded his board like a baseball bat.

Luke understood at once. "Joe, you got to come with us. We stick together, 'member?"

Joe looked from Sarah to Nate and back to Luke, then shook his head again.

Nate glowered at the boy. "Listen, you little—"

Sarah stepped in front of him. "Joe, please come with us. Cindy is used to having you near as well as Luke. She'll be worried if she can't see you, too."

Joe bit his lip, looking caught in indecision, so Sarah pressed on. "Just stay with us until Cindy is well. If you don't like it, I promise to help you find a new place to stay that's better than this one."

Luke tugged on Joe's arm. "Yeah, come with us. You know I gotta stay with Cindy. She'll be real scared like if she don't see you around too."

"Joe, please," Cindy pleaded before coughing seized her.

Still reluctant, Joe picked up his box and added it to a satchel in the corner. He shot a defiant glare at the adults, but picked up the carryall.

Sarah tried reassuring him with a smile. "You won't need the club now."

His look let her know he wasn't leaving the board, so she didn't argue. At least he agreed to accompany them. What she would have done had he refused, she had no idea. One thing she knew for certain. She would never have been able to leave a child in this horrid place.

How long had these children been here? How had they survived?

THREE

Sarah's thoughts flew to her own childhood when her half sister Pearl provided for her and their half brother Storm. Would she and Storm have been reduced to living like this otherwise? No, she knew, one way or another, Mama would have made certain she had a decent place to live.

A new wave of grief for the sacrifices Mama made and her death almost overwhelmed Sarah. She pushed her personal feelings aside and concentrated on saving these three children.

Their walk to the hotel attracted some inquisitive stares, but no one said anything to them. Nate's steps never faltered, except for a few turns in the alley when Luke warned them about traps. At the hotel they hurried up the stairs and into Sarah's room, in spite of the alarm on the desk clerk's face when he saw them. The two boys lagged behind staring at the lobby and stairwell as if they had never seen a place so grand, but Sarah urged them ahead with the promise of a tour later.

Sarah whipped back the cover of her bed and made a place for Cindy. Nate lay the girl down gently and threw the ragged blanket on the floor across the room. He slid the coat from her and tucked the sheet under her arms. Luke and Joe went to the other side of the bed, but divided their focus between Cindy and wide-eyed stares at the room.

Cindy's eyes opened. "Where are we?"

Luke stretched across the bed and patted her hand. "Ain't this a grand place? You 'member, this lady's gonna make you well, you'll see."

Cindy's gaze shifted to Joe, who nodded in agreement.

Sarah brought a towel and basin to the bedside table. "That's right, Cindy. You're going to stay here and get well. Joe and Luke will be right here with you."

She bathed Cindy's face and hands. Removed from the smoky shack into a warm hotel room, Cindy's breathing had already eased slightly. Sarah's mind raced ahead making plans. She needed Nate's room for the boys, and someone had to find the doctor. She'd deal with the Welborns tomorrow.

"Mr. Barton, may I ask another favor of you?"

He looked nervous, ready to bolt and run. "What is it?"

When he turned that golden-eyed gaze on her, she almost lost her voice. He was the handsomest man she'd ever met.

She said, "Perhaps you could tell the desk clerk we need a doctor. While you're there, you could get another room for yourself. I believe there's a connecting door between your room and mine, which makes it ideal for the boys."

She flushed, remembering the time she'd spent peeking through the keyhole. No wonder she thought of him by his first name. How could she think otherwise of a man she watched undress?

"First we better get a story straight. You can't just haul kids around without permission from their family unless you have a good reason."

Sarah blanched. Intent on saving these children, she never stopped to think about permission from anyone. Surely if anyone cared about them, they wouldn't have been where they were in the first place. Still, she had better do this right. She scooted a chair around to face the bed and sat down.

"All right, children. This is Mr. Barton. My name is Sarah Kincaid. You may call me Miss Sarah. Luke, do you have any family here?"

He looked sad and hung his head. "No, ma'am. When our folks died, the preacher kept us 'til he wrote letters and got answers. He sent us here on the train. Our mama's Aunt Sue was supposed to meet us and take us to her house to live, but she didn't never come."

"You mean someone put you on the train alone?" Sarah asked.

"Miz Simmons rode this far with us, but she had to leave us to catch another train. She said to wait on a bench in front of the depot 'til Aunt Sue come. We waited all day."

"Didn't anyone from the depot see you all alone and try to help you?" Sarah's blood started to boil.

"A mean-eyed man kept talking to us, kept saying we should come with him. He tried to pick Cindy up but she wouldn't let him. Kicked him hard. I got scared, but that's when Joe come and helped us get away."

"And how long ago was that?"

The two boys looked at one another, then shrugged.

"Do you think it was over this many days?" She held up all ten fingers.

Both boys nodded and Luke added, "I think it was a long time ago when Ma and Pa died. Reckon it was right after school started. When the preacher got a letter back, he said we'd be at Aunt Sue's in plenty of time for Christmas."

Nate decided to take over the interview. At this rate Sarah would take all night and into next week.

"What's your last name, kid?" he asked Luke.

"Davis."

He pointed to Joe. "You read and write your name?"

Joe nodded.

Nate took paper and a pencil from the desk and handed them to the boy. "Write your full name."

With his tongue caught between his lips, Joe slowly scrawled his two names.

Nate picked up the paper. He could barely read the awkward letters scribbled in varying sizes. For a kid his size, this one hadn't spent many hours in school.

"Josiah Edwards. Edwards is your last name?" When Joe nodded, Nate continued. "Listen Josiah Edwards and Luke

Davis. You stay here in this room with Miss Kincaid while I go fetch the doc and get this room thing arranged. I'll have the cook send up some food for your supper." Before he opened the door, he paused and turned back.

"I'll tell the desk clerk and doctor you're relatives of Miss Kincaid's. You've been visiting other relatives, and we met your train here. Got that?"

Both boys nodded. "Miss Kincaid, may I have a word in private?"

She followed him into the hall, worry marring that gorgeous face. Her petulant rosebud lips made him want to kiss them into a full-bloomed smile.

"Surely we don't have to lie about the children," she said, her disapproval obvious. "Or teach them to lie as well."

Just what he'd expect from a naive busybody. "We covered that. You think the people who run this hotel are going to let a single woman bring in three ragamuffin kids? You don't want them shipped to some orphanage, do you? Tomorrow I'll start asking around, see if I can find out anything about them. Unless we turn up some kin, stick with my story."

"Yes, I can see you're right." She turned a full smile on him. "Thank you for helping us. You're being very kind." Her smile slammed right into him, churned his gut into mush. And damned if those lavender-blue eyes didn't suck him right in. He'd better be careful or he'd be paying her to take his inheritance from him.

"You be thinking what you'll tell those people—Welborn, isn't it? They're not going to hang around while you play nursemaid to a sick girl."

The silvery tinkle of her laugh caught him off guard. "Now that's an unexpected bonus."

When she closed the door behind him, he stomped down the hall. If he didn't get roped into some of the durndest things just to make a few dollars—or get back what should be his.

Not only had he wasted a ten-dollar gold piece to get the room next to Miss Butter-Wouldn't-Melt-In-Her-Mouth

Sarah Kincaid, but now he had to spend more to get a second room on the same damn floor. Good thing he beat that swine Welborn at cards. He had to give it to Miss Priss Kincaid, though. She went with that Luke kid right off into a dark alley. Took guts. And stupidity. No telling what or who might have been waiting.

Remembering the encounters he witnessed with Welborn on the boat and with the kid, he understood several things. One, someone had instructed her in defending herself. Two, the shy and proper little lady had a temper. Three, she had a real soft spot for kids. Better file those facts away for the future.

When the food came, Sarah thought Nate had ordered enough for several meals until the boys stuffed down most of it. Their manners were atrocious and both were far too dirty to even be in the room with food, much less eating. Sarah insisted they wash their hands, but made no other criticism. She decided to choose her battles. She wanted the children to accompany her to Texas. Pushing now might alienate both boys.

She hoped the doctor hurried. If they were at home, Pearl would know exactly what to do. Sarah had a fair idea, but she had none of Pearl's store of herbs and remedies with her, not even anything to make a poultice or rub for Cindy's chest.

In the meantime, Cindy drank warm tea and swallowed some chicken soup. Her breathing grew worse from the exertion, but Sarah thought the nourishment would help. Who knew when or what the child had last eaten? She was asleep when Nate returned with the doctor.

Dr. Wells confirmed Sarah's fears. "She's got pneumonia. Needs at least a week in bed here before you take her on a train ride." He looked around the room, must have noted it was one of the more luxurious rooms offered by the hotel. "You'll be taking the sleeping cars when you leave?"

While waiting for the doctor to arrive, Sarah had decided to reserve one of the new Pullman cars straight through to the

Kincaid Springs depot. "Yes. We'll take a Pullman car all the way. We won't even have to change trains."

He scratched his chin. "You might be able to get away in three or four days if you can keep her in one of the beds on the train, then. I'll stop around tomorrow and see how she's doing."

When the physician left, Nate stood by Cindy's bed examining a key. "Going across the hall. I'll move my things and open the boys' room from the other side."

With the connection opened up, Sarah showed Luke and Joe their sleeping quarters. Luke took to it right away, bouncing on the bed in glee, but Joe looked wary. Nate strolled back in while she tried reasoning with Joe.

"You can both sleep at the same time. No one can bother you. Leave the connecting door open or closed, your choice."

Joe motioned to the hall door.

"You'll have the key and the door will be locked."

Joe shook his head and held up two fingers.

Before she could continue her argument, Nate walked to the armoire and shoved it in front of the hall door. "No one can come in now unless you move this for them." He pushed a washstand near the opening between the rooms. "When you're ready to sleep, you can push this in front of the door if you're afraid. Got it?"

Obviously puzzled, Joe nodded. His wide eyes watched Nate's every move.

Nate knelt in front of Joe. The boy stepped back, but Nate met his gaze and pointed to the door between rooms. "You can leave that door open or close it. It won't make any difference. No one here will ever bother you. Not in *any* way. Understand?"

Joe met his gaze but made no movement. Nate gave him the key and stood. He took Sarah's arm and ushered her into the room in which Cindy lay sleeping. The door closed behind them and they heard sounds of the washstand being moved.

My stars, she thought. If they won't trust me enough to leave the door opened all the way, how will I ever convince Joe and Luke to come with me to Texas?

"He's so afraid of being trapped and attacked. You'd think he would be happy to have such a nice place to sleep after that horrid shack he's been in for who knows how long."

Nate paused, as if choosing his words carefully, then said, "I suspect the boy's had some bad things happen to him."

Sarah snapped, "Of course, he has or he wouldn't have been living there in the first place."

"No, Ma'am, I don't think you understand." He looked back at the closed door between the two rooms and shook his head. "I believe that boy has had terrible things done to him." Owing to the line of work her mother was in, he hadn't expected her to be shocked. Maybe the rich folks she lived with protected her.

Sarah wondered why Nate repeated himself? She said, "I know he has. There's no telling who's been trying to steal that horrid shack from them. It's a wonder to me they've survived."

He turned her to face him and held her arms so she met his gaze. "What I mean is, I think he's been used as, um, as a girl by a man or men. Do you understand what I mean?"

"No, I . . ." His meaning jolted through her. A boy used as a girl? She'd read of such things happening in classic literature, but couldn't really understand it, found it hard to believe it happened in real life, especially in this day and age. "Oh. Oh, no."

She thought she might throw up, so she rushed to a chair and sat down. "You mean someone did . . . that. . . to him? Poor Joe, what a horrid life he must have had."

Tears gathered in her eyes and she struggled to hold them back. She still felt ill, nauseated at the thought. How could anyone treat a child that way?

Nate's voice softened and he knelt in front of her. "Sorry, I shouldn't have been so blunt. Didn't you notice how he moved away from me, how he watched my every move?"

She sniffed and pulled her handkerchief from her cuff to dab at her eyes. "I thought it was caution because he doesn't trust adults. I never thought of anything like . . . that."

He stood. "You'll have to give him plenty of room, Sarah. Sorry, I mean, Miss Kincaid."

"No, please, call me Sarah. You've helped us so much. And I'll call you Nate if I may." That's how she thought of him anyway. Nate with the strong shoulders and muscled chest. Nate with eyes like a wolf. Nate, who made her think silly schoolgirl thoughts and her body react in odd and startling ways whenever he came near.

"Yes, please call me Nate. That boy won't trust either of us easily, especially not me. Don't be upset or push him."

"As long as he'll stay here, I'll be happy. Time later to worry about convincing him to move with me to Texas."

"You need help here right now?" he asked.

My stars, yes, she needed help. She needed his strong arms around her to comfort her while she rested her head against his broad chest. She needed his smooth words easing her fears. Too many things had happened, too much to absorb and deal with.

Taking a deep breath, she stiffened her spine. "You've done more than enough. Cindy's sleeping and her breathing's easier. I'll sit with her in case she wakes, but thank you."

She wanted to tell him not to leave her alone. After the doctor's diagnosis for Cindy and the troubling revelation about Joe, she needed him to stay. He wouldn't even have to talk to her, but she needed his presence.

"Then I'll be right across the hall. About midnight I'll come over and take a turn watching the little girl."

"That's not necessary, but thank you again." She wished she could ask him to stay in her room tonight. What would he think, though? No doubt he'd take it as an invitation for much more. She almost risked it.

He opened the door. "Sarah, so you'll know, I told the doctor and desk clerk we're engaged. Seemed the easiest explanation for my being around." With a click he was out of the room before she could respond.

The nerve of the man. Telling people they were engaged

without even consulting her took gall. She worked herself into a state, but reason returned.

Nate was right. People would talk, and she hated to be the center of gossip. Lord knew she had more than enough of that as a child in Tennessee. She'd been so careful to avoid any impropriety in their new home when they reached Texas. True she'd helped Pearl with her restaurant for a few months until they'd sold it, but working for her sister really wasn't improper in spite of what Lily said. And hadn't she put up with Lily's shenanigans and tried to act every inch a lady for the past seven years?

She touched the ring on her finger. Rubies set in hearts. Scandalous to wear such fanciful jewelry while in mourning, but Sarah loved it. Mama had slipped it from her own finger and placed it on Sarah's, and Sarah wasn't about to take it off. Cal had given it to Mama to wear as a wedding ring, but it could easily be an engagement or betrothal ring.

Scooting an armchair beside the bed, Sarah wondered what being engaged to a handsome man like Nate Barton would be like. For one thing, he'd probably have kissed her good night. Her fingers touched her lips. She'd never been kissed, not by a man. Billy Jenkins when she was fourteen hardly counted.

Billy had caught her behind the church and planted a wet kiss on her lips before she knew what happened. Storm thought it was funny when she told him, but that's when Storm showed her ways to repel unwanted attention from a man.

She glanced at the proper little black-enameled watch pinned to her bodice. Nine o'clock. Only three hours and Nate would be back.

From the adjoining room she heard the scraping sounds of the washstand against the floor. The door opened a crack and Luke crept through. "Is she really gonna be all right?"

Though she had wondered herself earlier in the evening, Sarah nodded. "She'll be feeling better in no time. See, she's already breathing better."

He looked close to tears and patted his sister's hand where it rested on the covers. "I tried to take care of her, honest."

"Of course you did. I'll bet no other brother could have managed as well for so long, Luke. She's lucky to have you."

"You think so?" He brightened a little. "Joe helped me. I couldn't have done it without him."

"You make a good team. Why don't you go to sleep now and enjoy that nice big bed? In the morning we'll see about getting you cleaned up and into some different clothes."

"Joe won't sleep in the bed. He thinks it's a trick and he made him a place underneath. Got his club right beside him. It ain't a trick though, is it?"

"No, it's not a trick. Maybe when Joe sees how well you sleep in the bed, he'll change his mind."

Luke chewed on his lip then asked, "Suppose maybe I ought to stay in here and take care of Cindy? I could sleep on that little cot you had brought in for you."

"I'll stay with her. If she wakes up and is afraid or asks for you, I'll come get you. Mr. Barton will be back in a few hours to help me take care of her tonight, so you can rest easy. After all, you and Joe have been taking care of her a long time. It's our turn."

"If you're sure. It's been a awful long time since I slept in a real bed. I ain't never slept in one that nice."

"Then it's time you did. Good night."

"Good night." Luke slipped back through the door. This time he left it open a crack. Sometimes mere inches measured giant progress.

Nate worded the message carefully so the telegraph operator wouldn't be able to understand it. No telling when some key man was working with the law. Monk had said he would check for wires every time he stopped. Nate sent the same wire to four cities, all addressed as agreed to Mike Masterson. It was a clean name, one they hadn't used before, just as Barton was clean for him. He finished the message and handed it to the telegraph operator.

Delayed in Memphis Central City Hotel STOP Here until Friday then Kincaid Springs Texas STOP Nate Barton END

If Monk got one of the wires, he would get here before Friday and know who to ask for. If not, he knew where to find Nate. All Nate had to do now was go back to do his shift at babysitting for Miss Lovely-To-Look-At Kincaid and bide time.

"You what?" Mrs. Welborn clutched at her throat with one hand, her mouth agape.

"I'll be staying here in Memphis for a few days until the little girl can travel." Sarah braced herself for Mrs. Welborn's outrage. She wasn't disappointed.

"I've never heard of such a thing." Mrs. Welborn looked like a steam engine, cheeks red, breath huffing around her shrill voice. "Taking in beggars off the streets. Staying unescorted in a hotel. Traveling alone. In spite of Lily's efforts to educate you in the finer aspects of life, you obviously take after your mother."

"Thank you. My mother was a fine woman."

Mrs. Welborn's eyes bulged and her face reddened. "She was a trollop."

"That's quite enough about my mother. You didn't even know her." She took a deep breath to stay her anger. "These children need me and I'll stay until the little girl can travel safely. I'll hire a companion to accompany me on the trip."

"Hmph." Mrs. Welborn's nose tilted upward. "Probably find an adventuress looking for a chance to rob you."

"Perhaps. One thing I can guarantee, she'll be far more pleasant than you and your lecherous husband." With that, Sarah turned and left the Welborns' room.

Pausing outside the door, she fought to calm herself. She felt she might throw up—or pass out. My stars, what had come over her? Never in her life had she been so rude. True, Mrs. Welborn deserved her wrath for those awful comments about Mama.

Still and all, she couldn't believe she had spoken so harshly to a woman more than a generation older than herself.

Sarah regained her composure and hurried down the corridor to her own rooms. Once inside, she closed the door and leaned against it, closing her eyes in relief. My stars, it felt good to stand up for herself for a change, to speak her mind. It was even harder than she'd imagined, though. She wondered if she would ever be able to do so again.

Nate sat slumped in a chair near where Cindy slept. He looked up from the book he'd been reading. "Tough meeting?"

She opened her eyes and nodded. "Not pleasant, but it's over. I've placed an advertisement in this evening's paper for a traveling companion."

His eyebrows raised and he sat up straight. "You've what?"

"Since the Welborns are leaving today, I'll need a traveling companion. I've placed an ad in the paper."

He seemed to consider his words before he said, "I thought, since I'm on my way to Texas as well, I'd travel along with you and offer my protection as your traveling companion."

Of course you will, she thought. No matter how hard she tried to accept his assistance as generosity of spirit, she couldn't keep herself from questioning his motives. And wondering about the wounds hidden by the bandages she'd seen through the keyhole. The man frightened her at the same time her fascination compelled her to him.

You're just a rabbit, Sarah. This wolf will get you unless you're careful.

She said, "That's very kind of you. However, surely you realize it's not proper for a single woman such as myself to travel without an older female chaperone. I hope to find someone who is both pleasant and good with children."

Nate looked irritated, but said only, "I think I should accompany you as well, to assist with the boys and all. There are cads about who prey on women. My presence would discourage their interference." Then he took a deep breath and his face became inscrutable.

And who will protect me from you? Sarah wondered. "That's hardly necessary. I teach school in Texas. Each weekday I instruct twenty-five students of varying ages, so I'm quite capable of looking after three small children. In addition, I'll have the assistance of whomever I hire as companion."

His expression remained indiscernible, except for those tawny eyes. For a second, Sarah was sure anger sparked there. Anger and something else. Wolf or lamb, which was he? She thought she knew.

She drew herself up and continued, "Certainly you've been a great deal of help. I appreciate all you've done, of course. Sitting with Cindy while she's ill, making arrangements, watching out for the boys while I did errands and such. But with the companion I'll hire and in a private rail car, I assure you everything should go smoothly from now on."

"Caring for them night and day is a little different from teaching," he said. "And you might want my presence to ward off anyone like that Welborn fellow."

Had he known Welborn was a lecher? Recalling her encounter with the odious Mr. Welborn, she weakened. "You . . . You're welcome to ride in the Pullman car with us if you wish. There will be plenty of room and it should be a pleasant trip."

"I believe I'll take you up on that offer." He watched her as if he appraised her, but neither his voice nor his face gave a clue to his assessment.

Sara wondered at his thoughts. Was he up to something or genuinely offering his help? Either way, Cindy and the boys liked him, and they would enjoy having him near. If he traveled in the same rail car, Sarah would get to see him then, as well. Pushing down the sudden knowledge she also enjoyed his company, she wondered what he had to gain by accompanying them.

What sort of man volunteered to help with children who were not even related to him? Maybe a lonely man, one who longed for his own family. Maybe a man who had an ulterior motive, but what would it be? She didn't think it was seduction. After all, he'd made no unseemly moves. In fact, he'd been a perfect gentleman.

She slid her fingers to her waist, checking the money belt she wore. He couldn't possibly know about the money. What harm could come of his accompanying them?

She said, "There are so many people seeking to take advantage of travelers, it's true your presence might deter them if it doesn't take you out of your way." And if you're not one of them, she thought. "Where was it you said you're going?"

Nate looked back down at his book and said, "Oh, you may not have heard of it. Little place thirty miles or so West of Austin called Kincaid Springs." He looked back at her, his face a mask. "Say, isn't that an odd coincidence, Kincaid being your name?"

Panic gripped her. Could he have known her destination? She'd been careful not to mention a specific place in Texas within his hearing. "I . . . I live near Kincaid Springs. What takes you there?"

"I'm meeting business associates."

"What kind of business?" she snapped. She would have sooner pegged him as a gambler than a businessman. Handsome as the devil, she suspected he and sin were frequent companions.

"It's quite confidential. I'd be betraying my colleagues if I told you more at this stage."

"Oh." Possibilities whirred in her mind but nothing fit.

"I'm sure you understand. One word at the wrong time can sink a venture."

She didn't understand, but she nodded. "Yes, of course."

What kind of venture attracted Nate Barton? Probably something totally disreputable. No matter. A large and muscular man like Nate in attendance would deter any lechers like Welborn on the trip. She would take advantage of Nate's offer and then send him on his way when she reached the safety of her family. How hard could it be to dismiss him once she reached Kincaid Springs?

FOUR

Nate snorted at himself and threw his jacket on his bed. Who would ever have thought he'd be playing nursemaid? For that matter, who would believe Lucky Nate Bartholomew—make that Nate Barton—would be caught dead taking care of three brats and keeping his hands *off* a delectable feminine morsel like Miss Pure-As-The-Driven-Snow Kincaid? No one, that's who. He could hardly believe it himself.

A smile forced itself as he admitted a soft spot for the sick kid, Cindy. He laughed. That he had a soft spot at all came as another big surprise.

Cindy was a good little thing, though, and never complained or made any trouble. The two boys reminded him of himself, especially Luke. They were good kids in spite of helping lighten a few purses along the way and knowing some of the tricks of living by your wits. Who could find fault in that?

Joe obviously had had some horrible experiences and didn't trust anyone, not that Nate blamed him. Never let your guard down, that was his own motto. He'd do well to remember that now in spite of Miss Sugar-And-Spice, with her hair like pale moonlight and eyes the purple-blue color of a flower he'd seen once on a vine in New Orleans.

Would you listen to yourself?

Nate snorted again in disgust and sat down to take off his boots. At least the kids made a perfect excuse to stick like glue to Miss Goody-Two-Shoes.

Damned if she didn't have the nerve to wear his mother's

ring right in front of him. Yeah, so she didn't know it belonged to him or had once belonged to his mother. It didn't gall him any the less to see it on her finger.

Nate had searched through Miss Too-Good-To-Be-True's bags while she was off talking to the Welborns and arranging her newspaper advertisement. Cindy slept and the two boys were in their room. Nate'd found the sapphire and diamond earrings and necklace, but had left them. He wanted it all, all he had coming to him. She must still have the money belt on her. Since that first evening on the riverboat, he'd been careful never to touch her other than to offer his arm.

That would change. He had plans for little Miss I'm-A-Teacher before he left for New Orleans with all that was his.

With any luck, Monk would arrive before they left for Texas.

The chaperone she insisted on hiring—even though she claimed she was perfectly capable of taking care of twenty-five children—would make carrying out his seduction more difficult, but he thrived on a challenge. One way or another, that delectable damsel and all her assets would be his. Smiling at the thought, he lowered the lamp and crawled into bed.

Three days later, Joe and Luke squirmed on the sofa as if they would bolt at the first chance. They had been scuffling, but now sat wiggling and giggling at some joke shared between them. At least they had agreed to take baths and wear the new clothes she bought them. Cindy looked like a pale angel propped up against the bed pillows in her new blue nightie. Her breathing rattled less and her face shone like peaches and cream rather than the deathly pallor of a few days ago.

Sarah sat at the desk in her hotel room waiting for the fifth and final applicant for traveling companion to arrive. What would she do if this woman proved no more suitable than the others? She straightened the sheets of writing paper on the desk. Perhaps she should have wired Pearl to ask her advice. Or, she could have asked Storm to come escort her home.

No, what a silly thought. Surely she could hire her own traveling companion. Hadn't she wanted to do just that?

The first woman to answer the advertisement two days ago had been so frail and senile she would have been no help whatever with the children, and might actually have required care herself on the long journey. Sarah hated to turn her down, but there was no point in hiring someone like her.

At least Sarah was able to say no. A week ago she probably would have accepted her because she felt sorry for the poor woman. Sarah chewed her lip, remembering she'd slipped the woman some money before sending her away. Not the most businesslike reaction, but the woman needed assistance.

The second applicant came yesterday, a florid, rotund woman who spent most of the interview discussing her various ailments. My stars, one hour in that woman's company had caused a headache. Sarah shuddered at the thought of spending days on end with her. Turning her down was not difficult. The third and fourth applicants earlier this afternoon turned out just as unsuitable, and it wouldn't surprise Sarah to learn either of them was escaping prosecution for a crime.

A knock on the door prompted Sarah to say, "Remember our secret signals, and mind your manners."

Joe looked tall and proud in his new clothes but didn't seem to trust Sarah any more because of them. Nevertheless, he looked presentable when he answered the door and stepped back to admit a woman of medium build. Her hair was that peculiar soft shade some blondes become instead of gray, and her brown eyes sparkled. The lines in her face looked planted by a lifetime of smiles. She wore a white shirtwaist and plaid skirt. Sarah noticed both the top and skirt had been mended in numerous places, but with skillful stitches.

"Good afternoon, young man. I'm Mrs. Galloway. 'Tis about the advertisement I've come, the one for a companion to Texas."

Joe bowed and swept out an arm to indicate she should enter. Sarah motioned to the chair in front of the desk.

"Won't you have a seat, Mrs. Galloway? I'm Sarah Kincaid. May I offer you some tea before you tell me about yourself?"

"Now wouldn't that be lovely?"

Luke wheeled the tea cart over. His hair stood up like a rooster's comb on top, but he seemed proud of his new clothes and shoes. He gave Mrs. Galloway a plate and napkin while Joe offered her a plate of treats. Sarah poured the tea, and the boys helped themselves from the treat tray as if it were not the third time this afternoon they had done so. Luke set his plate on a table by the sofa, then fixed a plate for Cindy.

"What lovely children. Would they be yours, now?" Mrs. Galloway asked.

"I . . . in a way." Sarah launched upon Nate's story.

"I see," said Mrs. Galloway.

Sarah suspected the woman actually did see the way things were, so she asked, "Won't you tell me about yourself?" She felt the tension ease out of her shoulders. Finally, a woman who seemed pleasant and intelligent, suitable for the tasks.

"I'm a widow. I've been living with my widowed daughter, Betsie, God love her." A shadow crossed her face and her lip trembled, but she raised her chin and continued, "She just remarried and I thought she and her new husband would enjoy having the house to themselves. I'll find a new life out West."

Sarah wanted very much to be businesslike. She tried forcing aside the compassion which had surged forward during the woman's brief speech. Once more empathy surfaced, and this time Sarah gave in to the sensation.

"Have you any objection to children?" Sarah asked, not putting into exact words that the children would accompany her to Texas. She watched the two boys to see if they understood the implication of her question. Joe and Luke seemed engaged in a contest to see who could push the most tea cakes into his mouth. Good thing Mrs. Galloway's back was to them.

"None at all, especially not little saints like these."

Joe picked that second to choke. He dropped his plate, and

his cough showered crumbs across the carpet. The sound startled Mrs. Galloway and she turned in her chair. Joe looked at Sarah, then at Mrs. Galloway, his eyes wide with horror.

Sarah said, "Are you all right, Joe? Take a few sips of your tea, then please pick up your plate and the large crumbs."

Joe brushed up every crumb he could find. Luke helped while Cindy giggled until she started coughing.

Mrs. Galloway laughed. "Isn't that just like a boy?"

Joe looked relieved and went back to cleaning up.

Luke took him a new cake to replace the spilled one. "You talk different, Mrs. Galloway. It sounds nice."

"Now aren't you a smart lad to notice," Mrs. Galloway said. "I'm from Ireland."

"Is Ireland far away?" Cindy asked, her voice faint and gasping from giggling and coughing.

"Oh my, yes, lovie. 'Tis across the ocean I came on a big ship with my husband and daughter. My man's dead now, may the Lord have mercy on his soul. Been gone these three years it is. In all the world I've only me daughter left."

"Cindy is recuperating from pneumonia," Sarah explained. Behind the woman's back, both boys rubbed a finger on their chin, their signal that they approved of her.

Sarah said, "Mr. Barton, my, um, my fiancé, will be traveling by rail with us. I've reserved one of the special Pullman sleeping cars through all the way to Texas. We plan to leave the day after tomorrow. Will you be available to travel then? That is, if you want the position."

Relief flooded Mrs. Galloway's face. "Sure and that would be grand."

"Would it be possible to leave your daughter and son-in-law in the morning and help me get ready for the journey? I'll reserve a room for you here in the hotel if that's all right. It will make it so much easier on the day we depart."

Mrs. Galloway looked around the room, as if measuring its worth. "Sure and that would be grand. I'll be happy to help."

Sarah hastily took a sheet of hotel stationery. "You'll want to let your daughter know where you're going and where she can write you. This is my address in Texas. Once we're there, I'm certain someone in my family can find you a permanent position and place to live if you wish."

They agreed on a salary and Sarah fixed the departure details with her, then gave her a small advance on her pay.

"You can count on me, Miss Kincaid. I'll be here early tomorrow." Mrs. Galloway grew younger and straighter with each disclosure. By the time she left the hotel suite, her face beamed with a smile and her steps fairly danced.

Nate watched the woman leave Miss Sweet-As-Sugar-Candy's hotel room and walk down the hall to the stairs. Her walk told him she'd been hired. Well, she looked sharp, but not sharp enough to keep Lucky Nate Bartholomew—damn, make that Nate Barton—from getting what he had due him. The female hadn't been born who could best him.

He waited until the woman turned the corner to go down the stairs before he stepped across the hall and rapped on the door. Once inside the room, he watched the two boys rolling on the floor in a mock battle. He expected the prim spinster to be aghast, but she surprised him.

"You hire the lady who just left?" he asked.

She nodded. "Her name is Mrs. Galloway. I'll tell you all about her later. Right now, we have plans to make. You boys can wrestle later in your own room."

With a last gouge in the ribs, Luke rolled away from Joe.

Although she had her back to them, Sarah said, "Stop that. Would you both move the sofa near Cindy's bed and sit down so I can talk to all three of you at once?"

The boys looked at one another with wide eyes.

Luke pulled at her sleeve. "Miss Sarah? How'd you know I jabbed Joe after you said stop?"

"I have a brother and three nephews and I teach school

back in Texas. I know a lot about children." She smiled. "Besides, I used to be your age."

Nate tried to picture Sarah as a child scuffling on the floor with her brother. Nothing came. Immediately another picture planted itself in his mind, one where he and Miss-Pure-And-Proper rolled on the rug in the throes of passion. He pictured that golden hair spread across the rug, her bare skin inviting his touch.

Pushing that vision firmly from his mind for the time being, he took one end of the sofa and the boys lifted the other. They set it perpendicular to the bed just short of the pillows and Cindy's head.

Sarah moved her desk chair near the armchair already beside the bed. She motioned Nate to take the more comfortable chair and she sat in the wooden one.

Nate had spent the better part of two days looking for clues to the kids' parents, even went to Pinkerton's. Nate Bartholomew, as the respectable Nate Barton, hired a detective. Each time he thought about it, he almost laughed aloud.

Carefully composing his face, he hoped this wasn't going to take all day. He still had a little business of his own.

Sarah knew she had to choose her words carefully for the difficult battle ahead. In her mind she had gone over her words a dozen times. She prayed her plan worked. "As I said, we have big plans to make."

Arms across his chest, Joe looked ready to run for the door. Luke and Cindy gave their full attention. Nate looked as rapt as the kids.

"You know Mr. Barton and Mrs. Galloway are going to travel with me to Texas. I've hired a special railroad car to ride in, one with comfortable chairs, beds, a kitchen, and a privy."

Cindy's face screwed up and tears ran down her cheeks. "But you're my angel. I don't want you to leave us. I like it here. I love you."

Sarah's heart sang. She touched Cindy's hand and leaned over to plant a kiss on her forehead. "I love you, too, dear. And we can still be together. That's part of my plan."

Joe narrowed his eyes. Poor boy wouldn't trust anyone.

Luke slid to the edge of the seat and asked, "What do you mean you and Cindy can stay together? Cindy's my sister and I take care of her."

Nate flashed her a sympathetic look, but remained silent.

"Not just Cindy. All of us. You and Joe and Cindy and me, we can stay together. You three can come with me and be my children and live on a big ranch in Texas. We'll be a family."

Nate put up a hand. "Wait, Joe, hear all she has to say."

It was then Sarah noticed Joe poised to run for the door. The hall door, not the one to his room.

"Joe, please listen to me. I wasn't lying when I said I would find you a place as good as the one you had if you wanted me to. I meant it. But, please, just listen for a while and think about what I'm saying."

Joe settled back on the sofa, but looked unconvinced.

Sarah continued, "I live on a ranch with my sister Pearl and her husband Drake. They have a big house with lots of bedrooms. Cindy could have her very own room, and you boys would share a room like you do here until we get our own house. You could have a dog, and each have a horse."

The boys exchanged looks, and Luke seemed interested. Joe tried to hide it, but she could tell she had caught his notice also. Cindy's little face shone with fascination.

Sarah pressed on while she had their attention. "There will be other children your age to play with. You'd be warm in winter and cool in summer. We live near the river so there's lots of fishing and swimming in warm weather. My sister is about the best cook in the whole world and there are always lots of cookies and pie and cake around."

Cindy said, "Oh, I want us to go, don't you, Luke?"

Joe nudged Luke and made scrubbing motions.

Luke nodded and asked, "Would we have to take baths?"

Darn. That Joe sure knew how to fight dirty.

"Yes, you would," Sarah admitted. "But the house has one of the new bathing rooms. One of the men who works on the ranch, Mr. Isaacs, arranged an ingenious system where the water runs right to the bathing room. No one has to haul buckets of water to take a bath. There's even a boiler to heat some of the water."

Nate added, "I'll bet you'd have lots of places to run and get dirty again."

"That's right." She nodded. Nate seemed instinctively to know what to say to the children while she, a schoolteacher used to children, was having a hard time. "You could play by the barn, or in the meadow, or climb giant trees. My nephews built a play fort near the river. Sometimes my brother Storm takes them camping and they get to sleep under the stars and cook out on a campfire."

Joe nudged Luke again and made signs like digging.

"Would we have to work hard?" Luke asked.

"No, but you'd have responsibilities. On a ranch everyone has to do his fair share."

"What're res—resbilities?"

She looked at Nate for support. He leaned forward, elbows on his knees.

"Jobs you do. A man always has responsibilities. That's how you know you're not a baby anymore. I'll bet you two would have to help bring in the wood for the stove. Probably help feed the chickens, things like that."

She smiled her thanks at him, then turned back to the children. "You wouldn't have to work very much, just help out a little like my nephews do. The main job of children is to play and grow strong."

The two boys exchanged surprised looks, as if the concept of having play a part of their lives was new.

"Who are the other kids?" Luke asked.

"My nephew Robbie is six and Evan is almost five. They help me gather eggs each morning when I'm home. As Mr.

Barton said, they help feed the horses and chickens and bring in the wood for the stove. Then there's the baby named Parker, but he's too young to work."

She turned to Cindy. "I have two nieces, also. Katie is four, and Beth is three. You can play with them. They have dolls, a little doll house, a little tea set for parties, and a big swing in a tree by the house."

"Oh, let's go with her," Cindy pleaded with the boys.

Joe shook his head and motioned for Luke and Cindy to go.

Her heart broke. How could she leave this troubled child behind? She couldn't, of course, but she hadn't much time. She had already reserved the train scheduled to leave just over a day later. Maybe Luke would help convince Joe to go with them.

"You don't have to decide now, Joe," she assured him. "Think about it and we'll talk about this some more tomorrow."

Sarah explained her arrangements with Mrs. Galloway while they ate supper in the suite. Nate nodded as if he approved of all she told him, but his face wore that mask again. For some reason she couldn't fathom, she very much wanted him to think her mature and capable. She had no idea what he really thought or what kind of person he might be.

Was he a wolf waiting to pounce when she least expected it, or merely a helpful person? What would he have to gain? She could think of nothing except the funds in her money belt, and he knew nothing of those.

The boys played checkers until bedtime. Luke giggled and acted as if he hadn't a care in the world. Joe seemed worried. Over and over she caught him looking at each person in the room as if memorizing them, his expressive brown eyes sad.

Later, when the boys had gone to their room and closed the door, she said, "If only Joe could talk. I think he wanted to tell me something. I should have given him some paper and asked him to write me a message."

"I doubt he would tell you what he's feeling. Seemed worried about something, though. Probably the trip. He'll see things will be all right for him with you."

"I hope so. It breaks my heart to see him so untrusting."

"Give him time." Nate stood and picked up his hat. "You need help watching Cindy tonight?"

"No, thank you. She's already sleeping much better. Mrs. Galloway promised to arrive early tomorrow to help."

He bowed. "Then I'll say good night."

The next morning, Sarah wakened to the sound of the wind moaning against the windows. Her first instinct was to snuggle into the pillow and go back to sleep, but she remembered all she had to accomplish today. If she didn't hurry, Mrs. Galloway would arrive and catch her in her nightclothes.

She rose and chose a black wool dress. Mama had been gone less than two weeks, and already Sarah had tired of wearing the traditional black mourning garb. Mama hadn't wanted her to wear black, but Aunt Lily wouldn't hear of anything else and made her order several new black dresses made in St. Louis even before Mama died. How lucky for her, Aunt Lily wouldn't know the difference. When Sarah returned home, she planned to wear her own clothes in the soft pastels she preferred.

She finished brushing her hair and pinned it into a bun at her nape. The scrape of the washstand across the floor caught her attention. Luke slipped through the partially opened door.

"Joe's run away."

"My stars. How could he do that?" Sarah rushed to the next room. Sure enough, no sign of Joe. The wardrobe still blocked the hall door. Frigid air whooshed in an open window, moving the heavy draperies with each gust. She pushed them aside and peered out. A narrow ledge ran the length of the building and intersected with the roof of a balcony on the floor below. As she searched for a sign of the missing boy, the first snowflakes glided on the wind.

She closed the window and crossed the room. "Are all his clothes gone?"

Luke nodded. "Yes, even the new ones, and his stick, too."

"We have to find him. Dress warmly, I'll go across the hall and ask Mr. Barton to help us search."

Sarah rushed from the suite, thankful Cindy still slept. She rapped on Nate's door. He mumbled something unintelligible, then opened the door. Buttoning his shirt, barefoot and with his hair rumpled, he looked like an overgrown boy himself. That didn't explain the sudden urge she had to unfasten the shirt he'd just buttoned and wrap her arms around him. How could she think of such a thing when poor Joe had disappeared into freezing weather?

"Sarah?" Nate shook his head, as if he couldn't believe she stood at his door.

"Could you help, please? Joe's run away."

To her relief, he didn't waste time with questions. "Let me get my boots on and I'll be right there. Get a warm coat. It's snowing out."

As Sarah opened the door to her suite, she saw Mrs. Galloway down the hallway. Two porters followed with a trunk and two valises.

"Oh, Mrs. Galloway. Thank goodness you've come." She hurried into the room and held the door for Mrs. Galloway and the porters to follow.

Mrs. Galloway entered and took off her hat. "Top o' the mornin' to you! Why, Miss Kincaid, you look fair upset. Whatever can be wrong?"

Sarah tipped the porters and said, "Joe's run away and I must find him. Will you sit with Cindy while we search?"

"Of course. Now, don't you be worrying about a thing here, dearie, and just find that boy-o. Cindy and I will be fine."

Sarah tied on her warm velvet bonnet, then pulled her heavy cape around her. She grabbed up her gloves and wished she had given some to Joe. Perhaps he at least wore the new coat she bought for him. Oh, dear Lord, what if he had fallen getting down from the hotel window? She prayed he was all right and they could find him soon.

FIVE

A rap sounded before Nate opened the door and stepped in. He wore a long brown coat, black boots, brown leather gloves, and black hat. The red silk muffler at his throat seemed out of place with his other clothing.

"How long has the boy been missing?" he asked.

"We don't know," Sarah said. "He left sometime after Luke went to sleep last night and before he awoke this morning."

Nate strode to the boys' bedroom. "He take everything?"

Sarah nodded. "Yes. I hope he's wearing the warm coat we bought him." Fighting tears, she halted on her way to the door and put a gloved hand on Nate's arm. "I hope he's all right. He crawled out the window, didn't even say goodbye."

Tears sprung to her eyes, but she bit her lip and turned back to Mrs. Galloway. "We'll check back periodically to make sure you're all right here and see if he's come back."

The three hurried out into the cold and made straight for the place where Joe would have landed in his climb from the window. "At least he isn't lying here from a fall," Sarah said.

"Let's go to our place," Luke said. "He'd go there first."

They walked the few blocks to the alley leading to the shanty the three children had called home. Sarah ducked her head against the wind. Swirls of snowflakes grew thick and stuck to her eyelashes. Her nose already felt like an icicle, and she pulled her woolen scarf over her nose and mouth.

Luke led the way down the treacherous alley. He knocked

on the door but there was no answer. They heard movement inside. Luke knocked again and called, "Joe, open up. It's me."

The door opened a crack and a man of indeterminate age stood there. "Ain't no Joe here, kid. Get lost."

Nate stepped in front of Luke and shouldered the door open. He walked in and inspected the room as he talked. "We're looking for a boy. He used to live here."

Sarah followed and also looked around to be certain the men were not holding Joe there against his will. The room looked the same as the children had left it. A second man sat on a packing crate. The same fire burned in the same bucket and the same lantern glowed dimly from an upended barrel. Two pallets lay on the floor near the fire.

"If it's the kid we saw, he can't have this place back. I told him as much, but he didn't say nothing. Just run off."

"How long ago was that?" Sarah asked.

"Woke us middle of the night banging on the door. Offered to let him in 'til mornin', but he just backed up and run."

"Which way did he run?" Nate asked.

The man looked from Nate to Sarah, greed alight in his eyes. He stroked the stubble at his chin. "Mebbe I could remember more if I was to feel the comfort of money in me hand."

Sarah bristled. "I can't believe you would put money ahead of the safety of a young boy lost in this weather. He's mute and can't even ask for help. Now, tell us which way he went."

"La-ti-da. Aren't you the fine lady, ordering me like I worked for you? Well, I don't. Not yet. What's it worth to you?" The man's face scrunched into an evil grin and he extended his hand to receive payment.

Sarah pulled at the strings of her reticule, willing to pay the horrid excuse for a human if it helped them find Joe. Before she could pay, Nate grabbed the front of the man's clothing and jerked the lout several inches off the floor. His roommate stepped forward but one glare from Nate sent the second man back to his crate.

"You heard the lady ask you a question. I'd better hear an honest answer. Now."

The man sputtered and struggled but Nate held firm.

"Thataway," the man pointed farther down the alley.

"If we don't find him, we'll be back here for a long discussion." Nate let him go and straightened the man's filthy jacket. Then, he smiled and said, "Thanks for your help."

When they were back in the alley, the man slammed the door.

"You know where this leads?" Nate asked Luke.

"Sort of. We didn't go that way much. The people and places with food are the other way."

"Maybe the man lied to us." Sarah bit her lip and looked up the gloomy passage. "There must be a thousand places for a little boy to hide in this town. Should we split up?"

Nate shook his head. "I think we should stay together. One lost person is enough. Let's try this path."

Hours later, Nate and Sarah slogged through ankle deep snow. They had stopped for food about midmorning, more for Luke's sake than anything. Then they'd taken him back to the hotel room to stay with Cindy and Mrs. Galloway. There was no point in his continued exposure to the bitter elements. He'd already shown them all the places he knew where Joe might hide.

She'd give Nate one thing. The man was organized. Just an hour ago he stepped into a mercantile and purchased two lanterns, kerosene for them, and a blanket for Joe when they found him. Now they each carried a lighted lantern against the gloom of dusk.

Sarah knew Nate was worried, almost as much as she was. The temperature had dropped all day with the late winter storm. She felt as if she had trudged fifty miles since morning. Now she was so tired and frantic she could hardly speak.

Her voice sounded far away to her, "Let's go back and

make those men talk to us. You could beat them up. Make them tell us where Joe went." She knew she wasn't being reasonable but panic threatened to overwhelm her.

Nate pulled her into the shelter of a doorway. He set down his lantern and took her by the arms. "Those men don't know anything, Sarah. We have only a few more blocks to cover and we'll have made a circle around the hotel. Why don't you go back to your room and let me finish this?"

"No. Joe's my responsibility. I knew something was wrong last night. I should have asked him about it then." She put her head against Nate's chest and sobbed, letting her lantern dangle from her hand. He took the lantern from her and set it down, then slid his arms around her.

That poor child, alone in this horrible weather. Some good works she could do. She couldn't help one small boy who had nowhere to live. They had to find him soon. What was she to do?

Patting her back gently, Nate said, "It'll be all right, Sarah. We'll find him."

She sniffled and met his gaze. "But what if we don't? People freeze to death every winter in storms like this."

"Don't give up yet." He gave her a hug, then held her away from him. "Come on. If you insist on going with me, let's get this over with."

They were behind the rail depot now where a long line of warehouses stood. Some of the buildings were double-sided. On the depot side, the doors were boxcar high to allow for ease in loading and unloading. Doors also opened on this side to allow access for wagons. Some buildings had planked walkways and porch-like docks stacked high with crates. Many had walkways from one warehouse to the next.

He nodded to the first warehouse. "You stay here and look from this angle while I walk up there and look around the stacks of crates. Stay even with me so we don't get separated."

Sometimes all she saw was the glow of his lantern as he stepped behind crates, barrels, lumber or machinery. Walking on the road, she looked under the raised walkway. They had come almost a block when she saw a dark shape where two warehouses met, one set back from the other by several feet.

She called, "Joe!" On her hands and knees, she crawled to the huddled form.

Joe was curled into a ball, and he was crying. She heard steps overhead as Nate cleared the edge and jumped down.

Setting down the lantern, she wrapped her arms around the shivering child. He wiped at his tears and tried to pull away. She clung to him with all her strength.

"Oh, Joe. Thank God, we've found you. We were so worried." Cold fingers of icy wind flicked at them in the rapidly dropping temperature.

Nate crouched at the edge of the walkway.

Sarah motioned him to come under the dock with her and Joe. Nate's face, red from the cold wind, turned pale and his eye widened. She motioned to him and said, "Bring the blanket. Joe's freezing."

Nate shook his head in a burst of motion.

"Nate?" she snapped.

He grasped a plank overhead and then duck-walked as close as his reach allowed. He set the lantern close to Joe. "We've been looking for you all day, son." Nate glanced back at the road then at Joe. "We were worried about you." With a shake of his head he moved forward and slid the blanket around Joe.

Joe looked from Sarah to Nate, surprise registering on his face. Surely Joe knew they would search for him. Did he expect them to be angry? Did he think they'd just forget about him?

Sarah placed her hands on Joe's cheeks. "We love you. Surely you know we couldn't leave without you."

He shook his head and tears welled in his eyes. Sarah took pencil and paper from her reticule and gave it to the boy. She held her lantern so it shone on the paper.

"What's wrong? Why did you run away? Don't you like me?"

Joe wrote. *Yur good lady. I bad.*

She put her free arm around him and hugged him to her side. "No, you're not. You're a good person, Joe."

He shook his head and wrote laboriously. *Men made me do bad things.*

Nate said, "The men were bad, not you."

Joe's only response was to hang his head and Sarah heard him sniff, as if trying not to cry and almost succeeding.

She took her handkerchief and wiped Joe's cheeks and nose. Then she took his hand while she asked, "So you think I'm good?"

Joe nodded.

"Well, years ago a man—a relative—tied up my sister, my brother and me. He intended to kill us but my brother-in-law rescued us just in time. Do you think that made me bad?"

Joe looked upset and shook his head.

"If a bad man doing something to me doesn't make me bad, then how can a bad man doing something to you make you bad?"

Joe's expression registered astonishment. Clearly he felt responsible for all the wrongs done him in his short life.

She held on to his hand, afraid to let him go for fear he would dart off into the night. "Joe, we have to stay together. If you don't want us all to live here under this walkway with you, you have to come to Texas and live with us."

Joe laughed at the absurdity of them living under the dock.

Nate clapped him on the shoulder. "Come on, son. Luke and Cindy are waiting for you at the hotel. They've been worried, too. Let's get out of this place."

Back at the hotel, Luke cheered and Cindy clapped when Joe came in. He offered a shy smile, and seemed relieved.

"Come sit by me, Joe," Cindy commanded and gestured to the seat just vacated by Mrs. Galloway. "I'll tell you the story Mrs. Galloway just told Luke and me."

Nate picked up his hat and coat. "If you'll excuse me, I

have some last minute arrangements to make. I'll be here in the morning to help with our departure."

"The train leaves at half past six, so we need to leave the hotel a little before six," Sarah said.

He smiled and clapped his hat on his head. "I'll be here at half past five."

Sarah arranged for dinner to be sent to the room. She was too exhausted for food, but she knew the others needed the meal, especially Joe. When they had finished, she put the children to bed with Joe's promise he would never run away again.

"Now, Mrs. Galloway, your room is just down the hall, number 212." She handed over the key.

"I'll leave me luggage here for the morrow." Mrs. Galloway picked up a valise. "This wee bag is all I'll be needing."

"Good night, then." As soon as the door closed, Sarah shed her clothes and crept into bed beside Cindy. What a day she'd had. They'd all had. Surely tomorrow would be easier.

Fiona Galloway wrote the letter with shaking fingers. She didn't write well. It was illegal in Ireland for the Irish to attend school, so she was lucky to be able to read and write at all. Now she wished she had the words to say all that was in her heart, but she'd make do.

After she returned home from being hired, she'd tried to tell Betsie of the job. She'd wanted to tell her daughter good bye, but not a word would she say to the hard man her daughter had married.

Poor Betsie. If she didn't already, she would soon rue the day she'd wed that one. When that day came, Fiona wanted Betsie to have a place to run to, even if she'd gone against her mother's wishes to marry that bounder.

Betsie and Rolf had still been asleep when Fiona left. They'd been out late the night before visiting friends, Rolf's friends, of course. He'd insisted Betsie cut ties to her own.

Had Rolf been awake, Fiona feared he wouldn't have let

her take anything but the clothes on her back. That's why she'd left her things next door at Mrs. Murphy's in readiness for her departure this morning. Rolf would have a fit for sure, thinking she'd taken things he could have sold. Didn't Rolf have the house left Fiona by her own darlin' Finn, and all that was in it? No matter now. They were only things, and Betsie had the use of them as long as Rolf let her.

Fiona worried, though. Rolf Hirsch was not a man content, nor was he a man to work for what he needed when there were those to give it to him. He was handsome enough, it's true, if you overlooked the mean cast to his eyes and the hard look of his mouth. Nothing like her Finn with the laughing eyes and the easy smiles and a voice that would charm the leprechauns. She shook her head and sighed, then got on with her task.

Fiona addressed the letter carefully, then slipped it in another envelope with a note to Mrs. Murphy asking her to deliver Betsie's letter when Rolf wasn't around. Not for one minute did she trust that oaf Rolf to give Betsie her own mail without reading it first.

Fiona put in the bit of cash Miss Kincaid gave her in advance, or what was left after the ride in the carriage this morning and purchase of two skirts and shirtwaists yesterday. Fiona asked her daughter to keep the money hidden safe in case she ever needed to come to Texas. Heaven help Betsie if Rolf ever found it. He'd never let her keep the bit of money Fiona slipped in the letter if he knew about it.

Nate stepped into the saloon and moved to a table in the corner. Seated there was a tall, thin man dressed all in black. His solemn face suggested he neared middle age, but Nate knew him to be only thirty-one. Nate slid into a chair and placed his hat on the table.

"Got your message from the hotel clerk. You barely made it to town in time to catch me."

"Had me a bit of trouble in St. Louis," Monk said. "You leavin' tomorrow?"

"In the morning." He leaned back and grinned. "You wouldn't believe the set up. Traveling in a private car all the way through. Imagine, this trip I won't have to worry about anyone recognizing me."

Monk narrowed his blue eyes. "With Roxie's daughter?"

Damn. He'd forgotten what a soft spot Monk had for Roxie. He'd looked after her like a mother hen. Nate hoped Monk wasn't going to get all protective over Miss Better-Than-You.

Nate straightened in his chair. "With her and her traveling companion, and three kids. One of the kids is sick, that's why the private car."

Monk nodded. "Roxie had a little portrait of her daughter I recollect. Looked a pretty thing. She pretty in person?"

"Yeah, she's a looker. Pale hair and these eyes kind of purple, but kind of blue. Hard to describe. She's tall like Roxie, but doesn't look like her in the face."

Nate motioned one of the saloon girls over. He ordered a bottle of whiskey and two glasses, then turned back to Monk.

"Glad you got here before I left. We need to make plans."

Monk took the bottle and uncorked it. He poured some into each glass and set the bottle on the table. "So. What's up?"

Nate held his glass up and inspected the color. "Who you figure could help us pull a railroad con?"

Monk shook his head, sending a lock of his dark hair across his forehead. "Don't know. Iverson's dead."

"Damn. He was a good man. What happened?" Nate asked. Iverson was a deceptively respectable looking man who spoke like a Harvard scholar. Come to think of it, he had been at Harvard.

"Had one too many aces in Galveston. Shot in the heart."

"That'll do it." Talk of trouble with a card game reminded him of his own recent battle. He'd been playing straight, too. Who could have known the locals would protect a crook just because he was one of their own citizens? He shook his head. "How about Winfield?"

"He's in prison in Kansas. Turned real mean, I heard."

"Who's that leave?" Nate asked.

Monk shook his head. "I guess Hargrove's the only one I can think of."

"Damn. I hate that man. Never trusted him."

"Me either. But he can do the rich executive better than anyone I know, better than Iverson could." Monk tossed back the last of his drink and refilled his glass.

Except on very rare, thoroughly private occasions, two drinks was all either of them ever had, and Nate knew this would be Monk's limit. A man who drank too much sometimes talked too much. He also lost his edge for observation.

"Any idea where Hargrove is?" Nate asked.

"Last I heard he was up in Chicago, running a crap game. Had him a family, but heard his wife left and took the kids."

Nate snorted. "Not exactly big time."

"No, but he's in one spot." Monk twirled his glass. "That part don't sound too bad to me."

"Don't worry. When we get our money this time, it's off to New Orleans like we always planned. We'll start us up our own Lucky Times Palace and be set for life."

"I'd sure like that. That's what Cal wanted—you fixed up in one place so you could have a home and family. Me, too, I reckon. Always treated me like I was family."

Nate set down his glass and looked at Monk. "He sure as hell went a long time before he settled down."

Monk nodded. "It was Roxie what done it. After your ma died, Cal was lost. Roxie gave him back the reason to go on."

Bitterness erupted in Nate. "You'd think a son and adopted son would have been reason enough."

"Cal always set special store by you, but a kid ain't the same as a woman, and you know it." Monk gave him a quizzical look. "You still sore about that? I thought you got over Cal marrying Roxie. You sound like a kid who didn't get dessert."

Embarrassed his feelings showed, Nate said, "Yeah, yeah. I know Roxie was good for Cal. I'm sorry I didn't make it back in time to tell them both."

It was Monk's turn to look embarrassed. "My fault. I was the one sent to find you. Took me too long. Was me wanted to kick in to that poker game in Arkansas, too."

"No, you aren't to blame. We both should have spotted a crooked deal, but who'd think the town would turn into a mob?"

"I sure thought you were a goner there." Monk rubbed a hand across his mouth. "Seemed like such a good plan, you going out of town in a casket and them thinking you was dead."

"It was a good plan." Nate's fist hit the table as all the anger he'd felt then resurfaced. "Who knew the bastards would decide to plant me then and there?"

Monk said, "Ain't that the truth? When that sheriff held me for questioning, I was fair in a panic. If it weren't for the doctor getting me out of jail, I'd still be there."

"I durn near died before I dug myself out of that grave, though. Still can't stand small places."

The memory of the panic he'd felt left Nate's mouth dry as dust. It had even resurfaced tonight staring at the inky recess where Joe hid. He poured another drink and downed half of it.

"Lucky for you the undertaker was a poor carpenter. If that pine box had held together, you'd have died 'fore I got to you."

"Reckon so. At least things are looking up now. Tomorrow I'll be on my way to Texas, traveling in style."

"What about the kids?" Monk asked. "Where'd Roxie's daughter come by three kids?"

"Found 'em." Nate shook his head and chuckled. "It was the craziest thing. She found these three kids in a back alley shanty and took them in on the spot. Damned if she didn't rope me into helping her."

Monk laughed, "I'd like to have seen that."

"Before you know it, she'd reserved a private car and hired

her a woman to travel on the train with them." He told Monk about the Welborns, about the aunt who eloped, and about the three children.

"Sounds like a nice girl. Roxie was real proud of her. Hear tell she got there a few days before Roxie died."

"So I heard." He couldn't keep the resentment from his voice. The way she'd cut him when he offered his help on the train still stung. All this talk had brought back that plus all the pain of his father marrying Roxie and all the mistakes Nate had made in his life. He wanted to hit something, but only said, "She can be a prissy little snob when she wants to. Don't know where she comes off thinking she's a great lady, knowing what her mother did for a living."

Monk shook his head sorrowfully. "I know your pa loved your ma, but he loved Roxie, too. You cheatin' Roxie's daughter don't set right with me, Nate. She's almost like family."

"Look, The Lucky Times Palace should have come to me, and you too, if you weren't so stubborn. If I'd been there when Cal died, I'd have inherited his share. The way it was set up, half of the money from the sale should come to me."

He remembered the jewelry. "And damned if she's not wearing the ruby ring that was Ma's. She's got the sapphire and diamond necklace and earrings, too."

When Monk still looked unconvinced, Nate said, "You know I can't afford to file for my half in court, things being what they are in Arkansas and a few other places. It's best I stay dead on record, but I want my share."

Thinking about it got him mad all over again. "She's rich, I tell you. All the Kincaids are rich. Dammit, they've got a town *and* a county named after them. How many people you know can reserve a Pullman car when they want to travel? Tell me that. Hell, those folks won't even miss what we take."

Monk didn't look convinced, but said, "Reckon you're right. Say, if you're taking a rail car there, how we gonna pull the railroad bit on them?"

Nate sketched on the table with his finger. "I checked at the depot. The line from Austin to Kincaid Springs is one of those dead end tap lines. Going nowhere for them, but the start of a gold mine for us."

"Lord knows I could use a stake right now. Poplar Bluff didn't work out like I'd hoped, then there was a little trouble in St. Louis. I'm near busted."

Nate stood. "Come with me back to the hotel and we'll work out the details for Hargrove's pitch. You can bunk down with me unless you have somewhere else to stay. I had a big win on the riverboat so I can let you have some spending money. Stay out of sight until we've gone, then you hightail it to Chicago."

Sarah turned over and punched her pillow once more. Though exhausted emotionally and physically from her day's search, sleep had eluded her for hours. Recalling her remarks to Nate about being able to care for the children without his help, she groaned. And after he had rushed in, gun drawn, ready to rescue her in that dark alley when she first found the children!

Why had she been so snippy with him when he offered his help? She heard herself boasting about being able to teach twenty-five students and how caring for three small children was well within her capabilities. How could she have been so insensitive?

Pride goes before the fall. In her head she heard Pearl saying those words, and Sarah had been prideful, hadn't she? More, she had wanted to distance herself from the tawny wolf tracking her every move. Then that wolf had spent all day in the snow helping her look for Joe.

Nate had not reminded her of her boast, had not told her she should have watched Joe more closely, had never even complained. He only helped. Though her head told her this wolf might devour her, her heart argued. Remember how gentle he was with Cindy, her heart pleaded, and how kind to the boys.

She snuggled into her pillow but sleep evaded her. Over

and over, her thoughtless words replayed in her head. Regardless of Nate's intentions, she'd been rude to someone who offered help. Sarah hated rudeness.

Her tossing and turning disturbed Cindy. She reminded herself she never could sleep with a guilty conscience. With a sigh Sarah slid from bed and drew on her wrapper and slippers. Pacing the floor, she mulled over the day's events.

Nate had been organized and masterful. Not like Peter back home when he tried but came across instead as domineering, autocratic, and just plain bossy. Nate had been strong, encouraging, caring. She paced forward and back until she decided she had worn a path in the carpet design.

She remembered how his arms around her felt, reassuring her when she felt at her lowest. How secure she had felt enclosed within those strong arms, her head against his broad chest. She groaned again. And after she had spoken so harshly to him only a day or two before. She threw herself into a chair and rested her head against the back. Fatigue dragged her down, but sleep would not come.

There was no getting around it. Until she apologized, she would get no rest, and she desperately needed sleep. If Nate hadn't turned in, she had better get it over with and eat her helping of humble pie. Expelling a large sigh, she stood and walked across the room.

As quietly as possible, she opened the door and peeked into the hall. A slit of light shone under the door of Nate's room. Before she lost her courage, she moved across the hall and knocked on the door.

When Nate heard the soft knock, he and Monk had finished the last detail of their plan. Nate had just pulled off his boots and removed his tie. He and Monk exchanged questioning looks and Nate shrugged. Taking out his pocket watch, he saw the hands pointed straight up and down—half past midnight. Who would call now? The rap came again.

Motioning Monk behind the dressing screen, Nate opened the door. Sarah faced him, wearing her nightclothes.

"Sarah, is something wrong?" he asked. Could Cindy have taken a turn for the worse? Surely Joe hadn't run away again.

"No. Well, yes." She stepped inside the room and folded her hands demurely in front of her. "Pardon me for coming at this hour but I saw your light was still on and I have something to say."

When he stared, she must have realized she was hardly dressed for calling on a man in his hotel room. Miss Pure-As-The-Driven-Snow blushed and her hands clutched the front of her wrapper tight against her throat. Not before Nate caught a glimpse of a sheer linen nightgown with lace at the yoke, lace which revealed pale satin skin. Instead of the neat bun, her hair tumbled down her shoulders and caressed her breasts.

His blood boiled. Were Monk not hidden in a corner of the room, Nate feared what he would have done. He longed to touch Sarah's pale golden hair, pull her to him and kiss those rose petal lips. He yearned to carry her to the bed and spend the rest of the night in reckless lovemaking.

Mentally, he gave himself a swift kick and said, "After such an exhausting day, I would have thought you'd be asleep."

She stammered, "I couldn't stop thinking about you."

He smiled. Had the schoolmarm turned seductress? Maybe he could keep himself between her and Monk and his friend could slip out the door.

Blushing redder, she said, "My stars, that came out wrong, didn't it? I meant, I couldn't stop thinking about how rude I was to you the other day. Do you remember? We were discussing my plan to hire a traveling companion when you offered your assistance with the children on the trip. I assured you I could handle them with no help?"

"Ah. Yes, I believe I remember that conversation." He kept his features carefully neutral now. He would play this any way she wanted.

She continued, "Well, I was wrong, wasn't I? Joe ran away and I would never have found him without your help."

In his most soothing voice he said, "Oh, I'm sure you would have located him without my aid. However, I thought we made a good team for the task."

"Yes." She tilted her head as if the thought was new to her. "Yes, we did." She took a deep breath and shrugged. "Well, be that as it may, I want to apologize for being so rude and to thank you again for helping. In fact, when I learned Joe had left, seeking your help was my first thought."

Nate made a slight bow. "I was happy to be of assistance, especially since our efforts were successful." So he was her first thought in time of trouble? He savored that knowledge.

Sarah smiled and sent Nate's blood boiling anew. If she smiled like that more often, she could rule the world.

"Then there are no hard feelings?"

He shook his head. "None whatever, I assure you."

She backed a step toward the open doorway. "So, um, I'll see you in the morning?"

He gave a nod. "As we planned."

Still clutching her wrapper to her throat, she gave a little finger-wiggling wave and said, "Good night, then. See you in the morning."

When Nate closed the door, Monk stepped from behind the screen, a wide grin on his face. Nate shot him a glare and said, "Don't say a word, not a word."

Apparently Monk didn't consider chuckling as a word.

SIX

Excitement raced through Sarah. Home. She was going home at last, and all three children were coming with her. On the way to the rail car, Sarah sent a wire letting Pearl know when to expect her. She'd already wired about the children.

What her family must be thinking about this she couldn't imagine. Knowing Pearl, though, she would have bedrooms ready for the children—probably complete with books and toys. In today's wire Sarah included Nate and Fiona as possible houseguests. They filled all the spare bedrooms at the ranch, so she hoped no one else was visiting. No matter, she and Cindy could share until they found Fiona a position. Sarah had an idea for Fiona.

Nate carried Cindy, her head on his shoulder, holding her gently with one arm. Fiona herded the boys, trailed by porters carrying luggage. Her entourage in tow, Sarah located a conductor. When he discovered the group had reserved the special Pullman Palace Drawing Room and Sleeping Car, he led them to it with great deference.

"You're in luck here, folks. Here we are, seventy feet long it is, and hot water included." The conductor stepped aside and gestured to metal steps leading to the car from the train platform. "Go right on up. You'll find it equipped with every modern comfort and decked out fit for a queen."

"Thank you for your help," Sarah said.

He touched a finger to his cap. "Welcome, Ma'am. You and your husband and family have a nice trip."

Sarah started to protest, but Nate took her arm with his free hand and guided her in front of him. "This way, Sarah."

She paused on the open vestibule platform and glanced over her shoulder, certain she should correct the conductor's misconception. The man walked swiftly away, listening to another traveler as he moved beside the train. Sarah gave a resigned sigh and went into the car.

She jerked her arm from Nate's hand as she entered. Under her breath, she whispered intensely, "Why didn't you let me correct the man?"

"Believe me, it would have been time wasted. Never make unnecessary explanations."

"Hmmph. Is that your policy?" she asked.

"Always," he said firmly.

She glared at him but he only smiled.

Behind them Fiona gasped. "Would you look at this place? The hotel was grand, but it was nothing compared to this." She ran her hand over the intricate walnut panels. "My, this wood's so polished you can fair see yourself in it."

Sarah gestured around. "Let's choose seats, shall we? The train will get underway in a few minutes."

"Can I sit by a window?" Cindy asked.

Nate set her gently on a plush covered seat. "Certainly, Princess. We can all have window seats if we wish," he said.

"Oh, boy," said Luke as he sat across the aisle from Cindy.

Joe raced to the seat facing Luke and sat down. Each boy pressed his face against the glass. Porters stowed luggage and left, glowing at the tip Nate proffered.

A new porter in a crisp white coat approached and gave a slight bow. "Name's James. You folks be wantin' breakfast?"

"Oh, yes," Sarah said.

"We'll be underway in five minutes. 'Bout twenty minutes 'til your food's ready here. O' course, you can go on up to the dining car if you'druther."

Sarah glanced at her companions, but everyone watched her as if awaiting her decision. "We'll eat here, thank you.

And I asked for a bed ready for our little patient here." She brushed her hand across Cindy's hair. How wonderful to have the children with her.

James walked forward and paused several seats away. "Yes, Ma'am. It's right here with curtains all ready to close when she's sleeping. I left 'em open at the window, too, in case she wants to watch out at the scenery a while."

Cindy's eyes widened. "You mean there's beds in here?"

"Remember, Miss Sarah told you there are beds, dining room, and even a privy." Nate reached up and touched the sloping wood above the window. "Beds fold down from these panels, and our seats also fold over to make a bed."

"Oh, dear. And can people see us sleep?" Fiona asked.

Sarah touched the curtains beside the bed made ready for Cindy. "No, no! I believe we'll all have these curtains to close to offer privacy at night. We'll see how well it works at bedtime." She slipped off her coat and laid it across the velvet of the seat back, then bent to help Cindy remove her wrap. The boys had already thrown their jackets beside them.

The car gave a lurch and the adults took their places. Fiona sat by Cindy and Sarah sat across from them. Nate seemed to weigh his choices, and then sat beside Sarah.

Slowly picking up speed, the train pulled out of the station. Sarah's heart beat fast with the excitement of returning home. She felt like a victor returning from battle with precious plunder. Rescuing the children, being able to take them with her and provide them with a comfortable home, sent her spirits soaring. Teaching at her school provided a feeling of accomplishment. Saving the children meant much more. At last she had truly accomplished good works.

Glancing at Nate, she almost forgot she shouldn't trust him. He had been so attentive and the perfect gentleman. More, he was the most appealing man she had ever met. Whenever she found herself near him, warm tingles pooled in her stomach.

His arm brushed against hers, but not in an improper way,

and layers of clothing separated them. Then why did his touch send heat sizzling through her?

In her continual reading, she had often come across a description of someone or something being "breathtaking." Until she met Nate, she hadn't fully understood that term. This mystery man took her breath away. No matter what happened when they reached Texas, on this trip common experience united them. Why shouldn't she enjoy his company now?

Giddy as a schoolgirl, Sarah forgot her shyness and talked to her new family. She entertained them by relating her first train trip seven years ago when she moved from Tennessee to Texas. The boys sat wide-eyed when she told of the villainous attempt to shove Pearl off the train and how Pearl's husband, Drake, saved her. All the while Nate appeared politely attentive, but offered no comments or questions.

She still couldn't figure him out. He acted as if he had her best interests at heart, and certainly he was a wonder with the children and polite to Fiona. What thoughts shaped his mind, though? How did he come by the wounds those bandages covered? What kind of business did he have in Texas? Questions she needed answers for cluttered her mind.

Sarah looked at her ring. Small rubies and diamonds flowed left and right from a large heart-shaped ruby center stone, all set in gold. It could easily be a betrothal ring.

What would it be like if Nate really were her husband, if the children were theirs? She shook her head. What silly daydreams. Nate Barton was hardly the marrying kind, especially not to a spinster schoolteacher.

Still, she thought they looked like a family. Maybe people thought Fiona was the children's grandmother. Sarah had seen the admiration of those they passed at the depot. Women gave Nate a second glance, then looked at Sarah with envy. If Nate married, what kind of woman would he choose? A soft gong interrupted her fantasy.

"What was that?" Luke asked.

"Music to my ears for sure, son. Come on, that's the dinner bell." Nate picked up Cindy and followed the porter.

They passed the berth opened as a bed and made their way to the forward end of the car. James indicated to an elegantly laid table and said, "Ladies, please sit here. Sir, you can dine with your family or step into the smoking car."

Nate deposited Cindy and saw Sarah and Fiona seated. Then he said, "Well, men, shall we go into the men's smoking room or eat with the ladies?"

Luke giggled and he and Joe exchanged nudges at being addressed as adults and invited into the men's smoker to dine.

"Sit here, Luke." Cindy pointed to the empty chair.

Fiona said, "Miss Kincaid, perhaps you'd like to move across the aisle and sit with Mr. Barton? I'll see these little scallywags eat properly. We won't be disgracing ourselves in this fine setting, will we, Children?"

Feeling trapped, Sarah slipped across the aisle and let Nate seat her. He took the chair across from her. The silver service shone on the crisp white damask covering the table. Fresh flowers graced the crystal and silver vase anchored near the carved wooden panel between windows. Her gaze wandered to the lavishly appointed car.

"Remembering your journey to St. Louis or the one years ago?" Nate asked.

Surprised, she raised her gaze to meet those tawny eyes watching her. She answered, "Memories of the move to Texas filled my thoughts."

"Travel has changed a bit in the past few years, but similar cars were available then, weren't they?" Nate gestured around them. "Did you travel in a car like this one?"

She laughed. "Hardly. Drake's major concern was transporting the fine mares he'd bought from my father. At least, until someone tried to kill Pearl. We rode in very comfortable seats, but they didn't make into beds so we had to sit up all the way."

"A bit tiring. What about your recent trip to St. Louis?"

"My aunt and I shared a compartment with sleeping berths." She sighed and shrugged. "Of course, I had the upper one."

Sarah remembered Lily's complaints, and thanked heaven she had a more pleasant companion for this trip. She hoped Lily found happiness, but couldn't find it in herself to miss Lily's constant waspish comments and complaints.

The breakfast was plentiful and well served. When they'd finished, Sarah took Cindy to the ladies' toilet before tucking her into bed for a long nap. Cindy watched the scene passing by her window for a while. Then, clutching her new doll, she dropped off to sleep. Sarah tucked the cover under her chin and closed the curtains.

When she returned to her seat, Nate stepped out into the aisle so she could sit next to the window. She smiled her thanks and sat down. Fiona sat across from her. They chatted for a while, then heard Luke and Joe scuffling behind them.

Fiona said, "Saints preserve us, sounds to me like those boys need a distraction. I'll move back there for a bit and tell the lads a story or two."

Suddenly, Sarah's new confidence deserted her and she felt awkward and unsure of herself. How silly. It wasn't as if they were alone, for heaven's sake. The boys and Fiona sat right behind them, Cindy slept just in front of them, and two porters worked away in the tiny galley ahead. She didn't know what to say, though, and sat twisting her ring.

Nate picked up her hand. "Lovely ring. Unusual, too."

Her hand felt a perfect fit to his. His long, slender fingers curled around hers, snugging her palm against his stronger one. He examined the ring, holding her hand this way and that to let the stones catch the light. She couldn't explain the intensity of the heat spreading through her. My stars, he only held her hand!

Controlling her thoughts, she said, "It was my mother's wedding ring. She gave it to me just before she died."

She slipped her hand from his. Gathering her courage, she paused and then remarked casually, "That's why I was in St.

Louis." She turned to watch him. "I thought I saw you at the cemetery during her funeral."

Nate gave a little shrug and said, "It's possible, I suppose. I went to pay my respects at my father's grave while I was in town." He looked thoughtful. "It seems to me there was a funeral going on while I was there." He turned his head and met her gaze, those tawny wolf-eyes wide and innocent. "Could that have been your mother's service?"

She took a breath and plunged ahead. "Yes. And then you were on the boat, then in the same hotel. It seems strange."

Nate shrugged. "Yes, life is full of these coincidences. But then, I'm grateful. Otherwise I would never have met you."

"And would that have been so bad?" she asked, not meaning to sound coy, but wanting to hear his answer. And wanting it to be affirmative.

He took her hand back in his. "Ah, Sarah, it would have been a tragedy."

Blushing but pleased, she pulled her fingers free from his grasp again and folded her hands in her lap. "Tell me about your family."

"Nothing to tell." He made a dismissive wave with one hand. "They're all dead now."

"Everyone?" she asked.

"Well, my mother's parents are still alive back in Virginia, but I've never seen them." He looked at her. "They disowned my mother when she married my father, so I've no wish to meet them. I may have cousins somewhere. No one close."

"Oh, that's sad. Do you live in St. Louis?"

He paused, then said, "No." As if reluctant to elaborate, he took a deep breath before he added, "I live in New Orleans. I had business in St. Louis, but I'm finished there."

The flat finality in his voice made her wonder. What an odd turn of phrase. Still, he had been the man at the cemetery, she was sure of it. Perhaps it was all coincidence, as he said, but she still wondered.

Nate flexed his shoulders and said, "From what you told the

children, I gather you live with your sister and brother-in-law on a ranch outside Kincaid Springs. Tell me about your family."

"Pearl's my half sister and is thirteen years older than I. It was she who raised our half brother, Storm, and me. Storm's a year older than I am. I came to live with Pearl as a baby, but Storm was about five when he came. When she married Drake, he adopted Storm and me." She sat up straight. He might as well know the worst now. "You see, the three of us share a father even though we had different mothers."

His only comment was, "I see."

She sighed. "I suppose you do. I'm not ashamed of my family, but it's a subject I usually avoid. My father's legitimate son was insane. We only found out seven years ago he'd threatened to kill anyone our father married as well as Storm and me. That's why our father didn't marry my mother or Storm's. He's married to Storm's mother now, though."

"And Pearl's mother? Why didn't he marry her?"

"Before he knew about Pearl being on the way, his parents arranged a marriage for him with a woman from a wealthy family. I think he loved Pearl's mother, Jerusha Parker, but he isn't a strong man and gave in to his parents."

"I take it something happened to both women."

Sarah nodded. "Jerusha died when Pearl was about ten. About a year later, our father's wife went mad during the War and killed herself. "

"What happened to the crazy son?" Nate asked.

"He was the one I told Joe about when we were under the dock. You remember?" When Nate nodded, she continued, "Drake shot him in self-defense when he rescued us. That left our father free to marry Storm's mother."

"So, this Storm's mother is now your stepmother? Why didn't your father marry your mother instead?"

"My mother had already married a nice man in St. Louis. My father still lives in Pipers Hollow, Tennessee. He raises horses there."

"Do you ever visit him?"

"My father, his name is Quinton Walker, has been to visit us in Texas several times. Storm goes to see him in Tennessee, too, but I don't. I hate Pipers Hollow and never want to go back." He probably wondered why she didn't make a visit on this trip, since she was in the same state, but never again would she set foot in the community where she had received so much persecution growing up.

"Do you think of him or this brother-in-law who adopted you as your father?"

Sarah pondered a minute. "I've never been asked that before. I guess neither. In truth, I guess Drake's grandfather seems more like a father to me than anyone else in my life."

"His grandfather? Not this Drake?" Nate asked.

She smiled and shook her head. "Grandpa Kincaid is gruff on the outside, but really such a sweet man. His hair stands out like a silver lion's mane and he's tall and imposing. He treats me as if I'm a princess, as if he loves me. I have a room at his house for when I want to stay overnight in town. He's helped me invest any money I received, and is forever buying me presents. Spoils me at the same time he's strict. Does that make sense?"

"Not much. I suppose I'll understand when I meet him."

Nate stared out the window as the miles clicked away. After lunch both boys had fallen asleep on their seats and Fiona rejoined him and Sarah. Cindy napped in her bed. When she awakened, Fiona went to her.

He heard Fiona telling Cindy an amusing story while the boys played with their toy soldiers on the floor nearby. James lit the oil lamps for the evening. Soon he would make up the beds, probably while they ate their dinner. Sarah's eyes drifted shut and her head slid to Nate's shoulder. He gently edged her book from her hands and closed it.

An almost overwhelming desire to protect her swept over him, a strong need to gather her in his arms and hold her safe.

He cursed himself for a fool. This woman had his money, his mother's jewelry. He didn't mind the sapphire necklace and earrings so much, but the ruby ring was a present to Ma from Cal at Nate's birth.

Ma always told him it was her lucky ring, that someday he should give it to the girl who was lucky enough to win his love. Ma ran out of luck, though, when she tried to have other children. After several miscarriages, she and her baby girl both died. Some luck.

Cal was never the same after that. Seemed a part of him died with Ma. The closest he came to happiness was with Roxie. Nate closed his eyes against the pain of bitter memories.

How he wished he and Cal could have been closer. He wished Cal had let him call him Dad or Pa, but Cal wanted them to be buddies. Damn, there were lots of people to be his pal. Monk had been there as a friend. A boy needed his father to *be* a father. Too late now. Nate was alone in the world except for Monk, who was as much a brother to him as if blood united them.

When the conductor thought he and Sarah were married, a great clamp seized Nate's gut. He had no idea a simple mistake could cause such havoc. He was the one who started the idea at the hotel that he and Sarah were engaged. Why should he care what a bunch of yokels thought?

He tried to deny he liked the idea of people thinking they were a couple, that the kids were theirs. That kind of thinking was for saps with weak minds and strong backs. Besides, Sarah couldn't be much over twenty, so she could hardly have kids the ages of the boys. Let people think what they wanted.

So far, this trip had not gone as he planned. Sarah seemed immune to his charm. He'd tried taking things slow, but he thought he should step up the effort. Inexperienced as she was, he should be able to tear down those walls of reserve.

The dinner gong sounded. The boys, who had come to know that sound as well as Sarah's rules, set aside their soldiers and rushed to the toilet to wash their hands.

Nate put his hand on Sarah's arm and shook her gently. "Sarah, dinner's served."

She opened her eyes and sat upright. Her hands fluttered to smooth stray wisps of hair back into her bun. A flush spread over her delicate cheeks. "Oh, my stars, I do apologize for using your shoulder as a pillow. How rude of me."

He leaned near and spoke only for her ears. "Believe me, it was my pleasure. I volunteer to be your pillow at any time."

She blushed brighter and refused to meet his gaze.

Nate stood and offered his arm. "Shall we join the others?"

The dinner involved several courses served efficiently. They lingered long in the elegant setting. The boys excused themselves to watch James while he made several seats into beds and pulled down two upper berths.

"We want to sleep on top," Luke said.

Joe nodded his agreement. The boys got ready for bed and climbed up into their bunks. Sarah and Fiona excused themselves to make their own preparations in the ladies' room at the rear of the car. Nate sat across the aisle and pretended to read.

Soon the two women were back. Sarah wore a different wrapper over her nightclothes than she'd worn when she came to his room last night. This one was blue wool and it crossed over in front and buttoned up to the shoulder.

"Sure and it's glad I'll be to sleep in this bed," said Fiona. "Last night I was that excited about the trip I could hardly close my eyes, for all I was in that grand room."

Sarah held the curtain while the older woman slid into place. "You see how it works, Fiona. You close the curtains at the window, then pull this aisle curtain closed and you'll have complete privacy."

"Thank you, dearie. You'll be doing the same soon, I suppose?" Fiona asked.

"Oh, yes. I'll check on the children once more. The porter will be turning the lights down, but I'll ask him to leave one at each end of the car burning low in case anyone needs to get up during the night."

Nate watched while Sarah checked on Cindy in the area next to Fiona. He saw the little girl sleeping soundly, still clutching her doll. The boys climbed up and down from their beds, and Joe seemed upset. Luke finally lay down, but Joe came across the aisle and sat near Nate. Sarah apparently noticed Joe's concern.

She asked, "Joe, what's bothering you?"

He made motions to indicate that while he was sleeping, someone would grab him.

Sarah shook her head. "No, Joe. We'll all be right here. No one but us will come into the car, unless the conductor comes through. Now, up into the bed with you."

Joe climbed onto his bunk, but sat with legs crossed and a mutinous look on his face.

"Joe, you know none of us would hurt you," Sarah pleaded.

Joe nodded then leaned out and pointed first to the door at the end of the car, then to the other. He made motions to indicate someone opening the door and creeping in. Though still not as good at it as Luke, Nate thought he and Sarah were getting pretty good at interpreting Joe's sign language.

This impasse could go on all night, though. Nate stood and touched Sarah on the arm. "Let me try, if you will."

Surprise in her wide jewel-toned eyes, Sarah said, "Of course. I'm at a loss here."

Nate went to the galley and spoke with the two porters. Soon he returned with a load of empty tin cans, dinnerware, a piece of rope and some stout twine.

"How about I make you a burglar trap?" he asked Joe.

Joe's dark eyes widened. He nodded and scooted back against the back wall of his berth.

Using his knife as a punch, Nate worked holes into the cans. With the twine, he tied a knife or fork to make a clapper in each can. He took the rope and strung it across the berth inside where the curtains would close, then tied the cans to the rope. They dangled and made slight rattles with the movement of the train. He stood back, satisfied with his work.

"Now, watch what happens if I try to grab you." Nate lunged and grabbed Joe. The cans set up a loud clatter.

He put Joe back up on the bed and asked, "Is that good enough so you can sleep?"

Joe nodded and lay down. Nate pulled the covers over the boy, then closed the curtains. When Nate turned around, Sarah had tears in her eyes. She walked quickly to the rear of the car and sat down. He followed her and took the place beside her.

She sniffed and pulled a handkerchief from the pocket of her wrapper. "Will he ever get over this fear?"

Nate didn't know what to say or do. His arm slid around her and he patted her shoulder. "Give him more time. He's come with you. That's a major accomplishment."

Dabbing at her eyes, she said, "He's here, thanks to you. And now you've helped once again."

"It was my pleasure. I hope you'll call on me if there's anything else I can do." He meant the statement to carry heavy sexual innuendo, hoping she would offer him encouragement.

"Oh, thank you," she said and sighed. "I'll go off to sleep now the children are settled. See you in the morning."

He rose when she stood. Her wide lavender-blue eyes were still wet with tears and her thick lashes looked longer with the moisture clinging to them. When she flashed that time-stopping smile, his heart beat faster and a great invisible fist sent a blow to his diaphragm. Not only did the thoughts of seduction and revenge disappear, *all* thought left his brain.

"Good night," she said as she moved toward her bed.

He stammered, "Good night," before he made his way to the bunk below Luke's. He pulled the curtains before he took off his shirt and boots, but left on his pants. Accustomed to sleeping unclothed, he'd overlooked provision for communal arrangements like these.

Touching the healing wounds at his shoulder and side, he checked their progress in the dark. Skin formed nicely now and he no longer wore the bandages. Soon only scars would remain. He lay back on his pillow and drifted to sleep.

Inky blackness surrounded him. He fought his way upward, upward, clawing and pushing. He couldn't make it, couldn't breathe. Air, he needed air! Dirt filled his mouth and nose. Death closed in, he was going to die, suffocate in this grave. He gave out a cry of anguish.

Nate sat up, bumping his head, and swung his feet onto the floor. That damn dream again. When would that horrible memory dim? He longed for a peaceful night's sleep free of the nightmares that plagued him. Night after night it was either this one or the one where an angry mob dragged him off to be hanged.

Maybe it was the dark. He dragged open the curtains. At each end of the aisle a light burned low, sending a faint glow along the car. Nate took a deep breath and lay back down. Maybe now he could sleep.

He heard movement and Sarah appeared. Her wrapper was open. She didn't see he was awake as she checked on Luke. Nate caught her rose fragrance as she leaned in to peek at Luke in the berth above. When she stepped back, her glance met Nate's.

She clutched her wrapper to her. "I'm sorry if I wakened you. I thought I heard a cry, but it must have been my imagination. The children are sound asleep."

"I was awake." He patted the mattress. "Talk a while?"

"Um, I, well," she looked back over her shoulder toward her berth, "I'd better get back to sleep."

"Just for a moment," he said and patted the bed again. "Sorry I wakened you, but the cry was mine. I had a nightmare."

With a surprised look, she sat at his feet. "I can't imagine you having nightmares. Would they have anything to do with those?" she asked and pointed at the place on his shoulder.

He hated the fact that he'd revealed a weakness to her. Taking her hand in his, he ignored her reference to his healing wounds and said, "Just something I ate, I suppose. How is your bed?"

She looked like a rabbit caught in a trap. He enjoyed the

power of toying with her. With his free hand, he touched her waist, tugging her gently to him. Her eyes grew wider but she let him slide her along the seat. His hand moved to her back and pulled her near.

Her hands braced on his chest. That golden hair dangled across his chest and made tantalizing little curls bobble with the train's movement. Wide pupils stared at him from her deep lavender-blue eyes. Her rose petal mouth parted slightly and her tongue flicked across her bottom lip.

All at once it ceased to be a game. His desire flared. Blood pumped urgently, bringing life to his loins. He wanted to explore every inch of her exquisite body, to see into her mind, to touch her soul.

With her mouth only a breath away, he whispered, "Sarah—"

The train gave a lurch, toppling her onto him. She gave a soft gasp and leaped up. He reached for her hand, but she backed away. After one last astounded glance, she gathered up her skirts and fled.

He started to rush after her, but she slipped into the berth and closed the curtains behind her. A slamming door could not have been clearer. Nate turned around and threw himself onto his bunk.

Damn, he'd rushed her. He'd been thinking with the wrong part of his body this time and let his desire for her override his judgment. Now he'd put a wedge between them. Her pale face in the dim light as she stood in the aisle haunted him.

Had that been terror or disgust in her eyes?

SEVEN

Sarah sat on the bed and hugged her arms. What had come over her? She had wanted to climb in beside Nate, had let him pull her near. If the train's unexpected swerve hadn't suddenly jostled her to her senses, she would have kissed him. What more would she have done? Her face burned with shame. What must he think of her?

Thinking she'd quickly peek at the children, unseen by anyone, she hadn't even tied the sash of her wrapper. When she looked down, humiliation spread through her again. Undone ties at the throat of her nightgown let the lace yoke part to reveal the tops of her breasts. The dark circles surrounding her erect nipples showed through the thin cotton.

Nate must have thought her wanton, inviting his advances. Probably he thought she sought intimacy with him under the guise of checking on the children. Possibly he thought her one of those loose women who pretended to be circumspect in public. Oh, my, how could she face him tomorrow morning?

Her mind went over the scene. Nate had pulled her gently toward him, so he must have wanted her there. His wolf's eyes mesmerized her, enticing her near. Recalling how his warm, firm chest felt beneath her hands made her fingers flex. She had wanted to run her hands over his heart to feel the strong beat there and see if its pounding matched her own.

Longing to caress his broad chest, his strong arms, and run her fingers through his thick hair, she had let her guard down. She admitted she wanted to touch all of him, to explore the hidden delights his body might yield. Her hands touched her heated cheeks. My stars, was she as loose as the women who had worked in her mother's saloon?

Pearl had told her she would know when the right man came along because his touch would affect her differently from that of other men. He would make Sarah want things she had never experienced with a man. Was Nate *the one* for her? Or, did she have a carnal nature which had suddenly asserted itself?

Surely not. Peter Dorfman had courted her for several months but she had never wanted him to hold her, had never been tempted to kiss him. There were no tingles when Peter held her hand. Her skin sizzled when Nate touched her.

But what if she had given in to her base urges? Luke might have wakened and found them entwined on the bed beneath his, Fiona might have wakened, noticed Sarah's empty berth, and sought her. Anyone might have come along. The horror of such a scene washed over her and her cheeks once more burned in shame.

Even worse than what people might think, she would have given in to the careless behavior and broken her personal code of ethics. She had vowed never to act reckless in regard to intimacy. Until tonight, she had kept that promise to herself.

Sarah slid into bed and pushed open the window curtains to look out. Only an occasional light shone in the jet-black night. The steam heat of the coach clouded the cold glass with condensation. Her finger trailed a heart through the beads of hazy moisture. She sketched *NB* inside the heart, then paused, shocked at her action.

Good thing no one else would ever see. She found herself almost uncontrollably attracted to Nate. No one need know how much he occupied her thoughts. Believing his wounds were somehow the result of him being on the wrong side of the law made her wary. It did nothing to dim her fascination.

She let her fingers slowly trace *SK* beneath the other letters. Her initials. Were they? Sometimes she didn't know who she was. She thought of all the surnames she could have used—her mother's, her natural father's, Pearl's. Now her name was Sarah Rochelle Kincaid. So many names, but in her mind she was just plain Sarah. Just herself.

But who was she? People at home told her she was beautiful and clever. Inside, though, she felt dowdy and plain and sometimes a bit stupid and overwhelmed. Would she ever overcome the effects of the criticism and censure from townspeople in her early life? The whispers and outright name-calling caused Pearl to school her and Storm at home. Because of Pearl's personal experience with the horrors of bullies, she understood Sarah's fears and let her live a cloistered life at home until their move to Texas.

Even then, Sarah couldn't bear contention or confrontation, avoided any action which might cause disapproval. Maybe that's why she couldn't speak up for herself, why she always let people influence her. Until lately. When she'd found the children, she'd found the courage to speak and act on her own.

The heart on the window now looked as if it cried steamy teardrops down the pane. She prayed that wasn't an omen and rubbed at the damp heart with a corner of the sheet. Then, she closed the window curtains and drifted off to sleep.

Nate lay in his bunk cursing himself for ten kinds of a fool. Damn, why did he have to rush Sarah? When he saw the look in those enormous lavender-blue eyes as she backed away, he knew he'd made a terrible mistake. Whether her reaction had been fright at the suggestive nature of their contact or disgust at the thought of intimacy with him didn't matter. His hasty movements had caused her distress and damaged the trust he'd worked hard to build.

Things had moved along well until he pushed her. Slowly he had cracked that prim armor. She let him take a part in caring for the children, talked with him as if they were friends.

His timing was off tonight, that's all. He'd let opportunity press him into action when he should have continued his slow assault. Tomorrow he'd be the perfect gentleman again, but carry through his plan to regain what belonged to him. If he won over Miss-Soft-As-Velvet Kincaid in the bargain, so much the better.

Nate lay awake a long time. He wished the rocking of the train would lull him into a sound sleep free from nightmares. He wondered if he would ever again have a peaceful night's rest.

The morning after her encounter with Nate, Sarah hated to leave the warm cocoon of her berth. Knowing she had to face him eventually, she'd hurried to the ladies' room and dressed. As she rushed to help Cindy, he stepped from his berth and they collided. His hands on her arms braced her, and they stayed like that overlong as their gazes met. How easy it would be to lean into his embrace and let his strong arms hold her. She snapped back to consciousness and stepped away.

She managed to stammer out, "Good morning."

"Dare I say you look pretty as a picture this morning?"

His wolf's eyes stared into hers, freezing her limbs and thoughts. She wanted to say something witty, but found herself unable to speak or move.

From behind Sarah, Fiona said, "A woman never tires of hearing such words. Now be off with you, you young scallywag. Get to your chair and let us get these children up and dressed."

For the remainder of the trip, Sarah carefully acted with propriety. Nate remained the perfect gentleman, always attentive but never pressing. Every time his strong hand brushed hers, she wondered if it was an accident or planned. Each contact elicited the same sizzling response from her body. At night she lay in her bed longing for his touch, dreaming of his kiss. By the end of the trip, exhaustion claimed her.

She welcomed the chance to live in roomier quarters where she could see Nate in more normal surroundings.

On the day they finally drew near Kincaid Springs, her new family hovered around Sarah while she pointed out landmarks through the train window. She knew she babbled from excitement, but couldn't help herself. When at last they passed Pedernales Falls and the station came into view, she hurried the children into their coats and drew on her cape.

Nate picked up Cindy, whose recovery had progressed nicely. Her cough lingered and she still needed extra rest, but her eyes sparkled and her skin looked healthy. He draped the blanket he'd bought in Memphis around Cindy's head and shoulders as extra protection from the cold.

Fiona looked nervous, but Sarah patted her on the arm. "Don't worry, it's a friendly place. You'll be welcome and we'll find you somewhere of your own soon."

"Sure and it's lovely of you to be so kind. Fear's upon me, and I'll not lie to you." Fiona's face held apprehension, and her voice quavered.

They said goodbye to the porter, and Fiona helped Sarah herd the boys to the vestibule. Nate trailed, carrying Cindy.

"There they are." Sarah waved and called, "Over here."

Drake and Storm stood talking to Grandpa. At Sarah's call, they all looked up and walked to greet her. Grandpa reached her first and hugged her, then looked at those who accompanied her.

"Girl, it's 'bout time you got back." He shook his white mane and asked, "Doesn't that Lily beat all, leaving you on the spot like that?"

Sarah hugged Storm and Drake. The children watched with eyes like saucers. Fiona stood quietly behind the boys. Nate, still holding Cindy, stood beside her.

Sarah stepped back and gestured to her companions. "Let me introduce Fiona Galloway. She accompanied me from Memphis. Nate Barton was kind enough to help rescue the children."

"Now, who do we have here?" Grandpa asked as he looked from one child to the other.

Sarah introduced the children. Nate set Cindy gently on the station platform. She curtsied as Sarah and Fiona had shown her, holding the blanket as if it were a queen's robe. Each boy gave a slight bow when his name was called.

After rummaging through his pockets, Grandpa pulled out a paper bag and made a great show of opening it, peering in, and jiggling the contents.

"Anybody here like candy?" he asked as he extended the pouch toward the children.

"I do," Cindy and Luke called in unison and Joe nodded. Grandpa held the sack while each child selected a fat peppermint stick.

Cindy and Luke said, "Thank you," and Joe bowed elaborately.

Sarah explained, "Joe doesn't speak, but he makes himself understood in other ways. Now, shall we get our things? I can hardly wait to get home."

Cindy coughed, and Nate picked her up. Sarah reached up to make the blanket snug about the little girl.

The deep blue sky of a clear, cold day was overhead. In spite of the sun, Sarah could have sworn the north wind pierced through her. With Cindy in his arms, Nate held Luke's hand. Sarah guided Joe and they made their way to the wagon. Storm's horse was tied to the back.

Chester, Grandpa's handyman, helped load luggage. Joe and Luke tried to heave a trunk onto the wagon. Storm interceded and pretended he needed the boy's help, then told both he appreciated their assistance.

"I wired you I'd invited Mrs. Galloway and Mr. Barton to stay at the ranch for a while. Mrs. Galloway will be looking for a position with a family where she can live comfortably while she works for them. I insisted she stay with us until she finds a new position. Mr. Barton is meeting business associates in town. I invited him to stay at the ranch until they arrive."

Sarah saw the skeptical looks exchanged by Storm, Drake, and Grandpa. She stiffened her spine and prepared to do battle if necessary. For the first time in her life, she cared less about what these three men thought than following her own mind.

The closer the train had come to Kincaid Springs, the more she realized she didn't want to part company with Nate. He might not be around permanently, but she wanted to prolong her time with him. Hoping her attraction to him was only a fascination that time would dull, she wanted him near to find out.

Grandpa said, "I'll let you folks go on out to the ranch and get in out of the wind. Pearl would skin me alive if I asked you to my place before she gets a chance to fuss over you. I'll be out tomorrow to hear all about the trip."

Drake helped Sarah and Fiona onto the wagon seat and climbed up beside them. Nate set Cindy on his carpetbag in the shelter of the bench seat and tucked the blanket around her before he sat beside her. Joe and Luke climbed into the back near him and sat on the luggage.

Storm tucked a thick lap robe around Sarah and Fiona, then produced two more for Nate and the children. Drake clicked the reins and they were underway. The children peered around, fascinated by everything. Storm rode beside the wagon, occasionally dropping back to talk with Nate and the youngsters. Sarah heard Luke ask about the heavy rawhide chaps Storm wore.

She fired rapid questions about what had happened in the weeks she'd been gone until she was satisfied she'd caught up on all the news. Condensing Lily's elopement and the boat trip down the Mississippi, she elaborated on Nate helping her rescue the children and her subsequent hiring of Fiona.

When they reached the stones marking their entrance to the ranch lands, she pointed out their progress to her new family. Soon the sloping banks of the Pedernales River curved through the meadow. The willows and cottonwoods along the banks were bare now. She told the newcomers how it would look in a few weeks with wildflowers and new growth.

At last the ranch house came into view amid a grove of ancient live oak trees high on the hill. Solid quarried rock walls ambled this way and that, and a wide porch hugged the front of the house, which overlooked both meadow and river. Tall rockers across the veranda issued an invitation to relax and watch the world. She expelled a sigh. My stars, what sight could be more welcome?

She clasped her hands in front of her and said, "Oh, it's so good to be home."

Turning to look over her shoulder, she gestured to the children to move forward. She pointed to the house rambling across the hilltop and said, "There it is, children. That's your new home."

"It's like a castle, only not so tall," Cindy said.

Joe nodded and held out his arms to indicate large.

Luke called, "Look at the horses." He pointed to a paddock of Drake's fine breeding stock.

As they started up the hill to the house, four children ran down the road laughing and yelling. Drake stopped while they clambered onto the wagon.

"Aunt Sarah, you're finally back," Katie said from behind her and hugged Sarah around the neck.

When she turned around, she saw her three huddled close to Nate. They were silent and looked worried. Pearl's rowdy bunch were overwhelming even under the best of conditions.

Drake came to the rescue. "Hey, you monkeys. Quiet down. Aunt Sarah's brought you three new cousins."

Sarah said, "They're Cindy, Luke, and Joe. Now tell them your names."

Robbie and Evan introduced themselves. Katie gave her name and Beth's, who was shy because of her lisp. Katie added, "Is the man our new uncle?"

Sarah blushed, but Nate just smiled. "Name's Nate Barton. You can call me Nate. I'm hanging around your place a few days until some friends get to town. That all right?"

The children nodded and the wagon came to a stop in front

of the house. Pearl and the housekeeper, Maria, rushed out and introductions started all over.

Nate watched warily as they drifted into the house and the Kincaid children lured his three away to see their rooms.

His three?

Damn, when had he started thinking of them as his? He'd have to watch himself or he'd start fitting into this life like any other poor sucker.

No, not him. Not Lucky Nathaniel Bartholomew.

Hell, there was another thing he'd better remember. Nate Barton. Think the part, that was his way. Never let your guard down, even in your thoughts.

He'd almost lost his carefully schooled control earlier when he learned Sarah's beloved Grandpa was also District Judge Robert Kincaid, owner of the leading law firm in town. Damn, lately his only luck seemed bad. Regardless, he refused to let anything or anyone stand in the way of recovering his money. Judge or not, Nate had forced calm on himself and acknowledged the information without—he hoped—a change in his expression.

Now, he looked at his surroundings. Some place. Bright rugs covered the stone floors. The stone fireplace was big enough to roast an ox in. A sofa and three chairs clustered to invite conversation in front of the fire, with other chairs near tall windows. At the opposite end of the large room a spinet faced into the area and a guitar leaned against the wall.

Rustic in outside appearance, the exterior of the house blended in with the hillside as if it had always been there rather than built by man. Inside, it had all the refinements of elegant living with a Texas twist. Though not opulent, it spoke of quiet wealth, comfort, and good taste. A good place to launch his plan. A pleasant place to bide his time.

He sized up Sarah's half brother and brother-in-law. Both were tall men with black hair. Drake was taller, probably close to half a foot over six feet, and broad as a barn across the shoulders. Nate figured the man was mid- to late-thirties, and in great physical condition. The half brother, Storm, looked Indian, and was a little leaner and several inches shorter than Drake. Nate knew Storm was only a year or so older than Sarah, so he'd be about twenty-one. Both men were protective toward Sarah, and neither would make a good enemy.

It galled Nate to be beholden to any man, especially a solid citizen like either of these two. He'd always figured a man had to be soft in the head to farm or ranch. Working hard from dawn to dark in all kinds of weather was for suckers.

Nate Barton was above that sort of thing. He relied on his mind to get him through life. To have a free place to stay while he waited for Monk and worked on gaining his money and property from Sarah, Nate'd go along with this set up. He refused to admit he cared about staying near Sarah and the children. It wouldn't hurt to check on them, that was all.

"Why don't we go into my study and leave the women to catch up on all their gossip, Mr. Barton?"

"Make that Nate, won't you?" Nate said.

Drake led the way into a smaller room, but one large for its purposes of study and ranch office. Bookshelves lined two walls and a massive oak desk stood in front of them. Another stone fireplace, but one of normal proportions, centered on one wall. Beside it stood the most ridiculous rocking chair Nate had ever seen. Cowhorns formed the arms, curved over the back, and provided the rockers. The padded seat and back were covered in cowhide. Nate couldn't help staring.

Drake looked at it and said, "Sight, isn't it? My father bought it when I was a kid."

"Damnedest thing I've ever seen, but it fits this room," Nate said as he looked around. "Seems appropriate for a rancher, somehow."

"That's what my wife said when she rescued it from the barn loft." Drake walked to a sideboard. "Whiskey?"

Nate nodded. "Wouldn't mind a glass after the chill of the wagon ride."

Drake poured the liquor into three glasses then gave one to Nate and another to Storm before he took his own.

"To good friends and good times," he said as he raised his glass, then took a sip. "So, you met my sister-in-law in Memphis?"

Here comes the interrogation, but I'm ready.

"Actually, we met on the paddle wheeler coming from St. Louis. She traveled with an older couple. Welborn, I believe, was their name."

"Yes, so she mentioned in her wire from St. Louis. Friends of the Vermillions and my Aunt Lily," Drake said.

"No wonder she sent them on ahead," Storm said so low that Nate barely understood.

"I don't believe Sarah cared for their company," Nate confided. "Apparently they didn't approve of the children and refused to wait for Cindy's recovery."

At his use of Sarah's first name, both men looked at him, then at one another.

"Your sister insisted I call her Sarah after I'd helped her with the children. I hope you don't mind?"

Storm only shrugged.

Drake said, "That's entirely up to her." He drained his glass and set it back on the sideboard. "What sort of business are you in, Barton?"

Hell, here comes the pissin' contest.

Nate hoped he was ready. "Investments. Two of my associates are on their way here, but I expect it will be a week or two before they arrive." He took a deep breath and faced his host. "Of course, if it's inconvenient for me to stay here, I'll move into town."

"No need for that." Drake leaned a hip back on his desk and his eyes narrowed a bit. "No, I think it's best you wait here."

Nate took that to mean Drake wanted him here where he could keep an eye on Nate's movements and any contact he had with Sarah. Storm set his glass down. His face gave away nothing, but Nate remembered the look the two men exchanged earlier.

Storm smiled and said, "No point in your being on your own in a strange town when you can be here instead. Maria and Pearl are great cooks."

Drake smiled at Storm. "Cooking all you think about?"

"Never think about cooking. I think about eating," Storm said.

Drake looked about to shoot another question at Nate when a clanging sounded. He pushed off the desk. "Ah, well, there's the dinner bell."

And just in time, thought Nate.

"Well, what do you think?" Pearl asked as she and Drake readied for bed.

Drake tugged off a boot. "My money says he's up to no good. Says he's in investments. Damn, I'd sooner believe he's a gambler."

"Have you ever seen Sarah so talkative?" She couldn't get over the change in her shy sister. Pearl took off her dress and draped it over a chair.

With his second boot half off, Drake stopped and looked at his wife. "I swear she said more on the ride from town than I've heard her say in the whole seven years you and I've been married." He let the second boot drop and stood to take off his pants. "She talked a mile a minute the whole way here."

Pearl never tired of watching her husband undress. The sight always set her tingling with anticipation and desire. He looked as handsome tonight as he had the first day she'd seen him on a dusty street in her Tennessee hometown. Lucky for her he'd needed a wife immediately. Luckier still, she'd accepted.

Life had blessed her these past few years. She'd put the terrors they had faced behind her. After a rocky start, their marriage had been filled with love and happiness. She hoped Sarah and Storm could find the same love and contentment.

Sarah was no longer a child, Pearl knew that. Still, she couldn't help wondering about the man Sarah had brought home with her. There was something about Nate Barton she couldn't put her finger on. It was almost as if she knew him, but that was impossible. The feeling nagged at her, though, and only her sister's happiness kept her from asking more questions of him.

"She looks so happy." Pearl shed her petticoat and draped it atop the dress. "It's wonderful the change that's come over her. And the children seem precious. So sad to think of them on their own. I'm glad Sarah brought them with her."

"Yeah, honey." He smiled at her and set her heart fluttering while he continued, "She had a good teacher. Maybe those three are what brought her to life. Hope it's not that Barton fellow." He shook his head and repeated, "Never saw her so talkative."

"Not just the chattering, Drake. Did you notice she glowed with happiness?" Pearl untied her chemise and dropped it.

"Hope Barton doesn't cause her harm."

Pearl brought her hand to her throat. "Hurt her? You don't think he's dangerous, do you?" Then she understood. "Oh, I see. You think he might break her heart."

Fiercely protective, Pearl would sooner someone hurt her than any one of her family. "That would be terrible, just when she seems to be finding her own place in life. And she's so happy now."

"Barton looks the sort to be easy with the ladies." He pulled his shirt off and absentmindedly rubbed his hand across his bare chest. The muscles rippled in the soft lamplight.

When Pearl would have protested on Sarah's behalf, he raised a hand to ward off her objection and said, "I know, I know. Sarah is a good woman and old enough to know her own mind, but I don't trust Barton. Not at all."

Pearl worried at a knotted tie on her drawers. "While Sarah was checking on Cindy after dinner, Fiona let slip that, at the hotel and on the train, Sarah passed him off as her fiancé."

Drake paused to consider this tidbit. "Doesn't sound good. Wonder what brought that about?"

"Can you think of something to keep him here where we can watch him, but busy so he doesn't have so much time around Sarah?" Pearl asked as she crawled into bed. "Sarah wants him at the ranch with her and the children."

"Yeah," Drake said. "I'll tell him how much I need help with the spring roundup. Between us, Storm and I will keep him occupied. Be fun to see what a tenderfoot like him does with a few blisters on those soft hands."

Drake slid in beside her and gathered her into his arms. "Now, honey," he said as he nuzzled her neck. "How 'bout us keeping each other busy a while?"

Fiona sat in the rocker by the fireplace and looked at the room she'd been given. Though not as ornate as the hotel room in Memphis, it was far nicer to her way of thinking. An elegant room, yet cozy enough so a body could relax. Giving a lie to her thoughts, she leaned back in her chair and gave in to worry.

Here she was hundreds of miles from anyone she knew. Had she been a fool to come? What if there were no jobs available? Apprehension gnawed at her. That nice Miss Sarah would never turn her out on the streets, but she couldn't live with the Kincaids for any length of time. After all, she had her pride.

The situation at home had become intolerable and couldn't be allowed to continue. She couldn't keep avoiding her son-in-law or having Betsie feel forced to defend her. With any luck, Fiona could find a place soon. She only hoped it wasn't taking in laundry or something equally hard and low paying. Rocking gently, she resigned herself to hard work and loneliness.

She hoped she hadn't spoken out of turn when she mentioned Miss Sarah and Mr. Barton traveled as fiancés. How was she to know Mrs. Kincaid didn't know? Fiona's hurried explanation that it was for appearance's sake and nothing improper occurred did little to wipe the worry from Mrs. Kincaid's eyes.

Mr. Barton—oh, why couldn't she remember to call him Nate as he requested?—was a charmer. What a bold boy he was, though, and not to be trusted with an innocent lady like Miss Sarah. In Mrs. Kincaid's place, Fiona would worry about his intentions.

How complicated young people were. Perhaps being past courting age had compensations. Still, she couldn't help feeling life had passed her by since her Finn's death. At least she'd had twenty years with him. Hard as some of those years were, she'd always known she was loved and cherished. What more could a woman want? Exhaling another sigh, she rose to write a letter to Betsie.

EIGHT

Sarah slid into her seat beside Nate at the breakfast table and spread her napkin on her lap. She'd been up a large part of the night with Cindy and could have used a few more hours' sleep. Wasting part of her first day home, though, was not on her schedule.

In contrast, Nate looked alert and handsome in his white shirt and the cream paisley vest she admired. His brown and gold mane slicked away from his face and brushed the top of his collar in back. Those tawny golden eyes of his sparkled with what she hoped was pleasure when he saw her.

"Is Cindy gonna be okay now?" Luke asked.

Before she could answer, Fiona added her question from across the table.

"Ah, poor wee thing. Is the lass resting well now?"

"Yes, she's much better," Sarah said as she spooned scrambled eggs onto her plate.

"What?" Nate asked, alarm evident in his eyes. He stopped cutting his slice of ham to ask, "Is something wrong with the little princess?"

His obvious concern somehow lightened Sarah's fatigue. He really does care, she thought.

She smiled to reassure everyone. "The cold, the excitement, and all the moving about yesterday caused her a slight relapse. Pearl's given her a nice tea and syrup for the cough."

"Shouldn't we send for the doctor?" Nate asked, then

looked at his host. "I assume there's a doctor in town, isn't there?"

Drake stopped buttering the biscuit he held. "Dr. Percival, but there's no need to bother him. You'll soon learn my wife is far better at treating illness than most doctors."

"She learned very young from a woman in Tennessee," Storm added. "Ever since then she picks up more treatments talking to other healers and reading whatever she finds. She can help any ailment. Cures most."

"My question meant no disrespect to her abilities," Nate said. "Perhaps if you'd seen the child when we first found her, you'd understand my alarm. I'd not like to see Cindy, or anyone else, that ill again." He looked as if he wanted to add more, but said nothing else.

Joe and Luke, apparently sensing the tension between the adults, watched the exchange with eyes wide. The other children at the table also watched with unusual quiet.

Taking pity on Nate, Sarah said, "Cindy's already breathing easier and hardly coughs at all. She'll probably be able to play in her room with Luke and Joe and her cousins tomorrow."

Joe nudged Luke, and Luke asked, "Can we go play now?"

Sarah nodded. "Wear a coat if you go outside."

"Come on, we'll show you our fort," Robbie said. He and Evan took off at a gallop with Luke and Joe close behind.

Drake finished his biscuit and pushed back in his chair. "Say, Barton, you have anything special planned while you wait for your associates?

"Nothing in particular." Nate put down his fork and looked at Drake. "Something I can do for you?"

Sarah saw Drake and Pearl exchange looks and wondered at their conspiracy. Storm watched expectantly, as if waiting for an event. What was going on here?

Storm asked, "Do you ride?"

Nate shifted in his chair and looked from Storm to Drake as if wondering what they expected. "Yes. Not as well as you I'm sure, but I've ridden horses most of my life."

"Worst of the cold's over here. We're starting to bunch our herd for the spring roundup. All the hands are needed on the range," Drake said. "Wonder if I could recruit your help?"

"Drake," Sarah protested, surprised at the depth of her anger toward her brother-in-law. "Nate's a city man. He's not used to working on horseback the way you and Storm are. Surely you aren't asking that of him?"

Beside her, Nate placed a hand on her arm and said softly, "It's all right, Sarah." Then, he answered Drake, "Be happy to help if you need me."

"Great," Drake said. "You can probably fit into Storm's clothes, unless you brought some work pants with you." Drake said the word *work* as if to imply it was foreign to his guest.

Nate ignored the insult and looked at Storm as if gauging his size. "Appreciate the loan. Only brought business suits with me."

Storm pushed away from the table and stood up. "I'll get a shirt and pants and put them in your room." He looked out the dining room window. "Better get a jacket, too," he said and left the room.

Sarah fumed. Setting Nate up to help on the ranch made no sense. She didn't know who started it, but Pearl, Drake, and Storm were all in on it. Drake always started an early gather at this time of year to count and brand the new calves, but there was no shortage of ranch hands to help with the job. In fact, Drake usually had extra cowpunchers at the ranch because he hated to turn away anyone looking for honest work. She intended to get to the bottom of this, and she planned to do it soon.

Nate choked down his anger as he pulled on the brown denim pants borrowed from Storm. He stuffed the blue chambray shirt into his waistband and reached for the bandana. If Kincaid's help wasn't needed to cinch the railroad deal, he would have told Mr. High-and-Mighty Kincaid exactly what

he could do with his ranch . . . and several other things including body parts.

What could Nate do but agree, with Luke and Joe sitting
there watching him? Why it mattered what they thought of
him he couldn't say. Damn, he'd never had anyone look up
to him before. And not for what he could do for them or give
them, but just for being himself. He couldn't fail to measure
up in their eyes.

And Sarah. He exhaled and admitted it mattered what she
thought, too. Oh, he still intended to get what was his from
her. Maybe even sample Miss Sweetness-And-Light's charms
in the bargain. All the same, he didn't want to lessen himself
in her opinion now, though his mind refused to sort out the
reasons.

If Mr. High-And-Mighty Kincaid thought he could drive
Nate Barton away with hard work, he had another thought
coming. Let him pull all his tricks. By damn, he'd be surprised. Nate had a few tricks of his own waiting and he
planned to make the Kincaids pay extra for every hour he
worked here. With that to carry him through the day, he
clamped on his hat, jerked on the coat Storm left for him, and
stomped from the room.

Sarah checked on Cindy once more, then found Pearl in the
herb room. Pearl pulverized dried leaves for one of her medicines. Normally Sarah loved the blend of scents in this room.
Today, she hardly noticed.

"What is going on?" Sarah asked, arms akimbo. "Why did
Drake trick Nate into helping on the ranch?"

Pearl looked up but kept stirring the pestle into the mortar.
"You heard him. He said he needs help with the roundup."

"In a pig's eye he does," Sarah stamped her foot as she
spoke. "Don't think for a minute I missed that look you and
Drake exchanged at breakfast. Storm's in on it, too, isn't he?"

"Sarah, you're overreacting to a simple request." Pearl's

calm voice failed to soothe Sarah's anger, but Pearl continued, "After all, starting Monday you'll be busy again with your school. Nate would be bored all day out here away from town."

"Maybe so, but he's not used to ranch work and you know it. He's a businessman."

Pearl met Sarah's glare. "Ranching is a business."

"You know very well what I mean. Ranching is a hard business and Drake's good at it. But it's not Nate's business."

"And what is Nate's business?" Pearl asked.

"He's . . . he does, well, something about, um, investments."

"You don't know?"

Sarah fought the clutch of fear in her throat. She sat down on a ladder-back chair. "I don't know, do I? I . . . I mean, he never said, not exactly."

"What did he say?" Pearl asked.

Taking a deep breath and exhaling it, Sarah thought back. "At first, on the boat, he mainly said things about the weather, the trip. You know, the sort of chatty, impersonal things you say to strangers in a situation like that."

Sarah bit her lip a few seconds. "He did sort of keep himself between me and that odious Mr. Welborn. Did you know Mr. Welborn wanted me to let him into my cabin at night?"

"He never? Why the horrid man." Pearl put the pestle down and gave her full attention to her sister.

Sarah nodded. Talking about it unearthed the sting of his words. "He said terrible things about Mama, and how the apple didn't fall far from the tree. Then he threatened to tell the captain I sought him out and made indecent proposals to him if I didn't agree to his."

"What did you say?"

"Well, frightened as I was, the things he said about Mama made me mad as a hornet. I told him off, then jabbed him in the ribs to make him let go of me. For added measure, I stomped on his foot and gave him a hard kick in the shin."

Pearl laughed. "He deserved worse."

"He was still cursing when I went into the salon. Not long

after that Nate came in and spoke to Mrs. Welborn and me for the first time on the trip. That's when Nate started escorting me to and from my cabin, always staying between me and Mr. Welborn."

A staggering thought occurred to her and she looked at Pearl. "You don't suppose he overheard that awful little man threaten me? That he was protecting me?"

"Could be. He seems to think highly of you." Pearl stepped near and put her hand on Sarah's shoulder. "But, Sarah, it doesn't answer the question of what he was doing there—or here. Or what he does for a living, does it?"

"No, I guess it doesn't," Sarah admitted, though it hurt her to do so. She couldn't explain her loyalty to him. He had helped her when she needed him, been kind to her. In truth, she'd known him less than two weeks.

"Shouldn't you ask him?" Pearl asked.

"I . . . Well, I sort of did. He said he couldn't tell anyone until his associates arrived. Said it was confidential and he couldn't betray a trust." Sarah worried over her lack of information about the man she'd invited to her home. Her sister's home.

She leaped up and paced the small room. All her anger evaporated and she felt like crying. Even though she'd dreamed of him making his home in Kincaid Springs, what did she know about Nate? She'd pictured him with an office in town, guiding investments for important people. He must have an office elsewhere he'd return to soon.

Face it, it's not just an office you want him to have here. You want him to make his home with you.

Maybe all that pretending they were engaged started her fanciful thoughts. No, she admitted, she'd been attracted to him before that, even on the boat, even when she thought he was following her. She wondered how she could be suspicious of a man and captivated by him at the same time. If it weren't for the children, though, she would never have acted on that fascination. Would she?

* * *

The dust at the back of the herd choked him, the smell disgusted him, and the work might very well kill him. Worse, he hated the look on Drake's face, as if any minute he expected Nate to call it quits. Nate wanted to do exactly that, but he clenched his jaw and kept riding. He'd rot in hell before any cowpuncher forced him to give up.

Storm rode near and asked, "Everything all right?"

Nate nodded. "Fine."

Hell, he'd never told a bigger lie. The truth was he was so sore he could hardly sit in the saddle and he feared he'd be unable to walk once he tried to dismount. On top of that, he'd choked down enough dirt to raise potatoes. He refused to give up. Damned if he wouldn't fall down dead before he admitted he couldn't match endurance with a bunch of cow pushers.

"Want to come with me?" Storm asked.

"Might as well," Nate said and prayed Storm meant going in to town for supplies. "If it's all right with Drake."

"Yeah. Vincente saw some beeves down in a draw. Give you a break from the dust."

Anything had to be better than where he was now.

"Sounds good. I'll follow you." Anywhere away from here, he thought. Hell would be a treat after this.

Hours later, Nate amended his earlier opinion. Dragging a cow out of a mudhole was worse than the dust. Through it all, Storm treated him as an equal partner, never giving a hint of his thoughts. Nate figured he was a pretty useless ranch hand and gave Storm extra points for his tolerance.

Nate wondered about Storm. He must be a half-breed. Taller than most Indians, he had their dark coloring—except for startling purple-blue eyes like his sisters'.

Nate had shucked out of his borrowed coat to work in the protection of the draw. Early on he had lost his footing on the slippery ooze, which left him covered with mud and cow manure.

"Whew, I think I'll stay upwind of you. You'll look forward to a bath tonight," Storm said.

"A real bath?" he asked, hope supporting him.

"Zed Isaacs figured a way to store water for our new bathing rooms. Boiler to heat the water broke yesterday. Less Zed got it working better during the day, won't be a hot bath tonight."

"Sarah told the kids about the bathing room but I figured anybody as dirty as I am would have to take a dip in the river or the horse trough."

"Little cool for outdoor bathing," Storm said. "Maria's going to be plenty mad about those clothes, though." He looked down the draw and narrowed his eyes.

Nate followed his gaze, but saw nothing moving but a roadrunner scurrying across the sand from a mesquite tree to a clump of brush.

"Cow in trouble," Storm called as he rode off.

Nate let out a groan and followed.

Later as he released a calf, it ran smack dab into him instead of toward its mother. Backing away from the frightened animal, he tripped on a tree root and fell flat out on his back. He landed with a wham and slammed the needles of a huge prickly pear cactus across his right shoulder.

Storm helped him up and said, "I guess that's enough for one day. Let's go in for supper."

Nate almost wept with gratitude.

Riding into the ranch complex they met Drake and half a dozen of the ranch hands. Nate beat off as much of the caked and dried mire as he could, then stuck his head and arms under the trough pump. He slicked his hair back with his hands and flicked the water away.

Storm and Drake walked as sprightly as if they had just gotten up from the breakfast table. Nate staggered behind. The older children ran to meet them. Drake scooped up Robbie under one arm and Evan under the other. Storm picked up Katie and twirled her around. Damn, where did they get the energy?

"Hey, you're back. Rope any cows?" Luke called as he and Joe ran up. Their welcoming smiles soothed away a few aches.

He shook his head. "Not me, boys. But my horse and I pulled some out of the mud after Storm roped them."

When Joe pulled on Nate's sleeve, then pinched his own nose, Nate was so startled his knees almost buckled. He inwardly rejoiced. Joe had touched him for the first time, reached out without fear and touched him.

Nate made no mention of it but said, "I know, I smell bad. Cows are a nasty lot."

And that was the kindest thing he could say about the creatures. He hoped they had steak tonight. He'd really enjoy getting back at those cows by eating part of one.

But it was good to have the boys run up to meet him as he came back. He'd never had anyone that glad to see him return before. Nice to know he'd been missed. It almost made all his aches seem worthwhile.

"Hey, know what?" Luke asked. "Robbie and Evan have this great fort down by the river. They let us play in it all day. There's lots of other boys living here on this ranch and they played with us."

"That's great. What do you play in a fort?" He put a hand on the shoulder of each boy. Joe didn't pull away. At least the day wasn't a total waste. This place must be good for wounded boys. Maybe it wouldn't be too hard on lost souls like him.

Joe made shooting motions with his hands, then pretended to shoot an arrow.

"Ah, and who were the Indians and who were the soldiers?" Nate asked.

"We took turns. After that we were all Texas Rangers rounding up the Comancheros," Luke said, then he looked at the others. He whispered, "What are Comancheros?"

"Mostly some really mean men. They raided the settlers in Texas to sell horses, firearms, and things like that to the Comanches and others. Even kidnapped people to sell in

Mexico as slaves. I'm glad you two were the good guys," Nate answered.

"A letter came for you today," Luke said as he skipped ahead of Nate.

"A letter?" he asked. Who would send him a letter here? Hell, who would send him a letter anywhere?

Joe shook his head and made a tapping motion with his finger and held his ear as if listening.

"You mean a wire?" Nate asked and Joe nodded. Must be from Monk. Nate increased his gait and managed a stumbling trot up to the ranch house.

"It's in your room," Luke offered.

Nate stopped to kick out of his boots on the wide porch and traipsed down the hall to his room. The boys promised to see him at supper and went off with their new playmates.

The envelope lay on his wash stand. He ripped it open and sat in the rocker by the fireplace to read the message.

Delayed Stop Hargrove engaged two more weeks End

Damn. Two more weeks, plus travel time? How could he tolerate ranch work that long? He'd have to, no matter how much he hated it.

Hargrove must be in jail for the next two weeks. Nate wondered what charges landed him there. He disliked Hargrove and hated having to use him for the plan. The man knew how to impress an audience, though. He'd give him that much.

When Nate's turn in the bathing room came, he stripped and sank into the tepid water. A steaming bath would have felt good and a pillow for his abused sitter would have been a Godsend, but at least he could scrub himself clean. He pulled at the cactus needles, but couldn't reach most of them. Raw blisters on his hands hurt like fire, even holding them in the water.

All in all, he was in sad shape after only one day. How could he last weeks? Maybe he'd die before then and be free from this misery. Nate dressed and limped into the large gathering room to await dinner.

He hadn't let on to anyone, but Nate remembered Pearl from his brief time in Tennessee. That was when Cal went to persuade Roxie to come to St. Louis and Nate had tagged along. Nate shook his head. They'd had big dreams back then.

He and Cal had helped Roxie take an injured saloon girl to Pearl's house. He figured the girl was a goner, but Pearl's doctoring pulled her through. He probably saw Sarah and Storm at the same time, but only vaguely remembered a couple of young people. He remembered Pearl, though, and the way she ordered him and Cal around. Not that he would have recognized this attractive, well-dressed woman without knowing beforehand that it was she he'd be meeting.

Seven years ago she'd dressed in baggy, worn dresses with her hair in a braid down her back and had gone barefoot while she peddled her baked goods and did her folk healing. He was nineteen, but he hadn't changed all that much since then. Filled out a little, grown a few inches and a few scars. So far, there'd been no inkling she recognized him, though. She treated him with cool politeness and he knew she wished him gone.

Sarah hurried up to him and asked, "Are you all right?" Her blue dress turned her lavender-blue eyes more indigo and the lamplight darkened her golden hair.

"Are you injured?" Pearl asked.

Her concern seemed genuine, though Nate thought she viewed him with suspicion. He didn't scare off that easily. The Kincaids would soon learn that.

Nate flashed a smile. "If you don't mind, I could use some help pulling out the cactus spines in my shoulder." He thanked heaven the needles weren't lower.

Pearl said, "Come right into my treatment room."

Nate followed her and Sarah trailed him into a large room with windows along one wall. Beyond the windows he saw the garden with a fountain at the back of the house. The room smelled strongly of herbs he couldn't identify, but the aroma captured his interest.

He wondered where she obtained all these plants. Bunches hung from hooks along the ceiling. Others lay loose in baskets on a counter. Clear glass containers holding leaves, blossoms, or powders sat side by side along the counter. Opaque jars lined a set of shelves.

"Looks like a pharmacy in here," he said.

"It is a pharmacy, of sorts. I gather and process ingredients for many of my medicines." Pearl scooted a chair near her worktable then pulled on an apron. "Take off your jacket and shirt and sit right here."

Nate removed his jacket and draped it on the back of the chair. He looked at Sarah, who stood nearby. Would he bring Pearl's wrath down on him if he took off his shirt with Sarah present?

As if she read his mind, she said, "It's all right, Nate. I help Pearl sometimes."

He shrugged and unbuttoned his shirt.

When his hands left blood on the shirt, Sarah gasped. She pulled his right hand into hers and held it palm up.

"Didn't you wear gloves?" she asked.

"Yes. Storm gave me a pair." They hadn't helped much. Nate wondered how long it would be before he was able to shuffle a deck of cards and deal himself a winning hand.

Pearl said, "Here, put some of this salve on them." She took a jar from the shelf and gave it to Sarah.

Sarah opened the container and spread a thick, pungent ointment onto his palm. Her gentle motions soothed the raw skin but created a different ache low in his belly. She wrapped the hand in loose strips of cloth.

She smiled at him. "Now let's have the other one. The bandage is just to keep the salve from staining your clothes or rubbing off on everything you touch."

While Sarah worked on the other hand, Pearl pulled needles from his shoulder.

"Must be two dozen needles here. How'd you keep working with these in you?" Pearl asked.

"Didn't know I had a choice," Nate said, though in truth he'd received them near the end of the day when work was almost finished.

Pearl smiled, and this time the smile reached her gorgeous amethyst eyes. "You'll need to apply more of this salve and rebind the hands before you put your gloves on in the morning. You should use the same salve on the shoulder at bedtime. Untreated, those pricks become infected."

She washed her hands and dried them, then removed her apron. "If you'll excuse me, I have to see if Maria is ready to serve dinner."

"Thanks," Nate called as she left the room. He stood and pulled on his shirt, then looked at his hands.

"Let me help," Sarah said and secured each sleeve. "How do your hands and shoulder feel now?"

Her nimble fingers felt cool to his skin. Over the blending aromas in the room he caught the rose scent she always wore. Several strands of her golden hair curled at her cheek where they had escaped the hair piled into a loose knot atop her head.

He wished she would run those hands over him, and the thought caused an instant reaction in his body. Longing to close the door and sample her luscious rose petal lips, he instead said, "Thanks for your help. I'll be fine now."

What a lie. He expected to die of muscle spasms and fatigue before midnight.

She said, "If you'll tell me when you're ready at bedtime, I'll rub some salve on your shoulder for you."

He almost sank back onto the chair at the thought. At least he had something to live for.

Sarah gave him a bone-melting smile and said, "Why don't you join the others and I'll round up the children for dinner?"

When he returned to the family area, Nate recognized the Judge talking to two strangers.

Storm said, "Nate Barton, let me introduce our cousin Gabe who's a lawyer in Grandpa's firm. Then this is Zed Isaacs, who's responsible for the water in the bathing rooms as well as lots of other ingenious things around the place."

Older than Storm, maybe in his late twenties, Gabe looked like the other Kincaid men. Tall, broad shouldered, dark hair, blue eyes. Zed Isaacs appeared close to forty, tall and thin. His sad gray eyes watched the world as if resigned to disappointment.

On the other hand, Fiona looked ready to bolt at any minute. Though not related to the Kincaids, her appearance suggested differently. Dressed in a black skirt and shirtwaist, she wore her black shawl clasped tightly to her. With her champagne-colored hair twisted into a neat bun, she appeared the proper poor relation at a family gathering. Although her demeanor suggested calm, the uncertainty in her eyes revealed her distress.

Nate ambled over to her on aching legs. "Have a nice day?" he asked.

She smiled, worry temporarily removed from her face. "From the looks of your hands and the way you're limping about, I'd say my day passed better than yours."

"I certainly hope so. Otherwise you'd be dead." The dinner bell sounded, so he offered his arm. "May I escort you in to dinner?"

"Now wouldn't that be lovely?" she replied and slipped her hand onto his arm.

Her eyes twinkled when she smiled, making her seem younger than her years. He wondered what state of affairs brought a woman in her fifties to her current insecure circumstances. She had mentioned a married daughter, but not what caused her to leave her daughter's home for the uncertain life she faced here. None of his business, but what would she do? No wonder she looked worried.

* * *

Sarah cornered Grandpa after dinner on his way back from the privy. Because it was so important, she gauged her words carefully.

"How are you getting along without Lily to run your household?" she asked.

Grandpa's pained expression answered before his words, "Ah, girl, my nice orderly life is a shambles. Polly and Emily do their best, but the truth is they both need constant supervision. And that girl who comes weekdays needs taking by the hand."

"Have you thought of hiring someone as housekeeper to see to all the things Lily did for you?"

"Hmph. That Williams woman came around asking for the job, and I turned her down flat. Woman never shuts up. I don't want someone yammering at me all the time I'm home."

Sarah took his arm and walked with him. "What if you found a quiet, polite woman who could make your house as efficient as when Lily lived with you?"

"Now where would that woman be found, other than your own lovely self?" he asked and patted her hand where it rested on his arm.

"Mrs. Galloway is available. Of course, she won't be free for long. As soon as word gets around about a jewel like her, someone will snap her up."

"The woman who came with you on the train?" He looked thoughtful, then said, "She seems quiet enough, but that doesn't mean she can run a house like mine."

"Would you be willing to give her a chance to try?" Sarah held her breath, hoping he'd say yes.

He shook his head. "Hmmm, I don't know. What would I do if she doesn't work out? I'd hate to fire her and there I'd be, stuck with her."

"Oh, Grandpa, just give her a chance. I promise if she doesn't have your house just as you like it in a month, I'll find her another position myself."

"Well, I'd rather you come live with me and take on the

job, but I know you've got your school to teach." He exhaled a deep breath. "You know I can never refuse you anything. Bring her to the house tomorrow and we'll work out the details."

"Oh, thank you, Grandpa." Sarah planted a kiss on his cheek and gave him a hug. "You won't be sorry."

"I probably will, but we'll see. You know, you're different since you're back from seeing to your mother." He looked her up and down. "Seems that trip did you good."

"I'm still just me, Grandpa."

"Well, I've always admired you, girl. Still do, but you're perkier now. Have more spunk."

"Is that good?" She didn't feel different, but Storm and Pearl had both suggested the same thing.

Grandpa gave her arm a pat. "Yes, I like seeing you caring less about what people will think and more about what you want."

"My stars, Grandpa," she gasped. "That makes me sound horribly selfish."

"No, not at all. You're a fine woman, a joy to your family. As for me, I'm tired now, and I'm going home."

"We'll see you tomorrow." She gave him another hug and a kiss on his cheek.

Sarah decided to wait until morning to tell Fiona the good news. The excitement of it might keep her from sleeping well. Sarah smiled, thinking how pleased Fiona would be when she heard.

NINE

From Cindy's room Sarah walked toward her own. When she passed Nate's door, she saw it open and stopped. She'd forgotten her promise to put salve on his shoulder. Pausing in the doorway, she watched him.

He lay sleeping on his side, hands resting on the bed in front of him. She watched the rise and fall of his chest and ribs. No doubt his day left him exhausted. The covers were at his hips and the lamp burned low. He must have been waiting for her when he fell asleep.

His broad shoulders tapered to a small waist where the sheet dipped low enough for her to see he still wore his trousers. Tousled locks fell across his forehead and gave him the deceptive appearance of harmless innocence.

Yes, just what the rabbit thinks about the snare.

She stepped into the room and picked up the jar of salve and a towel. Dipping her finger into the ointment, she pooled a bit in her palm and held it to lend her body heat. Using her fingertips, she spread the unguent onto his broad shoulder, smoothing it in gentle strokes. He moaned at her touch and his eyes flew open.

"Sarah?" he whispered.

As he rolled over, she shoved the towel under his shoulder to protect the bed linens from the salve. His hand came to her waist.

"As I suspected, I didn't survive my day. I've died and

you're a ministering angel," he said. Tawny eyes heavy with sleep gazed at her and he offered a crooked grin.

"I apologize for not coming sooner to put the ointment on your shoulder."

All the time she spoke, she thought she shouldn't be in his room, not with him on the bed and no shirt on. Even with the door open it wasn't proper. But she had promised. More, she'd missed talking to him today.

"I tried to stay awake. Heard you with the children. What was all the commotion with Cindy?" he asked.

"First she was afraid to sleep by herself, so Katie wanted to sleep with her. Then Beth was afraid, so they're all three asleep in Cindy's bed."

"But she slept alone last night."

"Well, not much. I sat with her until she got to sleep, and because she was ill I spent a lot of time in there during the night."

"And now you're here." His eyes darkened and their power immobilized her. He pulled her toward the bed and she sat near him.

"I, um, I didn't mean to wake you. I thought I'd just rub some of Pearl's salve onto those needle pricks. They, um, they can get infected." Why should she feel so shy and nervous all of a sudden? They'd been seated side by side closer than this on the train for days.

His eyes watched her as if he were drinking her in. She saw the old wounds, those which had been under the bandages she'd seen in Memphis. Injuries still unexplained. She touched the one at his upper chest. "This salve would help keep those scars from pulling," she said.

"Would you put some on them for me?" His voice came low and husky and his gaze never left her face.

Dipping her fingertips into the jar once more, she gathered a dab of the unguent. With slow circular motions she spread it on the upper scar. Firm muscles beneath her hand rippled when he moved his arm across her lap to let his hand rest at her waist. As she widened the circles, her fingers absorbed the pounding of his heart beating in time with hers.

Unable to hold his gaze, she looked down at the jar and picked up more salve. She spread it on the lower scar at his side near his waistband. When she had made only a couple of circles with her fingers over the roughly healed injury, he gasped and grabbed her hand.

"I think that's enough for now." He took a ragged breath and sat up. "Let's try this instead."

His arms slid around her and he lowered his mouth to hers. The taste of him surprised her. He slid his tongue into her mouth. Surprised, she might have pulled away, but he held her fast and intensified his assault.

The room swirled about her and she sank into his kiss. His tongue came again, probing, tasting, teasing. In her wildest dreams she would never have imagined a kiss could be this potent. Following his lead, she touched her tongue to his and his grip on her tightened. He moaned and his bandaged hands moved over her back. Her bones dissolved and she molded herself to him. He broke the kiss to look at her, then settled himself against her again.

He pulled her onto his lap and she slid her arms around him. Trailing kisses along her neck, he whispered, "Sarah."

She let her head fall back onto his shoulder to give him access to her throat. His hand came to her bodice and fumbled with buttons.

The shock made her push away. "Oh, Nate. What are we doing?" she asked and leaped to her feet. "I . . . I shouldn't have kissed you like that. I shouldn't even be in your room."

"Of course you should. The door's open, you were only helping me."

"Was I?" Helping him to what? she wondered. Or, was she helping herself to his charms? My stars, where was her brain? In a few more moments she would have let him . . . Well, she didn't know what she would have let him do. She suspected it would have been whatever he wanted. Worse, she thought her needs matched his own and wished she could stay to explore what he offered.

"Maybe you could sit and talk to me for a while." He patted the bed then scooted up to rest his uninjured shoulder against the headboard.

"No." She edged away. "I, um, I should go to my own room. Yes, I should go." What must he think of her, kissing him like that?

"Please stay, just for a bit," he said.

She shook her head and pressed her hand to her throat. "No, no, I can't. I shouldn't be in your room. What on earth was I thinking?" But she wanted to stay, needed his strong arms around her.

"You thought you were helping a friend. And you were. There's no harm in that."

"There could be." If he knew how much she yearned to crawl in bed beside him, he'd be shocked. The knowledge shocked her. "You'd better go back to sleep. You need your rest. I should sleep, too."

He shrugged. "If you insist, but I'd rather talk to you. I've hardly been able to speak with you since we arrived."

"I know. Perhaps tomorrow. You had a hard day and tomorrow morning will come too early for you."

He groaned and let his head fall back against the headboard. "These ranchers are tough. I may die trying to keep up."

Backing to the doorway, she said, "You'll be fine. I have a feeling you're tough, too, in your own way."

He smiled. "Thanks, I hope you're right."

She stopped in the doorway. "At least tomorrow is Saturday."

When he raised his eyebrows in question, she said, "Everyone quits early on Saturdays so there's time to go into town." She hoped he'd choose to stay at the ranch with her.

"Thank God. Maybe I can keep up with Storm for part of a day."

"Good night." She pulled the door closed behind her and hurried to her room.

* * *

Nate had already left with the other men when Sarah came into the dining room. She wondered if she would have been able to meet his gaze after what happened in his room last night. Sighing, she wished she'd had the opportunity to see him. He'd said he hadn't had a chance to talk to her alone and that was true.

She chewed her lip and wondered at the effect he had on her. All her life she'd acted with propriety, especially since coming to Kincaid Springs. She wore a corset if she went to town, always appeared neat as a pin and in the proper dress for the occasion and time of day. On her trip to see about Mama, though, something changed.

Of late, two beings warred within her. The old Sarah, so careful to act properly at all times, offend no one, too shy to speak up for herself, did battle with an emerging and blossoming entity. This new-sprung Sarah wanted to protect her children, to make a home for them. Moreover, the just-out woman longed to expand her experiences.

Watching Mama die forced Sarah to evaluate her own life. Lily's abandoning her might have added to this change. Certainly finding her children drove her to seek changes in her life, required a set of new situations.

And Nate. Handsome, strong, wonderful . . . dangerous Nate. What about him created this yearning, a desire to do outrageous things that involved much more than kissing? She'd have to watch herself, be far more circumspect.

This evening she'd ask him to walk with her down by the river. Surely that was proper, right here near home. They'd be alone and Nate could talk to her all he wanted. Would he kiss her again? She hoped so and planned to give him the opportunity.

After all, there was no harm in flirting or kissing in a genteel way, was there? Her conscience asked, even if the kisses set her on fire and made her feel all sorts of things she didn't understand? No, she'd be proper, she simply wouldn't think those things. She'd kiss him and they would talk, that's all. That matter settled firmly in her mind, she told Fiona about Grandpa's job offer.

Fiona shook her head. "Oh, now wouldn't that be lovely? But, I couldn't possibly take the job."

"Why ever not?" Sarah gasped.

Fiona looked close to tears, and shook her head again. "It would never work."

Frustration shot through Sarah. "Why? Tell me why?"

"Sure and I saw the big house you pointed out on our wagon ride from the train station. Big as a castle it was." Fiona shook her head.

Sarah loved that house so much she found it impossible to keep the enthusiasm from her voice. "It's really charming inside. Drake loves to tell how Grandpa ordered it from a catalog. The pieces were shipped all the way from Chicago. Then, Grandpa hired a decorator who brought things from all over the world."

Sarah sighed. She always enjoyed staying in the lovely pink and white room reserved for her. Though she'd never let on to Pearl, she'd always wished she could live with Grandpa in town.

"What did I tell you?" Fiona asked.

Snapped from her reverie about Grandpa's house, Sarah said, "I don't understand. Isn't this what you'd hoped for?"

"In all my born life I've never so much as set foot in such a fine house. God love you for trying, but I'd be in bits every minute, don't you see? What would the likes of me be doing in a house like that? No, I thank you all the same, but I'll not be taking the job."

Sarah felt like screaming. "I don't understand. Please explain to me why you don't want the job."

Fiona's face showed surprise. "Not want it? Sure and I'd like it plenty. But, dearie, I would never be able to do a proper job of it."

Fiona pulled a handkerchief from inside the cuff of her sleeve and dabbed at her eyes. "Imagine me telling other women what to do to make a fine house like that run proper. Why, they'd . . . They'd laugh at me."

"Nonsense. Emily and Polly are both used to having someone tell them what's expected. They need supervision."

When the look on Fiona's face showed no change, Sarah tried another tactic. "And I'm worried about Grandpa. He's done so much for this county and here he is in his late years with his home in chaos. It's affecting his health, poor man."

She had Fiona's interest now. Fiona asked, "Is he ill then?" She clucked her tongue. "And he looks such a fine strapping man."

"Pearl has to keep him supplied in tonics. His diet needs to be carefully monitored, but there's no one to check on it. My Aunt Lily was so particular about everything. With her gone, I worry so about what will become of him." Sarah wondered if exaggeration counted as a lie. She hoped not.

"Well . . . I do know how to plan a man a good meal. I haven't forgotten so much as that. And I know about cleaning. I kept a good house, that I'll admit."

Sarah sighed. Finally they were getting somewhere. "You know how to clean, you're very organized, you're neat . . . And, Fiona, you need this job."

Fiona wiped her nose and smiled. "All right, dearie. Sure and I'll give it me best try. May the Lord have Mercy on us."

Sarah patted her arm. "You'll do fine, Fiona. Now, are you ready to talk to Grandpa?"

Fiona exhaled a giant sigh. " 'Tis nervous as a cat I am, but we might as well talk to Himself and be done with it."

That evening, Sarah and Nate walked slowly along the riverbank. She touched the branch of a willow heavy with buds, but no green showed. A few more warm spring-like days like this one and the trees would leaf out.

"Your limp's better. Are you getting used to riding again?"

Nate looked back where the house stood. "You may have to hitch up the wagon and bring it to get me back up that hill."

She laughed. They passed the makeshift fort and waved at the youngsters. So far, the children all played well together. Pearl's boys were younger than Joe and Luke, but several of the vaqueros' children were near their ages.

"I'm surprised you didn't go into town with Storm and some of the other men," she said.

"Too early for my associates to be there. I'd rather relax here and talk to you."

He took her hand in his. The sensation of his strong warm hand and the strips of cloth protecting it made her think of last night in his room. She wished she could have stayed there, could have explored the delights he might offer, the lessons he had to teach. What those delights might be, she could only guess from what she'd read and overheard of married women's conversations.

What would it be like to lose herself in abandon to him? Would the tingles she experienced at his touch heighten? She gave herself a mental shake. Such fancies could only lead to bad results. She meant to act properly in the future and not lose his respect. Gently retrieving her hand, she walked beside him on the worn pathway.

She ducked her head, but watched him through her lashes. Beside them the river glistened in the light of the setting sun. The same light caught in his hair and painted more gold into the browns.

"You folks sure have pretty sunsets out here," he said. "Sunrises, too."

"You should see it when there's been a thunderstorm with some of the purple clouds still in the sky. That's how my brother got his name, you know. His mother thought his eyes looked like the rolling purple clouds of a storm so she named him Eyes Like Storm Cloud. He shortened it to Storm

Cloud." She gave him a sidelong look and said, "Oh, dear, I seem to be babbling. Anyway, it really can be breathtaking."

He stopped and gently pulled her to face him. "I doubt it could compare to the breathtaking sight I see now."

Myriad sensations shot through her—pleasure, astonishment, wonder, sheer stark terror. What should she do? What should she say?

She stammered, "You . . . You're being kind."

Trees screened them from the house now. They were alone with only the birds and animals to keep them company.

"Far from it. Sarah, you're one of the most beautiful women I've ever seen. But more than that, you're intelligent, interesting, and, well, spunky."

She let out an exasperated sigh. "Spunky? People keep telling me that. What does it mean?"

He laughed at her chagrin. "You aren't afraid to stand up for what you believe. Look at the way you rescued the children."

Her gaze met his. "I couldn't have managed it without your help." She wouldn't have wanted to.

In spite of his bandages, he took both of her hands in his. "Yes, you could have. I know you would have saved them against any odds."

"Would you like to rest a bit?" She gestured to the trunk of a giant cottonwood felled by a storm. Drake had stripped the limbs and hauled them away, but left the massive trunk as a sort of bench. This was her goal. Here they could sit side by side again and discuss anything they wished in private.

They sat and she smiled up at him. Oh, dear, what should she say? "Um, did I thank you for helping me?"

"Yes, several times. I can think of another way, though," he said and pulled her near.

His gaze watched hers as he lowered his head. Shuttering her eyes, she leaned into him. She wanted this kiss, wanted to reclaim the sensations he aroused last night. Probing tongues danced together and fused in the fiery kiss.

Heat coiling in her core intensified and exploded through

her. She forgot her earlier resolve to remain calm and proper. For the moment she couldn't get enough of him. Her hands caressed his chest then slid around his neck.

He broke their kiss to swing his leg over and straddle the trunk, then snuggled her to him as he reclaimed her lips. She didn't understand her need for more from him, but she ached for whatever he offered her. The power of her desire astonished her.

When he worked his fingers loose from the bandages and let them fondle her breast, she moaned with the pleasure of his touch. He gently rubbed his fingers across her nipple and she pulled him closer. Even through the fabric, his touch seared her skin.

She craved more, more of this wonderful rapture surging through her. When she felt his fingers at her bodice fastenings, she didn't protest. Instead, she sank into his kisses and helped with the tiny buttons. He pushed the offending cloth down off her shoulders.

Whatever was to come, she wanted to experience all of this man and savor this moment. He broke the kiss to move across her face, down her neck, and across her shoulders, showering kisses as he moved. She threw her head back and arched to allow him complete access to her exposed heart. So transported was she that his mouth on her bared breast came as a surprise. The exhilaration spiraled through her.

She gasped and cried, "Nate." Not asking him to stop, only registering her pleasurable astonishment.

His hand touched her ankle, then moved slowly up in circular caresses. She knew she should pull away, should stop him immediately. Captured in his spell, she couldn't force herself to halt his lovemaking. Like the rabbit caught by the wolf, she was powerless to escape—only she had no wish to flee.

He slipped his fingers through the slit in her drawers and touched her most private place. She would have protested, but his lips reclaimed hers and she was lost. His finger moved across her feminine nub and stars exploded in her brain.

When his finger slipped inside her, she melted. He moved his mouth back to her breast. The suckling of his mouth and tongue strokes against her nipple kept pace with the delving of his fingers inside her. She had an almost overwhelming urge to move her hips in time to his strokes, but feared she would fall from the tree trunk and end this magic.

His arousal pressed into her side. If she had bones in her body she would have touched him, explored him as he explored her. She thought nothing could ever be more wonderful, but a new thrumming built inside her. Growing, blossoming, wave after wave of ecstasy grew. My stars, she had no idea anything could feel this good. She lost control, felt her body leave in an ascent to paradise.

"Nate?" she panted.

When his gaze met hers, his eyes were dark with passion. "Give into it, sweetheart. Let yourself go."

He sought her other breast. Only his arm bracing her kept her from dissolving across the tree trunk. With his fingers probing, he used a thumb to rake across her nub.

A flick of his tongue and he raised his head from her breast long enough to murmur, "That's it, sweetheart. Let yourself flow with the feeling."

The sensations increased until she neither heard nor saw her surroundings. She burst with pleasure and sank against him.

After a few gasping breaths, she opened her eyes. "Nate, what happened? I never dreamed, I mean—"

He held her against him and nuzzled her neck. "Pretty powerful, isn't it? Especially the first time."

She raised her head to look into his eyes. "You mean you can make me feel like that again?"

He chuckled and kissed the corner of her mouth. "Anytime you'll let me. There are other ways to give pleasure. It only gets better."

Wonderful news, but what enjoyment had he received? "And what makes you feel that way?"

He took her hand and pressed on his arousal through his clothes. "I can show you."

She moved her trembling fingers to fumble with the buttons of his trousers, eager to satisfy her curiosity as well as let him share her delight. He exhaled a sharp breath when she touched him. Her fingers tested the sensation of soft skin on his hard shaft.

Pearl had explained the ways of men and women long ago, and Sarah had seen statues of naked men pictured in books. Nothing prepared her for the transformation of the manhood part. She wondered how on earth it ever fit inside a woman's small place. As she pondered this, she caressed up and down his sex. He moaned, his eyes closed.

His arms braced behind him on the tree trunk and he threw his head back. He appeared lost to anything but her touch, and she took pleasure in this new power she had over him. She gripped his shaft gently with one hand. The fingers of her other hand probed the tip of his manhood. A bead of moisture appeared and she massaged it around the tip. He moaned and she thought he might fall off the tree trunk.

No one had told her she possessed this ability to reduce a strong man to a moaning slave. The ability to induce such overwhelming emotion sent her spirits soaring. She wanted to laugh with delight. Had she looked this oblivious to the world when he had touched her?

Suddenly she became aware of a familiar noise and paused to listen. The jingles and creaks of a rig caught her ear, wheels crunching on the pebble strewn path.

"Someone's coming," she said.

She leaped up and straightened her skirt. My stars, she looked a sight. Quickly, she buttoned her bodice and smoothed her hair. Her heart still beat furiously and her stomach jiggled inside her. She shook her skirts, hoping the wrinkles remaining didn't give away her recent conduct.

He sat up and stared at her through dilated eyes which

seemed unable to focus. In fact, he looked dazed, as if he hadn't heard her or couldn't register her words.

She pulled at his arm. "Nate, someone's coming along the trail. Straighten your clothes."

He shook his head and stood, tucking in his shirt and buttoning his trousers with trembling fingers. She stood beside him and took his arm. They strolled toward the oncoming buggy. She glanced down at her dress and smoothed out a telltale wrinkle.

The folly of what she'd just done struck her. What on earth possessed her to behave like a . . . a harlot? Yet, how could she regret the sensations she'd just experienced? She looked up at Nate. His composed features surprised her and his eyes wore that shuttered look he so often displayed. What did he think of her now? She wished she knew but she hardly knew what she thought of herself. They walked slowly while her mind whirled with conflicting sentiments. The rig approached rapidly with the horse at a trot.

"There you are, Sarah," Peter Dorfmeyer said as he pulled beside them. "Your absence from the house surprised me. Surely you knew I'd come to call this evening?"

"No, Peter. How could I know that?" She turned to Nate. "Nate, this is Peter Dorfmeyer, the banker from town. Peter, Nate Barton is here on business and staying at the ranch for a few weeks."

The two men eyed each other with hostility. Neither acknowledged the other with a greeting.

Peter looked at Sarah and said, "I'd been coming to call each Saturday for two months before your trip. It only stands to reason I'd resume my visits once you returned." He glared at Nate and huffed an exaggerated sigh. "Well, you both might as well get in and I'll take you back to the house."

As Nate helped Sarah into the buggy, she murmured, "At least now you don't have to walk up that hill."

TEN

At the house, Nate helped Sarah from the buggy. He held her waist and gazed into her eyes. She saw the light of amusement glistening in his eyes' wolfish depths and they shared a smile before he released her. Peter fumed his way around the buggy to escort her into the house. From her point of view, the way to handle the situation was to walk ahead of the two men.

Sarah invited them to sit in the living room. "I'll get some refreshments." She smoothed her dress again as she went into the kitchen. Did her appearance tell others what she and Nate had done? She'd die of embarrassment if anyone else knew.

Maria met her with a tray of tea and slices of chocolate cake left from dinner. Sarah thanked her as she took the tray and retraced her steps to where she'd left the two men. Nate sat in an armchair by the fireplace looking as if he owned the world. He smiled as she came in, jumped up, and took the tray from her. Peter's rigid posture kept him on the edge of the sofa, his face stiff with disapproval.

Nate placed the tray on a table and Sarah prepared to serve. A herd of small boys raced across the foyer. Luke and Joe left the others to venture into the living room. They stood near Nate and stared openly at Peter.

"Would you boys ask Cindy to come here for a minute, please, and come back with her?" Sarah asked.

She served the men while she waited for the children.

The boys soon returned with Cindy in tow. Apparently the girls had been playing dress up. Cindy wore an old dress of

Pearl's and carried a parasol. A long feather bobbled over the brim of the large-brimmed bonnet tied to her head. Her feet were poked into a pair of Sarah's shoes, clumping as she dragged them to keep the shoes from falling off.

"Peter, this is Cindy, Luke, and Joe. Children, this is Mr. Dorfmeyer. He manages the bank in town."

Cindy curtsied and each of the boys gave a little bow. Curiosity filled their faces as they glanced from Peter to Nate and back to Sarah. Cindy lifted the front of her skirts and clopped regally to Nate, her dress hem dragging behind her.

"Hello, Princess Cindy," he said as she climbed onto his lap and snuggled against him.

She giggled. "You always call me that, but we're playing house. I'm the mother. Katie and Beth have to mind what I say."

Sarah smiled at them, bursting with pride at their behavior. She ruffled each boy's hair and walked to lift Cindy from Nate's knee. She gave her a kiss on the cheek when she set her down. "Thank you for coming to meet Mr. Dorfmeyer. You may run along and play now."

The boys rushed outside and Cindy clomped toward her room to rejoin Katie and Beth.

Peter's nose wrinkled in distaste. "More of your students, I suppose?"

Sarah picked up her teacup. "Oh, no. Those children are mine." How wonderful to be able to say those words.

"Yours?" he stammered. "That's impossible."

"I found them on their own in Memphis and brought them here with me. In fact, Mr. Barton assisted me. I'm adopting them."

"That's hardly proper. I mean, it is bad enough you've built that school and insist on teaching those ragamuffin children there." His face had grown red and he looked about to suffer apoplexy.

Sarah paused, her cup halfway to her lips, then returned the cup and saucer to the table. "I beg your pardon. What do you mean, 'bad enough' I built my school?"

She had suspected his intolerance for those less fortunate than himself, but Peter had never been so open about it before. How could a man who'd had all the advantages of life begrudge any child the opportunity to read and write? Many of her friends thought Peter handsome. For the first time, Sarah noticed Peter's brown eyes were a bit too close together and his eyebrows rode like furry caterpillars across his brow.

"Well, really, Sarah." Peter shrugged. "It's not as if you're helping them. After all, teaching them to read and write only raises false expectations for those people."

Sarah fought her temper, but it boiled inside her. Who did Peter think he was, talking about "ragamuffins" and "those people" as if they were of no consequence? She believed every person, no matter how destitute, had the same rights. How could Peter talk as if the poor were somehow less human than those more fortunate in society?

Nate stiffened, but said nothing. He regarded Peter as he might an annoying insect just before he gave it a swat.

With an even voice belying her inner turmoil, she asked, "What sort of false expectations, may I ask? Do you think reading, being aware of the world around them, is somehow hindering their well being? Do you mean to imply that the ability to count money so they're not cheated is wasted?"

She watched Peter now, examining his appearance. He definitely had a weak chin. Worse, she feared he had no compassion. She almost felt sorry for anyone so shallow and with so little feeling for his fellow man. Almost.

Peter pursed his lips and poked his nose in the air. "Well, really, my dear, they're hardly likely to use those skills, now are they? The boys will become ranch hands or some such and the girls will clean their own houses or someone else's and have a dozen children. Never have enough money to bother counting."

"You don't know that. And what if it's true? School will enrich them in ways that will remain with them throughout their lives. You don't even know the children at my school." To her knowledge, he'd never even been in the schoolyard.

"Nor do I wish to. And now you've brought children you know nothing about into your home. It's commendable for you to feel sorry for them, my dear, but surely you don't intend to carry through with this adoption thing?" He speared a bit of cake with his fork as if he discussed the weather, not lives.

"I've already asked Gabe to draw up whatever legal papers are necessary. The process will soon be complete." She wanted to say more, wanted to slap that pompous smirk from his face, but kept her anger in control. After all, this man was a guest.

Peter's face turned red and he set down his plate. "That simply won't do. No, it won't do at all. Hardly fitting for a woman of your station. You must keep in mind the man you marry will want his own children, not a group of orphans bred in who knows what circumstances."

Nate stood and opened his mouth to speak, but Sarah interrupted. "The man I marry will welcome my children, and *these three are my children.*"

Peter dusted a crumb from his cuff. "They hardly fit in with a banker's image," he spoke as if he addressed a simple child. "Now, don't worry your pretty head about it, my dear. Leave it all to me. We can place them in a good home. You'll soon see it's best for everyone."

Fury seized control of her, a ferocious anger so great she found it hard not to strike Peter. He talked of the lives of her children as if he were placing a litter of kittens.

She stood, her hands on her hips. "Of all the nerve. For your information, they *are* in a good home. Peter Dorfmeyer, you are a pompous ass. Leave this house now and do not return."

Peter's face registered shock and he spluttered, "My dear, you don't know what you're saying. Why, with your family connections and mine, we'd make a highly suitable union."

He shot Nate a seething glare. "It's obvious you've been unduly influenced by outsiders. You'll come to your senses in time."

"Out," she yelled and pointed to the door.

Nate stepped forward. The look on his face made it obvious he intended to hasten Peter's departure.

Peter picked up his hat and crossed the flagstone floor. He turned and pointed at Nate. "You haven't heard the last of me, Barton." He turned back and stomped out.

Nate followed him to the door and closed it firmly behind Peter's retreating figure. Sarah collapsed back onto her chair. Since her money was in his bank, the chances of her escaping an encounter with Peter were nonexistent. She'd avoid him whenever possible, though, from now on. She might even move her funds.

Nate rejoined her and sat in the chair facing hers. He smiled and she saw the tenderness of understanding reflected in his gaze. "Lovely visit, wouldn't you say?"

His simple words dissolved her anger and she couldn't suppress a giggle. "Oh, my stars. I sent him off with a flea in his ear, didn't I? I shouldn't be surprised by his attitude and shouldn't have let it affect me. He's tried to tell me what to think and how to act since he started calling on me."

She met his look and her voice softened. "I never invited him to call, never even invited him to come again."

"Seems to feel he's doing you a favor," Nate said.

She giggled again. "Maybe he feels differently now. He'll probably not even speak to me in the future."

"I doubt his kind discourages that easily," Nate said.

Drake had accompanied Pearl to visit a patient an hour's ride away and they weren't expected back until late. Fiona presided over the games in Cindy's room. Sarah looked around to make sure no other household members overheard. She took a deep breath, but couldn't meet his gaze.

Twisting at a pleat in her skirt she forced herself to look up at him. "Nate, about what happened by the river—"

He leaned forward and placed a finger to her lips. "Don't spoil it by telling me you're sorry."

She looked at her hands, suddenly unable to meet his eyes. "No, um, not exactly. It's just that, well, I've never done anything like that before."

"I didn't for a minute think you had," he said. He took both of her hands in his. His strong hands cradled hers gently and his touch sent her senses reeling again.

"Sarah, you're a beautiful and intelligent woman. I enjoy being with you. That hasn't changed."

She raised her gaze to meet his mesmerizing, molten eyes. He hadn't said he cared for her, just that he enjoyed being with her. Did he have any regard for her, or was she just a convenient diversion?

She said, "I was afraid you might, well, you might think me a loose woman."

Storm came into the room and looked from one to the other. His eyes narrowed in speculation and his jaw clenched. Nate dropped her hands and scooted back in his chair.

Sarah felt her face flush. Her brother might be quiet, but he missed nothing that went on around him. "I didn't know you were back from town." Oh, dear, that sounded bad, as if it made a difference in how she acted.

"Came in the back." His face masked his thoughts, but Storm continued to look from Nate to Sarah. "Saw Peter driving away. Short visit?"

"He made some very insulting comments about Luke and Joe and Cindy." Sarah sighed and stood to face her brother. "You might as well know. I lost my temper and asked him to leave."

Nate rose also and stood at Sarah's side. She appreciated the gesture of support.

"Your business, not mine," Storm said. "Couldn't understand why you let him call here in the first place."

Astonished, Sarah answered, "You never told me."

Storm shrugged. "Like I said, none of my business." He

slapped his leg with his hat a couple of times before he added, "Say, Nate, a few of the boys are meeting in the bunkhouse now to play cards. Come on and join us."

Nate hesitated, then nodded to Sarah. "Will you excuse me?"

"Yes. Of course. It's time for me to round up all the children and herd them off to bed. I'll see you both tomorrow."

Nate knew a summons when he heard one, and made no mistake about Storm's invitation. Storm had wanted to separate Nate from Sarah and it worked. Nate had followed him to the bunkhouse without complaint. No use bucking against strength, and Storm definitely had the power here.

There was a card game all right. Nate's bandaged hands made play more difficult, especially with his fingers tender from burst blisters, but his past training didn't let him down. Careful not to win too often or take much from any individual, he remained several dollars ahead all evening. He wanted no more suspicions raised regarding him or his background.

No need to cheat with this crowd. His mind kept perfect record of who played what cards. An eager young kid chewed his lip when he had a good hand, another man tapped a finger on the table. In the first hour Nate picked up the signals from each player except one. Only Storm masked his thoughts to the world. Nate would figure him out, too, given time.

He tossed in four nines and let the kid win with three jacks. Nate caught a flicker of surprise in Storm's purple-blue eyes. So, Storm kept track of the cards as well. Good to know, but there was no proof he'd let the kid win, because the cards were scooped up and shuffled immediately. Nate had won enough, especially from a couple of the men he didn't care for. No point calling attention to his skill in games of chance.

Thinking of chance, being here was taking a big one. He knew the Kincaids had no wish to welcome a newcomer into their fold, especially in regard to Sarah. From his viewpoint, they were all overprotective of her. He had to admit she needed their protection where he was concerned and it rankled. Why hadn't they protected her from that arrogant Dorfmeyer?

Remembering Dorfmeyer brought back the calamity barely avoided when the man arrived. Damn, what had Nate been thinking? If Sarah hadn't heard that rig coming, they would have been compromised. By now he'd be on his way to a wedding with a shotgun at his back.

Would that be so bad? The thought hit him like a jolt of lightning. The misery of working as a ranch hand would definitely be softened with Sarah and the children to welcome him home each day. If he survived the hellish days, the nights would be heaven.

Why assume he would be working as a ranch hand, though? What would he do to support a wife and three children? Maybe he could open a saloon in town. Sure, as if Sarah would want a saloonkeeper for a husband.

He gave himself a mental kick in the rear. What a sap he was to even think about living here with Sarah and the children. He could never fit in, never make it in her world. Hell, she didn't even know his real name. Better to enjoy Miss Sugar and Spice's company while it lasted, take what he could, and get out. She'd be better off without the likes of him—as long as she avoided that Dorfmeyer jerk.

With the Kincaids's money in Dorfmeyer's bank, the man knew to a penny how much this clan had. Probably a fortune. Desirable as Sarah was, Nate figured a large part of Dorfmeyer's pursuit of her had to do with her money. And how does that make him different from you, he asked?

Damn, he hated to put himself in the same category with the likes of that ass Dorfmeyer. Nate refused to admit his immediate hatred of Dorfmeyer had anything to do with jealousy. The man had no redeeming qualities except a steady job.

He tossed in his hand and waited for the next round to be dealt. Storm's stoic expression didn't fool Nate. The man watched Nate's every move, knew when he won and lost. Nate had the eerie feeling Storm could see into his head and read his mind. Since Storm hadn't shot him yet, that couldn't be true, but he couldn't shake the sensation.

Nate joked with the men, had a couple of drinks, and played hail-fellow-well-met. When they ribbed him about being a tenderfoot, he joked with them. He neither said nor did anything to cause censure from anyone. Even when he won, he did so graciously. The men seemed to accept him, except for Storm.

Sarah's brother gave away nothing of his thoughts, but kept an invisible barrier between them. Nate would have liked Storm to extend the camaraderie offered by the other men. When they had worked together the past two days, Storm was friendly, polite, and even considerate. Something was lacking in him, though. Trust, respect, friendship, maybe all of those. As so often throughout his twenty-six years, Nate had the feeling he didn't measure up. Might never meet the standard. Aw hell, what did he care? He was leaving this burg in a few weeks anyway.

Sarah closed the door on the room Luke and Joe shared and walked down the hall to her own chamber. She rushed to her mirror and examined her face. No, she didn't look different. She'd been certain anyone could look at her and know she had let a man take liberties. A blush spread across her face as she recalled the episode by the river.

My stars, she had let him touch her . . . there. Not just let him, had urged him to continue. And in the open, where anyone might have seen them. What on earth had come over her?

Bliss, that's what. Wonderful, exhilarating rapture. She'd never experienced those sensations, hadn't known they existed. Her fingers touched her lips and she longed for his kiss. She hugged herself and recalled his strong arms embracing her, hands caressing her.

All her life she'd tried to do what was expected of her, to be perfect. Her every action balanced carefully had made her feel as if she walked on a circus tightwire. She had tried to please all her family and make them proud of her. She'd even been nice to Pearl's awful Granny while she'd lived.

For the past seven years she'd dressed as Aunt Lily insisted, helped Pearl with her medicines and patients, taught the children of Drake's ranch hands, sung in the church choir, learned the piano, served on community and church committees. She did whatever she could to make life tranquil, peaceful, and meaningful for those around her. True, she'd refused to go back East to school as Aunt Lily had wanted, but that had been fine with the rest of the family. Never before had she flaunted propriety as she had this evening.

In a fit of pique she had ordered Peter to leave and not re-turn. What would Pearl say? My stars, the man was one of the town's leading citizens! Just the same, Sarah would never welcome him in this house again. How could she have toler-ated his jibes and pokes at her school, at Pearl's medicines, at her way of life this long? If she was so undesirable, why did he come to call in the first place?

All the family had their money deposited in the bank Peter had taken over from his uncle, though the uncle retained own-ership. It was the money that prompted Peter's interest. His callous, unfeeling attitude toward the children ruined him for her. In the future, she'd find it hard even to be civil to him.

Wondering what had come over her of late, she prepared for bed. She still wanted respect and admiration from her family and friends, yet she had risked it all to explore the unknown with Nate. Knowing she acted foolishly hadn't stopped her. In truth, her body responded to him as if it was out of her control. There was no blaming him, though she knew her family would see the situation differently. Nate re-sponded as she had, as if he, too, couldn't help himself.

She slid into bed and hugged her pillow. This man and woman thing was even more a puzzle to her now she'd sampled it. Yearning for Nate's embrace, she wondered where this attraction led. She hoped he decided to stay in Kincaid Springs. Perhaps his business could be carried out from an office in town, but she didn't know, did she? So far, she had no idea what business brought him here in the first place. With a sense of despair, she burrowed into her pillow and drifted to sleep.

Nate took his place across from Sarah at the dining table. The past week had been hell. Storm and Drake kept him out from before dawn until after dark each day and he rarely saw Sarah all week. He wasn't stupid enough to think that an accident. The family conspired to make sure he and Sarah were never alone. He'd hardly had a chance to say two words to her on Saturday before Drake and Storm had all but dragged him with them.

He was beginning to wonder if any amount of money was worth what he'd endured this past week. For a start, a Texas ranch was a hellish place. Everything bit, kicked, scratched, stung, or poked. And that didn't even begin to address the bruises, blisters, raw places, sunburn, or protesting muscles.

At least he'd been allowed to sleep until seven this morning. Then he'd dressed and gone to church with the Kincaids just like last Sunday. God was probably laughing about that one. Sinner Nate invading hallowed ground two weeks in a row. What a joke. The walls hadn't trembled when he walked in, though he had wondered if they might, or lightning flash, or some other sign that he was where he didn't belong. Then Reverend Potter had shaken his hand after the meeting and said how nice it was to see him again and invited him back, as if he were as good as any other member of the community.

The last time he'd been to church was for Ma's funeral. She'd been a big one for attending services, though Cal seldom accompanied her. If she'd lived, her son might have turned out to be a solid citizen instead of a sham. The pain of what might have been almost choked him, but he pasted on his sociable smile and looked around.

Surely this was the whole Kincaid clan. The Judge's daughter Rosilee and her husband Sam Tremont were the only people he hadn't met before. The guests included the Tremonts, Gabe, Drake and Pearl and their five kids, plus him and Sarah and their three. Damn, there he went again, thinking of the children as his. And Sarah. He couldn't help thinking of her as part of him. He'd damn well better get over whatever moon-eyed thoughts he had there.

The chandeliers overhead sparkled in the sunlight streaming through gleaming windows. The polished floor shone almost as much as the mirror over the buffet standing against the wall. As far as he could tell, the best of everything decorated the long table. A crisp white linen tablecloth covered the table, but he could see from the legs and matching chairs that the wood was dark cherry. He'd wondered if the children were allowed to eat in here with all this silver, crystal, and china, but a count of the places revealed they were included, with a high chair for Parker.

This was the first large family meal Polly and Emily had prepared under Fiona's supervision. Fiona fluttered back and forth from the kitchen to the dining room in a state of anxiety. Several curls escaped from her bun to frame her flushed face.

Nate envied Fiona living in this lavish house in town. Lord, he wasn't sure he could survive life as a ranch hand until Monk showed up. Living here would suit him fine, though.

But he wouldn't give up, wouldn't give Drake or Storm the satisfaction of seeing him quit. He'd felt like it at least two dozen times this past week. Hell, he'd felt like it that often every day. Cleaning out stalls, beating the bushes for lost cows, and all the other nasty jobs saved for him had only made him tougher and more determined not to be defeated.

For the first time in his life he had stuck with a difficult job because he wanted the respect of the men he worked with. Not crooks like him, but ordinary saps. He had worked his tail off to surpass the expectations of cowpunchers. If that didn't beat all, what did?

Not just the men. Admit it, he thought, you couldn't bear to see disappointment in the eyes of Sarah and the kids. He had to concede it was good to come back at the end of the day and see welcome in their smiles. They'd meet him and walk him into the house. After he cleaned up, they'd all eat a good meal together. If it weren't for the stupid cows, it wouldn't be a bad life. Damn, he'd try to stick with it a while longer.

This wasn't right. Usually about now he'd be feeling great, enjoying himself and mentally ridiculing the suckers while he set his scheme in motion and waited for the payoff. He wasn't supposed to want to be a part of their lives, shouldn't be admiring them. Hell, this deal was giving him a headache. Too late, he thought with a sense of sadness, the scheme's been set in motion and it's too late to change things now.

Joe plucked at his sleeve. The boy's eyes widened and he motioned around them. He stretched his hands out as if indicating a large amount.

Used to interpreting Joe's mimed communications, Nate nodded. "It's big, isn't it? Must be over two dozen rooms."

From Nate's other side, Luke whispered, "It's the fanciest place I ever saw. Nicer than that place we stayed when you found us. Is this some kind of hotel too?"

"No, son, it's big as some hotels, but it's a house, the Judge's home."

To Nate's mind, it was much better than any hostelry because it was a home. He'd love living here, having beautiful things around him every day. Maybe when he got to New Orleans, he could find a place like this for himself.

He gave himself a mental shake. Who was he kidding? Living over a saloon with the bare necessities of furnishings was more likely. Except when he needed something fancier as part of a swindle, that's all he'd ever had. That and life from a suitcase, traveling from one rotten place to another.

Across the table, Cindy asked, "How many people live here?"

"Just Grandpa, plus Mrs. Galloway and Polly. Emily and

her husband Chester live over the carriage house," Sarah answered.

"I like it here," Cindy said. "I like Grandpa, too." She looked up at Sarah.

"I've always loved it here. When Pearl and Storm and I first came to Texas, we lived here with Grandpa for a while."

"Will he be my Grandpa?" Cindy asked.

"Yes, dear," Sarah said and hugged Cindy. She pointed down the table to Gabe Kincaid. "Cousin Gabe's making sure you and Luke and Joe are officially adopted by me so Grandpa will be your very own Grandpa, too. All my family will be yours."

"What about Nate?" asked Luke.

Nate met Sarah's gaze across the table. He saw the question in her beautiful lavender-blue eyes. Ah, hell, this was the hard part. With a growing sense of regret, he wished things were different, that *he* was different.

Being a part of this family, settling here for all time wasn't a possibility for the likes of him. Nope, these folks wouldn't want him around once they found out the truth about him. Too bad, but he'd known it couldn't last.

He realized Luke still waited for his answer, Sarah still watched. He put his hand on Luke's shoulder and gave it a squeeze. "Don't you worry about me, son. You'll be so busy going to school, exploring the ranch, playing with your cousins and all your new friends, you won't miss me once I've moved on."

Luke looked down at the table. "Yes, I will."

The light in Sarah's eyes died and she lowered her gaze, pretending to fuss with Cindy's new hair bow. Nate felt lower than a snake.

Joe pulled at Nate's sleeve and motioned to Nate, then to the floor.

"See, he wants you to stay here, too," Cindy said.

Fortunately, the Judge chose this time to tap his spoon against a glass. "It's good to have you all here. Let's bow our heads for grace."

After a prayer long enough to qualify as a sermon, to Nate's way of thinking, the Judge nodded to Fiona. "We're ready."

Nate thought Fiona needed to go lie down. The meal was exceptional, but she looked nervous and worn to a frazzle by the time it ended. The Judge had insisted she join them at the table, but she hopped up every few minutes to rush into the kitchen and check on one thing or the other.

After dinner, the women went into the drawing room. With furtive glances at the adults and whispered discussion about exploring the attic, the children rushed away, supposedly up to the old playroom. The Judge led the men into the billiard room. Gabe and Sam Tremont racked up the balls while Storm watched. Drake sat in a wing chair, legs extended, and his polished boots crossed at the ankle.

"Hear you're doing ranch work while you're waiting for your friends to arrive," Judge Kincaid said to Nate.

Nate looked at Storm and Drake. Slavery was what he'd call it. "I've tried to lend a hand."

"Drake tells me you're a hard worker and helped a good bit. Says you've got a sharp eye for detail."

What a shock. Nate had no idea what Drake thought of his efforts, though he knew the man watched him like a hawk. "Suspect he's being generous. I've no experience in ranching. Hardly think my efforts made much difference."

"You don't know my other grandson. Sam's boy, Lex, is in the state legislature. Used to work in my law office like Gabe, and I've missed him. Need another man in the office but haven't found one who measures up. Still looking for someone who spots the small details, follows up. Meanwhile, think you could take a stab at filling in while you're waiting around on your own?"

"You mean work in town in an office instead of on the ranch?" Nate thought he heard an angel chorus. He couldn't suppress a chuckle. "I think I could manage that."

The thought of working for an officer of the court gave him a few qualms. In fact, it scared him half to death. His policy had always been to avoid any contact with the law if possible. On the other hand, working for the man the town and county were named for would give him more credibility when he started asking folks for money. In the meantime, and this was no little thing, he'd be free of that damned ranch work.

Salvation at last. No more unruly cows, no eating dust or slogging through mud. No more dodging prickly cactus or scratchy brush. No more fearing lethal cattle horns or poisonous snakes. He could wear clean clothes and keep them reasonably neat all day. He almost hugged the Judge in gratitude.

"Fine," the Judge said. "Start in the morning at nine. Give yourself a day to see if you think you'll like it. If you take to the work, move your gear in here Tuesday."

Aha, now he understood. Get him away from Sarah, out of the same house, away from the children. The bastards were trying to trick him again. But trickery in a nice office versus trickery involving cows didn't take much pondering.

"You want me to stay here, with you?" he asked. He'd miss Sarah and the kids, but this place had definite merits.

"It'd be easier for you if you move in here, but you could ride in every day." The Judge must have read his mind because he said, "You'll have time most evenings to ride out to the ranch and visit."

Nate smiled and gestured around him. "Be hard to take this after looking at the back end of cows for over a week, but I believe I'll chance it."

The other men laughed.

Storm shook his head. "Feel sorry for you. When you're sitting in that stuffy office with Gabe, you'll miss being out in the fresh air."

He looked from Drake to Storm. "Hmm, let's see. Miss breathing in dust and sliding on muck, riding through all kinds of weather to sit in a nice clean office?" Nate pretended to weigh one against the other. He shook his head and said,

"Working with you fellas has purely been a pleasure, but I believe I'll take the chance and work with Gabe."

The Judge slapped him on the back. "Fine, it's settled. I'm presiding at a trial tomorrow morning, but Gabe will show you what needs doing." He turned to pour each man a drink from the decanter on the sideboard. "Now, Sam, tell me what you hear from Lex about that land reform bill."

A hearty discussion ensued on the evils of government interference and Nate stood at the side of the room and pretended to listen. Relief flooded through him. No more onerous ranch duties, but he hadn't sacrificed the Kincaids's good will.

Sarah couldn't find fault with him working for her beloved Grandpa. They'd still be able to see each other even though he'd be living in town. Now if Nate could only keep in good graces with the Judge and Gabe, he'd be all set when Monk arrived with Hargrove.

ELEVEN

Sarah dismissed school for the day. Carlotta Mendoza had filled in while she was gone. Since all the children were taught in one room, Sarah had worked out a plan to introduce some topics on a rotating basis so the older children didn't hear the same thing year after year. She kept a firm agenda for all the subjects, with cultural as well as scholastic sections covered.

Carlotta was a good friend and it had been kind of Carlotta to step in when Sarah received word her mother was dying. She knew Carlotta would like to teach the class all the time. Sarah had promised her that when the class grew too large for one room, Carlotta could be the other teacher.

The time to add the other schoolroom had arrived. Drake and Storm had promised to start construction whenever she gave the signal. Word of her innovative style and diverse subjects had spread. Several families from town sent their children to her school and her original class of eight had grown to twenty-five. More parents promised to send their children in the fall.

In truth she couldn't take credit for the curriculum. Sarah only repeated what Pearl had taught her and Storm. In turn, Pearl had learned a diverse range of subjects from a distant kinswoman who had been their neighbor in Tennessee.

Sarah wondered what would happen to the school without her supervision. Someday she would quit teaching to being her own childbearing. With a start she wondered why that thought popped into her head. My stars, she wasn't even married. Closing her eyes, she saw Nate's face and sighed.

He won't stay. He won't marry you.

Facing facts, she admitted she'd been dreaming of Nate since they met, especially since their time in Memphis. Her dreams on the train ride found her hoping he'd stay in Kincaid Springs and marry her. There, she'd acknowledged it, but it did nothing to lessen her longing. Her gaze went to the window, to the hill where she'd once planned to build her home. Now she wanted to live in town, to be near the office where Nate worked each day.

Foolish dreams. That's all they were. Futile yearnings of a spinsterish schoolmarm destined to sleep alone every night of her life. At least she had the children to comfort her. With a resigned sigh, she put on her bonnet and drew her shawl around her. When she stepped out of the school and pulled the door closed, she called the children—both hers and Pearl's two oldest—who had been playing nearby.

"Time to go home."

They walked together, Cindy holding her hand while the boys ran this way and that. As they came around the house, Sarah's heart skipped a beat.

"Hey, that's the horse Nate uses," Luke called.

Cindy let go of Sarah's hand to race ahead with the boys. Sarah felt like racing with them, but only quickened her steps. What would bring Nate here before the office closed on the first day he worked for Grandpa?

Inside, she found Nate conferring with Drake. Pearl and Storm sat nearby. What could be important enough for Drake and Storm to come in from the range this early in the day? Worried, Sarah removed her bonnet as she hurried over to them.

Her children had swooped down on Nate and he ruffled each boy's hair before he picked up Cindy. Nate smiled at Sarah.

"It's all right. We've finally heard from the Pinkerton agent. Gabe insisted I come tell you that the letter arrived."

"What does it say?" she asked, fear clutching her like a tangible thing. What if the children's relatives were found?

Nate gave Cindy a kiss on the cheek and set her down before he took a letter from his pocket. "There was no trace of any living family members for Luke and Cindy. From the piece of ticket you found in their trunk and the things Luke remembered, the Pinkerton man traced them to Somerville in Tennessee."

Luke's face lit up. "That's it, Somerville." Then he looked as if he would cry. "Oh, no, do we have to go back?"

Nate gave his shoulder a squeeze. "You're staying right here, but now we know about your other family."

Relief washed over Sarah and she sat down. Cindy climbed onto her lap and snuggled against her. Luke sat at her feet and Joe leaned against the arm of the chair. Her children.

Nate continued talking to Luke and Cindy, "The preacher you stayed with got a letter about a month after you left saying that your mother's aunt had died after a serious illness. By the time her things were being cleared away and someone found the letter directing her to pick you two up, the date had passed."

He looked at Sarah, "The Somerville sheriff wired the Memphis authorities, but no one could find the children. They're forwarding some papers and other things of the aunt's you might want to save as mementos."

"What about Joe?" Sarah asked.

Joe moved in front of Nate and stood staring up anxiously, a look akin to fright in his wide brown eyes.

"Pinkerton agent talked with a man named . . ." Nate referred back to the letter, "Reuben Ingles—"

Before Nate could finish, Joe bolted from the room and ran out the front door.

"I'll get him," Nate said and thrust the letter at Sarah as he passed her in a rush.

Nate raced after Joe, his long strides closing the distance between them. Joe rounded the barn with Nate on his heels.

The boy threw himself at the wall and sobbed as he slid to the ground. Nate grabbed him and, when Joe would have wriggled free, he hugged the boy close.

"It's all right, son. You didn't let me finish. Ingles can't take you. No one will make you leave here."

Joe stilled but his sobbing continued.

"The letter said Reuben Ingles has no legal claim to you at all. There's no reason why the adoption can't go forward."

Joe looked up at Nate, hope dawning in his eyes. Nate relaxed his grasp on the boy.

"Was he the man who hurt you?"

Joe shook his head. He pretended to take money from his pocket and hand it over.

"I see. Other men paid him for you."

Joe nodded and held up three fingers, which Nate took to mean three different men. Joe mimed watching, then running.

"So you ran away." Nate gave Joe a reassuring pat on the shoulder. "You were very brave to strike out on your own, son. I'm sorry you had to go through all that. You've had some rough times, but that's all past. You're safe now."

Joe shook his head. He mimed someone creeping, then grabbing.

"The Kincaids will protect you. They're your family now."

Nate hoped he spoke the truth. The letter had painted Ingles as a despicable character who wanted to be reimbursed for the loss of his stepson.

Joe shook his head and looked at the ground. Obviously sad experience had taught him about his stepfather's lack of redeeming qualities.

Nate exhaled a breath. Some men didn't deserve to live, to his way of thinking. He took Joe's hand. "Come on. The others will be worried about you. Let's go back."

He figured Joe was still plenty worried about his stepfather. "The Pinkerton man didn't tell Ingles where you are or who you're with. He wrote that Ingles asked, but the man wouldn't tell him. Ingles doesn't have any idea where you are."

Joe wiped away his tears, but he didn't look reassured.

On the way to the house, Nate said, "I'm real sorry your mother is dead, Joe. The Kincaids are good people and, like I said, they're your family now. They love you."

Joe tugged at his hand. With his other hand he pointed at Nate. A pain stabbed Nate's heart. He couldn't lie to this boy, not about this.

"Yeah, kid. I love you, too, but I'm not part of the deal, see? I don't belong here, not like you do."

More conversation was prevented because Luke and Cindy ran down the walk to meet them. Pearl's family stood on the wide porch awaiting their return.

Sarah hurried forward and hugged Joe. "No one can take you away now, Joe. When the adoption is final, you'll be my son by law. In my heart, you already are." She encompassed all three children in her arms. "We're a family and no one can change that. We'll stay together."

Over the heads of the children her eyes met his and he saw the regret there. Damn, he wished things were different. Once more, he wished he were different.

Nate went back to the law office, intent on finishing the work assigned him for the day. Gabe had said it wasn't necessary, but Nate knew they were pressed to get ready for an upcoming trial when Gabe would defend a man with the evidence stacked against him. Besides, Nate didn't want to get off to a bad start with Gabe or the Judge.

At six, Gabe went upstairs to his apartment. Later his steps sounded down the wooden stairway outside the building, no doubt on the way to the Judge's house where Nate was scheduled to join them for dinner and discussion of the week's work schedule. Nate vowed to do such perfect work here that the Judge and Gabe would be dazzled by his brilliance and hard labor.

Would you look at yourself? He almost hooted with derision

toward his newfound attitude. Here he was trying to please Mr. Dot-Your-I's Gabe and Judge Lord-Of-The-Manor Kincaid just as if he planned to stick around for years, as if this were a real job. If it weren't for making points with the Kincaids, he could be sitting in the saloon or lounging in the hotel right now.

He was just closing his desk to leave when the sound of banging startled him. Two bedraggled looking middle-aged men came in with broom, bucket, and a mop. Polishing rags hung from their pockets.

Damn, it couldn't be. Nate looked again. Double damn, it was. Incredulous at the sight of ghosts from his past, he re-opened one of the files on his desk and ducked his head. He recognized them but hoped these men wouldn't remember him.

"Howdy, Nate," Willard Ainsworth said and picked up a wastepaper basket to empty it.

Nate froze. These two old drunks could ruin all his plans. He wondered if they remembered his real last name.

"What are you two doing here?" Nate asked.

"We's a-working for the Judge, too. He give us a job to keep us out o' trouble," Burris volunteered.

Willard nodded. "We clean up here Mondays and Thursdays, do jobs for the Judge whenever he asks."

"Where you boys live?" Nate asked and prayed it wasn't on the grounds of the Judge's home.

Willard pointed West. "We got us a nice little house not fur from here. 'Course the Judge owns it, but he lets us live there long as we keep it in good shape and don't drink none."

Burris nodded. "And we have to do the Judge's biddin' when he wants, which is purt' near ever' day."

"I don't understand. What brought you to Kincaid Springs?"

The two exchanged looks, then looked at the floor as if embarrassed.

Willard mumbled, "We come to steal away Pearl and Sarah and that boy Storm. We was gonna take 'em West with us."

"You what?" Nate figured the two had been drinking and didn't know what they were saying.

"We didn't mean no harm, unnerstand? We wuz just goin' to pertect 'em, like," Willard said.

Burris scratched his stomach. "Yessir, we didn't mean to burn down Pearl's eatin' place neither. That were purely a accident. So wuz me gettin' shot when we tried to git the money off'n the train."

Willard nodded. "Burris is still troubled by that wound in his leg when it gits cold or damp."

Nate couldn't make any sense of the two's ravings, so he waved them away. "I expect we'd better all get to work."

His thoughts whirled in confusion. What did these men know about him? He barely remembered the time spent in that terrible Tennessee hick town. He had hated it, hated the people, and could hardly wait to leave.

Thinking back, he recalled these two hanging around, trying to get free drinks from Roxie or her customers. Jokes of the town. Maybe they were so drunk back then they hadn't even known who he was. What if they'd just heard he'd be working here and never made the connection?

He ventured, "Say, how'd you boys know my name?"

"Doncha 'member us, Nate?" Willard asked. "We wuz allus comin' in to Roxie's place back in Pipers Hollow. 'Member when you 'n your daddy wuz there?" Willard rubbed the stubble on his jaw. "Now, let's see, musta been jus' 'bout the time Pearl and them moved here."

"Maybe," Nate said. Damn, they did know him. He might as well come right out with it. "Anybody else around here know I was there?"

The two brothers exchanged puzzled looks.

Burris said, "Reckon Pearl and them do."

"No, no they don't, and I don't want to remind them," Nate said. "Can we keep it our secret, just between us three?"

"Reckon so, but I don't see why," Willard said.

Nate thought furiously. He couldn't make it sound too

important or these two would be sure to wonder about him and ask the wrong questions. Worse, they might report to the Judge.

"Makes me real sad, what with my daddy and Roxie both being dead now. Yes, it all makes me real sad. Like to forget I ever saw that place. Can you understand that?"

"Why sure, Nate." Burris scratched under his arm. "We gets sad sometimes, specially when we think about our mama dying. She don't know we done them bad things, though, which is good."

"She'd be proud of you both now. You got a good place to live and a good job. Me, too. Let's just forget the past."

Both men nodded and Willard said, "That's a good idee."

Nate closed the file and stacked it with the others on his desk. He felt ten years older and five times a fool. He should never have started this scheme with Roxie's daughter. Monk tried to tell him, but he wouldn't listen.

Nate stood. "Guess I'll see you around. Good night."

Nate hurried toward the Judge's home. He smiled and nodded at the people he passed, but panic rose inside him. What should he do? He felt an overwhelming urge to turn back, go to the livery stable and get a horse. His bag was still packed from this morning. He could take the next train out of town.

Calm down, he thought. You've gotten out of worse scrapes than this. Hell, you survived being buried alive, surely you can outwit two simpletons.

When he arrived at the Judge's home, Fiona met him in the foyer. "Himself and Mr. Gabe waited dinner for you. You can be going on in to the dining room."

The Judge sat at one end of the table like the lord and master he was, and Gabe sat at his right. A place at the Judge's left had been laid for Nate. Apparently Fiona wasn't dining with them tonight.

The Judge nodded as he joined them. "Glad to know Pinkerton's came through. Gabe briefed me on the letter."

"It's a relief to Sarah. She doesn't have to worry about stray relatives showing up to stop the adoption." Nate traced a circle with his finger on the linen beside his plate. "Joe was alarmed that his stepfather had been contacted. He's afraid the man will find him somehow and kidnap him. I tried to reassure the boy, but I can't shake an uneasy feeling about the man."

Over dinner Nate filled the other two men in on Joe's experiences at the hand of Ingles. They shared Nate's outrage.

The Judge said, "I fear you're right. Can't see a man like that giving up without making a bid for a payoff."

"Two odd men were at the office when I left. Hope it was all right to leave them there," Nate said.

The Judge laughed. "If there were no lighted lanterns on the desk," he said. "Had to put those two to work to keep them from killing themselves or someone else."

"Seemed a little simple," Nate said, hoping to lay groundwork to cover any remarks the two might make about him.

"Oh, they do okay cleaning up, surprising enough," Gabe said. "I guess you could say they need direction."

Nate frowned and shook his head. "They said something about setting a fire and getting shot. I didn't understand."

"They never make much sense," the Judge said.

Nate breathed a sigh of relief. If the Ainsworths mentioned him in connection with Tennessee, maybe no one would give any credence to their ravings.

The Judge continued, "When Pearl first came here, a man had in mind to kill her and the two young 'uns."

Nate nodded. "Sarah told me about that time. I believe Drake saved the three of them."

The Judge nodded. "Kincaids take care of their own, and Drake did what he had to. Lordy, it had been a bad time. Before we knew who was involved, Drake took charge of Storm and we had armed guards everywhere Pearl or Sarah went."

His somber face broke into a grin and he chuckled. "These two clowns came along. Not funny at the time, mind you, but it seems like it now."

"Why? What did they do?" Nate asked.

"First they failed miserably at robbing the train Pearl's money was on and Burris was shot. Next they burned down her restaurant trying to get in and kidnap her. They were caught when they tried the kidnapping a second time with two armed guards and Drake present."

"Not a bright thing to do," Nate offered. The thought of crossing Drake Kincaid made his hair stand on end. That the two men stayed alive surprised him.

"You said yourself they're simple," Gabe said and shrugged.

The Judge said, "There were mitigating factors, though. As long they have clear instructions, they do their job and stay out of trouble. They worked off their sentence and had no place to go and no money. I gave them a job. They haven't been up to any mischief to speak of since."

He speared Nate with a piercing look. "Gabe tells me you took to lawyering like a duck to water."

Nate shot a grateful glance at Gabe, then answered, "It interests me."

The Judge regarded Nate speculatively and chewed at his mustache. "Might ought to consider staying here and reading for the law. Need a good man, since Lex is off in Austin most of the time."

Not wanting to make a commitment but unable to make himself turn down the offer, Nate smiled and asked, "You making me into a project like the Ainsworths?"

Talk drifted to others the Judge had helped rehabilitate, and then on to the upcoming work scheduled. Nate let the other two men carry the burden of conversation. His mind worried over the Ainsworths recognizing him. He wondered who else from that Tennessee hellhole had migrated to this town.

The thought kept running through his mind that Kincaids take care of their own. Apprehension skittered along Nate's spine. What would Drake have to say to the man who cheated his sister-in-law, his family, and his town when it all came out? Not only Drake. The whole clan would be after Nate's blood with a vengeance no sheriff or posse could ever match.

* * *

Sarah heard Nate walk down the hall to his room after she was already in bed. Wishing she could go to him and talk, she pulled the cover snug against her. She needed to talk to him about the letter, needed to hear his opinion on Joe's stepfather. Admit it, she thought. You need to hear his voice, feel his embrace, for your own well being and not just for Joe or the other children.

Tomorrow he'd be moving to Grandpa's and she would seldom see him. Nate working for Grandpa was bound to be a good thing, though. She visualized Nate joining Gabe at Grandpa's law firm and staying in Kincaid Springs.

She lay thinking for what seemed hours, unable to turn off her thoughts and go to sleep. A soft tap at her door surprised her. The knob turned and she heard Luke's voice.

"Can you come talk to Joe?" Luke asked. "He's real scared and hid under the bed."

Sarah rose and put on her navy wool wrapper as she slid her feet into her felt slippers. She lit a lamp and brought it when she followed Luke back to the room he shared with Joe. At first when she couldn't see the boy she feared he'd run away again. Luke kneeled beside the bed and looked underneath.

"She's here. You can come out," Luke said. He backed away and looked up at Sarah. "He won't move."

Sarah set the lamp on the floor, knelt beside the bed and peeked beneath. Joe lay curled in a ball against the wall at the head of the bed. He looked terrified.

She pleaded, "Dear, you're safe here. Come out and let me tuck you into bed."

Joe shook his head.

Sarah pleaded, but Joe refused to budge. Short of dragging him out, she hadn't a clue what to do. On the train when he was scared, Nate had known how to placate Joe. Nate had calmed Joe earlier in the day as well when the letter upset him. Joe responded to Nate more than to anyone else.

"Luke, would you ask Nate to come here?"

Luke disappeared and soon returned with Nate. Nate's feet were bare and his pants only partially fastened. He rubbed his eyes and his shirt hung loose with the buttons undone. Sarah scrambled to her feet to greet him.

"What's going on?" he asked and yawned.

"Apparently the letter scared Joe more than we realized. He won't come out from under the bed."

Nate asked Luke, "He have a nightmare or something?"

"I reckon he did," Luke said. "He was kicking and thrashing around so much I couldn't sleep. Then he moved his legs like he was running and fell plumb out of bed."

Nate stood still a moment looking perplexed. "Guess I can give it a shot." He kneeled, then flattened himself and slid underneath beside Joe. His feet stuck out from under the bed as he wriggled himself so that his head was near Joe's.

Sarah lay down on the floor on the opposite side of the bed with her head almost under it and her legs stretched out behind her. Luke joined her and peered at Joe. Nate talked softly to Joe and she strained to hear his words.

"Bad dream?" Nate asked.

Joe nodded.

From behind her, Sarah heard someone enter the room. She bumped her head peeping at the newcomer.

"Some kind of new religion going on here?" Storm stood in the doorway, leaning against the jamb. "Reckon that bed's comfortable enough, but hardly worthy of prostrate worship." He wore his denim work pants but no shirt and his feet were bare.

Sarah rose and went to her brother. His room was next to that of the boys, so he must have heard the disturbance. "The letter from Pinkerton's upset Joe. He's had nightmares and now won't come out from under the bed."

"Heard the hubbub." Storm asked, his voice low. "Those Nate's feet I see sticking from under the other side of the bed?"

She whispered, "Yes, I couldn't get Joe to come out. He seems to have confidence in Nate, so I asked him to help."

Storm nodded and gave her shoulders a hug. "Unless you think I can help, you work this out and I'll get back to sleep."

Storm left and Sarah returned to her previous station. Nate held Joe's hand and talked to him. Slowly Joe uncurled his body and followed Nate out from his sanctuary.

Sarah rushed around and hugged Joe. "You know we'll never let anything bad happen to you if we can prevent it, don't you?"

Joe wiped tears from his face and nodded. He put his arms around Sarah's waist and hugged her, burrowing his face against her. Tears sprang to her eyes. It was the first spontaneous display of affection he'd offered.

"Come on, son. Into bed with you," Nate said and pulled a chair beside the bed. "I'll sit here until you're asleep. We'll leave the lamp burning low so it won't be dark."

Luke and Joe climbed into bed and Sarah tucked the covers around them. "Luke, it was good of you to come tell me when Joe was frightened. You're brothers now, and brothers and sisters look out for one another." She brushed her hand across the forehead of each boy. She wanted to kiss them, but feared they would rebel at that much mothering.

Nate sat beside the bed next to Joe. "Remember what I told you. It's okay to be afraid as long as it doesn't keep you from doing what's right."

Nate nodded at Sarah and she left the room. She couldn't stand the thought of not being included, though, and hovered outside in the hallway until Joe and Luke dropped off to sleep and Nate came out.

He walked with her, then stopped outside the open door of his room. "He thinks his stepfather is coming here after him."

"Do you agree?" she asked.

He shrugged. "I think it's more likely he'll show up asking you for money. I almost hope he does. I'd like to see the man punished for what he put Joe through."

She stared at his bare chest, at the unfastened top button on his trousers, and a sudden urge to touch his skin assaulted her. Shocked at her wantonness, she took a step back and stammered, "Thanks for your help."

She raised her gaze to his and her knees almost buckled. His wolf's eyes blazed with passion in the light from the lamp she carried. He stepped toward her and cupped her face in his hands to brush a gentle kiss across her mouth. Only a touch, really, but it ignited the passion smoldering within her. It must have affected him in the same way. He released her briefly, then pulled her inside his room and closed the door softly behind them.

She set the lamp on a table, then moved into his arms. He smiled before his mouth possessed hers, his tongue probed and darted within. No longer was his kiss soft or hesitant. He tasted of the brandy he must have drunk earlier in the evening at Grandpa's. She melded her taste with his.

He broke the kiss and gripped her shoulders. His chest heaved with ragged breaths and passion darkened his tawny eyes. "Sarah, get out of here before I lose all control."

She reached behind her to turn the key in the lock. When she turned back, his eyes showed surprise as well as his desire. He tipped her face up with his finger.

"Do you know what you're doing? I won't be able to hold you and not ask for more."

"I want more, too." She extinguished the lamp and slid her arms around his waist under the loose shirt.

"Sarah, I need you more than you can imagine. I can't restrain myself much longer." He wrapped her in his embrace.

"I've already lost whatever restraint I had," she said and pressed her face against his bared chest.

He moaned and reclaimed her lips, his kisses insistent and persuading. Unable to resist the lure of his muscular shoulders, she moved her hands across them and pressed him toward her. He broke away to shrug out of his shirt then push the wrapper from her shoulders. She let the wool slide down her arms until it dropped to the floor. When the ties to her nightgown were released, it, too, pooled at her feet.

The touch of cool air on her skin did nothing to cool her ardor. Standing bare as a babe in front of him, she wondered at his thoughts. Did he find her beautiful, did he think her too bold? She might have crossed her hands modestly over her breasts, but he swung her into his arms and carried her to the bed. He laid her gently on the sheets, then crossed to the windows and opened the curtains wider. Light from the full moon slanted across the bed.

He said, "I want to see your wonderful body."

When he returned to her, he claimed his place beside her but propped himself on one elbow.

"You don't know how I've dreamed of this," he said as he spread her unbound locks across the pillow. "Your hair is the color of moonbeams." He raised several curls and let them slide through his fingers. "Strands of silk against my hand."

He trailed kisses softly across her shoulder. "Soft, so soft," he murmured before pressing his lips to hers. His hand cupped her breast and his thumb moved across her nipple.

Pleasure spiraled through her. She wanted more of him, wanted to reclaim the ecstasy she'd experienced by the river. Moving her hands to his trousers, she worked to undo the rest of the buttons.

His hands stilled hers and he raised his head to meet her gaze. "Are you sure? Do you have any idea what you're doing?"

Though she hadn't planned this now, she knew she must proceed. Tomorrow he would leave to stay with Grandpa and she might never have another opportunity to know his intimate touch.

"I'm positive, Nate. I've yearned for you so." She didn't tell him she also knew he didn't return her love. She couldn't go through life wondering what if, wishing she hadn't let a chance for magic slip away. This might be her only chance to share this with him. No one else would ever do. It had to be Nate.

He rolled off the bed and shucked his trousers, then rejoined her. Starting a trail of kisses across her eyes, he moved along her cheek to the corner of her mouth, and down her throat. His lips, teeth and tongue worked magic with her breast when he claimed a nipple with his mouth. His hands caressed her, cherished her, worshiped her.

She felt a woman adored and desired. This man drove her mad with his touch. How could she resist this chance to experience all he could offer?

He moved his mouth to her other breast and his hand sought the juncture of her thighs. He parted her legs and slipped his finger inside her. She felt moisture gather as his finger slid in and out.

Clinging to him, she begged, "More, Nate. I need more."

His apologetic voice pierced her fog of ardor. "I don't want to hurt you, but there'll be pain just at first."

"Now, Nate, I need you now."

He poised over her and pressed his manhood against her tender entry. She needed without understanding exactly what she craved. Her whole being cried out to him to sate this overpowering urgency within her.

She felt him inside her and marveled that his manhood fit so well. Her arms and legs circled him, pushing her body up to meet his.

He kissed her. "Are you ready for me?"

"Yes, yes, yes. Please hurry."

His mouth claimed hers and she lost herself in his kiss. He thrust into her feminine folds. She felt pain and stiffened in surprise. He paused but his lips continued their sorcery.

Memory surfaced of the pleasure she had found at his hands by the river. Surely this would be even greater once the pain subsided. Ecstasy awaited and this time he would share it with her. When his movements renewed, only pleasure radiated from her core.

"You're doing fine, sweetheart," he coaxed. "Stay with me."

Lost in his spell, she climbed to the heavens, rising with

each fevered movement. His thrusts grew more rapid, his breathing more labored. When she thought she would explode from pleasure, she felt the burst of his release as her own erupted. Together they floated back to earth.

She clung to him and he rolled off her, cuddling her to his side. He kissed her hair, her face, her eyes, then nuzzled her neck. Never had she felt so cherished.

"That was even more wonderful than I'd dreamed," he said. He held her and she heard his breathing return to normal as drowsiness claimed him.

"I love you," she whispered as he drifted off to sleep.

She longed to remain wrapped in his arms, but she feared discovery. Embarrassing as it might be for her if their liaison were discovered, it would be worse for him. She wanted no unpleasantness for him because of this wonderful experience. Even though she wanted him to stay in Kincaid Springs with her, she didn't want it to be because her family coerced him to marry her. What kind of union would that be?

With a mixture of elation and regret, of fulfillment and yearning, she slipped from his arms. She pulled on her nightgown and stepped into her slippers. Clutching her wrapper around her, she unlocked the door. She retrieved her lamp and closed the door softly behind her.

In her room she cleaned the evidence of their union from her thighs. She wondered at the linens on his bed and vowed to slip in and check them before she left the house in the morning. Only when she'd made her way to her bed and lay curled beneath the covers did she relax.

Then she touched her stomach and heat spread in a flush across her face with the knowledge of the risks she'd run. What if they'd planted a babe and Nate left? Overcome with remorse for her wanton actions in disregarding propriety and her strict moral code, she berated herself. Her reputation would be ruined, her family shamed. The child would never know a father, would suffer the horrid taunts hurled at Sarah as she grew up.

Dear Lord in heaven, what had she been thinking about? Nothing, that's what. Actions based on emotion, on the burning need within her that caused her to act without a care in her head for consequences. How many times had she heard Pearl caution women on the ways to avoid pregnancy? Sarah should have taken those precautions, but it was too late now.

After all the years of concern over the opinions of others, she couldn't prevent the thoughts from surfacing now. She bit her lip in anxiety. She was a Kincaid now and an important part of the community. It was her duty to set an example, to be a credit to her family.

Never would she try to abort a child as Aunt Lily had done. No, she'd face whatever she must. If a child came from tonight, at least she'd have a sweet reminder of her time with Nate. Sarah prayed her situation would work out for the best, that if she had conceived, Nate would stay in Kincaid Springs and ask her to marry him before anyone knew of the pregnancy.

TWELVE

After a restless night, Sarah forced herself awake. Already she heard the sounds of people rising. Doors closed and feet trod in the hall. Someone, probably Storm, whistled a tune. The smell of fresh bread and coffee wafted into her room and her stomach rumbled.

She moved and her body reminded her of the lovemaking she and Nate had shared during the night. Tender tissues protested when she sat on the side of the bed but did nothing to diminish the soaring of her spirit. How sweet he'd been, how tender, yet passionate. Surely he felt something more than lust for her to have been so gentle and considerate.

Her dream resurfaced of herself and Nate sharing a life together. Cindy, Luke, Joe, and the children to follow shared a place in her fantasy. There would be boys with their father's tall stature and strong physique, girls with their father's tawny eyes and thick lashes. They'd live in a house filled with love and laughter.

She would love having his children, with him by her side. Her hand pressed her stomach. Already a baby might be growing. How wonderful to have a little boy like Nate.

Oh, Lord, what if he left? The thrill of the possibility of pregnancy weighed against the shame of being unwed with a child. If the shame were only hers, she would not worry. Blame would fall on their child, though, and Cindy, Luke, and Joe would also share her disgrace.

She hugged her arms and rocked on the side of the bed.

At least she had known happiness for one brief night, even if it never came her way again. She still had her three children and the memory of Nate's lovemaking. Lonely it might be, but she could live with only that.

And if a baby grew within her, she would confront that situation, too. She would not be cowed, would not hide herself away. No, she would rejoice in her child and get on with her life.

The realization that she could face whatever life brought her, though it meant facing disgrace, startled her. She wanted to be known for her good works, true. Suddenly she knew she would accomplish those acts with or without Nate, regardless of whether or not she carried his child. Though she hoped he would decide to stay with her, she would not let even him deter her from her chosen path.

If she must live alone all her life, a lifetime without Nate, she had this experience to savor. One night to last through eternity. She prayed there was more, but either way she would survive. Moreover, she would succeed with her school and with her children. Her resolve renewed, she stood and dressed for the day.

Dawn crept through the windows and nudged Nate from slumber. He reached for Sarah as he awoke, needing to feel her against him once again. He rolled on his back as the memory of their previous night's lovemaking swept through him. The miracle of her passionate response, the sweet satin of her skin, the way she fit in his arms made his longing spring anew. Burrowing into her pillow, he inhaled the lingering of her rose fragrance.

He had thought once he conquered her, she would be out of his system and he could get on with his plans. Fool, he cursed himself. His desire for her had increased tenfold rather than diminished. Recollection of the many names he had called her made him wince. They were all wrong. She was

Miss Heaven, Miss Paradise. Miss Too-Good-For-The-Likes-Of-You.

Despair enveloped him and he pressed his hands to his face. Dear God, help me. How had he come to such a place in his life? Now he wanted all those things he had wasted a lifetime scoffing at. He wanted this job at the law office, a cozy house, his family with him each day. Most of all, he wanted Sarah.

He threw back the covers and sat up on the side of the bed. Maybe there was a chance. Maybe he could forget about the swindle and go on as he was now. Monk would go along with him. All they had to do was convince Hargrove to move on.

Nate stood and reached for his trousers. He saw the spots of blood on the sheet and winced. He'd never been with a virgin before, had no right to this one. At least he could protect her name. Whipping the tattletale sheet off the bed, he folded it into a small square and stuffed it under the mattress' center. From the armoire, he took out a fresh sheet and remade the bed.

Fearing he'd dallied too long, he hurried through his preparations for the day and went to the kitchen for breakfast.

Everyone else in the household was in the dining room, some already seated.

Nate nodded. "Good morning."

He received greetings from the others and sat beside Sarah.

"You recovered from your rough night?" Storm asked.

Sarah blanched and her mouth dropped open.

The shock of the question caused Nate to drop his napkin and he bent to retrieve it. Could Storm have known Sarah came to Nate's room? No, he'd never be this calm if he had. Shotguns would be involved if anyone here knew what had transpired between him and Sarah.

Storm stared from Sarah to Nate. "What time did you get Joe settled down and get him to sleep?"

Nate realized he'd held his breath at Storm's first question and only now resumed breathing. Sarah answered before he could.

"Nate sat with him until he fell asleep and he seemed fine when I checked on him later." She looked at Joe a couple of seats away. "You're all right this morning, aren't you?"

Joe nodded and seemed embarrassed at the reminder of his weakness.

Nate smiled at him and said, "We all have nightmares at times."

Joe flashed Nate a look of gratitude before he lowered his eyes again.

"I have nightmares sometimes," said Robbie. "Then Mama comes in and holds my hand until I go back to sleep."

Storm nodded. "That's what she used to do for me when I had bad dreams."

Joe watched Storm, his eyes wide with speculation, as if finding it hard to believe this large man had ever been a small boy with nightmares.

Drake addressed Joe. "Son, you're part of our family now, and we'll do everything we can to take care of you. You remember that, all right?"

Joe nodded. He looked at the people around the table as if seeing them for the first time. For the first time since Nate had known the kid, a kind of peace showed on Joe's face and he dug into his breakfast.

Drake turned to Nate and asked, "How do you like the law office so far?"

"I'm surprised at how much I enjoy it," Nate answered. "It's little stuff, of course, since I don't know how to do much yet. Still, there's an order that makes sense."

"Don't know how you could like dusty books and boring papers more than being out with the cows and horses," Storm said.

Nate shook his head. "There's no comparison. Cows lose hands down."

"So, you moving to Grandpa's today?" Drake asked.

"Yes, that's the plan," Nate answered. After what happened last night it was for the best, but he longed to hold Sarah again. How sweet it would be to lie with her each night and wake with her in his arms. Good thing he was moving away from the temptation of her only a few doors down the hall.

Drake pushed back from the table and tossed his napkin beside his plate. "Well, don't be a stranger. You're welcome to change your mind anytime and move back here."

Nate had his doubts as to the truth of that, but he appreciated the statement anyway. For some reason it made his leaving a little easier. He didn't feel he was being shut out completely by his move into town. Damn, if Drake knew Sarah had spent half the night in Nate's room, things would be different.

In the rush to get everyone off to their day's activities, Nate had no time alone with Sarah. He thanked Pearl for her hospitality, then told his three youngsters goodbye.

"Remember, you're a real family now. Look out for one another and for your new Mama."

Cindy's lip trembled and the two boys nodded solemnly.

"Hey, why the long faces? I'll be back in a few days and I'll also see you when you come to town. You'll have lots to tell me then."

At last, as he tied his carpetbag to his saddle, Sarah came to speak with him. Pearl watched from the porch and the children danced around him, so he couldn't hold Sarah, couldn't tell her any of the things he longed to say.

"You'll come back sometimes, won't you?" Sarah asked.

"Every chance I get," Nate answered. "Will you be coming to town?"

She smiled up at him with her perfect rosebud mouth. "Every chance I get."

He wanted her so much he almost forgot to tell her about the bed. He leaned forward pretending to check his saddle and murmured, "I put the stained sheet under the mattress and replaced it with a fresh one."

Her cheeks flamed and she lowered her eyes. "Thank you. I meant to do something like that."

He placed his hand on her arm. She met his gaze and he said, "Perhaps when I come back, we can go for a walk by the river."

Her smile appeared wistful. "That would be nice. We can, um, talk then."

Damn, he hated to leave her. All the more reason to go. He bid a final goodbye and rode into town. He'd dallied over his goodbyes until he would need to ride straight to the livery and head for the office. When he arrived, Nate asked the stable boy to take his bags to the Judge's house and Nate strode toward the office.

Gabe and Nate labored hard through the morning. Work had stacked up since Lex Tremont had been gone, plus Gabe was preparing for a trial. Nate figured he was being given busy work, things which needed attention but which any halfway intelligent person could do. He found that not only could he do the work, he enjoyed it. Gabe's approval seemed genuine.

Gabe and Nate had just returned from a quick meal next door at Granny's Lunches when Sheriff Liles came in and stopped at Nate's desk. At the sight of the badge and holstered gun with a hand resting on it, Nate's throat constricted and his mouth went dry as cotton.

His mind whirled, wondering how he had he slipped up. Had his past caught up with him the moment he'd come to work in town? He braced himself and looked up at the lawman.

Sheriff Liles asked, "You going to the ranch after work?"

Nate relaxed and leaned back in his chair. At least he wasn't under arrest yet.

"Hadn't planned to go today, but I can if you need me to. Why do you ask?"

"Got a wire this morning from Pinkerton's in Memphis. Someone broke into their office a few days ago. Might have been searching for Miss Sarah's information on those kids. Leastwise, her file was spread all over the desk."

Nate felt a chill slide down his spine. "Ingles."

Sheriff Liles nodded. "You got it. Pinkerton agent figured it was this Ingles fellow. No proof yet, but thought you folks should know."

Gabe asked, "You think he's coming here?"

Nate said, "As fast as he can. He'll try to get money out of Sarah or hurt Joe. Maybe both."

"Hell of a thing when Pinkerton's is burglarized." The sheriff took a piece of paper out of his pocket and unfolded it before he handed it to Nate. "Here's the wire. I copied off this Ingles's description and I'll be looking for him if he shows his face around here. They're mailing me a drawing."

"If he's coming, he'll be here before you get the drawing," Nate said. He looked at the wire. Why had they waited so long to send word? Calculating the travel time by train, he said, "He may be here now."

"That's what I figured, too. Don't worry, I'll keep my eye out for him."

Nate gripped the wire and fury boiled inside him. "So will we. He's a sorry excuse for a man."

"The Judge told me as much when he sent me over here." The sheriff tapped Nate on the shoulder. "Now look here, if you see this Ingles, you let me know and I'll take care of him." The sheriff tipped his hat and walked out.

Nate's first thought was to ride to the school and warn Sarah. The urgency of that action would only frighten Joe and heighten his fears. So far Ingles hadn't been sighted anywhere nearby. There was no certainty the man was even involved, though Nate's gut told him Ingles was responsible for the break in at Pinkerton's Memphis office.

Face it, though, Nate couldn't be leaving work every day to ride out and tell Sarah the latest news. Gabe needed his help with defense preparations for a trial set to begin in two days. They still had a lot of research and organization ahead of them before Gabe would be ready. In fact, Gabe had plans for the two of them to work late tonight. Best to think this out and act with calm and as little disruption as possible.

Though he had no real obligation to anyone but himself, Nate found he enjoyed his association with rules and regulations here in this office. Everything looked quite a bit different from this side of the law. Not that he cared about some sap who got caught with his hand in the till and said he was innocent. They all say that.

Still, if he could work things out with Monk and convince Hargrove to move on, this could be his chance to stay here with Sarah and the children. He couldn't afford to shirk his share of the load and endanger that chance. He shook his head in disbelief. Imagine him worried about missing work.

Gabe's voice snapped Nate from his thoughts. "What're you planning?"

Nate picked up a sheet of paper and his pen. "I have to get word to Sarah without frightening Joe. "

Gabe nodded his agreement. "Yeah, she needs to know, but she's still in school. Why not send word to Drake or Pearl now? They can tell her in private without spooking the kid."

"Good idea, that's what I'll do," Nate said. "I'll send a note to Drake and one to Pearl. They can tell Sarah and Storm and help keep a look out for Ingles."

Gabe looked out the window and stood up, "There's Burris and Willard across the street. I'll get them in here and they can take your messages." He left and soon returned with the two bedraggled Ainsworth brothers.

Nate wasn't sure these two were trustworthy. "We need you to take a message to Drake Kincaid's place. Can you find it?"

Willard nodded. "We been there lots of times. Knows just where it is."

Nate wrote a note to Drake and one to Pearl. He enclosed a note for Sarah with Pearl's. When he'd finished, he blotted each of them dry and folded them into envelopes. He scrawled a name on each of the envelopes.

"This is very important." Nate handed Burris and Willard each an envelope. "Take this straight to Pearl at the ranch house and then find Drake out on the range or wherever he is.

Don't let anything keep you from getting these to Drake and Pearl. Wait for an answer from Drake. Okay?"

"You can count on us," Willard said.

"Yessir, you can count on us," Burris echoed.

Nate gave each man a coin and sent them on their way. After they left, Nate tried to keep his mind on the work before him, but his thoughts kept drifting to Joe. Poor kid. He'd had a rough life and had only recently learned to trust.

If Ingles showed up to threaten Joe, it would break down that hard-won confidence Joe had in the family who loved him. Nate included himself in that list of people, but knew he didn't belong. Not yet, anyway. Maybe there was a chance. In his heart he tried not to dwell on the possibility but the kernel of hope slowly grew.

The afternoon wore away and Burris and Willard tromped in.

Willard said, "See if'n this makes sense." He drew himself up and puffed out his chest as if reciting on stage. "Storm's gonna move his horses over to the pasture by the schoolhouse. Then two of his men gonna watch during the days 'n case that mean man tries to come to the school."

Burris beamed a smile. "That's right. We said you could count on us, didn't we?"

"That's good. Anything else?" Nate asked.

"Pearl says you both come to supper soon," Burris said. He peered over Nate's shoulder and read the papers spread on the desk. "What're ya doin', Nate?"

"Gabe is defending Mr. Billingsley on Thursday. He has me copying some of the facts so he can organize the case more easily."

"That's the fella what they say stole money from the bank, ain't it?"

Willard cuffed him and said, "You know it is. We seen him taken to jail, don't you 'member?"

Burris nodded, then asked, "Reckon why that Mr. Dingle always has so much stuff from the bank in his trash?"

"What?" Gabe asked.

"You know, that Mr. Dingle at the bank. Willard and me picks up his trash."

Willard cuffed his brother again. "Now Burris, you know the Judge said we ain't s'posed to tell anybody what folks has in their trash. It ain't good business."

Gabe held up his hand to silence Willard. "What kind of stuff from the bank?"

Burris scratched his head and looked thoughtful. "Oh, you know, them bitty pieces o' paper they put around stacks of money? Well, there wuz some of them. And letters with the bank printin' on 'em. Stuff like that."

"Ain't been none lately, though," Willard said. "But we did find some letters on real nice paper. I allus saves the good paper so I can make my lists on it."

"You know when it stopped?" Gabe asked. "Would it have been about the time Billingsley was arrested?"

The brothers looked at one another, then both nodded. Gabe's elation with this new development had him hug each of the brothers. They each stepped back in surprise and regarded him as if he'd lost his mind.

Gabe laughed. "You two may have saved a man's reputation and put a crook in jail. Don't say anything to anyone about what you told us."

"You can count on us," Willard said.

"Would you be able to help us some more?" Nate asked.

"Why, sure," Willard answered.

"You get all the papers you got from Dingle together and we'll come by tonight and look at them. Can you do that?"

"Yep," Willard said and Burris nodded agreement.

The Ainsworth brothers left and Gabe and Nate went back to their work. They had new evidence to gather and new facts to check. They worked until almost seven.

Gabe stood and stretched. "Let's call it a day here. You've been a big help."

"I'd say the Ainsworths were more help." Nate put down his pen and straightened the papers on his desk.

"They were a real find, but I don't know how convincing their testimony will be and most of that rubbish has been burned by now. Finding that precedent in Illinois will definitely make a difference."

Nate lapped up the praise. He had wondered why Gabe went to such lengths to defend a man everyone in town thought guilty. "You interviewing those witnesses again tomorrow?"

"Yes, and then I'll see the accused again. It's all coming together." Gabe doused the lamp and closed the door behind them.

Nate started down the plank sidewalk and Gabe joined him.

Gabe said, "I need to ask Uncle Rob's opinion on something so I'll walk with you. Then I'll go by the Ainsworths' house and see what they have."

He didn't want Gabe talking to those two without him around to make sure they didn't let slip they knew him. He said, "I'll go with you. Be interesting to see what they have. The Judge trying the case?"

"Yes, he'll preside at the trial."

It didn't seem fair to Nate, having relatives involved in positions of power in the same trial. Not that he'd ever thought the law was fair anyway.

As if reading his mind, Gabe said, "Out here we have to make do with the people at hand. Don't think for a minute Uncle Rob will give me an inch just because I'm a relative."

"I never thought the Judge would show favoritism," Nate lied. Privately he thought the Judge would find little ways to slant the case in favor of his great-nephew. After all, Gabe actually worked for the Judge.

"The defendant had the choice of waiting for another judge to travel here, but he wanted to get this over as soon as possible. If you haven't already heard, Uncle Rob has the reputation for being firm but fair."

"Like with the Ainsworths?" Nate asked.

"Sure. What good would it have done to send those two to prison? They worked off their fine helping people here in the community. For instance, Uncle Rob had them making repairs on the homes of some of the poor and elderly hereabouts."

"Makes more sense than jail time if they're not dangerous," Nate agreed and wondered what the folks in that Arkansas town would think of that theory. For himself, he figured it was better than a mob who threatened lynching then buried him in an unmarked grave.

"Yes, and ever since they worked off their fine, Uncle Rob makes certain they always have enough work to keep them honest." Gabe laughed. "Isn't it funny that they may save an innocent man from jail?"

They walked the rest of the way in companionable silence while Nate wondered how firm and fair the Judge would be with someone who sullied his favorite, Sarah.

When Sarah left school at the end of the day, she saw Storm waiting for her. She noted several of his horses pastured nearby and wondered why. This land usually was reserved for hay with grazing only in time of drought.

Her three and Pearl's boys clamored for a place on the horse Storm led. He let Cindy sit on his saddle with Joe sitting behind her. Luke, Robbie, and Evan rode bareback on the other horse. Storm led the two mares while he walked with Sarah.

"It's nice to see you taking some time off in the afternoon," she said. Lowering her voice so the chattering children couldn't hear, she asked, "What's going on?"

"Bad news." He handed her an envelope with her name in a masterful scrawl. "Open this later. Guess it tells you about a wire Ben got today from Pinkerton's. Joe's stepfather may be on his way here. Nate thinks he'll try to blackmail you or snatch Joe. Maybe both." Storm explained about the breakin at the Memphis office of Pinkerton's and the file with her name and address lying open.

Sarah's knees almost buckled with the news. Storm reached a hand and gripped her elbow to steady her. She wanted to cry, to pull Joe off the horse and hold him, to ride to town and ask Nate to hold her. For Joe's sake, she pushed all those feelings inside and fought to remain calm. "That's why the horses are here?"

"Figured I'd leave two men here with the horses all the time you're in school 'til this is settled. Joe won't suspect anything, but it'll keep you protected in case that man tries to get to you or Joe while you're having classes or walking back and forth."

"Poor Joe wouldn't be able to sleep a wink if he knew. He might even run away to keep that horrid Ingles from finding him." Sarah didn't think she could bear losing Joe. He was a part of her, as much as if she'd given birth to him.

"Pearl and Drake agreed with Nate it'd be best to keep Joe from finding out about this. Might never amount to anything, so no point in him worrying all the time."

Sarah agreed. "He's still fretting over that letter from Pinkerton's yesterday. No telling what this news would do to him."

"Reckon he'd have nightmares for sure then, even worse than last night. We'll all be keeping a look out for him and the other kids. This is a mean hombre and there's no telling what he'll try if he shows up."

As they approached the house, Katie and Beth ran out, calling to ride horses, too.

"Uth, too. Uth ride, too," Beth lisped.

"Uncle Storm, we want to ride," Katie shouted.

Storm gave Sarah a sardonic grin, then turned to swing his nieces onto his horse with Cindy and Joe. Sarah watched the children laughing as Storm led the horses around the grounds. Why couldn't life be as simple as this?

Sarah pressed Nate's note against her and pushed down the panic clawing within her. Praying she could keep Joe's evil stepfather from harming the boy, she hurried into the house to confer with Pearl.

Drake sat at the table drinking coffee while Pearl and Maria prepared the evening meal. He put his cup down when he saw her enter. She wished Nate was here, but rejoiced that Drake and Storm lent their support.

Pearl handed her a cup of tea and joined Drake at the table. Sarah sat across from them.

"Storm fill you in?" Drake asked.

Sarah nodded and rested her hands on the table, still clutching her envelope from Nate.

Pearl reached across the table and gave her hand a gentle squeeze. "We've talked it over while we waited for you to return. It's not as bad as when Quin tried to kill us, but we have no idea when or if this Ingles will come or what he might try if he shows up."

"You think Cindy and Luke are in danger, too?" Sarah asked.

Drake nodded. "I think all of the children as well as you and Pearl are in danger. I'll be going with Pearl on any of her sick calls. Storm said he'd go with you wherever you go except school and he has his men watching there."

"I don't want Joe to know," Sarah said. "He's already so frightened."

"Right," Drake agreed. "I've asked a couple of the vaqueros to work near the house but told them not to mention why they're here. We've talked to Zed and Miguel as well. The children will have someone watching them anytime they're outside."

Sarah looked at her sister and the brother-in-law who'd taken her into his family. She felt tears fill her eyes. "I never meant to bring trouble to the family. I only wanted to help these children the way Pearl helped me, the way you both helped me."

"It's not your fault, Sarah," Drake said. "No way any of us could have left those kids on their own."

Pearl patted her hand. "Drink your tea, then go lie down a bit. Storm is watching the children until supper's ready."

Sarah sipped the honeyed herbal liquid, welcoming the warmth to her throat. As Pearl had suggested, she excused herself to go to her room. Safe in her own domain, she opened the letter from Nate. It repeated the news she'd had from Storm, then added that he wished he could see her, but Gabe needed his help on the Billingsley trial. He promised to see her at the first chance and assured her everyone would help her secure Joe's safety.

She pressed the note to her face and closed her eyes, hoping for Nate's scent. All she smelled was paper and ink. Disappointed, she turned back the coverlet and lay down. She hugged the pillow to her, wishing it were Nate. Even though he was stuck in town, she knew she could depend on him to do whatever was necessary to keep Joe safe. She hoped she could depend on him for more.

The next afternoon in the law office, Gabe prepared for a last interview at the jail with his client, Roy Billingsley.

"You're sure you need me?" Nate asked. He hated the idea of setting foot in any jail, even as a visitor. Who could say when a visit might become permanent?

Gabe insisted, "All you have to do is sit there and take notes while I ask Billinglsey questions. I'll be interested in any thoughts you have on tomorrow's defense."

Billingsley was the man Gabe would defend on embezzlement charges early in the morning. He swore he was innocent, that he never took as much as a sheet of paper from his employer. With reluctance Nate gathered up lap desk, paper, pen, and portable inkwell.

The sheriff welcomed them to the small jail. Nate looked around the office. He'd never had much time to look at this

side of a cell before. The wall was covered with wanted
posters tacked several deep in no apparent pattern. Nate let
his gaze move from one to the other, then froze as he locked
on one near the corner.

It was a bad likeness but there hung his picture. His side-
burns were longer in the drawing, and he wore a mustache.
The name given was Lucky Bartholomew, alias Ace
Bartholomew. Nate's limbs locked in place. He tried to look
away, to move across the room, but he could only stare. He
wanted to rip the hateful paper down, but he dared not make
any move to call attention to it.

Gabe moved a chair near the cell.

"Hey, Nate." Gabe called. "Grab a seat and come back
here."

"Sure thing," Nate said. He chose a ladderback near the
poster. After a glance to make certain no one watched, he
pulled the poster down and slid it into the lap desk he balanced on the chair seat. Sure enough, another face stared at
him in the vacated space so there was no telltale empty area.
He carried everything in and sat near Gabe. Picking up the
papers, he took a single sheet and laid it atop the poster. With
a sigh of relief, he opened the inkwell and prepared to take
notes.

THIRTEEN

Nate's spirits soared, and he whistled a jaunty tune on his way to the Judge's after work. Gabe had praised him highly for his assistance with the case. Nate had turned out two wills and done some probate work, land deeds, and other odds and ends this week under supervision. In no time, he would be able to work on his own, be like a real lawyer. Then he could ask Sarah to marry him, make his home here with her and the children.

His reaction to Billingsley at the jail also surprised Nate. The man pleaded his innocence, and Nate had believed him. Strange how talking to the man made all the difference. He'd written down everything Billingsley had said, then he and Gabe went over it at the office.

Gabe was a darn good man at his job. He'd prepared his client for the questions the other side would ask tomorrow. Gabe felt confident about the case and gave part of the credit to Nate, though Nate knew the Ainsworths' testimony would be the most important.

For the first time in longer than he could remember, he felt good about himself. He'd done work to be proud of this week, nothing he had to hide from anyone. Not that he wasn't proud of himself for tolerating the ranch chores. Lordy, that was hell, but he hadn't given up.

Drake and Storm both treated him differently now. More like an equal, with less suspicion lurking in their eyes. No, he hated the cowpunching, but he actually enjoyed his work with Gabe. He'd found a future here.

As he passed the hotel, two men stepped out. Nate stopped in his tracks. They made a strange pair. One tall thin man with dark hair, and a short portly man with silver hair and the demeanor of one used to others serving him.

"Hello, Nate," Monk said.

Though his lanky friend was a welcome sight, he couldn't say the same for Monk's rotund companion.

"Mr. Barton, how nice to see you again," Hargrove said loudly so that several passersby stared.

Damn. How stupid to think for even a moment that life might work out for him. He might be lucky with a deck of cards, but he was definitely unlucky in life. By now he should know that.

"You don't look glad to see us," Hargrove said, his brown eyes narrowing.

Cautious of the situation he'd created and wondering how to proceed, Nate said, "Guess we need to talk." Nate saw Burris sitting on a bench outside the Novak's Mercantile across the street and motioned him over.

"Howdy, Nate," Burris said and looked at the other two men with curiosity.

Nate said, "These men are the business associates I've been expecting. Could you take a message to the Judge that I'll be dining in the hotel this evening and will arrive at his home before bedtime?"

"You can count on me, Nate."

Wearily, Nate said, "I know." He gave Burris a coin and sent him on his way.

Turning to the two men, he said, "Let's have dinner and then we can talk in your room."

Upon entering the dining room, they were led to a table next to Peter Dorfmeyer. The man's glare left no doubt about the ill will he harbored for Nate. When Nate and his companions took their seats at the nearby table, Dorfmeyer threw his napkin on the table and stomped out.

"Friend of yours?" Monk asked, his blue eyes twinkling.

"We had a few words." Nate didn't want to explain in front of Hargrove.

Much as he hated Hargove's presence in town, Nate welcomed his friend Monk. It was good to have him here, someone who knew him, warts and all. Monk's friendship never faltered.

Nate changed the subject by asking about their trip, then tried to focus on the conversation in spite of the despair clutching him. He wondered how best to approach Hargrove. A bribe came to mind, but Nate had used up most of the stake he won on the riverboat. He probably owed the man for the fine clothes that Hargrove now wore.

After dinner, they moved to Hargrove's suite.

"Damn, a suite." Nate looked around the room. "Must be the best in the hotel."

Hargrove drew himself up. "It is the Presidential Suite. It's important we maintain our image of the wealthy magnate."

"Don't worry, Nate. I had a run of luck waiting around in Chicago," Monk said.

Nate spun and faced Hargrove. "What were you in jail for?"

"Chit of a wife showed up asking for money for the kids." Hargrove's jaw jutted out defensively. "I couldn't let her start that, now could I? Had to teach her a lesson. A man has a right to hit his own wife whenever she needs it."

"You think so?" Nate asked, furious with the man. In Nate's opinion no real man ever needed to hit anyone weaker than him. And what kind of jerk wouldn't want his kids to have enough money to live on? Nate's hatred of Hargrove grew.

"One of her brothers tried to intervene, some property was damaged. It all turned quite ugly." Hargrove shrugged and looked as if wife beating and brawling were ordinary occurrences. For Hargrove they probably were.

"How're things here?" Monk asked.

"Fine. Things are just fine."

Nate paced the room hoping the right words would come to him. Monk had known him most of his life. No doubt he realized Nate had cooled on the idea of this deal, but then Monk hadn't wanted it in the first place. Hargrove was another kettle of fish.

"You don't look fine. Is there something wrong?" Hargrove asked.

"Yes," Nate answered honestly. "I want to shut down the deal."

Hargrove looked aghast. "Shut down? After I came a thousand miles on a wretched train to get here? Not bloody likely."

"I'm willing to pay for your time and trouble. How much will it cost me?" Nate asked.

"Hmph," Hargrove snorted. "I hardly think you can afford to reimburse me for as much as we stand to make from this town."

Nate crossed his arms and faced Hargrove. "How much?"

"Ten thousand," Hargrove said. "Cash. Now."

Monk leaned against a wall, watching as if he had no stake in the arrangement.

"You know I don't have that much cash," Nate spit out.

Hargrove displayed a malicious smile. "Precisely. So we continue with the scheme as planned."

"We wouldn't clear that much each on this. It's just a small town."

"It's also the county seat." Hargrove looked pleased with himself. "I asked around in Austin. There's a lot of money here. And these Kincaids hold a great deal of it."

"I won't do it. I won't help you, won't go through with it." Nate stood towering over the little dandy.

Hargove's eyes narrowed and he glowered. "Ah, but you will. Perhaps you'd prefer a few sheriffs learn your whereabouts, like the one in Arkansas? Or maybe these Kincaids would like to learn your background?"

Monk stepped forward, "Sorry, Nate. Guess I talked too much on the trip here. It made such an interesting tale to pass the time."

A sickness descended on Nate. If he were the murderer those folks in Arkansas accused him of being, Hargrove would be dead. Monk couldn't have known Nate would change his mind, though, wouldn't have seen any reason to keep the tale a secret.

He looked at his old friend and said, "It's all right, Monk. Guess it does make a good story." To Hargrove, he said, "You can't rat me out without incriminating yourself."

"Yes, I can," Hargrove answered. "A few wires, letters, and you'd be in jail for life—or the guest at a hanging party. I'd be long gone to the next sucker station." He took out a fat cigar and lit it. Blowing a haze of blue smoke Nate's way, he said, "Face it. You'll go through with this or say goodbye to your freedom."

Hargrove had Nate over a barrel. Monk would be his only witness he wasn't guilty of murder in Arkansas, and that he only fired in self-defense after being shot twice himself. Who would believe the word of another con-man against Lone Pine's leading citizens? All his other schemes would come out, years of dodging the law revealed. He couldn't face Sarah hearing how worthless his life had been. And what would the children think? Better to be damned for one act of theft than for a dozen others, including murder.

Hell, what had made him think fate would ever let him go straight, be a family man? All the bad things he'd ever heard about himself flitted through his mind and a black cloud of depression settled over him.

Believing he could never make life with Sarah work, he gave up. "I hate it, but I don't have the cash to buy you off."

Hargrove chomped on his cigar and rubbed his chubby hands in gleeful anticipation. "Here's what we worked out on the way. You take us around tomorrow and introduce us to some of the swells in town."

"Can't," Nate stalled. "Have to help with a trial tomorrow."

When Hargrove's eyebrows raised in question, Nate

explained about his job at the law office, living at the Judge's home, the big trial, and his limited part in it.

"Perfect," said Hargrove and chuckled. "You've done well setting yourself up here."

Nate agreed to wangle an invitation for the two men to dine at the Judge's home the next evening. It was the first hurdle in the plan.

Dread pricked at Nate. He had a sense of darkness closing in on him, as if he were once again trapped in that coffin. This time there was no digging his way out.

Sarah smoothed the skirt of her dark purple dress. Used to pastels, she had unaccountably wanted this vibrant color the moment she saw the fabric on the shelf. She had to agree with Pearl that it made her eyes look more purple than blue.

Feeling terribly selfish, she had asked Carlotta to teach so she could attend the trial. Cindy, Luke, and Joe accompanied her. Cindy wore a dress in the same purple fabric, and she saw Cindy mimic her motions and press a fold from her skirt. She smiled, remembering how she used to copy Pearl and then Aunt Lily. Luke and Joe were too busy gawking at everything to pay any attention to her or Cindy.

Though she wanted them to share her pride in Nate's accomplishments, she gave them the choice of coming with her or staying at school. They wanted to see Nate at work and promised to be quiet and still. So far, they'd all three done well, but she wondered what several hours on this hard bench would do to their behavior. Already it numbed her posterior and had her shifting positions.

This would be the first case Nate had worked on that came to trial. She conceded that Gabe was in charge, but she knew Nate helped and couldn't miss seeing him at work. Spectators pressed closely against each other and the latecomers lined the courtroom walls. Sarah secretly applauded her forethought at urging the children here early so they secured a seat in the first row. Mrs. Billingsley and her two children also arrived early and sat across the aisle from Sarah.

Gabe entered with Nate and put a stack of papers on the table in front of the spectator section. Nate's eyes widened when he saw her and she saw the pleasure wash over him. He stepped over to the rail separating the first row from the section used by officials of the court.

"I had no idea you'd come," he said to her, then spoke to each child in turn.

"We had to see your first case."

"Hardly mine," he protested but smiled that heart-stopping smile of his and turned to sit beside Mr. Billingsley.

Nate looked handsome in his black suit, gray vest, and crisp white shirt. Sunlight pouring through the windows picked up the golden highlights in his brown hair. His wide shoulders flexed and she remembered feeling them under her hands. Warmth pooled in her stomach and she felt herself flush for her wanton thoughts.

Grandpa came in and everyone stood. Sarah had not attended a court session in many years and marveled at how regal Grandpa appeared. The preliminary routine was handled swiftly, Grandpa rapped his gavel and the trial began.

Sarah had always liked Mr. Billingsley, though she didn't know him well, and enjoyed seeing him at the bank. He was friendly without flirting and always asked after her family members by name. When she returned home and learned he'd been accused, she believed in his innocence and was pleased Gabe had agreed to defend him.

Glen McDougal acted as the prosecuting lawyer, and he started the proceedings. He went on about how Peter Dorfmeyer had caught the accused with shortages and insisted there was no doubt of Mr. Billingsley's guilt. Throughout Mc-Dougal's speech, Peter puffed up like a rooster strutting in the barnyard.

Sarah couldn't help comparing Peter to Nate again, which left Peter severely lacking in many respects. In retrospect, she wondered why she had tolerated Peter calling on her as long as she had. Watching him testify against his employee, she wanted to stick a hatpin in Peter's pompous hide.

The trial proceeded through the morning and the children wiggled in their seats. She wanted to wiggle in hers. Then it was Gabe's turn and all her attention focused on the drama unfolding. Gabe called witnesses to Billingsley's dedication to his family, bank clients who testified the man was polite and helpful, and his minister testified he had helped numerous members of the community in times of trouble.

Gabe winked at her and said, "I'd like Willard and Burris Ainsworth to take the stand together."

The two brothers looked better than Sarah had ever seen them. Their neatly trimmed and combed hair—or what hair there was in Burris's case—and fresh-shaved faces made them look years younger. They'd suffered a scrubbing, from their appearance, and that and clean clothing improved their aroma. Sarah thought the two looked normal in their new state.

A ripple of comment flowed across the courtroom as the two men stepped up to the witness bench. The sheriff's deputy scooted another chair so both brothers could sit after they were sworn in. Sarah could tell each was very proud of being called to give evidence but wondered what either could possibly add.

Gabe asked, "Willard, would you tell everyone your occupation?"

"We does odd jobs for folks."

"Is one of those jobs hauling off trash?"

"Yessir. We hauls trash for most ever' body in town. Ever' Tuesday we makes the rounds."

Gabe turned to the second brother. "Burris, do you ever go through the rubbish you collect?"

"Why, sure. Sometimes folks throws away good stuff."

A snicker sounded behind Sarah.

"And did you find items from the bank in the trash of anyone here?"

Burris leaned back and smiled. "Sure did."

Folks in the courtroom whispered at the disclosure. Grandpa rapped his gavel for silence and quiet returned.

Gabe said, "Now I know you don't like to tell what people put out for you to haul away but, Willard, would you tell everyone what you and your brother found in the trash that pertains to this case?"

Willard nodded. "We haven't never told what anyone throwed away, but you said we got to now. We found stuff from the bank inside a tin." He looked at Grandpa and explained, "We thought it might have a cake or some cheese in it, you see."

Sarah was surprised when Nate shouted, "Sheriff, stop that man."

She turned in time to see Ben Liles grab Joe Dingle's arm.

Peter stood and asked, "What are you doing with my assistant?"

Grandpa rapped and shouted, "All quiet!"

Gabe nodded and said, "Thank you, Your Honor. Now, Willard, will you tell us whose trash this tin was in?"

"That there Mr. Dingle. Had a real good chair, too, what we put in our house." Willard pointed to the back.

Gasps echoed through the room and everyone swiveled in their seats to look at the man being held by the sheriff.

"You can't prove a thing," Dingle shouted at them. "You have only the word of those idiots against mine."

Grandpa stood and rapped his gavel. His frown would have wilted the bravest of men. "I will not have this continued disruption. Sheriff, bring Mr. Dingle to the front here and keep him quiet while this trial is in session." That accomplished, he nodded to Gabe. "You may continue."

Gabe said, "Did either of you save any of the things you found in Mr. Dingle's rubbish?"

Burris rummaged in pockets and pulled out several wrappers from stacks of bills. Willard pulled out a sheaf of papers folded in thirds from his pocket.

Gabe accepted and displayed them to the jury and the other attorney before he placed them on the table. He picked up the first paper. "This letter, addressed to Mr. Dingle, discusses arrangements to meet and finalize the purchase of a house in Austin." He picked up another sheet. "This agrees to the terms of a lease on a store in Austin and says the lease will be held for his signature."

Gabe turned to Mr. Dingle. "Dorfmeyer must pay you a lot more than he paid Billingsley."

A glare from Grandpa silenced the wave of tittering that undulated across the room.

Gabe had the Ainsworths step down and called Mr. Billingsley.

"Who had access to your cash drawer and keys besides you?" Gabe asked.

Sarah saw the hope in poor Mr. Billingsley's eyes. He sat up straight and said, "Only Mr. Dorfmeyer and Mr. Dingle."

Peter looked as if it had finally dawned on him he had the wrong man. He stood and pointed at Mr. Dingle. "Where did you get the money to buy a house in Austin and lease a store there? And why would you, when you're working here?"

Dingle's face turned red with fury and he shouted, "You think I liked working with you, you arrogant bastard? Listening to your boasts and hearing you put me down day after day? I should have gotten your job when your uncle retired, but he passed over me to give it to an empty-headed braggart like you. Not because you know anything about banking, 'cause you only know how to lord about, but because you're related. I figured the bank owed me for putting up with your family all these years." He turned to Billingsley. "Sorry, Roy, someone had to get blamed and I couldn't figure a way to make Dorfmeyer take the fall."

When all the trivialities of dismissing the case and binding Dingle to jail were dispensed, Sarah and the children rushed to congratulate Gabe and Nate.

Nate swung Cindy up in his arms, and ruffled the hair of each boy. "You certainly got an exciting introduction to court."

Gabe accepted the thanks of the Billingsley family, then offered, "Lunch is on me if anyone's interested."

"Can we go to Granny's?" Sarah asked.

"Sure. Everyone ready?" They stopped when they overheard Peter tell Mr. Billingsley he no longer had a job at the bank.

Sarah spun on her heel and put her hands on her hips. "Peter Dorfmeyer, this man has just been proven innocent. What do you mean he no longer has a job?"

Others milling in the courtroom gathered to listen.

Peter flicked an imaginary speck of dust off his cuff then pushed his nose into the air. "Once he's been accused of embezzling funds, depositors can no longer trust him."

"I trust him," she said and sent her best glare with her statement.

Several onlookers murmured agreement.

A patronizing smirk appeared on Peter's face. "Now, Sarah, dear, women have no head for business. Don't fret yourself over something that doesn't concern you."

Nate stepped forward, but Sarah pressed a hand to his arm to stay him.

She leveled a glare at Peter and said, "If you don't give Mr. Billingsley a raise and promotion to your assistant, I am going to move my money to another bank. I'm sure my family will do the same."

"I know I will," Grandpa said from behind her. "Wouldn't mind opening my own bank right here in town."

Peter gasped at the thought of Grandpa as competition. He looked around him at the sea of unfriendly faces and his eyes widened in fear. "Now, now. There's no need to be hasty. Billingsley, you can have Dingle's old job. Be on time tomorrow."

He turned to Sarah. "I don't know what's come over you since you got back from Tennessee. You used to be so proper and now you're speaking out in public against your friends. I believe it has to do with your new associates."

"If you have something against me, don't take it out on Miss Kincaid," Nate said in spite of Sarah's restraining hand on his arm and the fact he carried Cindy.

Peter speared Nate with a glare. "I'll be making inquiries about you." With that threat, he turned and stomped out of the courtroom.

Grandpa said, "Hmph. Let's go eat."

Over a meal at Granny's Lunches, the men reviewed the case. Diners stopped by to congratulate Gabe and he graciously included Nate in the praise. Sarah was so proud of Nate. He might be used to grand financial schemes in his business, but he had pitched in to help her family while he waited for his business associates.

The children stared at everything in the restaurant, especially the case of desserts. At this time of day most of the clients were businessmen. Rhoda and her daughter Bayla bustled back and forth. Rhoda's husband, Abe Kline, took diners' payments when he wasn't waiting tables or helping in the kitchen.

Rhoda and Abe delivered their plates heaped with food, and Abe stopped to chat. He and Rhoda had graciously moved two of the square tables side by side so the family could eat together. After introductions to the children, Abe looked at them and inclined his head in Sarah's direction.

"She tell you this used to belong to her?" he asked.

Luke said, "No, sir." The other two stared at Sarah.

Sarah explained, "When Pearl and I first came here, I helped her turn this into a restaurant. We worked here, hmm, I guess most of a year before Rhoda bought it from us. Then she and Abe married and he started working here with her."

"Talks more than he works sometimes," Rhoda said with a wink as she passed by.

"Still uses Sarah's recipe for applesauce cake," Grandpa said. "Best cake I ever put in my mouth."

Sarah flushed with pleasure. "It's a family recipe. My mother gave it to me. Said it was something her mother made, but without a frosting. Then someone who'd once worked in a confectioner's shop in Denver showed her how to make the icing."

"Then we'll all have applesauce cake for dessert, won't we?" Nate asked the children.

Joe nodded and Cindy and Luke said, "Yes," in unison.

After they finished the meal, Gabe made a big show of groaning at the expense when he paid the group's lunch tab. They left and walked along the sidewalk toward the law office.

"The Judge was right. Best cake I can remember," Nate said. "And that frosting. Man, I—"

"Well, hello, Mr. Barton."

Sarah turned and watched two men approach. She liked the looks of the tall one ambling toward them the same way Nate walked. Something about the short round one put her off. Unlike his companion, he strutted toward them. She couldn't say what about him annoyed her, but the feeling remained. She watched Nate closely, wondering at the way he tensed.

"These are the business associates I've been expecting," he said. He set Cindy on the sidewalk and made introductions.

Sarah's stomach churned and she wanted to scream at the two to leave, to let things continue as they were with Nate helping Gabe. Surprised she could, she extended her hand and greeted the two men.

Mr. Masterson took her hand in his and his pale blue eyes met hers. "It's a real pleasure to meet you, Ma'am. I can't tell you how much I've looked forward to this."

Mr. Hargrove made a fuss of kissing her hand. "My dear," he said. "What a pleasure."

She wanted to wipe his kiss off, even if she had put her gloves back on before they left the restaurant. She didn't like men who called her "my dear" when she didn't even know them.

Face it, she scolded herself. You don't like him because you're afraid his coming will mean Nate leaves you. She listened to the men talk about some railroad and forced herself to pay attention.

"We can explain our plan better if we have a chance to show you our maps and figures," Hargrove said. "You'll see what a fine opportunity we offer for investment in this town's future."

Hargrove seemed enthusiastic, so she guessed it was something good for the community. Maybe whatever it was would need a local representative and Nate would stay.

Grandpa agreed to see the men at his home for dinner. Free of his day's work, Grandpa said he'd wait until the next day to fill out the papers concerning the trial and headed home. They stood at the office door now and she expected Nate to leave with his two associates. He bid them good day and went into the building with Gabe. She and the children followed.

Inside the office, Nate said, "If you don't mind, I'd like to help out here during the day. I can take care of some of the backed up papers before I have to leave."

Sarah's heart broke a little and she wanted to sit down and bawl. The kids looked sad, too, when they heard Nate mention leaving.

"You're efficient and a fast learner," Gabe said. "Great to have you if you can spare the time."

"My associates do most of the actual planning. I'll meet with them and other investors in the evenings. We hope to have a town meeting tomorrow."

"I . . . We'd better be getting out of your way," Sarah stammered. She had to get out of the room or she would embarrass herself by crying. "Thanks for lunch, Gabe. Congratulations to both of you on winning the case."

Nate frowned and said, "Sarah—"

"I'll see you soon. Guess we'll come to the town meeting tomorrow. Don't forget our picnic on Saturday." She turned and fled with her three children in tow.

Across the street Maria's grandson, Javier, waited for her. She signaled to him and went to the buggy. He joined her and took the reins.

"Thank you for waiting," she said, choking back tears.

"You all right, Miss Sarah?" Javier asked.

"Fine, I'm just fine." Inside she fell apart, but she stiffened her back and sat as Aunt Lily had taught her. Nate had never promised he would stay. In fact, he'd said he was only waiting for his associates.

Why did she think he'd change his mind just because she wanted him to? Even when they'd made love, he hadn't made any promises. She'd asked for no assurances, had known she could have only that one night. So why did she feel so abandoned?

Nate felt like pond scum. He worked as fast as he could, hoping to block out the sight of Sarah's face, the hurt and disappointment he'd seen there and mirrored in the faces of the children.

"Hey, you trying for the office record?" Gabe asked.

Nate looked up and blinked. "What?"

"I've never seen anyone accomplish so much in a few hours. You got a devil chasing you?"

Nate exhaled. That was exactly what he had, but he smiled and reassured the man he'd come to think of as a friend. "Wanted to help out as much as I could. Won't be so stacked up until you can get someone in here to work with you permanently."

Gabe met his gaze, his face inscrutable. "Frankly, I'd hoped that would be you." He held up his hand to stay Nate's protest. "I know, I know. You said it was just until these men arrived, but I had in my mind you might stay after their business was concluded and they'd left. Especially since you and Sarah seemed to hit it off so well."

Nate shrugged. "I hold Sarah in high regard, believe me,

but I have other obligations." Like staying a free man. Free to do what? He hadn't figured that one out. Run a saloon. Cheat the next sucker? Suddenly it didn't matter. He cared only for now, today, the few days he had left here.

"You're not already married are you?" Gabe asked.

"Phfft. Definitely not, but I'll have to leave soon for other reasons." To beat the sheriff out of town, just like so many other times.

"Well, if you change your mind, you have a place here. Grandpa'd probably make you a partner in time."

"Thanks," Nate said, trying to keep the frog in his throat from making his voice croak. "You can't know how much the offer means to me."

And he couldn't tell Gabe. Not his future plans. Nothing about his real life. Not even his real name. Still, for the first time in his life he'd done honest work to be proud of. Men he'd come to admire like Drake, Storm, Gabe, and the Judge actually sought his assistance, valued his opinion.

He'd work as hard as he could while he remained. This one thing would stand out in his rotten life as something worthwhile he'd done. One place where he'd done the right thing. Maybe someone would remember his work and not hate him too much for what he was going to do to this town.

FOURTEEN

The day after the trial, Sarah rode in to town with Pearl and her family. They brought the wagon so there would be room for her and all the children. Storm rode his horse as usual.

They came in for the big town meeting Nate and his two friends had called at the town school, where such meetings usually were held. The town buzzed with word of the meeting and speculation on the reason. People crowded into the school until only standing room remained. Soon people were wedged there also. From the faces she saw, people from nearby ranches and farms were there. Her family wasn't late, but they would have had to stand had Nate not saved them seats at the front.

She shifted her weight and flushed. No one guessed her secret. She'd slipped something from Pearl's stores of medical supplies, and the knowledge of her duplicity worried Sarah.

Not that regret played a part in her reaction, or embarrassment. No. Awareness might be a better word. Guilt plagued her when she remembered the pessary she had inserted before she left home. If the opportunity arose to carry out her plan, her preparation insured that no child would result.

Sarah had lent her support to Nate's project even though it would take him away. Her community meant a lot to her. If this would help the people who lived here to prosper, then she would assist in any way she could.

Nate stood by the teacher's desk. Charts and maps were tacked up on either side of him. Wearing his black suit again, he had never looked more in command. He looked so handsome it made her ache.

His fine voice demanded attention. "Thanks for coming. I've met many of you while I've been in town. Here are my associates, Mr. Michael Masterson and Mr. Henry Hargrove. Mr. Hargrove is from the Kansas and Texas Railroad, and I'll let him tell you his plan."

Hargrove strutted to the center and cleared his throat. "Friends, we have a wonderful opportunity to offer the citizens of Kincaid County." He used the schoolmaster's willow pointer to trace the route on the map as he spoke.

"We propose to start a train line from Austin through Kincaid Springs and straight West to Sierra Blanca, then one to El Paso. That means growth and prosperity for this community, friends. Participation now means the greatest profit for you folks later."

Hargrove went on to explain the investment, the interest rate, terms of yield, and how soon building would commence until it made Sarah's head spin. He took questions from the audience, but few were opposed. Peter stood against the wall near the front, a frown on his face through the entire meeting. Occasionally he took notes, but he said nothing.

Sarah sat worrying her handkerchief. She didn't want the town to change. It was a lovely place now, the prettiest she'd ever seen. Still, she couldn't be selfish. Maybe the people who seemed so excited wanted others to move in and bring growth for the town. This Hargrove would leave, though, so it wasn't his town to change. She guessed the railroad needed the new revenue that growth along the line would bring.

Sarah waited through the meeting and afterward while people lined up to buy their shares of the venture. Storm escorted Lorena Osterman home and Drake and Pearl readied their family to leave. Nate stepped over to ask if he could take her home in Grandpa's buggy. She agreed, but sent the children home with Pearl and Drake, with a reminder of the picnic they had planned for tomorrow. All three children promised to go straight to bed when they got home.

She found a seat away from people clamoring for a share in Hargrove's plan or asking more questions before investing. Mr. Masterson's job appeared to be taking money and writing out the certificates, then recording it in a ledger. She watched Nate as he answered questions, usually deferring them to Hargrove. After all, Hargrove was the railroad man and it was his plan. Refusing to think of this as Nate's project, she preferred to think of him as working at the law office and only lending a hand to the other two men. She had no idea how Nate or Mr. Masterson fit into all this. Perhaps Nate would explain it on the ride home.

Nate watched Sarah, sitting prim and proper at the back of the room and looking like the beautiful subject of an important painting. She'd worn her hair a new way tonight, piled on top of her head, and she sat ramrod straight with her hands folded in her lap. Knowing she waited for him made him proud.

He excused himself from the few remaining investors and strolled her way. She rose and gathered her shawl about her as regally as a queen donning her ermine robes. When she looked at him with her gorgeous lavender-blue eyes and smiled, his heart skipped at least two beats.

He returned her smile. How could he not? "Sorry to keep you waiting, but we can go now."

Placing his hand at her back, he guided her out of the school and to the buggy. When they sat side by side, he clicked to the horse and they drove away.

"Were you successful?" she asked.

"Yes, thanks." He slowed the horse so they could converse.

"I'm glad." She smiled and the warmth of it shot through him until she said, "I invited as many people as I could."

No, surely he'd misunderstood her. "You . . . you what?" he asked.

"I know this is really important to you, so we came in early and I stopped by to see as many people as time allowed and encouraged them to come tonight."

Oh, damn, now he'd involved her in his scheme! He didn't want any of the blame for his swindle to spill over onto her when he left town.

"Thanks, but, um, you shouldn't have gone to that trouble."

Though it was too dark for him to see her reaction now that they had left the lights of town, he heard the hurt in her voice. "You're not displeased with me for helping you, are you?"

"No. No, of course not," he assured her with as much enthusiasm as he could muster. "It was very gracious of you. Hargrove can handle everything, though. He's an expert at his job, which is why I leave everything to him now that he's here."

"Will you be leaving soon?" Once again he heard the sadness in her voice. Hell, he hated lying to her, but he couldn't seem to stay away from her either.

"In about a week, no more than ten days. We have other towns to cover." Not for him.

He was through with this crap, no doubt in his mind about that. After this he was going to New Orleans and never pull another deal like this one or any other. Unless the plan skirting around in his mind worked. He prayed he could pull it off.

"Yes, I guess you would. Will you spend several weeks in each one? Maybe I could bring the children and visit," she said.

"No, not like here. I came ahead because, for a change, I had the time. It will be a rush from now on. We'll be on the move almost constantly."

She pointed at a narrow road and surprised him. "Turn right here. Let me show you my school."

He looked at her but she refused to meet his gaze. Blood pumped through his body. She couldn't mean what he thought. No, there had to be some other reason for the detour.

Soon her small schoolhouse appeared outlined in the bright moonlight from a cloudless sky. The building stood nestled among a grove of live oaks. A dozen or more horses grazed nearby, the only sign of life. To the side of the small building playground, swings stood like lonely sentinels waiting for the school day's clamoring children. Two privies stood behind the playground.

Stopping the buggy near the hitching post, he helped her down. She took the key from her reticule and opened the door. Moving as if from memory, she lit a lantern and kept the wick low.

She gestured around her. "Well, this is it."

He took the lantern from her. Examining each picture, piece of sculpture or rock she'd set out for the children to see, he moved slowly around the room.

"It reminds me of a museum I saw once in Chicago. Natural science and art combined."

"Some of these children will never see a museum. If they stay in our school they learn to read and write well, but many will never leave this county and will have low paying jobs with little chance for any luxuries. I want them to know about the beauty as well as the drudgery of life."

What a wonderful person she was, helping people every day. Imagine what good she would do here. Just looking at her made him smile.

"If I'd had a teacher like you when I was a kid, I would have done a lot better in school."

She returned his grin. "If you had a woman teacher, I'll bet you had only to ply her with that smile and she let you get away with murder."

Embarrassed that she had guessed correctly, he marveled at her knowledge of human nature. He would have thought she could see that he didn't deserve her or her trust. This minute he should whisk her out of here and deliver her home before he had a chance to sample what he thought she meant to offer him tonight.

A week. Unless his plan worked, he probably had seven more days left in this town, ten at the most. Most of those he wouldn't even see her. Try as he might, he couldn't force himself away from her.

He saw her two natures warring within her and knew she fought the same battle. It wasn't proper for her to be here alone with him, much less carry through the invitation her gaze proclaimed. She stepped toward him and her beautiful lavender-blue eyes almost mesmerized him.

He set the lantern on her desk and tried to explain his reluctance. When he took her hand in his, he saw his mother's ruby ring on her hand. No longer did he resent her having it.

Cal had the ring made for Nate's mother on the occasion of Nate's birth. The ruby hearts symbolized eternal love. She had treasured it, intended that it someday go to Nate's wife. How angry he'd been when Cal gave the ring to Roxie, and angrier on learning the rubies had passed on to Sarah. Now Nate took pleasure knowing that the only woman besides his mother who'd ever been important to him wore that symbol.

"I should never have taken you in my room that night. I can't honestly say I'm sorry it happened, but I wish I had been strong enough to resist sullying you."

"As I remember, the feeling was mutual, and I'm glad we were together. I felt fulfilled, not sullied, and I want it again. Now." She placed her hands on his chest and lifted her lips to his.

He cupped her face in his hands and stared into her eyes. "Sarah, you know I can't stay? Don't think this will change that." He wished it could, prayed it would, wished he could hold her forever.

"It's because you can't stay that it's so important. I never asked for false assurances. I want to savor your body while you're here. I want a lifetime of memories."

Dear Lord, save me from myself. He wanted to weep or crumple in a heap at her feet. "Don't. You don't know what you're doing. You could get pregnant, if you aren't already."

"I would love to have your child, Nate. If I've already conceived, then I'll raise our child with pleasure and pride. But I, um, I'm wearing a, um, a pessary to prevent conception."

He stared at her, slowly understanding her words. Of

course, she would know of a pessary from her sister. The idea still astounded him. "You? You're wearing—"

She pressed a finger to his lips to silence him. "Please don't think poorly of me. It's not because I'm cold or calculating, as it might seem. I know you're leaving, and this may be the last time we have a chance to share this between us."

She turned away. "You know my mother and father weren't married, that my mother put me with Pearl to help me. I would never willingly subject my child to the taunts I heard. At the same time, I'd never do anything to stop a pregnancy once it began. I've known women to do that, but I could never kill my own child."

Knowing what it must have cost her to resort to the device, he took her shoulders and turned her to him. "Of course not, sweetheart. You were wise to be prepared knowing I can't resist you when we're alone." He kissed her forehead, her eyes. "In all the world, no one is more loving and compassionate than you. You're also the most desirable woman I've ever known."

He heard her sigh of relief. With a flick of her wrist she doused the lamp. Only a slice of moonlight filtered through the trees outside the windows, but it showered across her.

She took the combs from her hair and it spilled like moonbeams on her shoulders. After unfastening the buttons of her dress, she let it slip to the floor. "I wish we had days to explore one another, but we can't stay here very long or someone will come to investigate."

"Sarah—"

"Shhhh." She took his hand and led him to the cloakroom where she kept a single bed. "I have this for children who become ill at school."

His arms cradled her, but still he protested. "Sarah, you're a beautiful, wonderful woman, but I can't give you what you need, what you deserve."

She leaned into his embrace. "This is what I need from you," she whispered before her mouth claimed his.

He couldn't get enough of the taste of her. His tongue

brushed against hers. She met his probe and matched her strokes to his. His blood boiled and his heart banged in his chest like a parade drum on the Fourth of July. Her fingers kneaded his back and pulled him close.

She slid her hands to his chest and worked to undo the buttons of his shirt. He broke his embrace long enough to divest himself of clothes.

When he stood as naked as a babe, he lowered his mouth to her cheek. After raining a trail of kisses down her neck and across her shoulders, his teeth tugged at the ties of her chemise.

"I'm glad you left off the corset," he murmured.

"It seemed best, considering what I had planned for you." She unfastened her petticoat and drawers and kicked them aside.

Reaching out, she took his hand to guide him to her. He joined her on the narrow mattress. She scooted back and jumped.

Startled, he asked, "What's wrong?"

She giggled. "The bed is narrow and my backside is pressed against a cold wall."

"Mmm. I can warm you." He rose and pulled her to the center of the cot then spread himself over her.

Hating the narrow space, he wanted her in his bed, in his room. He needed her with him to stave off the nightmares, to feel her soft, sweet body next to his all night. He craved the pleasure of waking to find her curled next to him.

The hard, hot evidence of his need pressed against her abdomen but she didn't move away. Instead, she spread her legs and thrust herself to him. The sensation of her warm skin moving against his manhood almost caused his undoing.

"Now, Nate. I need you now."

No more than he needed her. He'd hungered to feel of her, to taste. So long. He'd been hungry so long. Before he knew her, before he knew only she could meet this terrible hunger aching inside him.

Slipping his fingers to her soft core, he started at the string he found there. The pessary ribbon, of course. That his sweet innocent Sarah wore a pessary for him made him hate himself more, but he lacked the willpower to halt their lovemaking.

"Now, Nate," she begged. "Please now."

Delay meant the risk of discovery, but he intended to go slow for a few more minutes, wanted to stretch their loving out. Suddenly he couldn't wait. Her urging heated his already boiling passion. Sliding his manhood into her intimate folds, her moist heat spurred him forward and he plunged inside her, deeper, deeper.

Intense pleasure reverberated through him in steadily increasing waves. His lips claimed her rigid nipple as his palm cupped her other breast. Her fingers threaded through his hair and she pressed him to her.

When he moved his hand between them to find the pulse of her femininity, she moaned with delight. They moved together, bodies synchronized in rapture. When he thought he would explode from pleasure, his release came and she cried out his name from her own zenith. He lay atop her braced on his forearms, her head cradled in the nook of his shoulder. Gently he kissed her hair, each eye, then rolled off her to stand.

Wishing again he could keep her with him all night, he knew he had to get her home soon or their absence would arouse suspicion. He hurried to dress, unwilling to create trouble for her with her family. A soft curse escaped his lips when he banged his toe as he searched for his clothes and boots.

She called out, "Wait. I'm used to the building and I know where things are."

As soon as they were dressed, they left the school. She locked the door behind them and he helped her into the buggy.

He joined her and sat hunched over, the reins in his hands. "I'm not proud of taking you like a thief in the night, Sarah. But I'm grateful for the time we've had together. I can't tell you how much I wish things were different."

She slipped her hand through his arm and gave him a pat.

"I wish they were different, too, but I'm also grateful we've had all we have."

Nate flicked the reins and they made their way to the ranch house. It was dark when they arrived. He walked her to the door and kissed her forehead. "I'll see you tomorrow in town."

Sarah hated that the door had to be kept locked now because of that horrid Ingles person. She unlocked it and slipped inside, closed it and went toward her room.

Storm sat in the main room and stood when she came in. Puzzled, she asked, "You just get home?"

He looked uncomfortable. "No. I rode by the school on my way home from Lorena's to check on the horses. Saw Grandpa's buggy in front and you and Nate inside. Seemed a strange time to be looking at the school."

"You were waiting up for me?" she asked, astonished he would think it necessary. An angry retort sprang to her mind, but before she spoke she realized his concern was justified. The very thing he hoped to avoid had happened.

"I just wondered is all." He paused, eyeing her suspiciously and waiting for her to explain.

She strove to remain calm and said casually, "Of course, we had to wait in town until all the people were through asking questions. Since Nate had seen that school but not mine, I showed him through. Unlike that stupid Peter Dorfmeyer, Nate immediately saw what I had tried to create with the artwork and science displays. He said it reminded him of a museum he'd seen in Chicago."

Storm regarded her closely. He chewed his lip a few seconds then asked, "What else did he say?"

Suddenly it was all more than she could stand. The sneaking around, the chances she'd taken, the threat to Joe, and Nate's impending departure. She rushed to her big brother and put her face against the front pocket of his favorite blue shirt. His arms went around her to pat her back gently.

"Oh, Storm," she sobbed. "He's not going to stay."

"I know. I know," he said as she sobbed against his chest.

* * *

By Saturday, Sarah's frazzled nerves had her jumping at every sound. She spent all her time worrying about Nate leaving and whether or not Ingles would appear. The children were too smart not to notice something was going on, but so far she'd been able to keep knowledge of the Pinkerton wire from Joe.

He watched her warily, though. Clearly his guard never relaxed and she knew he expected his stepfather to appear at any minute. Maybe he noticed he was never alone, never without an adult nearby.

She'd promised the children a trip into town as a treat. They planned to shop, then go for a drive and picnic with Nate after the law office's one o'clock Saturday closing time. After church on Sunday, all the Kincaids planned to gather at Grandpa's, but this afternoon would be just Nate, Cindy, Luke, and Joe with Sarah. Their family. She sighed and wished it were so.

Cindy looked sweet in her new blue gingham with a matching blue bow in her blond curls. Both boys were scrubbed and their hair slicked down—not that Sarah expected it to stay that way for long. She hoped Nate liked her new green sprigged muslin dress. She'd finished it only this morning. Pearl had pressed it for her while Sarah herded the children through their preparations. When they were ready, she carried the picnic basket and tucked it behind the buggy's back seat. Storm rode his horse near.

"Say, I believe I'll ride in with you and make sure these two boys don't rob the bank."

Joe smiled while Luke and Cindy giggled, oblivious to the look exchanged by Storm and Sarah. The children climbed into the buggy and Sarah clicked to start the horse.

A few puffy white clouds dotted the brilliant blue sky. Bright green leaves already decorated the willows along the river, and forsythia bloomed where Pearl and Sarah had planted it along the trail through the ranch. A soft breeze cooled the effect of the sun's rays.

In town, Sarah pulled up in front of the law office. Storm helped Sarah down from the buggy.

"I'll be around if you need me," Storm said. "Promised Zed I'd get him some stuff at the hardware store."

"We'll be fine. Thanks for the escort."

Storm pointed a finger at the two boys. "I'll be watching you. No bank robberies."

The children laughed and ran to the law office. Sarah followed them inside. Gabe and Nate stopped working to talk to the three youngsters.

"Can we go outside?" Luke asked Sarah. "We brought our marbles so we could play quiet."

Sarah nodded. "But only if you stay where I can see you from the window. I need to speak with Gabe about the adoption. Then we'll go to the mercantile until Nate is through here."

Cindy stayed with Sarah, but the boys rushed outside. Eager to get everything finished, Sarah pelted Gabe with questions. He answered patiently, though he had nothing new to tell her. It took time, she knew, but she was so eager to have the children officially hers.

A shout startled her and Luke burst into the office.

"A man grabbed Joe and took him," Luke cried.

"Where did they go?" Nate asked as he stood and reached for his hat.

He led Luke outside and the others followed.

Luke pointed at the back of the building. "A man grabbed Joe. He tried to grab me too, but Joe pushed me out of the way and jumped at the man." Luke looked up at Nate, wonder in his voice. "Joe talked, Nate. He talked. He yelled at me to run get you."

"Sarah, I'm taking Storm's horse. You get the sheriff, then tell Storm and Drake."

Sarah raced to alert the sheriff, Luke and Cindy on her heels.

Nate had left his gun at the Judge's house, so he turned to Gabe. "You have a gun in there?"

"Yeah, and I'm coming with you," Gabe said. They rushed

into the office where Gabe opened a drawer and took out a gun belt, strapping it on as he followed Nate. "I know the area around here."

They hurried outside to the street and Gabe called to a passing rider, "Tom, we have an emergency. Let me borrow your horse and your gun."

Gabe tossed the gun to Nate and mounted the horse. The two men rode South as Luke had pointed.

Rage drove Nate like a beast. He directed his anger at himself for letting Joe be kidnapped, and at Ingles for daring to harm Joe. Storm's horse was a fine animal easily able to out-distance the one Gabe rode, but Nate had to let Gabe take the lead. They rode through territory Nate had never seen.

Soon Gabe held up his hand and halted to look for tracks. They were at the top of a rocky ravine. Apparently Ingles had made no attempt to hide his trail.

"He has to be making for the caves," Gabe said. "Let's cut him off."

Not a cave, thought Nate. No, not a dark, confined hole in the earth. His belly knotted in fear. Dear God in heaven, have mercy. His heart pounded so hard he thought Gabe must hear. What will I do? How can I go into a cave?

Gabe turned his horse and angled West. In spite of his ter-ror, Nate kneed his horse forward. After a few minutes they topped a rise and saw a lone horseman in the distance. The rider stopped in front of a limestone cliff face. No doubt, it was Ingles. The man dismounted and dragged an uncooper-ative child behind him as he entered a small cave opening.

Thank God they were in time, but how could they rescue Joe? Gabe pointed to a group of trees about fifty yards from the cave. Once there, Nate slid off his horse and tied the reins to a tree limb while Gabe did the same.

"Any idea where we are?" Nate asked.

"Yeah. We're on Holsapples' place."

Could Nate force himself to enter that cavern? He'd have to do it. Somehow, he had to conquer his overwhelming fear of black, closed places and help Joe. Sweat gathered on his lip and forehead. His hands shook with the memory of being trapped in the coffin. Joe depended on him, though. With an iron will he forced his legs to support him and move him toward the dreadful hole.

"You know this place?" Nate asked.

"Yeah, but never been in that cave. No idea how big it is."

"I'll let you know," Nate said. He walked toward the cliff wondering if he could force himself inside the yawning abyss.

Gabe followed and they circled to avoid observation from the opening should Ingles be watching. They moved as silently as possible for two men in western boots over rocky terrain. When they were beside the entrance, they paused to listen. Nate heard shouts, but couldn't understand the words. He held the gun and Gabe drew his own from its holster.

Suddenly Joe cried out as if he had been hurt. Nate lost all thought for his personal demons. Forced to stoop to fit through the small tunnel-like entrance, he almost crawled for five feet. Suddenly the burrow widened and he stepped into the cavern. After the bright sunlight outside, the shadowy recesses blinded him. He had time to register two figures before he heard a gunshot. The force of the bullet turned him as he felt the white-hot sting in his shoulder.

Before Nate or Gabe could return the fire, Ingles grabbed Joe and held him as a shield. Ingles pointed a gun at Nate while his other arm imprisoned the youngster's neck.

"Drop your guns or I'll kill the kid."

Nate's fury fueled emotions so violent they shocked him. Never had he been a violent man. Even when he killed the man in Arkansas it was only in self-defense, more a reaction to attack than aggression. Now he wanted to shoot Ingles, to watch him die for all he had put Joe through, all the terror he still forced on the boy. But he was no gunman and feared his shot would strike Joe instead.

Nate's mind saw the scene as if he were not a participant in the bizarre drama. A single lantern glowed on a boulder. He absorbed the dank smell, registered the whiskey bottles scattered across the ground, the half empty one beside the lamp. Ingles's wild gaze darted from Gabe to Nate.

Joe sniffled and his wide eyes implored Nate. "Nate?" he called in a hoarse whisper. The sound of Joe's voice after so many weeks of silence startled Nate.

The villain struck Joe with the gun. "Stop yer whinin', brat. You'd best go back to not talkin'."

Rage clouded Nate's judgment and he almost rushed Ingles, but his partner tried reason.

Gabe's calm voice remained level. "Drop the gun and release Joe. You won't get away, Ingles, so make it easier on yourself."

"You bastards have ruined my plan," Ingles shouted. "Now you have to die."

Nate followed Gabe's lead in spite of his unreasonable desire to strangle Ingles with his bare hands. "See reason, man. Give up."

"If you make a move, I'll kill the kid. I'll throw him off the ledge."

For the first time Nate saw the inky black of nothingness behind Ingles. "Look, I know you want money," Nate said. "The Kincaids are wealthy. They'll reward you if you return Joe to them unharmed."

Ingles took a step backward. "They would have paid plenty if you two hadn't shown up. I had plans for those kids, all three of 'em. If those swells wouldn't pay, I'd sell the brats in Mexico. Now you've ruined everything."

The man fired once more and took another step back, dragging Joe with him. He stood only inches from the edge.

"It's all your fault things went wrong. I had it planned out good. I'll make you sorry you ever crossed Reuben Ingles 'n then I'll deal with those rich folks. Drop your guns and step over to the edge here. Do it now."

Gabe and Nate exchanged looks. Gabe dropped his gun. Nate made a show of dropping his, then they both lunged for Joe. Nate felt Joe's shirt slip from his grasp as Ingles stepped back. Joe reached for Nate and mere inches separated their hands before Ingles pulled Joe over the edge. Ingles's scream echoed through the cavern and Nate fell to his knees in defeat.

"No!" Nate shouted in despair.

So close, he'd almost snatched Joe. Sorrow and anger overwhelmed him. When the last reverberation of Ingles's cry died, Nate lay with his head on his arms. Tears ran down his cheeks. Joe had trusted him. He failed Joe, and it had cost the boy his life.

Through the silence, soft sobs caught Nate's attention. He inched to the precipice and looked over the edge. Nothing showed in the ebony depths, but he heard muffled whimpers below. He rose and staggered to the lantern and returned to the rim. Nate extended the light over the edge. Joe lay on a narrow shelf about fifteen feet down. The boy's leg stuck out at a crazy angle. There was no sign of Ingles.

"N- . . . Nate?" Joe tried to turn and moaned at the effort.

"Joe," Nate called. "How bad are you hurt?" And how could he get to him?

"Can't bend my leg or raise my arm."

"Hang on, son. Don't try to move. We'll get you out of there."

Gabe said, "You talk to the kid and keep him still. I'll get the rope from Storm's saddle."

He left and Nate reassured Joe that help would soon reach him. Gabe returned with a pair of leather gloves and a rope he tied to a large boulder. He fed the line to Nate who made a loop and drew it around his waist.

Gabe looked up and down Nate's frame and frowned. "Damn, Nate. You're gushing blood top and bottom."

Nate looked at his shoulder. A growing crimson stain spread across the shirt. He pressed a handkerchief to the wound.

Gabe inspected Nate's back. "Looks like that one is clean through the top of your shoulder, but I meant the one in your leg."

Nate glanced at the hole in his thigh where blood spread in a sticky flow. "Guess he got me again with his last shot." His attention had been so focused on saving Joe he hadn't felt the slug hit him.

Gabe removed his string tie and took out a handkerchief. He pressed the linen square to the wound on Nate's leg to staunch the flow, then used the tie to wrap as a tourniquet.

"That'll do for now," Nate said. "I have to get to Joe." He gave the line a test tug to make sure the rock and knot would hold his weight.

"Man, you're in no condition. Let me."

"No, I have to help Joe. I don't even know where we are. Couldn't go for help if we need it." Nate tested the rope again to be sure the rock would hold his weight. Facing the dark abyss made him dizzy with fear. Sweat poured across his brow and he thought he might throw up. He had to do it, though, had to rescue his boy.

Gabe nodded and pulled on the gloves. "I expect the posse is on its way by now. They should be able to follow our trail." Gabe set the lantern near the edge and guided the line while Nate slid over into the chasm.

Clearing the lip of the cave floor and edging down, Nate thought he might pass out. He forced himself to look directly in front of him, to pretend the wall jutted from firm ground outside with sunshine all around.

"N-Nate?" Joe asked.

Nate looked down and regretted it. He fought the wave of nausea sweeping over him, battled to remain conscious.

"I'm coming, son. We'll get you out of here." He felt his feet touch the shelf and sank beside Joe. As he did so, a chunk of ledge broke off and dropped into the nothingness. Not enough light spilled over from above for him to see clearly. He touched Joe gently.

"How bad are you hurt?"

Nate ran his fingers lightly over the arm. He felt the limb and up to the shoulder where it felt as if the arm had pulled out of the socket. He traced the leg and discovered the break there.

"The arm's not broken but it will take Pearl or the doc to fix it. Leg's broken. How about the rest of you?" Nate asked.

"Guess I'm banged up some."

From above Gabe called, "How is he?"

"Broken leg and dislocated arm." Nate slipped the rope from his body and dropped it over Joe. He widened it and carefully worked it under the boy's arms, being gentle with the injured limb, then tightened the loop. The movement caused another large chunk of the shelf to break away.

Nate yelled up, "He's ready to come up." To Joe he said, "Use your good leg and arm to push away from the rock so you don't bounce against it."

He tried to brace Joe's body to lessen the pain. As the rope tightened, Joe gave an agonizing cry. His injured limbs dangled helplessly.

Gabe asked, "You want to wait until I can get help and send down a stretcher?"

"Can't wait," Nate said. "Shelf's breaking away each time I move. Soon there'll be nothing left."

"I can do it," Joe said.

"I know you can. You're a brave boy. Gabe is going to lift you up. All you have to do is brace yourself."

"What about you?" Joe asked.

"Soon as you get up there, Gabe will take the rope off you and send it back down for me."

Nate watched Joe inch up. He felt dizzy again, so he sat down. Gabe pulled the boy to safety then leaned over the rim to talk to Nate.

From a thousand miles away Gabe called, "Here comes the rope. Let me know when to pull you up."

Nate couldn't focus. He heard more rock give way. Only a few feet remained, not even enough for him to lie down. Lying down sounded real good.

"Nate, grab the rope," Gabe shouted. "Nate!"

FIFTEEN

Nate fought the fog closing in on him. Why was it so dark? The coffin! He had to get out. Something hit his chest and he batted it away. Sound penetrated the haze smothering his brain. Someone shouted his name. He forced himself to concentrate on the words. His name . . . Who called his name?

He focused and realized faint light spilled from above. Silhouetted against the glow over the rim, Gabe dangled a line which hit Nate's chest again. His fingers closed around the rope's loop, and the rough hemp rasped against his skin. He tried to rise, but his injury-weakened limbs failed him.

A large section of his resting place disappeared and he almost fell with it. He listened for the sound of rock crashing against the chasm floor. Seconds ticked by before he heard the thuds far below. Only a two-foot space remained to spare him the same fate. His legs hung from the narrow bench, dangling into hell yawning below him.

This time he wouldn't cheat death. The scent of his life's blood soaking his clothing taunted him. Even the small amount of energy required to secure himself in the hemp's circle of safety eluded him. At least he'd saved Joe. Even if he wouldn't see the boy grow to manhood, the evil Ingles would never bother Joe or Sarah again.

Dear God, happiness had been so close. He squeezed his eyes shut, yet saw Sarah's beautiful face as clearly as if she stood before him. In his mind's eye her perfect rosebud mouth smiled and parted for his kiss.

No! He wouldn't give her up, not yet.

He heard Joe's faint call, "What's happening?"

Gabe muttered something, then shouted, "Nate, put the rope around you. Now, Nate, now!"

With a final thrust, he pulled the loop around his body and the last part of the rock shelf crumbled. He fell!

Heart-stopping seconds passed, then his body snapped as the rope jerked taut and he dangled like a clock's pendulum. He prayed for all his worth, prayed for his sorry life as he swayed in midair—that the rope around the boulder held against his dead weight, that the boulder securing it didn't dislodge.

"Nate, why aren't you up here?" Joe asked.

Joe's newfound voice wavered as if from fear, but Nate couldn't answer. The rope squeezed all air from his lungs. He heard Gabe reassure Joe but couldn't decipher the words. Pain and fatigue pushed all response from his mind.

Gabe hauled him upward, but Nate hadn't the strength to help. Each ragged wrench banged his body against protruding rocks. The rope bit into his flesh as he swung and crashed in a slow ascent toward safety. When he reached the edge, Gabe dragged him over, then dropped cross-legged beside him in obvious exhaustion.

"I sure thought you were done for." Gabe gasped and wiped a hand across his face as if to blot out the thought.

"Me, too," Nate answered, his voice croaking from a sandpapery throat and mouth dry as a desert. "Thanks. Couldn't help. Guess lost more blood 'n I thought. Weak as kitten. Chest hurts like sonofabitch."

"Rope probably broke some ribs when you fell. Bad jolt when the ledge broke off. Damn near lost you and me both." He helped remove the rope from around Nate's chest. Looking as weary and frightened as Nate felt, Gabe ran a hand through his hair and said, "As God is my witness, I didn't think I could pull you up those last few feet."

Nate tried to stand but fell back to the cave floor. He

crawled to where Joe lay and Joe stretched out a hand to meet his. He cradled the boy against him.

"You're safe now, son."

Gabe stood. "Neither of you can ride." He covered them with a dirty blanket he found with Ingles's things in the corner. "I'll go for help. Be back soon as I can."

After Gabe left, Joe looked at the edge of the cave floor and shuddered. "Is . . . is he . . ?"

"Yes, he can't hurt you again." Nate patted Joe gently.

Joe sobbed, "I'm glad. I hated him. He hurt my mama real bad. That's why she died. He was always hittin' her."

"Soon you'll be with your new mother. She'll take good care of you and love you so much you'll forget all the bad things that have happened. Don't ever forget your real mama, though."

"I don't think I can forget any of this." Joe tried to curl himself against Nate, then winced and moaned.

"Don't try to move yet, son," Nate said and inched closer to shield the boy. "Guess you won't forget completely, but in time it will dim in your mind so it's not so frightening. The Kincaids will make sure you have lots of good memories to crowd out the bad ones, make them seem less important."

"Maybe they can help you have good memories, too. You know, so you won't have those nightmares you told me about."

"Wish they could, but I won't be around that long. Don't forget I'll have to leave in another week or so."

"I wish you'd be my pa," Joe sobbed.

Nate felt like weeping with him. "I do too, but I can't."

"I promise I'd be real good and do lots of extra chores for you. I bet Luke and Cindy would, too."

"Son, it's not that I don't want to. Guess I'll always think of you three as my own youngsters."

"Then why don't you marry Miss Sarah and we could be a real family? Don't you love her?"

"Yes, I suppose I do." The knowledge came as a shock to him. It didn't make things any easier. Nate wished it was simple, but things had become too complicated. "You know your stepfather was bad and that Gabe and Storm and Drake are good men?"

"Yes." Joe sniffed and rubbed his good arm across his face.

"Well, I'm not a good man like the Kincaids. I'm not as bad as Ingles, but I've done bad things. It's too late for me. Promise you'll always be good. Make the Kincaids proud of you."

"I'll try, but I wish you'd stay. You could say you're sorry if you did something bad."

Saying you're sorry after stealing folks' money wouldn't make much difference. Maybe they'd wait for the trial before they hanged you was all.

Last night Monk and Hargrove collected amounts of money that staggered Nate's imagination. Hargrove was right when he said Kincaid Springs had lots of wealthy residents. He could talk Monk into helping him get rid of Hargrove, but the chances of Nate's plan succeeding were slim. He exhaled and sucked air at the pain. Best to concentrate on the problem here and now.

"How're you doing, Joe?" he asked.

"I'm scared. Reckon I'll ever be able to walk again?"

Nate smoothed the hair from Joe's face. "Of course, but not for a few weeks while your leg heals. Good thing your Aunt Pearl knows lots of medicines to speed up healing."

"She's my aunt? Guess I never thought of that."

"You've got a big family now, son. They all love you and want to help you however they can."

"You think I could call Miss Sarah my mama?" Joe asked.

"I think she'd like that a lot. She'll be real happy you can talk again, too."

Waiting in town, Sarah fumed and fussed at the delay while the sheriff gathered a posse. How long must she wait, could she afford to wait? What if Nate and Gabe hadn't found Joe? She paced, worry making her frantic.

"Now, Sarah, you've got to be patient," Grandpa said. "Ben is a good man, but he has his way of doing things. I'll take Luke and Cindy home with me. They can make use of the playroom."

"Thank you." She bent and gave each child a hug, then cupped each child's chin. Luke and Cindy were in tears and she had no words to reassure them yet. "Be good for Grandpa. I'll see you as soon as I find Nate and Gabe and we get Joe back."

She watched them walk away with a breaking heart. What if they failed? After all they had lost, how would she tell Luke and Cindy if they lost the boy who'd become a brother? Storm stood at her side, the reins of Grandpa's horse in his hand.

She looked up at her brother. "If I follow you, we can find them. You're the best tracker of anyone in town."

"We should wait for Drake. He's on his way." Storm looked toward the end of town. "I see him now."

After conferring with Drake, Storm and Sarah set out on their own. Drake promised to light a fire under the sheriff and his posse and follow close on their trail.

Storm led, holding his speed to allow Sarah in the slower moving wagon always to keep him in sight. The trail kept to the road only a short distance before going off across open range. At least the wagon's trail would be easy for Drake to follow.

She spotted a lone rider coming toward them. "Isn't that Gabe?" she yelled at her brother.

Storm dropped back beside her. "Yes, and riding as if the hounds of hell are nipping at his heels."

Her heart lurched. "Something bad has happened."

They met up with Gabe, who looked ready to drop.

Before he could say anything, Sarah asked, "Where's Nate?"

Gabe quickly told them what had happened. "Some rough terrain. Not sure the wagon can make it, but we need it."

"You want to climb up here and tie your horse to the wagon?" Sarah asked.

Turning his horse as he spoke, Gabe said, "Think I'd better lead the way. Follow me."

"Sarah, let me drive." Storm tossed him the reins of his horse and climbed up beside her in the wagon.

They followed Gabe across the rolling prairie, bouncing and rattling over the rough ground. Her bonnet came off and they let it roll across the ground with the wind.

She gripped the wagon seat with both hands. Even though he no longer had to worry about his stepfather, poor Joe would be scared and in terrible pain. Nate might even bleed to death unless they reached him soon. Possibilities flashed through her mind and she willed the horses to move faster, faster.

"I hope we don't lose a wheel on one of these bumps," she yelled at her brother above the noise of the wagon.

"Or break an axle." Storm spoke without taking his eyes from the land in front of the galloping team of horses. "Need to get there fast, though, and see how bad their injuries are."

"Haven't been this frightened since Quin tried to kill us."

"It'll be all right," Storm reassured her. "We should be near. We're on Holsapples' place now, and I remember the caves are on this side of his land."

Fortunately, the terrain remained fairly flat until they came to the rugged slope where the caves were. Storm stopped the wagon at the top.

Gabe pointed down a rugged bank to where the land flattened out before a cliff. "You see the horse tied in that copse of trees? Look right and you'll see the cavern entrance."

In wet weather it would be impassable, but the spring rains hadn't arrived to soften the ground. At last, she shaded her eyes and watched the opening in the cliff's side. Soon she would see Nate and Joe. Her heart pounded with anticipation.

Storm stood on the wagon seat. "Looks like a passable incline over there." He sat down and grabbed up the reins.

"Not so fast going down," Sarah cautioned. If they wrecked the wagon, their wild ride would be for nothing.

Storm grinned at her and they bounced down the incline. They halted in front of a cavern opening where Gabe waited.

"I have to see them," she called and jumped from the

wagon as it slowed to stop. She raced through the entrance to reach Nate and Joe. She had to bend at the waist and knees to get through the narrow tunnel. As soon as the crawlway spilled her into the cavern, she spotted her two.

They lay on the floor of the cave, Joe's head pillowed on Nate's arm. A single lantern cast an eerie light across the small cavern. The filthiest blanket she had ever seen covered them. She dropped to her knees and pulled it back.

Hoping she concealed her horror at the amount of blood covering Nate, she said, "Let's see how badly you two are hurt."

Nate smiled as if to reassure her. "Joe's leg is busted and his arm's out of the socket. He's banged up pretty bad from the fall, too. Been in lots of pain but he's been brave."

"Joe," she said softly, fighting back tears. She couldn't cry, had to be strong for Joe's sake. "Can you be brave just a little while longer? Storm's going to carry you and put you in the wagon so we can take you to town."

"Good," he said. Though she knew he'd shouted a warning at Luke earlier, the sound of Joe's voice now startled her.

Storm lifted Joe, but stopped at the cave's short tunnel-like entrance. "Not sure how we can get him through the opening." He turned around. "Even if I can stoop low enough and still carry him, don't see how I can keep him from bumping that leg against the sides."

Sarah said, "We'll use that blanket as a travois and pull him the short distance through the narrow crawlway." She folded the blanket in half and laid it out at the mouth of the cave.

Storm carefully placed Joe onto the blanket.

He touched Joe's hand. "Don't give up yet, Joe. This'll be bumpy, but it'll be short." He backed out of the cave, slowly pulling Joe with him. Sarah followed, talking encouragement to the injured boy. As soon as they cleared the narrow opening, Storm picked Joe up and put him in the wagon.

Sarah tucked a lap robe around him then gave his hand a squeeze. "I'll be right back as soon as I check on Nate," she said and raced back into the cave.

The posse, led by Drake and Sheriff Liles, thundered up and men swarmed everywhere. Drake and a couple of the posse members followed her into the cave while Gabe talked to the sheriff.

Sarah hurried to Nate. He struggled to his feet supported by Drake and one of the posse. Sarah hurried to him.

"Careful now," she said. "You've lost a lot of blood."

"Guess that's why everything keeps spinning around."

When they reached the narrowed exit, Drake asked, "You need us to pull you through on the blanket?"

"No, I can crawl. It's walking alone I can't manage."

Drake braced Nate as he knelt. He looked as if he might pass out, but he appeared to fortify himself and crawled forward. Sarah followed in time to see Storm help Nate up and into the wagon where he collapsed beside Joe.

She climbed in beside them and searched for anything to help them. Grabbing the filthy blanket and folding it into a pillow, she slipped it beneath Joe's head, then sat beside him and took his hand. She leaned against the wagon's side.

"Would you be more comfortable with your head on my lap?" she asked Joe.

He squeezed her hand. "No. Hurts to move."

She longed to baby him, to snatch him up and cuddle him in her lap, but knew he thought himself almost grown. "You're very brave, son. It won't be long before we're back in town and we'll have you in a nice soft bed at Grandpa's."

Joe closed his eyes, but didn't release her hand.

"What about you?" she asked Nate. "Won't you rest your head on my lap? There's nothing left to make you a pillow."

"Might get blood on your dress." He lay with his head on the bare boards of the wagon bed.

"Every bounce of the wagon will bang your head where you are. Scoot over here and put your head on me."

He moved his head to her lap. She let her hand rest on his good shoulder, careful to keep her fear from her face.

Drake called to Storm, "Will you ride ahead and make sure the doctor's on his way to Grandpa's?"

Storm retrieved his own horse and took off for town. Gabe and Drake conferred with the sheriff, then Drake tied his horse and the one of Grandpa's Storm had ridden from town to the tailgate, climbed onto the wagon seat and took the reins.

While they moved out, Drake explained. "Gabe's pretty tired, but he's staying with the sheriff and showing him what happened. He's going to look through Ingles's things and see if there's anything of Joe's. When they're through, he'll meet us at Grandpa's."

She let go of Joe's hand to reach for the picnic lunch she so carefully prepared that morning. With all that had happened, it seemed days ago. Wishing she had some cool water, she took the jar of lemonade from the basket. After pouring some into a cup, she offered Joe a drink, then Nate. Each downed some of the sweetened liquid.

They took a longer, less tortuous route back to town and at a more sedate speed, but Joe moaned and gasped at many of the dips and bumps. He didn't complain, though. Nate stiffened but made no sound.

Sarah said, "I know you're both in pain, but we'll be at Grandpa's soon."

Joe's eyes remained closed, but Nate answered Sarah's questions until he'd explained all that happened in the cave.

When it seemed as if they'd ridden for hours, Drake turned the wagon onto the river road.

"I recognize some landmarks. Town is only a few minutes away," she reassured her injured passengers.

"Can't say I'm sorry to hear that," Nate said, then gasped as the wagon hit a pothole.

Drake called over his shoulder, "I see Grandpa's house. Looks like Doc's buggy in front."

"Better take me in the back," Nate said. He met her gaze and a half grin appeared. "Fiona won't want me bleeding on her clean floors and carpets."

Sarah brushed the hair back from his face. "Under the circumstances, I think she'll overlook any extra cleaning involved."

Drake pulled the wagon up to the portico, the closest entrance for a wagon. Grandpa opened the door and stepped out, Storm and Chester following closely. Luke and Cindy were with them and clambered up into the wagon to see Joe and Nate.

"Stay back, children," Sarah said. "Let Storm and Drake help Nate and Joe into the house."

Grandpa said, "Been watching for you. Doc's upstairs in Storm's room getting ready to set Joe's leg."

Nate looked down at the fresh blood on his makeshift bandages. "I'll wait my turn in the kitchen. Lots of hot water is going to be required, so I might as well make it as easy as possible." He struggled and sat up.

Storm scooped Joe up and strode into the house with him. Joe looked at Sarah, silently pleading for her to come. Torn between her two injured men, she hesitated a second.

Nate pushed at her gently. "He's trying to be brave but he needs you with him."

She smiled her thanks and hopped down from the wagon. She gave a last glance over her shoulder and saw Drake and Grandpa lower the tailgate and help Nate slide out of the wagon while Chester controlled the horses.

She raced up the stairs to the room Storm used when he stayed at Grandpa's. Inside it, Fiona stood beside the doctor.

"Pearl's on her way," Fiona said. "Himself sent those odd brothers to get her."

The bed had been stripped of its coverlet and blankets and extra sheeting folded across. Strips of binding and two splints lay at the foot of the bed. Kettles of heated water were nearby on the wash stand.

The doctor uncorked a bottle and poured a milky liquid into a spoon. "Swallow this, young man. It will ease the pain."

Dr. Percival and Fiona busied themselves while waiting for

the laudanum to take effect. Using a pair of sharp scissors, he cut the clothing from Joe's injured leg, shoulder and arm. When Joe's eyes closed in slumber, the doctor told Storm, "Need you to hold him. First we'll get his arm set back in the shoulder."

Accustomed to helping Pearl with her healing, Sarah found herself unable to help in this instance. She held her breath and cringed when she heard the slight snick of the joint reseating itself. Even in his drugged sleep, Joe moaned. Then the physician started work on the leg.

"We're lucky it's a clean break and didn't shatter. He probably won't even limp once this heals," he said as he bathed the skin from ankle to hip. When he'd finished he lay the splints alongside Joe's leg and moved the bandages near. "Need your help again, Storm. You hold his body and I'll straighten the leg. Mrs. Galloway, I'll need you to hand me the bandaging."

Sarah could stand it no longer. She took Joe's hand and murmured soothing words softly in his ear. Whether he knew what she said or not didn't matter. Comforting him helped her get through the process. Joe moaned and tried to throw off her hand when the doctor set the leg. Fiona reeled bandages to Dr. Percival as he bound the splints in place.

"Well, let's see the other patient," the doctor said as he gathered up supplies. "This lad will need more of the laudanum to ease the pain for a few days." He gave a quick list of instructions and Fiona nodded.

Sarah smoothed her hand across Joe's cheek. He looked so pale and helpless. She'd almost lost him, almost lost both him and Nate. Now the crisis had passed, her knees wobbled and she nearly broke down. Tears gathered in her eyes, but she held them in. Her hands shook and she longed to crawl up on the bed beside Joe and sleep away today's terror.

Fiona placed a hand on her arm. "Are you all right, dearie? You've gone pale as a ghost."

Dr. Percival stopped, gave her a surprised stare, and opened his bag. He retrieved his smelling salts and held them out to her. Fiona hurried to take them for Sarah, then stopped when Sarah spoke.

"I'll be all right. It just hit me they both could have died." She forced a smile. "Joe will be a long time recovering from this. I don't even know how seriously Nate is injured."

Storm moved to her side, peering into her face as if for reassurance she wouldn't faint. He gave her a gentle hug. "I'll stay with Joe. You go see to Nate."

"And I'll step across the hall and make sure Nate's room is ready for a patient," Fiona said.

"Thank you." Sarah hurried from the room and down the stairs to the kitchen.

Pearl had Nate sitting in a chair with his shirt off and his trousers cut away from the leg wound. Polly and Emily hovered nearby, both wringing their hands.

"Oh, Pearl," Sarah said with relief. Pearl's medical bag sat open on the table. "I'm so glad to see you here. Fiona said Burris and Willard went to get you."

"I just arrived. Thought I'd get started cleaning this one up while the doctor worked on the other," Pearl said without pausing in her ministrations. "It'll save Dr. Percival time."

The doctor heard her as he entered the kitchen. "Thank you, Pearl. I hope you'll give the lad upstairs some of your herbs to help his bones knit. Be hard to keep a boy that age still for long." He set his medical bag on the table beside Pearl's, then bent to examine Nate's wounds.

"Shoulder wound is clean through. Pearl, you work on that one some more while I look at this thigh."

He tut-tutted and shook his head. "Nasty one here. Have to get that lead out, and it's deep. Better give you some laudanum, too."

"No, I don't want that stuff. Give me a swig of the Judge's whiskey and I'll be ready."

Polly headed for Grandpa's study. "I'll fetch the bottle."

"Needs stitching, don't you think?" Pearl asked the doctor while she cleaned the shoulder.

He nodded. "Yes, and you'd best do them. Your stitches are neater than mine and leave less scarring." He sponged at the leg, but blood continued to seep from the bullet hole.

Polly returned with a bottle of the Judge's best whiskey. She took a glass from the cupboard and poured the glass almost full. "Here you are, Mr. Nate."

"Whoa, we're trying to ease the pain, not pickle him," Doctor Percival said. "Go easy on that now."

"Thanks, Polly." Nate took one large gulp and set the glass on the table within easy reach. "Good stuff. Shame I'm not in a position to enjoy it."

The doctor took his instruments from his case and laid them on the table.

Pearl folded a soft cloth and placed it between Nate's teeth. "This will help, not as much as the whiskey, but at least you won't bite your tongue."

The physician probed and Nate's knuckles grew white where he clutched the chair arms. Sweat beaded on his brow, but he made no sound. At last the doctor held up a bullet. Nate removed the pad from his mouth, exhaled and took a couple of deep breaths.

"Got it, by golly." Doctor Percival dropped the metal into a pan. It clattered and rolled around the basin. "You did fine, Barton. Most would've passed out from the pain."

Nate offered a half grin and wiped his brow with the pad. "Wish I had."

"Now you better put that pad back in your mouth. Have to sew you up tight in all three places so they'll heal. I'll leave that to Pearl here and go on home for my supper. Not as young as I used to be, you know."

"Thanks, Doc," Nate said.

"Thank you, Dr. Percival," Sarah said to the elderly man. "I'll see you out."

"No need for that. I've been coming to this house since it was built, took care of Rob's wife, God rest her soul. Know my way about."

Pearl worked swiftly, giving directions to Sarah without pausing in stitching Nate's shoulder. "Take some of the purple coneflower, and mint. No not that mint, the other one. Now, some of that last packet there, the ginseng. Yes, make Nate a tea of those. Better add some honey when it's ready."

Nate bit one pad and pressed a second to his thigh to slow blood flowing from the insulted wound. He looked pale and Sarah feared he had lost too much blood. While the tea brewed she started beef boiling in some water for a broth, hoping it would give him strength without upsetting his stomach. She made plenty, enough for Joe also to have some when he woke up, then set it to the side so it could simmer slowly all night.

Pearl finished sewing each wound together, applied a salve and then bandages. Polly and Emily left to check in on Joe upstairs, but Polly soon returned.

"Emily's checking on the two young ones in the playroom," Polly said.

When she finished the binding, Pearl left to get Drake.

Sarah poured the tea into a cup and added a dollop of honey. "This will help you heal faster. Pearl will probably leave you a tonic to help build your blood." She sat across the table from him so she could watch him.

Nate made a face. "Hope it tastes better than this."

A laugh escaped in spite of her concern. "No, it tastes much worse."

He raised an eyebrow and dumped some of the whiskey into his cup. She pretended to be offended, but failed. Knowing he sat here strong enough to drink on his own filled her with joy.

Drake sauntered in followed by Grandpa and stopped beside Nate. "Let's get you up to bed before this hits you."

Nate set his cup down. "I can make it on my own now I've been patched up." He tried to rise, then fell back to his chair. He put both hands on the table and looked up at Drake. "Guess I do need a little help after all."

Grandpa said, "Reckon you'll feel a lot worse tomorrow

and the day after. I believe the third day's the worst one for this kind of injury. Pearl's doctoring will pull you through without the fever most folks get from wounds that bad."

"If I feel worse in three days, you'll be having my funeral," Nate said.

Drake hauled Nate up out of the chair and helped him stand. He pulled Nate's arm over his shoulder. "If you're able, let's get it done so you can rest."

With Drake's support, Nate wobbled along until they got to the stairs. He stopped and stared at the steps. "Lordy, do I have to climb those?"

Drake pulled him forward. "Come on, we'll go slow."

Sarah followed close behind them. "Think how good it'll be to settle into a nice, soft bed."

"Magic words," Nate said and grabbed the stair rail to help propel himself upward while Drake lent his help.

In Nate's room, Drake and Grandpa helped Nate undress while the women looked in on Joe across the hall. When they returned with Storm at their heels, Nate lay in bed and looked almost asleep. He opened his eyes when they entered.

Drake said, "Unless you need me here, I might as well go on home. You coming, Pearl?"

"Yes, I think both patients will be fine now, though they'll both have some pain." She took Sarah's hand and said, "I've left salve, tonic, and herbs for more tea for Nate, and herbs and a tonic for Joe. You know what to do about their food and how to care for them as well as I do, but you've only to send for me and I'll come right away. Would you like us to take Cindy and Luke with us?"

Sarah looked at Nate, saw the brief shake of his head. She sighed, happiness spiraling through her. He wanted her children here with him.

"Grandpa, is it all right if they stay?"

"You know it is. Like having younguns around again. Takes years off my age."

Sarah hugged him. "Thank you. They can help keep Joe

entertained. There's that big playroom upstairs plus the yard if they need to be rowdy or noisy."

Pearl nodded. "I'll send Javier back with clothes for you and the children."

"Please remember Cindy's doll," Sarah asked. "She sleeps with her every night."

"I'll remember. I'll send some books and the checker set to help entertain Joe."

"Your bunch coming for dinner after church tomorrow?" Grandpa asked.

Drake looked at Pearl and she nodded. "Only long enough for the kids to pester you while I check on the patients." She gave him a hug and kissed his cheek. "They love coming here, but you'll have your hands full without our crowd."

"I like having family near. Matter of fact, Lex and Belle will be back home next week with their two. Rosilee's opening their house and airing it Wednesday or Thursday. 'Course, they won't stay long, but it'll be nice to see them again. Have to have a family celebration for all of us while they're here."

Nate's eyelids closed. They popped open, then dropped closed again. Sarah shooed everyone from his room, then checked on Joe. She sent Storm home with Pearl and Drake. Joe slept soundly, thanks to the laudanum, and Fiona sat by his side.

She smiled when Sarah came in. "This one's sound asleep. I told Polly to feed your other two and let Emily put them to bed. I hope you don't mind."

"Oh, Fiona, thank you. Can you stay with Joe while I slip up and say goodnight to them? The excitement has probably left them exhausted but keyed up."

"Now, dearie, I'll be staying with this one a bit. Emily promised to come in at one to relieve me. I'll toddle off to bed then and sleep like a rock, I'll bet. I always do." She made a shooing motion with her hands. "You get yourself some sleep. I expect you'll also be checking on Nate. If Joe needs you, I'll hurry 'round for you."

"Thank you. I don't know how I could manage without you."

"It's my pleasure to be able to help you after all you've done for me, though I'm sorry that it's such a sad thing has given me the opportunity. Don't you be worrying yourself at all. Polly's older and needed in the kitchen, but Emily and I can take turns with this boy-o as long as needed. Himself won't complain when a little dust collects if it's for his family's sake."

Sarah hurried to check on Luke and Cindy. She thanked Emily for helping and the woman said good night. The children were already in bed, but tears ran down Cindy's cheeks.

"I need my dolly," she sobbed.

"Javier is bringing her to you. He'll be here soon."

"Are Joe and Nate gonna be all right?" Luke asked.

"Yes, but it will take some time before they'll feel well. They're both asleep now, but tomorrow you can talk to them."

Each youngster lay in a separate child-sized bed. Sarah tucked the cover around Luke, then turned to Cindy. Tears ran down her cheeks and she hiccuped a sob. Sarah dried her face.

"As soon as Javier brings your dolly, I'll bring her to you." Sarah pulled a large rag doll from a shelf. "Why, look here, this nice soft baby looks lonely. She's probably been hoping a pretty little girl would come along and cuddle her. She'll keep you company until your dolly comes." She snuggled the soft toy beside Cindy."

Placated, Cindy sniffled but curled against the doll.

"You'll leave a light, won't you?" Luke asked.

"Of course. And you remember where Joe and Nate are sleeping. I'll be in one of those rooms if you need me."

Sarah lowered the wick of the wall lamp so it cast a soft glow across the room. Soon both children slept. Creeping quietly down the hall and stairs, she left a trail of wall lights shedding soft light.

She returned to Nate's room. He slept, so she moved an upholstered armchair near his bed and sat down. The terror of the day left her exhausted, but she wanted to be near Nate.

Gabe peeked in and set a supper tray on her lap. "Polly figured you'd rather eat up here."

She lifted the napkin and inhaled. "I wouldn't have thought I could eat a bite, but this smells heavenly."

"Brought some things Joe might want from his stepfather's bag. Picture of a woman we thought might be his mother. I left it all in Uncle Rob's study for you to look at before you show it to Joe."

"Thanks for all your help. You saved Nate and Joe."

"No, I helped Nate save Joe, but he would have found a way without me."

"Oh, Gabe, he couldn't have gotten up that ledge without you. He told me how you saved him, how you had to pull his dead weight because he was too weak to help. I can never thank you enough. Without you, both Nate and Joe would have shared Ingles's fate."

Gabe looked embarrassed and changed the subject. "Reckon I can sit with him tonight if you like."

Sarah assessed him. His lanky frame sagged in fatigue. The skin near his eyes was pinched. Though tall and broad as the other Kincaid men, she thought even baby Parker could wrestle this one to the ground tonight. She wondered how he even made it up the stairs, much less carrying her tray of food.

"No, you need rest as much as he does. I'll stay. Fiona's with Joe. I'm so nervous from all that happened, I couldn't sleep a wink."

"Then guess there's no use both of us staying awake. If I don't sleep about three days into next week, I'll see you tomorrow." He closed the door softly as he left.

Surprised at her hunger, she wolfed down everything on the tray. The food supplied an energy boost and she settled down to watch Nate sleep.

Sarah thanked God for sparing Joe and Nate. Knowing how close they'd come to death left her trembling. She had some extra time now to be with the man she loved. Almost losing him forced her to acknowledge a new facet of her love for him. He mustn't leave her and the children. Could she convince him to stay with her?

SIXTEEN

Nate shifted uncomfortably and moved higher on the pillows piled at his back. Damn, his strength refused to return. He chafed at being in a sick bed for the past couple of days, but lacked the energy to do more than cross the room.

Tapping at his door alerted him to a visitor before Monk stepped into the room.

"Hello, Nate," Monk said. "You look better 'n yesterday."

"Feel like I been pulled through a keyhole. You come alone?" Nate asked. When Monk and Hargrove had visited Sunday afternoon, Hargrove strutted about making a nuisance of himself until Nate fought the urge to yell and throw something at him.

"Yeah, Hargrove's at the hotel. Sarah said I could come on up by myself."

He speared his good friend with a stare and raised an eyebrow. "You calling her Sarah now?"

Monk nodded and smiled. "She insisted. She's fixing your lunch tray. Nice girl. Roxie'd be real proud of her."

Nate figured Roxie would be mad as hell if she knew what he'd been up to with her daughter. At least Sarah had used the pessary that time at her school, but she could be pregnant from the first time in his bedroom at the ranch. What would happen to her if he'd planted a baby and then had to leave or the sheriff hauled him off to jail? For one thing, he'd never even see his firstborn.

Damn, he'd made a mess of everything so far. At least he'd

gotten Joe off that ledge before it gave way. For once in his life he'd done the right thing and it paid off. Maybe it made up for a few of his mistakes along the way.

He snapped from his reveries and decided to get on with his rat killing while he had Monk alone. "I've been searching for a way to call this off, Monk."

"Figured as much. How you going to get Hargrove off the scent? He's been out signing up folks left and right. You being a hero and all, folks are way too trusting."

"Damnation. Help me, Monk," he pleaded. "I'm looking for a way out of this. You know I'll make it up to you later."

"Nothing to make up. We're friends, aren't we? Besides, I promised your folks I'd look after you. Haven't done too good a job, but I tried."

"You've done as well as I'd let you." Not a man used to apologizing, Nate took a deep breath and spoke fast. "You were right back at the hotel in Memphis. I never should have started this with Sarah or the Kincaids, shouldn't have involved Hargrove for sure. I've been scouring my brain thinking of ways to call it off and keep Hargrove from sicing the law on us."

"Glad to hear that, Nate." Monk met his gaze. "Your folks treated me like a son. Roxie did, too, after her and Cal hooked up. Would have made 'em all real proud if you settled here with Sarah."

Nate leaned back and closed his eyes, pinching the bridge of his nose. "Don't know if I can pull it off." He exhaled and lowered his hand, then met Monk's gaze.

Monk stared at him as if something worried him. "Sure be good if you can. Just let me know what you need from me."

Nate watched Monk step to the end window with a view of the town. The heavy green damask draperies were tied back and allowed light to filter through a hanging of ivory lace panels. Monk parted the curtains and stared out. Something bothered him and he'd eventually spit it out. Long ago Nate learned there was no hurrying him. The worse the news, the longer it took to tell.

Four years' difference in their ages never divided their friendship. They were as much brothers as if by blood, though Monk had repeatedly refused any claim on Cal's saloon. Nate guessed he'd made it clear to Roxie, too, or she would have left part of it to Monk.

Nate was only nine when his folks found Monk begging outside a saloon and took him into their home. After suffering miscarriages through the years, Nate's mom died with her newborn baby three years after Monk joined their family. Cal sank into his own misery and left Monk and Nate mostly to their own amusements while he became depressed and cynical.

When Cal met Roxie on a chance stop at the saloon she ran in Pipers Hollow, he came back talking of no one else. He walked differently, smiled more, a man reborn. Monk had been off on some fool errand, but Cal dragged Nate down to that wide spot in a Tennessee road to meet Roxie while Cal convinced her to join up with him at The Lucky Times Palace.

Not that Nate blamed Cal so much now. Knowing Sarah had put all that in a different perspective. A smile from her rosebud lips or a sparkle in her lavender-blue eyes lifted his spirits. If he lost her, he wouldn't be fit company for anyone.

More often than not over the last few years he and Monk had traveled together. Nate avoided St. Louis after he and Cal quarreled, but Monk checked in every few months while Nate waited somewhere else. Since their teens they'd talked of having their own saloon in New Orleans. Monk must be pretty mad at him for messing up that dream.

Monk stood at the window a few minutes, then turned back to face Nate. "Nice town. Wouldn't mind settling here myself."

The admission surprised Nate. "Nothing I'd like more, but I think it's too late for both of us."

"Maybe not, maybe you can come up with a way. You're good at planning."

Monk paced the room, then stopped beside the bed. "Didn't want to be worrisome with you laid up and all, but there's things you need to know and I got to tell you like it is."

He dropped into the chair beside Nate's bed. "Banker fellow, that Dorfmeyer, has been talking against you to folks. Mad as a hornet 'cause people are calling you a hero. Says he's sent off inquiries on all of us."

"We used clean names. Won't be anything on you or me." The thought struck Nate. "Hargrove always uses his real name. Damn, if Dorfmeyer's nosing around hits the right spot, Hargrove could sink us before I have a chance to row this boat to shore."

Monk hunched, elbows on his knees. "Banker says he contacted the railroad people."

Hell, that would do it. "Did he?"

Monk shrugged. "Hargrove blustered around and got the telegraph operator to admit the banker hadn't sent any wires. Reckon Dorfmeyer wrote letters, though. Can't say I blame a banker being cautious, but he's a mean son of a gun."

"Pompous ass. Thanks for filling me in." He looked at his friend. Something still worried him. "What else is it?"

"Something else I didn't tell you."

"Yeah, what?" Nate asked. It must be bad if Monk hesitated.

"Hargrove." Monk spit out the name as if it were a curse word. "After he got out of jail back in Chicago, he told me he'd meet me at the train station. I collected my stuff and waited there for him. When he showed up, he was all agitated, excited like. His hands were skinned up and he was in a big hurry to leave."

Nate sank back against his pillows. "Any idea why?"

"All he'd say was he'd taught his wife a good lesson this time. Made me sick to my stomach. If I hadn't already told him about the deal, I would have got shut of him then and there."

"So, you think he beat her up again?"

"Yeah. Don't know what else." Monk whirled to face him. "I tell you, I wish I'd never found that man again. He's not like you and me. He's plain old scum. Never has a kind thought for anyone, not even his family, only for himself."

Surprised to hear easygoing Monk speak so vehemently against anyone, Nate agreed. He'd hated Hargrove more each time he saw him. "I'd like to get shed of him and call a halt to this whole mess."

Monk nodded. "Hope we can."

He sat up and his efforts sent the room spinning in his brain. Refusing to give in, he swung his legs over the side of the bed. "Damn, weak as a newborn. Doc says I have to stay here another few days. Hell, can't afford to waste my time in a sickbed with Dorfmeyer and Hargrove working at one another like two roosters at a cockfight."

"Looks to me like you got no choice. I seen dead people look livelier than you do. What're you trying and I'll help?"

Nate shook his head and was immediately sorry. "Got to do this on my own. Walk a bit now and then, get back some strength." Using the chair to help pull himself up, he winced at the pain when he put his weight on his injured leg. He felt blood ooze and looked down at the bandage's fresh red stain.

"Hellfire and damnation, can't even pee without a fuss." He stepped behind a screen to the commode chair and used it, then limped back to bed and sank against the pillows. "I tell you, it's humiliating to be this feeble."

He heard glass and china rattle against a metal tray. Sarah must be bringing his meal and one to Joe across the hall.

Monk grinned, "Leastwise you get good care from the prettiest nurse in the country."

A couple of days later, Sarah mulled over her latest problem while she made a late night check on Luke and Cindy in the third floor playroom. Luke slept with his boots lined up beside the bed and tomorrow's clothes ready on a chair. Both Cindy's dolly and the large rag doll were nestled with her beneath the cover.

Sarah planted a soft kiss on each sleeping child. How dear they were to her. Luck certainly smiled on her the day she found them and Joe. In spite of her niggling worry, she gave thanks for her blessings as she tiptoed downstairs to the second floor and looked in on Joe.

Such a good boy, he hardly ever complained and needed the laudanum only at night now. Storm had made him crutches and Pearl had padded their arm rest tops. Soon Joe would be hobbling everywhere, no longer imprisoned in his room by his broken limb.

Thinking him asleep, she leaned over and kissed his cheek. His eyelashes fluttered open and he smiled a drowsy grin. A soft sigh escaped him, then he dropped back into slumber. With a sigh of her own, she left the room, letting the door stand ajar in case he called out during the night.

She tapped softly on Nate's door, then stepped into his room. He sat up in bed playing solitaire.

"I thought you'd be asleep by now." She couldn't resist stopping by anyway for a chance to see him when no one else might observe her.

He met her gaze. "Same goes for you. I've spent so much time resting the past five days I can't sleep at night. As many times as you've run up and down the stairs, though, I'd think you'd be run ragged."

"I've sat down a lot, too. If I were teaching, I'd be standing all day."

"Maybe, but you wouldn't be teaching fourteen to sixteen hours a day." He stacked his cards and put them on the bedside table. "Tomorrow I'm going downstairs and walk outside."

Her heart gave a tug. When Joe started walking with his

crutches and Nate healed enough to be up and around, she would have no excuse to stay at Grandpa's. She'd be back at the ranch and might never see Nate alone again.

In spite of her reluctance, she pasted on a smile and said, "Glad you feel well enough. Lex and Belle are coming tomorrow. I expect everyone will be here for dinner tomorrow night. Maybe you'll feel well enough to join us." She sank onto the chair by his bed and clasped her hands in her lap.

"Something wrong?"

She hated to burden him, but could contain her worry no longer. "Oh, Nate, I think I made a terrible mistake insisting Fiona work for Grandpa."

He looked incredulous. "Where could she find a better place than here?"

"Nowhere, of course. But," she sought the words to explain her surprise and dismay, "they . . . argue. All the time. If Fiona says black, Grandpa says white."

"Maybe because you're tired and worried about Joe, you overreacted."

"I don't think so. No one in our family acts like that. I haven't known Fiona long, but you know how friendly and easy to get along with she was on the trip here. It's not like Grandpa to act that way, either."

Nate took her hand and tingles shot up her arm. "Hmm. Guess they need time to adjust to one another's ways."

"What if they never do? Oh, my stars, I should never have meddled. I meant to help, but I've created a difficult situation for two nice people." No easy solution presented itself to solve this dilemma. She'd worried about it for days.

"Nonsense. Grandpa needed a housekeeper. Never find a better one than Fiona. Place practically glows in the dark."

"Yes, and she said she likes it here." She sighed. Maybe she had overreacted. "Oh, perhaps I'm worrying for nothing. I certainly hope so." She stood and leaned over him to plump the pillows. "Let me fix these. They're all lumpy and lopsided."

He leaned forward, then moved lower to lie back. His head rested on the fluffy pillow and he watched her as if he expected more from her. Her breath caught in her throat. The pounding of her heart sounded loud as the drum of a brass band.

"Did you tuck the children into bed and kiss them goodnight?" he asked, his arm snaking around her waist.

"Yes, before I came in here. They're all three sleeping soundly. Luke and Cindy even remembered to put away the toys." She recalled Joe's crooked grin when she kissed him and it brought a smile to her face.

Nate looked up at her and moved his hand in slow circles at her waist. "Do I get a good night kiss, too?"

Awareness hummed through her body. Her mouth went dry as she remembered their last kiss. Almost without realizing it, she flicked her tongue across her lips.

His arm secured her as she leaned back to meet his stare. Those wolf's eyes blazed with passion. Mesmerized, captured by his gaze, she fought her growing desire. Try as she might, she could think of nothing but his touch and the way it made her feel, and her longing for it once again.

"Will, um, will you go right off to sleep as they did?"

"I don't think so." His strong hands settled at her waist and tugged her gently toward him.

She allowed him to guide her until she sat at his side. His tawny mane needed a trim and an errant lock fell across his forehead, taunting her to brush it into place. Her fingers tingled in anticipation, needing to touch his thick silken hair.

"I've thought about this all day," he said and pulled her into his embrace.

Being wrapped in his arms felt like coming home. Unbidden, a sigh escaped her. "Lord help me, so have I."

She stretched out beside him. Her hand rested at his waist below the bandages protecting his ribs, and her breast brushed against his chest. Leaning on one elbow, she pushed up to lean over him. Her unbound hair spilled across his chest. He pulled her to him and his mouth possessed hers. She melted into the molten kiss.

At first fiery and demanding, he softened the onslaught. He nibbled at her lower lip, then his tongue teased the edges of her mouth. Heat coiled at her core and she sought more of his taste, craved more of his touch. She slid her hand to cup his strong jaw, pressing him to her. Her tongue met his and mated in a sinuous dance. Tasting, delving, exploring.

A moan of pleasure escaped her when his hand found her breast. She arched with pleasure, her head tipped back. As she broke the kiss, her soft moan escaped. His lips trailed the tender line of her throat. How she had longed for his touch.

She wanted to caress his skin, wanted his hands on her bared body. As if they shared the same thoughts, he sought her dress. Her hands slipped under his shirt, skating along the planes of his hard abdomen to stroke broad chest muscles.

When he eased away, she followed him seeking his lips again, craving more of him.

He gripped her arms and gasped, "What are we doing? Anyone might come in and see you here like this."

His gaze traveled along her and she knew what he must see. Tousled hair, kiss-swollen lips, the front of her dress undone.

"Then let's lower the light." She roused herself enough to extinguish the lamp. With no moonlight shining, inky night surrounded them. "Everyone's asleep but us."

"Sarah," he whispered in the darkened room. "I won't deny I need you here with me, in my bed. But think about the risks."

"Right now I can think only of you." She lowered her head to his chest. How right this seemed. She belonged with this man.

"I want you, sweetheart, but, besides the fact that we shouldn't, I haven't the strength to do much."

"Let me then. Tell me how." There must be a way, she must experience his wizardry once more.

His hand seared a path along her bared shoulder. "Then heaven help you, for I need you too much to resist this chance."

She lowered her head to meet him. Gentle as a butterfly's kiss, his lips trailed her brow, her cheek, and nipped at the corners of her mouth. She wanted more of this enchantment. While he teased and enticed her with his mouth, he slipped her dress from her and tugged at the ties of her chemise.

Her trembling fingers found the buttons of his shirt and she opened each one, then pushed the shirt aside. He stopped long enough to remove the garment and his drawers, all he had worn in his sick bed. At the same time, she removed her petticoat. The muted rustle of soft cotton in the quiet night was barely audible over their deep breaths.

His hoarse whisper stopped her. "No, let me."

Her hands stilled. He tugged the chemise up, and his mouth closed briefly over her freed breast. A wave of desire started there and coursed through her body. He paused to slide her drawers down, the fabric tickling her sensitized flesh. One by one he rolled her stockings off, his lips trailing kisses on the bared skin. Delicious sensations shot through her making her shiver with anticipation. Soon she was bare as a babe, reveling in his touch.

She felt his hands glide slowly over her as if he memorized the feel of her. Her bones melted from the heat of his loving attention. She lay languorously under his spell. Belonged only to him. No other man would ever know her this way.

He slid a hand to the juncture of her thighs and she parted her legs to allow him access. His finger slid into her femininity as his thumb nudged against her bud. Lightning jolted through her. The ecstasy of his gentle thrusts sent her writhing against him, the sweet ache building and creating a hunger for more, more.

When the waves of joy pinnacled and lessened, she pressed her lips to his shoulder and touched the tip of her tongue to his heat. She trailed her mouth over his nipples and sought to bring him pleasure as he had her. His quick intake of breath signaled her success.

She touched his manhood, the soft outer skin a contrast to the rigid shaft within. He moaned. Her fingers slid over the velvet length, and felt a dewy drop bead at the tip. She ran one hand down, cupping him, enjoying her exploration, and felt his body tense. Power surged through her.

"Come to me," he whispered. "Climb on top of me."

Belatedly, she remembered his injuries. "Your wounds? How can we, um, do more?"

He pulled her onto him and she stretched against his length. Her legs rested atop his and she felt the bandage on his thigh and ribs against her bare skin. The hot, hard proof of his desire pressed against her belly, promising fulfillment to the burning need deep within her. But how could he share in the motions of lovemaking and not aggravate his injuries?

"The wounds," she repeated.

"They'll be all right. Pull your knees up beside me."

She followed his instructions. The tip of his rigid arousal pressed against her moist feminine folds and she took him into her. The hard length of him stroked the fiery ache burning deep inside her core. She heard his sigh of pleasure before he spoke.

"You're in control now."

Though he couldn't see her in the darkened room, she shook her head. "No, I have no control. My need for you rules me."

He pulled her shoulders down to let him suckle her breast. Fire surged through her. Longing to cry out in a haze of joy, she willed herself to be silent. She braced her hands against the pillow on each side of his head to keep her weight from his injured shoulder and ribcage.

His hands gripped her hips while his lips worked beguiling magic on her rigid nipple. She wanted to take more of him inside her, needed to fill herself with him. He thrust upward and they moved in concert, slowly at first then increasing in speed. Each time she took him deeper.

All sense of time and place abandoned her. Only the two of them existed in the world. She soared among the stars. Rockets burst and showered around her. Every fiber of her thrummed with electrifying pleasure. When she thought she would explode from the sheer ecstasy of the moment, a stunning rapture erupted within her. The warm sensation of his seed shooting into her accompanied her peak.

Sated, she spilled herself across him using her forearms against the bed to protect him from her weight. He held her close, his hands skimming along her skin. She breathed in his scent, hoping to inhale a part of him to savor. At last, she roused enough to slide to his side and nestle against him.

"Did we reopen your wounds?" Her fingers traced the bandage at his shoulder, seeking the moistness that would indicate fresh blood.

"I've never been better in my life." He kissed her hair, her brow, her eyelids.

"I wish we could stay like this forever."

"So do I, sweetheart. I want to hold you through the night and wake with you beside me in the bright light of day."

Though she had promised herself not to, she said, "If you stayed in Kincaid Springs—"

His hand cupped her jaw and his thumb slid to silence her lips. "Sarah, I never said I would stay. There are things I can't control. Believe me, if I can work things out, I will."

Hope blossomed in her heart. "You mean, you might stay?"

He heaved a mighty sigh. "Oh, hell. There are so many complications, things I can't tell you about. Things that would anger you and make you hate me if you knew."

"Nothing would make me hate you. I don't have to know everything about you, just what you want to tell me, just that you want to be with me. All I need is you with me for as long as you'll stay." Wanting forever, needing it desperately, she feared voicing it would drive him from her.

She heard the catch of his breath but he said nothing. Perhaps there was nothing to be said. Perhaps this was all he could provide. At the same time, she sensed their deepening bond these past few days. Since he had rescued Joe, there had been a difference in him.

Lying in the dark, she pictured Nate's mischievous smile, the twinkle in his amber eyes. In her mind she saw the way he talked to the children, the way they sought his attention. She had caught him watching her time and again as if he committed to memory each move she made. Luke and Cindy visited him several times each day, and he chatted with them as if he were a part of their family. Several times he had even donned the robe Grandpa lent him and limped across the hall to sit with Joe and talk or play checkers.

Suddenly, the realization of tonight's folly hit her. She recalled the hiding place of the pessary at the ranch.

She hadn't used the pessary tonight.

Tonight she might have caught a baby, and it was at her instigation. His willingness did nothing to lessen her responsibility. Driven by her love for him, she'd taken yet another step away from propriety.

As appalling as exposing a child to the shame of an unwed mother might be, she yearned for Nate's child. Moreover, she wanted half a dozen of his children, and she wanted him with her to raise them. They should share whatever life brought, grow old side by side.

How could the ladies claim merely to endure their husbands' attention? They must not feel the connection, the love, she held for Nate. She could no more deny his touch or her need for it than she could deny her need for air to breathe. If that branded her a harlot, then so be it. Her love was strong enough to carry that slur.

But she wanted Nate to stay in Kincaid Springs with her. He didn't know it yet, but he belonged here. There must be a way to convince him to stay. She had shared her body, her children, her family with him. What else could she offer?

SEVENTEEN

Laughing and chatting adults and squeals from children formed a din that rivaled any carnival. Nate navigated slowly down the stairs. He'd had the devil of a time making himself presentable. Already tired from dressing and sprucing up, he relied heavily on the cane Drake had brought him and kept one hand firmly on the banister. He thought he knew how Samson had felt after Delilah had shorn his long locks.

As amazing as Nate's brief time with Sarah had been last night, it had drained him of the little strength he'd regained since the cave incident. Not that he made any complaint. Though he had tried to resist the temptation of her body for her sake, he was glad she persisted. Her passionate response humbled him, made him grateful to be a man. Her man. Recalling her beguiling lovemaking caused his body to respond in ways he'd best forgo for the present. He sought a distraction, and concentrated on the steps and the people.

Ahead, Storm carried Joe, who held crutches for use after they were down the stairs. Luke and Cindy cavorted with their new cousins, weaving through the throng of adults. He spotted two children he didn't know, a boy of about five or six with chestnut hair and a younger girl with hair as red as fall sumac. When the children spotted Joe, they raced toward him clamoring for his attention.

Sarah stepped forward and made shooing motions with her hands. "Not too close. Give Joe room to move the crutches."

Nate followed the crowd into the large parlor. Pearl and

Rosilee Tremont spoke to a woman with her back turned toward him. Gabe and Drake stopped in midconversation with a stranger: A few inches shorter than the other two men, he had a shock of dark rusty hair and a face in which smiles had left their tracks. He stepped forward and extended his hand.

"I'm Lex Tremont and you must be Nate."

Nate shook his hand. "Guilty as charged. Nice to put a face with your name after hearing so much about you."

"Same here. The whole town's afire with talk of your rescue of Joe."

"Gabe did as much as I did. In fact, he had to rescue me as well as Joe. I'd be a goner if it weren't for him.'"

"You almost were anyway," Gabe said. "After you left for town in the wagon, the sheriff noticed the rope pulling against the rock frayed almost in two."

Nate felt himself pale, but forced a smile. "Guess I owe Storm a new rope."

Lex put a hand on Nate's shoulder. "You've met my parents, but let me introduce you to my wife." He kept his steps slow enough for Nate to keep abreast. "Belle, darling, this is Nate Barton, Sarah's friend who rescued Joe."

Nate watched her turn and the ready smile on her face freeze. He felt as if a mule had kicked him. Damn, it was the doxie he and Cal had helped to Pearl's place back in Tennessee that time. If he'd met her on the street, he would never have known her. Only because of the association with Pearl and Sarah did he recognize the sophisticated beauty before him now as the shy young saloon girl of seven years ago.

From the panic he saw in her eyes, he knew she remembered him, probably remembered his real name. Did her husband know her previous occupation? True, she'd hardly been with Roxie more than a few weeks before that customer beat her near to death. That must have ended her career as a soiled dove. He held his breath, wondering if she'd denounce him.

As if she fought for air, she nodded and said, "A pleasure to meet you, Mr. Bart . . . Barton."

He took her hand and bowed over it. "The pleasure is mine, Ma'am."

Fiona called them in to dinner and they flowed toward the dining room. Fiona had set the ten children at the table in the kitchen.

When the adults had gathered around the table, the Judge said to Fiona, "You've miscounted. There are only eleven places here. We're one short."

"Can't I count as well as anyone? This is a family gathering. I'll be eating in the kitchen to keep an eye on the wee ones."

"You'll eat in here. Polly and Emily can watch the children."

She speared him with a glare and crossed her arms. "They have their hands full cooking and serving. It's help they'll be needing, and it's help I'll be giving."

The Judge stepped toward her and crossed his arms. They looked like two playground bullies, each daring the other to cross the battle line. "Then you should have asked the day girl to come."

The others in the room stilled and shifted uncomfortably. Sarah chewed her lip as her gaze darted from her adopted grandfather to Fiona. Clearly she felt the cause of any disagreement between the two. Nate hated the worried frown marring her beautiful face.

"Ahem," he cleared his throat. "Why don't we put Joe in charge. He's the oldest and very reliable."

Sarah's glorious smile rewarded him for his effort.

Pearl also flashed a smile. "What a good idea. I'll step in and tell him and remind the other children to be good."

"I'll help Fiona set another place." Rosilee opened the sideboard drawer to get silver flatware then found a crisp damask napkin that matched those at the elegantly laid table. Belle took a dinner plate and crystal from the large side cabinet. They hurriedly arranged a twelfth place at the table.

Pearl returned from the kitchen. "The children are settled in, had their blessing, and are eating. Emily is ready to serve us now," she said and let Drake help seat her.

The others followed her lead, Nate choosing a seat as far from Belle as possible. Sarah slipped in beside him. When everyone but Fiona had settled at the table, the only place left was that at the foot of the long table opposite the Judge, the place usually reserved for the hostess. With a last glare at the Judge, Fiona sat down and snapped her napkin across her lap.

The Judge said, "This is a special evening, no mistake about that. We're celebrating several things. Belle and Lex and their family are back in our midst, and for that we are thankful. Nate and Gabe saved Joe from his rascal of a step-father. Though it's too bad the man died, we're thankful Joe was spared, and that Nate survived the rescue and his injuries are healing." He followed that with one of his sermon-length blessings.

From around the table three or four conversations sprang up simultaneously. Nate heard talk of horses, cattle, Austin, law, and someone's new dress. He lost track of any one thread, and concentrated on looking occupied with his food. Inside, his stomach battled a knot of worry.

Belle darted anxious glances his way. He figured he cast a few her direction, too. She sat at the Judge's left and Nate sat at Fiona's left. He couldn't understand the conversation at the other end of the table, but he saw that Belle seldom spoke.

Neither did Nate. Mostly he smiled and pretended to listen to the conversation around him while his mind searched for a solution. Should he confront Belle, pretend he didn't know her, try to strike a bargain with her? So far, he hadn't a clue. He let his chin drop on his chest and cursed to himself. As if Hargrove wasn't a big enough problem, now Belle appeared.

"You're not eating. Is something wrong?" Sarah asked so low only he could hear.

"Not much of an appetite today." Turmoil churned his stomach and he thought he might have to excuse himself and go lie down. Any minute he expected Belle to point a finger his way and denounce him. He forced down the bile in his throat and toyed with food on his plate.

Across the table, Storm said, "Man, you look pale as a sheet. You all right?"

He pasted on a smile and lied, "Not used to being up so much since the cave business. Guess I'm tired, but I'm fine."

The aroma of warm apples and cinnamon drifted from a tray of hot pie slices as Polly brought in dessert. She set a saucer of the warm sweet and a little pitcher of cool cream in front of him. Worried as he felt, his nose sent a perk up message to his stomach. He ate a few bites of the best pie he'd ever tasted, but his roiling stomach threatened to reject it if he ate more.

From Nate's right, Fiona announced, "Pearl baked the apple pies for us. Her own special recipe."

Dinner finally ended and they all trooped into the parlor. At the Judge's request, Belle played the piano and sang. Nate hadn't known about her musical talents. Her clear, sweet voice should have soothed his nerves. At least she couldn't tell anyone about him while she sang. When she had finished and all the goodbyes were said for the day, he exhaled his relief.

Giving fatigue as his excuse, he sought the sanctuary of his room upstairs. With minimum preparation, he crept into his bed and collapsed. He couldn't live like this much longer. The ups and downs of fear, deception, passion, regret, and wariness wrought their havoc on his mind and nerves.

One more day he had avoided exposure as a fake. But how long would Belle keep her silence?

Sarah floated down the stairs on Saturday morning. Luke and Cindy raced ahead of her.

Fiona greeted them, "Now wasn't it a lovely evening we had?"

Sarah nodded as she helped Cindy fill a plate from the sideboard array of oatmeal, eggs, biscuits, gravy, and thick slabs of fried ham. "Yes, it's good to have Belle and Lex back with Sammie and Rosie." She settled Cindy at the table, then turned to help Luke. "I enjoy our family being together." *All* her family, with Nate included at her side. She peered around Luke and glanced into the hall. "I checked on Joe and Nate before I came down. Nate wasn't in his room."

"No, he rose early and went to the law office," Fiona answered. "Said he needed to get some work done for Mr. Gabe."

Sarah's spirits rose another notch. Working for Gabe. Maybe today Nate would arrange to stay on in Kincaid Springs.

Nate had been asleep when she peeked in on him last night, so she hadn't spoken to him alone. Visions of them together sprang to her mind as she ladled oatmeal into her bowl and sat down.

Grandpa gave her shoulder a pat as he passed her chair. "Joe coming down?"

"No, last night's exertion was too much for him. He had a rough night. I should never have let him come downstairs. I felt guilty this morning, but last night I hated to keep him cooped up while everyone else was down here."

"We need to send for that costive old quack Percival?" Grandpa asked.

She shot him a reproving glance for his reference to Dr. Percival. "No, but I had to give Joe laudanum during the night and he's groggy and in pain today. I think he'd better wait another week or so before he spends much time on the crutches."

Grandpa placed his heaping plate on the table and took his seat. Quick as a flash, Fiona snatched his plate and removed the ham and gravy and substituted a bowl of oatmeal and a dollop of baked apple slices to round out the scrambled eggs and biscuits.

Sarah suppressed a giggle at the indignation on his face.

He turned up his nose at the oatmeal. "I don't eat baby pap."

"You know very well it's oatmeal. 'Tis my belief oatmeal is the main breakfast food for hearty men all over Scotland." Fiona paused. "Kincaid is a Scottish name, isn't it?"

"You've heard me say as much, and this Scot happens to

own this house. A man should be able to eat what he darn well pleases in his own home."

Fiona stood her ground, hands folded respectfully in front of her. "Pearl gave strict orders about exactly what you're to eat. She said 'tis how she helped you with your rheumatism."

He glared but gave a resigned shrug. When Fiona turned her back, he stuck out his tongue at her and the children giggled.

Grandpa asked Sarah, "Are you going back to teaching Monday?"

"Yes, Carlotta loves taking over for me, but I've played hooky long enough. Fiona said she'd care for Joe while I'm at school. That is, if you don't mind."

"Now, girl, we've been over this. You know I'd be much happier if you lived with me all the time. House is too big for one old man, even with several—" he looked at Fiona and raised his voice, "*insubordinate* staff members to keep him company. Needs young folks here brightening up the place." Fiona merely smiled.

For several years, Grandpa had tried to get Sarah to move in to town and live with him. His house was only ten minutes in the buggy from her school, so it wouldn't make her trip long.

"Thank you, Grandpa."

Fiona looked thoughtful. "You know, 'tis too bad Joe doesn't have one of those fancy chairs with wheels I saw once. An old lady sat in the one I saw and someone pushed her about. Wouldn't it be fine for the lad?"

"You mean a wheelchair?" Grandpa asked. "Now, wait a minute." He bent his head and steepled his fingers over his stomach. "Seems to me George Bingham had one of those when he broke his leg some years back. I'll take the rig out and see if he still has it."

"Judge Grandpa, sir?" Luke asked.

Grandpa smiled at him. "Call me Grandpa, son. Plain Grandpa."

"Grandpa, I reckon Cindy and me could build us a fort in that little barn. There's hardly anything in it."

"We'd be neat and not bother your stuff 'less you said we could," Cindy added.

"Now that's a real good idea. Soon as I get back from Bingham's place, I'll help round up some things for you to use." He turned to Sarah. "Why don't you let these two ride with me? They haven't seen that part of the county."

The children looked so excited, she hadn't the heart to say no. "All right, if you're sure you don't mind."

"Now don't be losing the children," Fiona cautioned.

Grandpa glared at her. "Hmph. Raised me three of my own plus one of the grandchildren. I'm not likely to start leaving a youngun here or there after all this time."

He and the children left, but Fiona didn't move from her spot. She sat staring at her hands and Sarah thought she saw her wipe fingers across her cheek. Suddenly, Fiona said, "Excuse me a moment." With that, she rushed from the room.

Certain Fiona had been crying, Sarah hurried after her. She followed her upstairs to Fiona's suite. Sarah rapped on the closed door, then opened it. Sure enough, Fiona sat in a chair by the fireplace, sobbing into her handkerchief.

"Whatever is wrong?" Sarah asked. She pulled another chair near and sat down, then took Fiona's hand.

"Himself's a good man, and there I was chastising him."

This didn't make sense. "Fiona, there has to be more to it than that. You've been at each other's throats all week. I swear you argue like two old married . . ." Sarah stared at Fiona, whose blush broadcast the accuracy of Sarah's statement.

"That's it, isn't it?" she asked. My stars, Fiona and Grandpa acted like some married people she'd seen. "You and Grandpa are sweet on one another, aren't you?"

Fiona stopped sniffing long enough to say, "As if the likes of me could marry a man like Himself, or"—she gestured around her—"live in a house like this."

"You already live here. The only change would be marrying Grandpa." Sarah smiled. Grandpa and Fiona in love. Who would have guessed? "Has he asked you?"

"That he did and I told him he'd gone soft in the head in his old age."

Sarah leaned back in her chair. "My, I'm sure that soothed his aching heart."

"Now don't you go making fun of me." Fiona bristled. "I know me place in life. It's lucky I am to have this fine position, but I'll not be making Himself a laughing stock by wedding him."

"Oh, Fiona. Do you know how long it's been since Grandpa's wife died? Do you have any idea the number of women who've tried to capture him over the years?"

"Well, of course they would. He's a fine figure of a man and full of interesting things to say. But me mind's made up."

"You're a fine figure of a woman and full of interesting things to say. For him to even ask you after all these years is a miracle. Please, if you care for him at all, say yes to him."

"I can't, dearie, but I thank you for not being offended by Himself's offer to me."

Sarah clasped both Fiona's hands between hers. "On the way here on the train, I thought people would think you were the children's grandmother. It was a lovely thought, and now it can be true if you let it."

"Thank you for that, too." Fiona withdrew her hands and gave a final dab to her eyes. "Well, I can't be pining away here when there's work to be done. You check on Joe and I'll be about me business running this household."

Fiona hurried back downstairs. Sarah walked slowly toward Joe's room lost in thought. What could she do to help Fiona see how perfect she and Grandpa were for one another? Pearl might have an idea. She'd ask tomorrow after church.

Nate had intended to put in a full day at the law office, but his body defeated him. Fatigue weighed him down and he had to call it a day shortly after eleven. He closed the last file as the door opened and Lex stepped in.

Nate's heart leapt to his throat and pounded. He felt sweat bead between his shoulders. Hell, he'd known something like this was coming since he spotted Belle last night. At least Lex hadn't brought the sheriff with him. Nate braced himself for guns, fists, threats or all three.

"Gabe around?" Lex asked.

"No, he caught the train to Austin this morning to visit his folks."

"Oh, yeah. He mentioned it last night. Guess I forgot."

Sure you did, thought Nate and took a deep breath. Might as well get it over with. "Anything I can do for you?"

"Maybe." Lex's somber expression must be a departure from the nature that put the smile lines on his face. In fact, his large brown eyes looked almost fearful, and his freckles stood out against skin gone pale as paper. "My wife thought she might have met you somewhere. You know her?"

And you mean in the Biblical sense, Nate thought. He recalled the shy, backward girl he'd known in Tennessee. That girl and the one he'd met last night held no resemblance, were in fact different people. "No, I can't say I ever met Mrs. Tremont before last night." She had a different last name back in Tennessee, but Nate couldn't remember it.

Lex chewed his lip and turned his hat in his hands. "You're sure?"

"If ever I had met a woman of your wife's beauty and sophistication, I'm certain I could never forget her."

Lex heaved a huge sigh and looked embarrassed. "Told her I'd ask you for her. She must have been mistaken."

If only it could be this easy. Nate couldn't believe he'd get off with a simple denial. "Perhaps she met someone who resembled me." He pasted on a grin. "Please tell her how happy I am to make her acquaintance now. Her singing and playing last night was concert hall quality. Has she given recitals?"

"No, no, nothing professional." Lex relaxed visibly and his love and pride for his wife shone from his eyes. "She used to play the piano for the Presbyterian Church here before we went to Austin. Now she just plays for friends and relatives, and at home for me."

His smile returned and Nate marveled at the transformation. No wonder Lex had success as a politician. With his wide smile illuminating his face, friendly-as-a-puppy-dog look, deep resonant voice, and Kincaid money behind him, he couldn't lose.

"Well, glad you're helping out here." Lex looked around as if reminding himself of the place where he once had worked. "Spent close to thirteen years here. Gabe said he and Grandpa had asked you to stay when your business friends move on. They offer you a partnership?"

"They mentioned me staying on, but no details were mentioned. Never got that far. I have a lot to work out before that could happen." An understatement.

"Like to hear how it all turns out. 'Course I guess I will. You can't keep a secret in this town." The worry returned to Lex's face.

"I'll let Gabe and the Judge tell you. Guess I'm kind of private. Never was one to give out details myself." That ought to reassure him if he still harbored doubts.

"Well, I'd better get home and let you get out of here. My wife and kids are waiting for me to take them on a picnic. I put a lot of store by my family." With that veiled warning, he turned and left.

Nate moved to the window and watched Lex walk away, then turned back to get his coat and hat. In spite of his denials, he hadn't convinced Lex that he offered no rivalry for Belle. Or, maybe Lex simply wanted to protect his wife from any gossip. Perhaps, hearing about the railroad scheme, he worried for the town. How could Nate assure him he posed no threat if he stayed?

Hell, he met one setback after the other. He'd better get to Monk and see how things were coming along. No sooner had the thought popped into his head than Monk stepped through the door, carrying a box.

"Saw Tremont leaving." He set the box on a table and opened it. "Got this at the hotel. Thought we could eat here in private and talk." He set out two thick sandwiches.

"Man, I'm ready for this." Nate pulled his chair up to the table, ready to dig in. "Where's Hargrove?"

"Having him a nap. Bastard had a girl in his room most of last night. Guess he didn't get much sleep."

"How much money has he raised?"

Monk met his gaze. "You ready for this? Almost fifty thousand."

"Damn. Bet he's about ready to pull out, isn't he?"

"Tuesday morning. It don't look good, Nate. He knows you want out and knows I always side with you. He's suspicious and he's trying to shut me out. Wouldn't be surprised if he tried to slip out on us."

"I suppose Dorfmeyer is still nosing around, too."

"Like a dog after a bitch in heat."

"I swear to you, if we get out of this, I'm never pulling anything again."

Monk nodded agreement. "You got a plan?"

"I've had several. None worth a damn."

"What're you gonna do then?"

"Pray a lot." Nate shook his head, wondering how this would all end and afraid he knew. "I'm still working on it. Give me time."

Monk stood and sighed. "Time's running out."

Nate joined Sarah on one of the pews usually reserved for Kincaids or Tremonts. They were three rows from the lectern. The children wiggled in front of them with their cousins, except for baby Parker who sat with Drake and Pearl. This morning Sammie and Rosie Tremont crowded onto the pew also to make a line of nine squirming bodies.

"Good to see you, Mr. Barton," someone from across the aisle said. "Sure glad you rescued the boy."

Nate nodded and smiled. On the way into the church he'd been stopped a dozen times and offered congratulations and good wishes. He'd never seen the like. Everyone who hailed him as a hero made him feel worse and better all at the same time.

Sarah touched the heads of Luke and Robbie and the boys pivoted in their seats to look at her. "No giggling and wiggling or you'll have to sit with the adults."

"Yes, Ma'am," they said in unison before they turned back. Both boys' shoulders shook with muffled giggles.

Sarah looked at Nate and rolled those beautiful lavender-blue eyes. An angel in a dark blue dress made of some kind of rustling silky fabric, her hair hung in ringlets on one side beneath her hat. Sunlight from the window over the altar caught her curls and turned them to molten gold on her shoulder. He ached to touch her, hold her in his embrace. Seeking to derail the track of his lustful thoughts, he concentrated on the other people in the sanctuary.

"Guess I know most of the folks here," he whispered to her, shocked, as he spoke the truth. Never hung around to know folks who went to church, but now he knew most of this bunch.

"Yes, and they all know how you and Gabe rescued Joe, and about your injuries." She turned to smile at someone behind them and turned back around. "Your friend Mr. Hargrove just came in. Shall we ask him to sit with us?"

Anger shot through Nate. "No, and he's not a friend, just a business acquaintance."

"Your friend Mr. Masterson isn't with him."

"Mon—Michael's catholic." Nate refused to look at Hargrove. The nerve of that weasel. His only purpose could be using church contacts to squeeze a few more dollars out of the townspeople. Which is what you planned the first time you came here, he reminded himself.

He refused to believe he was ever as bad as Hargrove. For one thing, he'd never in his life hit a woman. For another, if he had children he'd never deny them money for food and clothes.

Face it. You're as bad as he is in other ways. You're either a cheat or you're not, and you've cheated for years.

After church they filed out, and Nate received more good wishes. People went out of the way to shake his hand. They admired him, looked up to him. It felt good, damn good.

Never before had he realized the importance of fitting in, being a part of a community. If only it could last. Unless he could outsmart Hargrove, these folks would soon be cursing him.

As if on cue, Hargrove stopped him. "Well, good to see you walking so well, Barton." He nodded at Sarah. "Lovely service, wasn't it, Miss Kincaid?"

"Yes. Excuse me, Mr. Hargrove, I need to speak to Mrs. Potter." Sarah smiled at Nate, then hurried to the reverend's wife.

Nate and Hargrove walked to the outskirts of the crowd and stood beneath a large cottonwood. "You've become quite the family man." Hargrove smiled maliciously. "Sweet little skirt."

Nate longed to put a fist down the man's throat. "What do you want?"

"Can't I seek spiritual guidance the same as you?"

"That'll be the day. Why did you come?"

"I just wanted to remind you of our bargain. You've been avoiding me, Nate, my boy." He looked around smiling and nodding at those passing by. "I meant what I said. You try to cross me and I'll have the law on you so fast you won't have a chance to slip through the noose this time."

Hargrove paused and smiled while a couple passed by. "How would that piece of tail feel about sharing her wares with a murderer? And would she like being implicated as well? If it comes to that, how would you like her to share your blame?"

Nate gripped the man's arm in what would appear a friendly way. Hargrove's florid face paled. "Now listen, and listen good. Do not ever say anything disrespectful of Miss

Kincaid again. Not to me, not to anyone else. Got that?" He released Hargrove's arm.

Hargrove straightened his jacket sleeve. "So that's how it is, eh? Spun her a web and you're trapped in it?"

"Enough of that. She and her family have been nice to me. I never meant them any harm."

"Ha, that's easy to say now. You're the one who came up with this, or have you forgotten?"

"No, I can't forget. I wish like hell I'd never heard of you or this rotten railroad deal."

Nate's gaze sought Sarah. She talked with Mrs. Potter and Pearl, but she caught his gaze and smiled. When he looked back at Hargrove, the man's eyes narrowed in speculation.

"Well, well. Lucky Bartholomew, in love. Who would have thought it? This is indeed interesting. Just see you remember my warning or I'll take her and her family down with you."

"You remember what I said." Nate threatened, though inside he quaked with terror. He had to find a way to protect the Kincaids, especially his beautiful Sarah.

Hargrove walked away, shaking hands and chatting as he moved through the crowd lingering outside the church.

Sarah appeared back at his side, Luke and Cindy in tow. "You look angry. Is everything all right?"

He smiled down at her. "It is now. Shall we go home?"

"I wish it really was our home," Cindy said. "I like it there at Grandpa's."

"Me, too," Luke said, then peered up at Sarah. "I'm sorry, Mama. I like the ranch, too."

"Don't worry, Luke," Sarah told him. "It's all right to like both."

"They're both nice in their own way," Nate said. "I have to agree with Cindy, though. Even though it's a wonderful ranch, I prefer the Judge's house."

"I stayed at the ranch with Pearl and Drake so I could help her with her healing. Now, she has a woman training with her and doesn't need me, so I started the school."

"So, you wouldn't mind living in town?" he asked. If he could pull it off, maybe they could find a small home near the law office or on the edge of town nearest her classes.

"At one time I had a home site picked out not far from the school, but I think I'd prefer town. It's a short drive in a buggy to teach, as Luke, Cindy, and I will find out tomorrow."

"Back to work or school for all of us tomorrow." Nate wanted to savor this day in case it was his last with the people he'd forever think of as his family. "Let's get Joe up in that wheelchair and make the most of our day together."

EIGHTEEN

"Come on, children," Sarah said to Luke and Cindy. "Scoot this way so we save room for Rosie and Sammie."

"Mama, how come Rosie gets to come to school?" Luke asked. "She's too little."

"She's not, is she, Mama?" Cindy asked. "She's my new friend. And my new cousin."

Sarah's heart expanded a little each time the children called her Mama. "Rosie is young but she always behaves and works hard."

They stopped in front of the Tremont home where Sammie and Rosie waited at the gate. Sammie held his sister's hand in his and Belle watched from the porch. She waved as her children climbed into the buggy.

Sarah floated through the day. Students welcomed Sarah back, curious about Joe's adventure. She used their interest to teach them about caves and the dangers lurking within them. And bats. Children loved hearing about bats.

All during the day, Sarah's gaze kept wandering to the little anteroom. Through the doorway, she spied the cot she and Nate had used for their brief tryst. Each time her gaze fell on the narrow bed, she recalled how Nate's hands felt on her body, his sweet and gentle touch. She longed for that caress again, for the rapture he brought.

Warm tingles swept through her and pooled at her core. My stars, how could she concentrate on teaching with that reminder of his lovemaking taunting her all day? She walked to the back of the room and closed the door, shutting out the sight.

With so much to be accomplished, the day passed quickly. She dismissed the children and gathered her things for the trip to town. Before she could leave the building, Belle rushed in. Her perfectly groomed attire warred with her frantic expression.

Belle smoothed a strand of escaped hair back under her bonnet. "Sammie, you and Luke take Rosie and Cindy to play on the swings. You watch them now, so they don't get hurt."

Luke grabbed Cindy's hand and called, "Come on, Sammie. We'll race you."

The four children tore out the door.

"I'd thought we agreed I would bring the children by your house. Is something wrong?" Sarah asked. "It's not Grandpa is it? Nothing's happened to him, has it?"

Belle shook her head and looked as if she'd been crying. "No, no. nothing like that." She wrung her hands and paced in front of Sarah's desk. "You'd best sit down, because I have to tell you something you won't like hearing."

Puzzled, Sarah pulled the room's only other chair near for Belle and returned to her own behind her desk. Belle sat down, then jumped back to her feet and started pacing.

"I've worried myself sick about this since Friday night. Lex thinks he took care of it, but he didn't. I don't want him to know about this. That's why I came here, so we could talk privately."

Wondering what could be so serious, Sarah waited impatiently. She wanted to get home and visit with Joe before dinner. All at once, a horrible foreboding dropped over her like a veil. She didn't know how this concerned Nate, but she sensed it did. Just when he'd said he would try to stay, something bad must have happened to prevent it.

Belle paced in a short arc in front of Sarah. "I tried to tell Lex this would happen some day. He said it didn't matter. Well, it does. It matters to me, and it will to you, too."

Sarah absorbed the other woman's anxiety. "Belle, please get to the problem. You're tying me in knots."

"I'm sorry," she said as she whirled and paused before the desk. "I wanted to keep the secret, but you need to know." She sat in the chair, hunched as if she had suddenly aged fifty years. "You know when I worked for your mother in Pipers Hollow and those men helped Roxie bring me to Pearl?"

Sarah nodded. "How could I forget those horrible times? You were hurt so bad we thought you'd die."

"One of those men was Cal, the man Roxie married after she left Tennessee." Belle took a deep breath. "The other was his son, Nate. Your Nate. Not Barton, Nate Bartholomew."

Sarah's world crashed and shattered around her. Her breath left her body and a terrible knot balled in her stomach. She strove for calm, but it escaped her. "Are you certain? Maybe he only looks like the other Nate, maybe the first name's a coincidence."

Belle shook her head. "No, they were there several days before Quin beat me. I spent a lot of time talking to Nate." Her eyes pleaded for understanding. "He . . . we, um—"

Sarah put her elbows on the desk and rested her face in her hands. She wanted to shut out the hateful words. "I don't want to hear about it," she cried.

"I have to tell you the rest," Belle persisted. "It's not so bad. I'd only been there five or six weeks when Cal and Nate came. You know I had nowhere to go when Roxie took me in. She said I shouldn't start taking men as customers, that she would let me stay until I found someplace to go."

She stopped talking a few seconds, overcome with sobs. "She was such a nice person, Sarah. You should be very grateful to have such a good mother. She wouldn't have let your father turn you out the way mine did. Anyway, one night this man offered me a lot of money because I was new."

"Quin?" Sarah said her half brother's name like a curse. Hearing it brought back the terror of him trying to kill her and Pearl and Storm. The horror of watching Quin die from

Drake's gunshot. Oh, dear Lord, her aching heart could bear no more of this.

Belle nodded at the name. "The only man I'd ever been with was George, and just one time, when he told me he had no intention of marrying me I left him. I thought if Quin gave me as much cash as he had promised, I'd have enough to last until I could find a job as a maid or governess or something."

"So you went with Quin?" Sarah shuddered at the thought of Belle exposed to Quin's twisted evil.

"Yes. And he was rough. He . . . He hurt me. I was scared. He told me if I told or tried to leave town he'd kill both me and Roxie. I believed him. After that, I took any customer who offered for me. It was awful and I hated it."

"What has this to do with Nate?" Sarah asked while tears streamed unhindered down her face. Her broken heart sought escape. If only she could go home and lock the world away until she could talk to Nate. If only he were here to pull her into his embrace and explain all this away.

"He knew what I felt inside, sensed it. He showed me how it could be between a man and a woman. Not pretending he loved me or anything, just showing me how it should be for me." Belle broke into heaving sobs and had to pause again.

Sarah's world crashed further with every sentence from Belle. As if it weren't bad enough to know he lied, she had to find he'd had sex with her friend. She almost hated Belle for having shared Nate's body, for knowing him first.

A part of her knew it a ridiculous reaction, for she hadn't even known Belle or Nate then. He was an attractive man in his midtwenties. He must have had lots of lovers over the years. The woman part of her wanted Nate to be only hers, refused to share him with anyone.

She wiped her own tears and pleaded, "Please, Belle, you don't know what this is doing to me. If you have to tell me this, for the love of God, finish."

Belle regained control and said, "You don't know how much Nate's kindness meant. I swear to you, I was close to killing myself until he was so kind to me. You see how much I owe him, how I could never forget him or be mistaken about it being the same man. Oh, he's grown a bit taller and broader through the chest and shoulders, but there is no mistaking, he's the Nate who saved my life."

She dabbed at her face and eyes with a lace handkerchief. "I'd decided there could be no tenderness or happiness left in my life until he showed me differently. It probably meant nothing to him, but it meant the world to me. Then Pearl saved me again twice over when she healed me and gave me a chance to come to Texas and marry my precious Lex."

Sara leaned her arms on the desk and buried her face in their shelter. "Why did he lie to me? Why?" She hadn't asked him to stay, hadn't asked for promises of any kind. Why couldn't he have told her the truth?

Belle shook her head. "I don't know. I've worried for three days about it. I can't talk to Lex about it for fear he'll know how well I knew Nate. It must have something to do with this railroad thing."

"I don't see how it could." Adding to her distress, another realization sprang into Sarah's whirling mind. She looked up. "Belle, that means he should have had half the money from the sale of Mama's saloon. He should have Cal's share."

"Why didn't he claim it?" Belle asked.

"Mama thought he was dead. There'd been a wire from some sheriff that he'd been killed in a gunfight."

Oh, the bandages she'd seen through the keyhole. They'd been from gunshots. But why did the sheriff think Nate died? And why hadn't he asked for his share of the inheritance?

Feeling as if lead weighed down her limbs, Sarah rose from her chair. "None of this makes sense. I'm going to confront him as soon as he gets home. He has a lot of explaining to do."

Nate and Gabe looked up when Marcus Novak, the owner of the Mercantile which housed the post office, entered.

The man clutched an envelope in his hand as if he guarded a treasure.

"You delivering the mail now, Marcus?" Gabe asked.

"Mr. Barton got another one of them letters from Pinkerton's. I figured it was important." He handed the letter over to Nate.

"Thanks," Nate said as he examined the envelope. Should he open it now or wait until the merchant left?

"Say, you working for them Pinkerton's or something?" Marcus asked, his nose twitching with curiosity.

Nate had no idea how to answer. He smiled and shrugged. "Guess you could say it's something like that. Had a little business with them recently."

"Did you bring the rest of the mail, Marcus?" Gabe asked.

The man looked astounded. "Well, no, Gabe. 'Course not. You always come to the store to get it. I just thought this might be something real important Mr. Barton needed to see right away."

Gabe shook his head at the man's reasoning.

"And I appreciate it," Nate said. "Real thoughtful of you to take time to bring it to me."

Marcus nodded, looked torn between desire to learn the contents of the letter and the need to get back across the street to his store. Duty won and he said, "Reckon I'll get back 'fore my wife sends for me."

Nate thanked him again then slit the envelope open. He unfolded the single sheet of paper with an odd sense of dread.

It was from the same Pinkerton agent Nate had hired in Tennessee, the one who had warned them of the break-in and tampering with Sarah's file.

Dear Mr. Barton,

A curious thing happened today and I can only offer the information as a possible warning. Two men came into the office this morning to engage my services in a search for a Henry Hargrove, reported to be traveling

*with Monk Magonagle and Nate Bartholomew. Their
description of Mr. Bartholomew fits you exactly and the
names are quite similar. In the event they had the name
wrong and are searching for you, I feel obligated to
alert you. They said they live in Chicago and assured
me they had no wish to harm anyone, merely searched
for Mr. Hargrove on family business. I declined their
request to represent them. After so many years in this
business, I can read people. I didn't like what I saw in
these two.*

Nate refolded the letter and slipped it into his pocket.
Trouble was marshalling around him. He wondered how soon
Hargrove's brothers-in-law—and he had no doubt of the two
men's identity—would trace him here. Hell, who else was
likely to turn up to add to his misery?

Decision time had arrived. He had to make a choice to run
or stay and face the consequences. Get away with enough
money to open his own place in New Orleans or face possible imprisonment, maybe hanging? Sarah's face appeared in
his mind. He saw her eyes filled with love, her golden hair
spread on his pillow and her lips seeking his. In an instant,
that vision faded and he felt again the terror of the coffin in
Arkansas, the desperation he experienced at the hands of a
mob.

"Trouble?" Gabe's voice snapped Nate back to the present.

"Isn't it always?" He exhaled and reached a decision.
"Gabe, sorry, but I have to leave right now to take care of this.
Will you meet me at the Judge's in an hour? I'll explain then."

Gabe's perplexed expression didn't slow his response.
"Sure. Something I can do for you now?"

"No, this is something I have to work out myself."

Nate hurried toward the hotel. On the way he sought out
the Ainsworth brothers and stopped long enough to send them
on an errand. He had to catch Hargrove and warn him, talk
him into leaving the money.

Nate rushed into the hotel lobby and almost bumped into Dorfmeyer. This day just got better and better. When he tried to excuse himself and hurry by, Dorfmeyer grabbed his arm.

"I'm watching you. I don't think for a minute Hargrove works for the railroad. I've written to headquarters and also the authorities in several cities. Chicago, Memphis, St. Louis, Little Rock, New Orleans, and Fort Worth. Any day now I'll receive answers. I'll be surprised if at least one of those places doesn't have all three of you on a wanted poster. We'll see what a hero you are when the people of this town find out you're a fake."

Not bothering to lie or deny the accusation, Nate said, "You'll never have Sarah. Why don't you give up?"

"I was doing fine until you showed up." Dorfmeyer's voice rose an octave and his face flushed red. "If you hadn't filled her head with nonsense and pretended to approve of her adopting those brats she would have been mine by now."

"You mean her money, don't you?" Nate pulled free of his grasp. "You're wrong. Sarah would never have given up her children and would never have married a weasel like you." He pushed by the banker and hurried inside.

A glance into the dining room and bar assured him neither Monk nor Hargrove was there. Nate climbed the stairs and rapped on the door to their suite. Monk opened the door and stepped back to allow Nate to enter. He looked as worried as Nate felt.

"He's packing up." Monk kept his voice low and nodded toward Hargrove's room. "Been drinking all afternoon. Says he's leaving tonight."

"There's no train until morning."

"Bought him a horse at the livery stable. Has it waiting all saddled. Told the man there he has to ride West to make arrangements with the next town on the rail line."

Nate told Monk about the letter. "Don't know how they tracked him to Memphis, though."

"We rode the riverboat from St. Louis to Memphis just like

you did, even stayed at the same hotel as before. Hargrove's wife had connections to the law, from a big family I think. They'll use their connections to track him."

"I figure those two could get here as quick as the letter. If they're not already in town, they're on the way."

Monk nodded. "Banker fellow latched on to Hargrove talking about Chicago." He looked at Hargrove's room again. "Couldn't stop him bragging about what a big man he'd been there."

"His bragging may get him killed. If news of Dorfmeyer's inquiry reached Hargrove's kin, they have his exact location."

"Not for long," Monk pointed out.

"Might as well get this over with. Will you get your stuff ready to follow him in case I can't convince him?"

Nate walked to Hargrove's room. Sure enough, the man had piled clothing on his bed to make room for the money in his carpetbag. He looked up as Nate entered, but kept shoving money into his valise.

Nate leaned against the doorframe. "Had an interesting letter today."

Hargrove raised his head in a flash, then turned his attention back to the money. "Yeah, what about?"

"Seems two men are looking for you. Tracked you as far as Memphis. Figure they're on their way here."

That arrested Hargrove's hands and he paled. "What two men? How'd you find out?"

Nate inched closer to Hargrove hoping to distract him and catch him off guard. "They tried to hire a Pinkerton agent know. Wanted to find you for some 'family business' the said."

"How long ago?" he asked, his eyes darting to the door window, and back to Nate. Fear in Hargrove's eyes proved th matter in Chicago wasn't as settled as he'd indicated to Nate

"The date's not important. The letter reached me, so the could be here, too."

Desperation tinged his voice. "I'm leaving tonight."

"So I see." He walked toward his quarry, intending to seize him before he could take the money from town.

From nowhere a gun appeared in Hargrove's hand. "Don't think you can stop me just because you went soft over some skirt. Wife's brothers want to roast me alive. This is more money than I've ever had and I need it to make a clean start."

"There's nothing clean about you. So, you plan on cutting Monk and me out?"

"Maybe not. Here's the deal. I'll wait at the Windsor Hotel in Fort Worth 'til Saturday. If you aren't there to divide up the money by then, I keep it all and head West. You turn me in and I spill all I know about you and make sure that little lady and her family get blamed right along with you."

"You're making a mistake—"

Hargrove interrupted, "I don't have time for lectures. Turn around."

Nate hesitated but when Hargrove waved the gun, he turned. A whack thudded against his skull, the room spun and turned black as he fell.

Nate came to with Monk bending over him. He tried to rise but his head almost exploded.

"How long was I out?"

"Just a few minutes. Hargrove's gone, though. Told me you wanted to talk to me as he left. I came in and found you on the floor unconscious." Monk helped Nate stand.

"Said he'd wait at the Windsor Hotel in Fort Worth, but I don't trust him. Can you follow him?"

Monk nodded. "You coming or staying?"

"I have to explain to Sarah and her family. If they don't hang me or shoot me, I'll come after Hargrove."

Monk looked torn by indecision. "Maybe I should wait here for you, hang around outside town. Don't want to take a chance on a crowd like that one in Arkansas with no one to help out."

"No. If Hargrove's kin find him, they could wind up with all the money. You stick to him like glue. If they show up, you take the money and get out of the way. I have a feeling they aim to finish him off this time."

"You're right, but I sure hate to leave you here alone," Monk still hesitated.

"Go on. I'll be fine," Nate said as his friend prepared to leave. He hoped he'd be all right. What if he landed in jail before he could attempt to retrieve the money?

When his friend clutched his hastily packed bag in his hand, Nate said. "Monk? If I don't show up, you take the money and head for New Orleans like we planned. Set up in style."

Monk shook his head slowly and gave a sad smile. "I'm through running, Nate. With or without you, I'm coming back to tell Sarah I'm sorry."

When Monk had left, Nate moistened his handkerchief from the water pitcher on the wash stand. Pressing the wet cloth to the lump on the back of his skull, he headed for the Judge's house. He'd rather face the cave again than what he had to go through in the next few hours. With any luck, he'd survive. Whatever the outcome, he had to face his demons now.

Fiona met Nate at the door. "Himself and Gabe are in the study. Sarah's upstairs in her room in a frightful state. Said for you to come up first thing when you got here."

She must have talked to Belle. Well, at least that would save some explaining. "Drake and Storm are on their way. Would you ask them to wait in the study with the others until I get back down, please?"

Nate hurried up the steps. He tapped on the door, then walked into the room. He didn't know whether to expect tears or anger. He found both, but the icy fury frightened him. He had lost her, lost everything he valued.

"Why?" she asked. Though her voice held only restrained anger, her beautiful eyes were red and puffy from crying.

"Sarah, I don't know where to start. Please let me explain to you." He started toward her, but she stepped away.

"Don't you dare come closer. You stand right where you are and give me answers."

"It started long ago, but let me get to the part where Cal died. I didn't know, because I was on my way to St. Louis when it happened. Then, I got shot and accused of something I didn't do in a little town in Arkansas. By the time I got to St. Louis, both Cal and Roxie had died."

"I knew that was you at the cemetery during Mama's funeral. You skirted around it, but it was you."

"Yes, the day I got to town. The bullet wounds were infected and I could hardly stand, but I wanted to come to the funeral, pay my respects to Roxie and Cal both."

She shook her head as if trying to understand. "Why didn't you stand with the others? Why didn't you tell me who you were?"

"I couldn't." Lord, he hated to get to this part. He took a deep breath and looked into her eyes. "The sheriff would have arrested me if he'd known I hadn't died in Arkansas."

When he saw the disgust in her eyes, he pleaded, "Please, you can't make me feel more shame than I already have in me. But I've changed since we met. I'm a different person now, a man who wants to settle down in a respectable life and have a family, this family. You and Joe and Luke and Cindy." Oh, dear God, how had it come to this? Why couldn't he have learned this lesson some other way?

"Phffft." She crossed her arms and glared. "You used me, used my family. You let me give myself to you, risk my reputation, when all the time you were planning to steal from my family, from the whole town. When I think how I helped you cheat everyone, told them you could be trusted . . ." Her voice broke and a single tear escaped to trickle down her cheek.

He wanted to rush to her and fold her in his embrace, but he knew she would reject his consolation.

"Sarah, please come downstairs with me so I can explain all this to your family at the same time I tell you."

"No. I've heard all I want to." She thrust a jewelry case at him. "I'm keeping the ruby ring because Mama put it on my finger. You take this necklace and earrings. They're gaudy and flashy, just like you. You can give them to your next conquest."

"Sarah, there won't be anyone else. You're the only woman I'll ever want. The ring was my mother's, too. She wanted me to give it to the woman I love, but Cal gave it to Roxie. It made me angry and we fought over it, but now I see how right it was. I want you to have it."

"Then I don't want it." She tugged at the ring but apparently she couldn't slide it from her finger. "When I can get it off, I'll make sure you get it, wherever you are. I'll make arrangements to have half the money from the sale of the saloon sent to you—if you aren't in jail and if anyone knows your whereabouts."

"Please, Sarah. Give me one more chance. Come downstairs and stand with me while I talk to your family."

"My family?"

"I asked Drake and Storm to come here so I can explain what I've done and ask them to let me fix it, or at least allow me to try. They're down in the study with Gabe and the Judge. I can't keep them waiting much longer."

"Then get out and go make your excuses." She took a step toward him and poked his chest with her forefinger. "How can you fix this, you slimy coyote? Can you make me a virgin again? Can you replace the children's trust in you when they hear everyone in town curse your name? And you slept with Belle!"

"Sarah," he pleaded. "Give me another chance, Sarah—"

"Get out," she screamed. "Out, do you hear?" She shoved him into the hall and slammed her door.

Sagging in despair, he slipped the jewel case into his pocket and moved toward the stairs. When he passed Joe's doorway, Joe called to him. He sat in the wheelchair, which he inched forward with his hands on the wheels.

"Nate, Mama's been crying. Is everything gonna be all right?" Worry added age to his ten years.

Nate knelt and hugged Joe to him. "Son, I think this time I've messed up too much for it to ever be all right again."

"You're gonna try to fix things, though, aren't you? You're real smart and all. If you try real hard, you can."

"Yeah, I'll try real hard," he echoed. "Whatever happens, though, you remember I love you and your mother and Luke and Cindy." He hoped he could see Luke and Cindy before he left, if he was allowed to leave.

"Nate, please come back and be my pa. I know Mama would stop crying then."

"I'll try, son. I promise you I'll do my best."

He hurried downstairs wondering how it could possibly work out. Sarah hated him now. Even if he got the money back and made things right with the townspeople, he'd be lucky if Sarah ever let him see the kids again.

The Judge sat at his desk. Gabe and Drake sat in front of the fireplace, even though the weather was too warm for a fire. Storm stood at the window. All four men were taller than he, and all save the Judge in prime physical condition. Nate wondered if they would pulverize him before he had a chance to finish his explanations. They looked at him expectantly.

Nate's mouth felt lined with cotton and perspiration beaded his forehead. No use beating about the bush, get on with it.

"Before you take any action, I hope you'll listen to all I have to say." Nate took the wanted poster from his jacket and unfolded it with trembling hands. He tossed it on the desk for the Judge to see.

The Judge picked it up, looked from the poster to Nate and back again. "This you?"

"Yes. I'm a fake, a swindler. I came here planning to cheat you all and the other townspeople of as much money as I could get. Then I got to know you, liked you, wanted to stay here and settle down, quit the business of cheating folks."

"So why didn't you?" Drake asked.

"I tried. Hargrove wouldn't call it off, made some serious threats. He's run out with the money, but I know where he's headed. Monk—the man you know as Michael Masterson—is following him to make sure he doesn't lose the funds he took from the town."

"And what makes you think this Monk won't take the money and disappear?" Gabe asked.

"He didn't want to start the fraud in the first place, wants to settle down here himself." He looked at each man, then continued. "My father was Cal Bartholomew, the man who married Sarah's mom. In fact, Cal and I were in Pipers Hollow when Drake and Lex took Pearl and her family away. Monk and I grew up together. He thought a lot of Roxie, is real fond of Sarah."

Storm advanced on him. "What about Sarah?"

"I . . . I don't know. She's not very happy with me right now. If I can get the money back, I hope she'll forgive me."

"I think you took advantage of my sister." Storm grabbed the front of Nate's shirt and pulled him up. "You better make me believe you didn't take liberties with her."

Nate didn't know what to say. He wasn't about to tell anyone he and Sarah had been intimate, but he wouldn't lie anymore. His pause must have been all the confession Storm needed. Storm dropped him and sent a steel fist into Nate's jaw.

"Now, Storm, let's hear all he has to say before we take any action," the Judge said. He came around to help Nate up.

"How'd you get the lump on your noggin?"

Nate stood and tested his jaw. Not broken. He touched his tongue to his teeth. Miraculously, all were in place. Storm stood ready to pound on him again so Nate stepped back to straighten his clothes.

He touched his fingers tentatively to a lump the size of an egg. "Hargrove didn't want me to delay his departure."

Gabe said, "In Nate's defense, I noticed a reluctance on his part to talk about this railroad thing. He kept telling everyone Hargrove was only a business associate, not a friend. Told me he was trying to work things out so he could stay here."

Nate flashed him a look of gratitude. "I tried to call it off from the first. Hargrove threatened to turn me over to the sheriff, to implicate Sarah and all of you if I didn't go along with the original plan."

He shrugged. "I've done some stupid, petty stuff. This is the first big scheme I pulled. The thing I'd had the most trouble with happened when I wasn't in the wrong. Fact is, when I was in Arkansas, I was in a card game. One of the players who lost heavily accused Monk of cheating."

Nate paced back and forth in front of the Judge's desk, trying to ignore Storm's angry stare. "You don't know him, but Monk's nickname came because he lives like a monk. Except when I've led him astray, which has been way too often in the last few years, he never cheats, never chases women, goes to mass as regular as he can. He didn't cheat in that card game."

He ran a hand across his face, wishing he could wipe away the memory. "The sore loser pulled out a gun intending to shoot Monk, who as usual was unarmed. I pulled my gun and told the man to put the gun down. Instead he shot me twice. I fired back once."

He pointed to his biceps. "I aimed for his arm so he'd drop the gun, but I missed." Nate shook his head. He still couldn't believe it happened the way it did. "Maybe he turned to make his next shot. My bullet went right into his heart. The onlookers were all locals and the guy who died was wealthy. They were going to hang me, but Monk talked them into letting me see a doctor."

"Hmph," the Judge said. "A doctor before they hanged you?"

"Yes. Monk's a talker when he has to be. He convinced the sheriff—who was one of the men in the card game—I had to be well enough to stand trial. The sheriff took me to the doctor's office with the angry mob on our heels talking lynching."

"So, how'd you get out of that one?" Gabe asked.

"Monk talked the doctor into telling the mob I died. Then he bought a casket and brought it into the doc's office. I climbed in and Monk nailed it shut. The plan was to get me on the next train out of there, taking my body home for burial."

He shook his head again. "Didn't work like that. The sheriff insisted on a burial right away, then called Monk into his office for questioning. By the time Monk got loose and came back for me, I'd dug my way out of the grave. Like to have smothered."

The horror of it clutched at his middle and a shiver skittered through him. His voice shook and he felt clammy. "Monk told Hargrove about it when they met in Chicago. Hargrove threatened to wire the sheriff and tell him how I escaped."

"So, why have you herded us together?" the Judge asked.

"I plan to go after Hargrove and bring back the money. He's gone to Fort Worth, but he has some angry kinfolks on his trail. In case I don't live through it, though, I wanted you to know the truth."

"And what makes you think we'll let you leave this room alive?" Storm asked.

NINETEEN

Drake pushed to his feet and crossed the room. After placing a hand on Storm's arm, he said, "Storm, let me take over."

Storm threw Nate a glare before he stepped aside.

"What about Belle? If you were at Roxie's when Lex and I were in Tennessee, you must have known Belle."

Avoiding the subject of how well he knew Belle, Nate answered, "It was Cal and me who helped Roxie get her to Pearl's place. Neither Pearl nor Sarah," he looked at Storm, "nor you recognized me. Guess all of us focused on Belle. Thought she was dying."

Storm nodded. "She almost did."

"What I want to know," Drake persisted, "is whether you're going to tell people Belle worked at Roxie's. Lex wants a career in politics, and details like that could hurt his chances as well as his personal life."

The Judge stepped forward as if he wanted to be certain he heard this answer word for word.

"I told you I want to help this family, not hurt you further. Belle recognized me. She sent Lex to ask me if I remembered her. I lied and said no because I saw it worried him. No reason anyone needs to know anything about Belle being at Roxie's. Has nothing to do with who she is now."

"Well said," the Judge muttered and patted Nate on the arm.

Storm looked incredulous. "Grandpa? You siding with

him? How do we know he's not telling us what we want to hear same as he told Lex?"

"He could be in Timbuktu by now if he hadn't meant what he just said. Nothing to keep him from hightailin' it out of here with the other fellow. I figure he's seen the light, just like he says."

"That's right," Gabe added. "You all know I hate lies of any kind, but he's come to us when he could have left town. I say we give him a chance to make it right."

Nate waited for the other two verdicts. Panic clutched at his gut and made him physically ill. What if they kept him here? He knew Drake carried a lot of weight with the others. Right now Drake looked pensive, Storm angry. Nate held his breath.

"He leaves, I'm going along to keep an eye on him," Storm said. "Make sure he comes back, with or without the money."

"Might not be a bad idea." Drake looked at Grandpa. "Think Ben would deputize Storm and me? Won't give us any authority outside this county, but it might go a long way in persuading Hargrove."

The Judge brightened. "Let's get Ben over here and find out. Yep, you two along might help convince this Hargrove fellow to part with his ill-gotten gains." He tugged the bell pull. When Emily stepped to the door, he said, "Ask Chester to fetch the sheriff pronto."

Fear gripped Nate in a mighty hold. Perspiration gathered between his shoulder blades and across his forehead. What were the chances of the sheriff letting him walk out of here? Damn, no matter what the Kincaids said, Nate would be in jail within the hour.

"Badges will give you some credibility with the law whenever you catch up with this man." The Judge returned to his desk chair and sat down. "Now let's work out the details."

"You say he's headed for Fort Worth?" Drake asked.

"Windsor Hotel. Monk'll wire if Hargrove makes a wrong turn. In case I've already left," Nate looked at Storm and rubbed his aching jaw, "or in case I'm in no condition to travel, he's wiring the Judge any change in plans."

"You saying even if we throw you in jail, your friend is still bringing the money back?" the Judge asked.

Nate nodded. "Yes, sir, that's his plan. Like I said, Hargrove has a gun and Monk doesn't. He has to rely on outwitting and out talking the man."

The Judge stroked his chin. "Hmph. Thought he was a real quiet man when he was in town. But sounds like he can be a talker when he has to."

They heard the arrival of a newcomer, listened to his heavy tread and the jingle of his spurs as he strode down the hall. Desperation seized Nate. He should have left a note to explain and hurried after Monk and Hargrove on his own. No way in hell would a sheriff let him go after learning all he'd done.

Sarah's head ached from worry and she knew her heart would never heal completely from Nate's betrayal. Sensing something terrible had happened but not understanding the tension, her three children appeared wary and anxious, so she displayed a calm and smiling countenance for them. Inside, she felt just the opposite. Her dream world had shattered into a thousand pieces with knowledge of Nate's duplicity.

She made it through the school day without breaking down, and kept herself composed until she and Luke and Cindy made it to Grandpa's. Fiona greeted them at the door and took Sarah's carryall with her teaching supplies and set it aside.

"Did they make it away all right?" Sarah asked as she hung her shawl on the hall tree. Unable—or unwilling—to face Nate this morning, she remained in her room until time to leave for school.

"Yes, dearie, just as planned." Fiona gave Sarah's shoulders a hug. "Go have a bit of a rest. I'll bring an after-school snack for the children to Joe's room."

"Hurray," cheered Luke as he bounded up the stairs with Cindy at his heels.

Sarah smiled her thanks and followed the energetic children. Leaving Luke and Cindy regaling Joe with all that happened at school that day, she went to her room. Once the door closed behind her, her careful façade collapsed and tears flowed freely. She sank into her chair and dabbed at her eyes.

She had thought it would all work out. Nate hadn't promised he would stay, but she wanted it so badly she had believed it possible. Lost in thought, she sought to recall each word or look, every tender touch they'd shared.

How gentle he'd been. Tingles surged through her body at the memory. A fire built in her belly when she remembered the lovemaking they had shared. Other memories doused the flame. Nate lied to her, planned to cheat her family and the town.

A tap at the door preceded Fiona's entry. She carried a small tray holding a cup of tea and some cookies. After placing the tray on the table by Sarah, she took the chair across from her. Sarah hastily dried her eyes.

"Thank you," she said.

"Now, dearie, I know you're upset with Nate. I've been in bits about the whole thing meself. He's a bold boy but he'll be fine and return to you soon."

"He can return or not, it doesn't matter to me. All I want is for Drake and Storm to get the money and bring it back so no one is cheated." She pressed her hands around the cup to steady their trembling.

"It's yourself will be cheated if you think that. Nate loves you, I'm sure of it. That boy-o loves the children as well, and they love him."

Sarah almost choked on the tea and replaced the cup in the saucer. "He's a cheat and a fraud."

She looked at the ring on her finger. She hadn't minded losing the flashy sapphires and diamonds. If they were even real, they weren't anything she would ever wear. The ruby ring was different. Though now much of the pleasure of it had gone, she hadn't taken it from her hand after all. Mama had placed it there the day before she died and asked Sarah to wear it in memory of her. How could Sarah part with it after that?

Fiona's gaze showed her sympathy. "If you don't mind me saying so, if that was true once, Nate must have changed. Maybe he was a cheat at one time in his life, but he faced your family and told them everything. That took a lot of courage."

Sarah sat mute. The pain inside her barred reply.

"And will you look how hard he worked with Gabe? I hear he worked just as hard at the ranch with Storm and Drake. He could have been sitting up at the hotel living the easy life instead."

Sarah sniffed and said, "It was part of his trickery. He wanted to appear dependable so we'd trust him more."

Fiona ignored that comment. "Didn't he save Joe when a lesser man would have waited in town for the posse? You know yourself Joe might be dead if Nate and Gabe hadn't gone after him or if Nate had waited before he got the lad off the ledge."

Sarah nodded and took a deep breath. The memory of how close they'd come to losing Joe still haunted her. "Even mean people do nice things once in a while. It doesn't take away the bad things they've done."

"And good people do bad things once in a while, dearie. It doesn't make them bad people, though, now does it?"

"He's ruined my reputation." Sarah hated the memories stirring in her. "I encouraged people to invest in the railroad because I trusted him."

Suddenly she remembered how upset he'd been when she told him what she'd done. Now she realized he hadn't wanted her involved, but she had wanted him to owe a part of his success to her. She'd hoped he'd decide to stay because of it, that he might even love her. She pressed her hands to her cheeks.

"Oh, Fiona, I've been such a fool. How long before people know there's something amiss? How will I ever face them? They'll all hate me and hold me responsible. I'll never be able to hold my head up in this town again. I might even lose my students. No one will want me teaching their children."

"When he brings back the money, people will forget soon enough. It may be bad for a bit, but give it time."

"What if he doesn't? What will happen if he disappears or can't get the money?" Sarah's shattered heart ached.

"Seems to me he would already have run if that were his plan, but he won't be disappearing with Drake and Storm along." Fiona looked somber and shook her head. "Sure and if they don't recover the money, now that would be bad for your boy-o and for the folks in town. Listen, dearie, in here," she placed a hand over her heart, "I feel it'll all work out somehow. You'll see. Give it time."

Fiona patted Sarah's hand and quietly left the room. How could anything work out now? She forced down some chamomile tea, hoping it would calm her. Leaving the cookies untouched, she rose and washed and dried her face.

She had done things she never dreamed she'd do with any man, let alone without benefit of a marriage ceremony. Somehow the impropriety seemed less important now. All that mattered was keeping Nate near. She still had her children, but would she ever have Nate to make their family complete?

Sheriff Ben Liles tried to keep a positive outlook on recent events, but the scheme Rob Kincaid and his kin talked him into worried him as he walked along Main Street. He hoped he hadn't been a durned fool. It didn't make sens from a sheriff's standpoint to let Nate leave town to go after the money. Sometimes, though, you just had to go with your gut instincts.

He knew he wasn't the best or brightest lawman in the state, but he was honest. At least, he upheld the spirit of the law. By damn, he gave the county a day's work for a day's pay.

Ben met Gabe coming out of the law office. They'd both watched the train pull out this morning with Drake, Storm, and Nate on it, then gone off to their respective offices.

"Going for your mail?" Ben paused while Gabe locked the door of the law office.

"Yeah. I quit trying to get it early in the day," Gabe said and fell in step as they crossed the street to the Mercantile.

"Yep, that Marcus is a stickler for his routine. Don't matter the mail bag is dropped off each morning. No amount of pleading or cajoling can make him put it in the boxes until after his lunch is finished."

"That's the truth," Gabe said. "Surprised the heck out of me when he brought a letter to Nate yesterday. Didn't bring me my mail, though."

Ben laughed. "Sounds like Marcus. I like that Nate myself, even with all I know about him. Figure Sarah would be better off with him than with that banker."

"I have to agree with you, there. Something about Dorfmeyer irritates me, especially after he treated Billingsley so rough." Gabe pulled open Novak's Mercantile door and the little bell attached to it rang.

"How's business, Marcus?" the sheriff asked as he waited his turn at the section of letterboxes lining one end of the counter. Gabe opened his and extracted several letters, then stepped aside for Ben.

"Brisk for a Tuesday," Marcus replied. "Can I tempt you gents into trying these new cigars? Just came in on this morning's train."

Gabe shook his head, but Ben stepped up to the counter.

"Reckon not, but I'd like another pouch of tobacco and some rollin' papers." Ben slipped them into his pocket and laid down coins to pay for his purchase.

"You see the two fellows what got off the train this morning?" Marcus asked. "Said they was looking for that Mr. Hargrove on some family business. Got right back on the same car when they heard he'd gone."

Gabe stepped forward. "You say they got back on the same train they came in on? That means they're riding with Drake, Storm, and Nate."

"Sure thing," Marcus said and nodded his head. "I was picking up my supplies and the mail and I seen it all. Never heard of anybody doing that. Stayed in town less than thirty minutes. Ain't that something?"

Gabe faced him and Ben saw the indecision in his eyes. What did Gabe expect him to do? This was a sorry business, this thing with Nate and the other two. He'd be happy to see it all settled down.

The bell on the door sounded as Peter Dorfmeyer hurried in, thrusting a sheet of paper at the sheriff. "I knew something about Barton and his friends was phony. Here's the proof, Sheriff. What do you intend to do about it?"

The smirk on the banker's face was enough to make a man want to take a swing at it. Damn, he hated that pompous Dorfmeyer's hide more than ever right now. It'd be like the know-it-all to blab this all over town and get him in hot water, along with the Kincaids. Imagine the nerve of that weasel, courting a sweet girl like Sarah Kincaid.

Ben tried to appear a lot calmer than he felt. "Now Dorfmeyer, unruffle your feathers. What proof are you talking about?" He heard the bell ding again and knew someone else had entered, but didn't turn.

Dorfmeyer had an even more superior expression on his face than usual. "I wrote off to several places asking if those three were wanted. Well, that Hargrove is. Probably the others are, too. I just got this wire from Chicago asking tha

Hargrove be turned over to the authorities. Looks like that's your job."

Ben jerked the paper from the banker's soft white hands. He hated a man with hands that soft. Even pushing a pen wore a few calluses. Looked like countin' money would, too.

"Let me see." He scanned the wire. Sure enough, Hargrove was wanted in Chicago and elsewhere for a number of crimes. "Hank the Hustler, eh? Well, Dorfmeyer, you can rest easy. Matter's being taken care of."

"How? What are you doing to bring this Hargrove and his cohorts to justice?" Dorfmeyer demanded and stood glaring.

Ben folded the offending paper and slipped it into the pocket beneath his badge before anyone else saw it. Gabe watched silently. Ben tried to think what he should say, what he should do to head this off. A dozen thoughts flashed through his mind. None fit the bill.

Crime happened seldom in this county. Mostly he got drunks on Saturday night, occasionally a fight, and a ton of petty stuff needing his attention. Robbers had hit the bank twice, and both times he'd recovered the money quickly and sent the robbers to jail. Three times in the fifteen years he'd been sheriff here he'd failed at his job, though, and it weighed heavily on his conscience.

The first time was seven years ago when Drake brought his new family here. A madman had threatened Pearl and her kin. The culprit killed one man and injured another before Drake shot the cowardly son-of-a-gun. His second big failure occurred recently when he fell short at protecting that boy Joe from his no-account stepfather. Nate and Gabe had to save the child. Both times he'd been only minutes behind the rescue, but those minutes would have cost lives if someone else hadn't taken over.

Now he had this thing with Nate Barton or Bartholomew, his friend, and this Hargrove. Ben admitted he'd slipped up there because of Nate's association with the Kincaids, plus the fact he'd taken a liking to the man. Matter of fact, he still liked him, but not enough to let him ruin the town. He hoped the Kincaids knew what they were doing this time.

Ben realized Gabe still stared at him, he guessed waiting for his lead in an answer. What should he say? Dorfmeyer's temper seemed ready to explode and Ben had better come up with some excuse soon.

From behind the counter, Marcus spoke up, "Good thing Nate's working for Pinkerton's, aint' it?" He beamed with pleasure at knowing something he obviously thought a secret.

Dorfmeyer paled, "What do you mean, Novak?"

Marcus looked at Ben as if for approval. "Why, I guess it's all right to tell the secret now since they've gone after Hargrove, ain't it sheriff?"

Dumbfounded, Ben could only stare, nod, and wonder what the hell the storekeeper meant.

Marcus looked proud enough to bust his buttons. "Being the postmaster, I know a lot about folks. Barton got letters from Pinkerton's 'cause he's working for them. Took him his last one myself yesterday."

Dorfmeyer whirled on Ben. "That right?"

Skirting a direct answer, Ben said, "Don't know about him getting letters, but I took a wire to him from Pinkerton's." Lord, he'd have to go to church twice on Sunday for that stretch of truth.

Gabe's eyes widened but he remained silent. Ben saw Otto Holsapple peek around the dry goods aisle, and he had his foreman with him. The bell dinged again, and Ben saw Rob come in and stand quietly near the door.

Dorfmeyer turned to Gabe. "You know about this?"

After a second's hesitation, Gabe pulled at his ear lobe and said, "I was there when Ben brought the wire, and I saw Nate open a couple of letters from Pinkerton's while he was helping out at the law office."

Looking from Gabe to Ben, Dorfmeyer demanded "Where's Hargrove and Barton and the other man now?"

Ben pulled at his collar. Durned if he knew what to say, bu

figured he might as well work a little truth into this conversation. "Hargrove knocked Barton out last night and slipped away. Barton, Masterson, and two of my deputies have gone after him."

"That where Drake and Storm were headed with Barton this morning?" Holsapple asked.

"Yes," Ben admitted. "Deputized them both and they went after Hargrove with Barton. His friend was already on Hargrove's trail."

"What about our money?" Holsapple's foreman asked.

"Yeah, what about the money all the townspeople put up?" Holsapple wanted to know. "If Hargrove's a crook, then that means there's not a railroad coming through. How're we going to get our money back?"

Rob Kincaid stepped forward and held up a hand to silence the men. "They know where Hargrove's headed. They'll be back with all your money. All we have to do is wait here."

Dorfmeyer turned on his heel and stomped out of the store. Marcus worked his cigar spiel on Holsapple and the other man while Gabe talked with Rob.

Ben felt a mighty sigh heave out of his chest. He sure hoped Rob spoke the truth. There'd be hell to pay otherwise.

Nate rubbed his neck muscles in fatigue and stared out the window. They'd had to change trains in Austin, and had traveled at what seemed a snail's pace yesterday and all last night. At last this phase of the hellish trip neared an end. Storm hadn't said three words to him since they boarded the train. Never the talkative sort, Drake had not said much, either.

Nate recalled the trip from Tennessee with Sarah and the children. They'd traveled in luxury instead of the day coach in which he now rode. He closed his eyes and conjured Sarah's beautiful face in his mind, her perfect ivory skin, the smile of her beautiful rosebud mouth. He could look at her forever, longed to hold her in his arms at least that long.

His eyes opened. She hadn't smiled the last time he'd seen her. Tears she tried to hide pooled in her lovely lavender-blue eyes when she ordered him from her room. Though he'd told the children goodbye, Sarah refused to see him the day he left Kincaid Springs. He stared out the window and wondered how this would all work out. Would he ever hold her again?

He saw buildings indicating that a station was near. At last, the conductor called "Fort Worth," and the train slowed to a stop. They left the car and the depot and walked two blocks to the Windsor Hotel. Storm pulled up and stared at the shabby place.

"He's here?" Storm asked. "Expected him to choose a fancy place, with all that money."

Nate said, "Knows the fellow who runs this. Feels safer here." Nate saw the worn carpet as they entered the lobby. "Doesn't look like much, does it?"

Relief flowed through him when he spotted Monk sitting in the lobby reading a newspaper. Monk looked surprised when he saw Nate's traveling companions, but stood and walked across the lobby to meet them.

"He still here?" Nate asked looking around the reception area.

Monk nodded. "Has him a girl in his room."

"Where's the money?" Storm demanded.

"With him. Won't let it out of his sight." Monk looked at Storm and Drake, then back to Nate. Staring at the bruise on Nate's jaw, Monk asked, "Your escorts helpin' out?"

Nate shrugged. He wasn't sure how helpful Drake and Storm planned to be after he recovered the funds. "Sheriff deputized both of them in case it makes any difference with Hargrove or the local law."

Drake said, "Our badges have no jurisdiction here. Ben figured if there's any trouble, the association with the law would help clear us."

Monk's eyebrows raised. "That include Nate and me?"

"Reckon so." Drake nodded. "Leastwise, that's our plan."

Nate said, "Let's leave our bags and get on with it while Hargrove has his mind on other things."

After the three newcomers left their bags at the front desk, Drake asked, "You have a plan?"

"Yeah. Grab the money and hightail it out of here." Nate asked Monk, "You know how many exits this place has?"

Monk nodded. "Two, front door and through the kitchen to an alley for deliveries."

Nate nodded to Drake. "Monk and I will confront Hargrove and you and Storm cover the exits."

"Wait, I'm not leaving him alone with the money," Storm said and sent Nate another glare.

"With us at the only two exits that money's not going anywhere unless we let it," Drake told Storm.

Storm glared at Nate, apparently the only look he cared to share. "Well, I'm not letting you out of my sight."

"That's just the way I want it," Nate said. "You won't hesitate to stop Hargrove if it looks like that money's headed someplace other than where it belongs."

Monk raised a hand to stop the bickering and said, "I'll take the back."

"Hope Hargrove's had his money's worth from his doxie." Nate looked at Storm. "Let's get this over with."

Monk headed for the kitchen and Drake took a seat in the lobby with a view of the stairs. Nate and Storm headed up the steps and paused at Room 312 to draw their guns. Nate listened, heard muffled sounds from inside, then kicked in the door.

The woman riding Hargrove screamed and tumbled off, then leaped to her feet. She wore a fancy red corset, black garters, and black stockings. And nothing else. Her dress and petticoats hung over the back of a chair with Hargrove's coat. Brilliant red curls stuck out in disarray, and their glaring color didn't match the dark patch of hair clearly visible above her thighs.

Hargrove rolled off the rumpled bed and grabbed his

trousers from the bedpost. "What's this, a double cross?" he asked while he shoved his legs into his pants and covered his now drooping pecker. "Why'd you bring the injun with you?"

Nate kept the gun pointed at him. "We came to renegotiate our terms." He fished a few coins from his pocket and tossed them onto the bed. "Ma'am, take these and get your clothes on."

The woman snatched up the coins and grabbed her petticoats and dress. In a second she had them on, fastened, and the coins stuffed into her bodice. Her frightened gaze darted from Hargrove to the men with guns.

In spite of his shorter stature, Hargrove's stocky build hid powerful muscles. "So, you planned to cheat me all along?" Hargrove asked, pulling on his shirt and adjusting suspenders over it.

"No, I have some jewelry worth as much as your share would have been." From the corner of his eye, Nate caught the surprise in Storm's eyes before he continued, "You take the gems and get out and I'll take the money back to Kincaid Springs. Fork it over now."

"Like hell I will." Hargrove looked like a bulldog ready to fight. "You won't fob me off with some glass. That money is mine." He jerked the woman in front of him and pulled a knife from his pillow in one swift movement.

The knife tip touched the woman's throat and a drop of blood showed. "Both of you drop your guns and kick them over here or Amie dies."

The bastard would do it, Nate knew. He and Storm looked at one another, then dropped their guns and kicked them toward Hargrove. All the while, the woman called Amie made pitiful gurgling sounds and tears streamed down her face.

Hargrove looked at Storm. "Injun, you get the two valises from under the bed and set them over here by me."

Storm bent to retrieve the satchels from their hiding place. Nate waited for the instant Hargrove focused his eyes only

Storm. As Storm raised up, Nate grabbed Hargrove's arm and pulled it away from Amie's throat. Nate's grip forced Hargrove to drop the knife, but the brawny oaf shoved Amie at Nate. He stumbled and lost his purchase.

Storm reached for his gun but Hargrove kicked him in the chin and sent him reeling backward. Nate pushed Amie behind him and reached for the gun lying just beyond his fingertips. Hargrove intercepted him. They grappled and tripped over the ladder-back chair.

Amie wedged herself in the room's corner and slid down the wall behind her. She cowered there with her head pressed to her knees and her hands over her head, weeping copiously. Apparently, she thought if she folded herself into a small enough ball, she'd be overlooked and safe.

Storm saw Nate's predicament and tried to get around the struggling men to one of the guns on the floor. Hargrove managed to twist so that he kicked the guns. They skidded across the wooden floor toward Amie. Hargrove's coat that had hung across the fallen chair lay beside them, and he pulled a gun from the jacket pocket and pointed it at Nate, who released Hargrove and rolled away.

"You cheating bastards have had it now," Hargrove said and waved the gun. "Both of you get over there by the windows."

The men's labored breaths and Amie's soft whimpers suddenly filled the quiet room. She had made no attempt to slip out the door or grab one of the guns that had come to rest near the frills and folds of her dress.

Nate rose and fought the panic engulfing him. He knew if he and Storm moved as Hargrove demanded, the man would still need to kill them to have time and a clear path to gather the bags and exit the door. A guy as smart as Storm knew it, too.

"Listen, you two-bit lying cheat, Nate offered to let you leave alive with the jewelry," Storm snarled. "You try anything else, you won't be breathing when you leave this hotel."

"Oh, yeah? I'll show you! This is what I think of injuns, especially smart-assed rich ones." Hargrove pointed the gun at Storm's chest and cocked it.

"No!" Nate shouted and stepped in front of Storm.

TWENTY

The bullet drove into Nate's chest. At such short range the force threw him backward against Storm. They both fell to the floor. Hargrove reached for the cases, but pulled a gun from his boot. As Storm tried to rise he slipped on the folds of Amie's dress. He fired at Hargrove, but Storm's shot went wild as he fell back to the floor. Hargrove fired a wild shot as he yelled a curse and sprinted from the room in his stocking feet.

Nate struggled to his feet. Storm groaned and held his ankle. Nate called, "Get the bags and go down the back to meet Monk. I'll go after Hargrove."

Nate caught the gun Storm tossed him and followed Hargrove to the stairs. He stumbled down the steps. Breaths came in short, shallow gasps. His chest felt as if a train had hit him head on. If he had to climb up instead of descend, he didn't think he could make it and keep up with his quarry.

At the second floor landing, Hargrove turned to look over his shoulder. He spotted Nate, but Nate didn't stop. He couldn't fire because of people in the hall and on the stairs. Oblivious to the crowd, Hargrove fired. The shot whizzed past to thunk against a door. Frightened people screamed and scattered.

Hargrove fired again and the bullet struck the wall beside Nate. Splinters stung his face. Hargrove turned and bolted down the next staircase. Nate straggled behind, gasping for breath.

Nate saw Drake poised in position to intercept Hargrove. Before Drake could make a move, the two men from the train who had looked for Hargrove turned from the reception desk and walked to the bottom step. Hargrove stopped and raised his gun to fire. In unison, the two newcomers shot Hargrove before he got off his own round.

Hargrove fell forward and rolled down the remaining few steps. He came to rest in the lobby amid screams from a woman near the door. One man stepped forward and toed the body to test for life. Apparently satisfied, he backed away. Guns still drawn, the two men backed toward the entrance.

The second man called, "Nobody move. This is a family matter. Now it's settled, don't make us shoot anyone else."

They disappeared out the door and Nate heard horses' hooves pounding away. The whole incident lasted only seconds.

Drake rushed to Hargrove, and turned him over.

"You there," the hotel clerk called to a child peeking through the door, "get the sheriff."

"Should I go for the Doc?" a bystander asked.

Drake shook his head. "Too late for that. He's dead. Anyone know the two men who shot him?"

No one spoke up. Nate descended the stairs and looked down at the body. "It was the men from the train. Shot him and ran."

Drake nodded. "Had horses waiting out front. I couldn't get a shot at them without risking bystanders."

"Guess you'll have to talk to the sheriff," Nate said.

"Maybe." Drake said. "Where's Storm?" he muttered low.

Nate nodded at the dining room. "In back with Monk." He brushed wood needles from his cheek. His face still stung but he didn't think any splinters were embedded in his skin.

Drake pulled a handkerchief from his pocket and gave it to Nate. "You might want to cover up the hole in your jacket then see why you're not dead from the shot that made it."

Nate tucked the linen into his pocket and draped it over th

hole. It hurt like the devil, but he didn't feel blood running down his chest. Before he could check the severity of the wound, the sheriff entered the hotel. People stepped aside to allow the lawman access.

"What happened here?" he asked.

Several people started talking at once, so the sheriff held up his hand. "One at a time. You," he nodded at the desk clerk, "tell me what happened."

The clerk pointed at Hargrove's lifeless form. "This man, Mr. Hargrove, he was coming down the stairs and these two fellas was waiting here by the desk. They'd just asked his room number. Soon as they saw Mr. Hargrove, they pulled their guns and shot him. Didn't say nothing, just shot him."

"That it?" asked the sheriff.

The clerk nodded. "Well, after they killed him they said it was family business and we shouldn't make them shoot no one else. Then they ran out the door and rode off."

The sheriff stood and looked around at the crowd gathered. "Anyone else have anything to add?"

Nate noticed the clerk omitted mention of the shots Hargrove fired earlier, yet he had to have heard them. Others in the lobby must have also. No one else mentioned it either. People backed up and shook their heads. Probably things like this happened all too often in this seedy establishment.

Drake and Nate stood still. Nate's chest hurt so badly he could hardly breathe or stand. He composed his face and tried to look like an innocent bystander, mildly curious but uninvolved.

The sheriff asked for a blanket and covered the body. Drake and Nate moved to a front corner of the lobby, then slipped out the door and made their way around to the back of the hotel. Monk and Storm waited at the edge of the alley.

"You saved my life, stepping in front of me like that," Storm said. "He would have killed me for sure at that range. How bad did he get you?"

"Don't know." Nate could hardly breathe. His ribs felt

gripped in a vise. "Chest hurts like a sonofabitch. You have the money?" Now they were safe, the starch had left him.

"Here," Monk said and showed the two valises.

Nate put his hand inside his coat, but felt no wetness. When he looked, he found no red stain, no hole in his shirt. Patting gently where the bullet entered, he grinned.

"Well, I'll be damned." From his inside jacket pocket, he extracted the box Sarah had thrown at him.

The misshapen top of the case looked like a flower where it bulged up from the bullet's impact. Nate tried to open it, but couldn't. Storm took out a knife and pried up the lid.

Sapphires and diamonds twinkled up at them. The bullet missed the necklace and lay embedded in the open case between the earrings.

Storm turned the case over. A point protruded. "Bullet almost went through the case."

"I'll be damned," Drake echoed. "That saved your life."

"Sarah saved me, made me take it back," Nate gasped. "So I planned to use it to pay off Hargrove." He opened a few shirt buttons and checked his chest. A massive bruise already showed, huge and swollen with a center the size of the case.

Monk looked and shook his head. "Probably cracked your ribs. Lucky if they didn't puncture your lung."

Storm nodded to the jewels in his hand. "Those real?"

Nate nodded. "Sarah called them flashy and gaudy, and she's right. Worth a lot, though."

Monk said, "Cal won them off this wealthy financier. Said they were worth thousands and thousands."

"Where's the woman, that Amie?" Nate asked. All they needed was for her to start talking to the sheriff.

"Gave her twenty dollars and told her to forget all she saw and heard," Storm said. "She allowed as how she couldn't for get fast enough to suit her and took off down the alley."

"You look ready to pass out, Nate." Monk turned to Drake. "Reckon we could go somewhere and sit a spell while w talk?"

"Reckon so. Masterson, you have a room here?" Drake asked.

"Room 204, head of the stairs," Monk said. "But the name is Magonagle. Michael Magonagle. Folks call me Monk."

"I believe Nate mentioned as much." Drake turned to Nate and asked, "Can you make it up the steps to Monk's room?"

"Think so, if I can go slow," Nate said. "Wouldn't mind lying down a bit."

The men chuckled and Drake said, "Might as well go up there and wait. Three hours until the next train to Austin."

Now that Nate knew the money was safe and he wasn't dying, all he could think about was seeing Sarah again. Surely she would speak to him if he stayed in Kincaid Springs. How long could a woman stay mad? In Sarah's case, he figured it would be a long time. Now he had forever.

Sarah's ragged nerves neared a breakdown. She'd fretted over Nate, vacillated a dozen times on her actions should Nate dare return. Hating him for betraying her, she longed for him to return and hold her close in his strong embrace.

Once again she'd made it through her school day without losing control. She had to admit the children had an extra recess, but otherwise she'd shown no leniency to her mood. Better to stay busy and have less time to think about Nate. Now that they were home, Cindy and Luke played with Joe in his room and had no need of her for a while.

So far, no one had called at Grandpa's demanding his money back or decrying Nate for the crook she knew him to be. She decided a walk might calm her and set out to visit Belle Tremont. At least she could talk openly with her—unless Lex was there.

She passed two people who smiled broadly. Each man tipped his hat.

One said, "Afternoon, Miss Kincaid. Looking forward to seeing Barton again."

Puzzled, she only smiled and said good day. When she came up even with the law office, she slowed and couldn't resist looking in the window. Gabe saw her and motioned her in. She sighed as she opened the door to enter, wishing Nate were still at work in the office and not a criminal.

"Sarah, come in and sit a spell," Gabe invited with a wave of his hand at an empty armchair by the window.

He stopped his work and joined her in the matching chair separated by a little table. "I came to see you after work yesterday, but you were in your room."

She blushed, hating to admit she had shut out everyone but the children. Fiona had brought her meals to her, but she hadn't even spoken to Grandpa since Nate had left. Cowardly it might be, but her heart couldn't take more. Since her world had shattered around her, keeping up her front during the day at school and being cheerful for her children took all she had to offer until this mess settled one way or the other.

Gabe went on, "A curious thing happened yesterday when Ben and I were at Novak's Mecantile. Dorfmeyer came in with proof that Hargrove's a crook and is wanted in several places."

Sarah's agitation increased. She clasped her hands in her lap to keep from wringing them. "Oh, no. What did you do?"

Gabe held up his hand. "Don't upset yourself. Let me finish my story." He stretched his long legs in front of him and crossed them at the ankles. "Ben looked as nervous as I felt and I waited for him to say something. Then Marcus Novak spoke up about how Nate was working for the Pinkerton's."

Sarah stared incredulously. "But . . . But that's not true," she sputtered. "He told me himself he planned to cheat us and then had a change of heart." Nate's confession ended the dream world she had envisioned. She knew he would never have admitted his duplicity if it were not so.

"Marcus knew Nate received a couple of letters here from Pinkerton's, so he assumed Nate worked for them."

"What did you and Ben say?" She leaned forward, eager to hear Gabe's answer to her question.

"Ben admitted he brought a wire to Nate from Pinkerton's." Gabe pulled at his ear lobe and refused to look at her. "You know I hate lies worse than anyone, but, well, I kind of lied by omission. I admitted I'd seen Nate open a couple of letters from them here in the office."

"But that wire and one of the letters were about Joe."

He nodded. "That's right." He exhaled a huge sigh and sat upright. "Lord knows I hated not to confess that, but they need a little more time to get the money and get back here."

"So you protected them?" she asked, unable to prevent surprise creeping into her voice.

"Them, our family, Ben, even the townspeople. Why get everyone upset if it all works out without it?" He shrugged. "Besides, I have no idea what the last letter was about. He read it at his desk. That's when he asked me to meet him at Uncle Rob's in an hour, then he disappeared toward the hotel. Next time I saw him, he had an egg-sized lump on the back of his head and had asked Drake and Storm to meet him also."

"I, um, I didn't know about his head." Her fingers kneaded gathers in her skirt. "Well, you see, I was pretty upset."

He grinned at her. "I'll say. We heard you way down in Uncle Rob's study. Don't think I ever heard you raise your voice before."

She felt a blush flare again. "Anyway, what about Mr. Novak's story?"

"He's telling everyone in town how Nate and Masterson were agents sent to capture Hargrove and how Drake and Storm have gone to help since Hargrove knocked Nate out and got away."

More lies, she thought. What would it mean, though? All she could say was, "Oh."

"Yes, exactly. Now Nate's even more of a hero than after he rescued Joe."

She looked at him. "As long as he comes back with the money, that is."

"Well, yes," he admitted, then reached over and patted her arm. "Don't worry, Sarah. He and the money will be back."

"I hope you're right. Losing all that money would be horrid for folks. I'd pay them all I could, but I don't have near enough."

"What will you do about Nate when he comes back?"

She couldn't hide her surprise. "Are you so sure he'll return?"

"I am. I only worked with him a short while, I know, but I like him in spite of all that's happened. He's a hard worker and efficient. Helped me out a lot, I can tell you. I'll be glad to get him back."

Shock reeled through her. "You don't mean you'd let him work here after this? That Grandpa would let him?"

"Think about all he's done, Sarah. Saving Joe, staying instead of running, confessing to us, trying to make it right." He leaned forward, elbows on his knees, and met her gaze. "Think about the way you were before you met him."

Eyeing him suspiciously, she asked, "What do you mean?"

"Don't misunderstand. You were a jewel as bright as your lovely eyes. But you were a copy. Part Lily, part Pearl, part what you thought everyone wanted you to be. Always proper. Spoke only when spoken to, and then never more than necessary."

"But he—we—" she stopped and pressed her lips together. She felt a blush heat her face, horrified at having almost admitted what she and Nate had done, the lovemaking they shared.

Gabe held up his hand to stop her. "I don't want to know what went on between the two of you when you were alone. All I know is you've blossomed into a real person of your own. I like the new you." He grinned at her. "Even when you yell."

Sarah forced a smile. "I'll try to yell more." She rose and told him good-bye.

No longer intent on talking to Belle, Sarah turned back toward Grandpa's. Mulling over Gabe's remarks, she realized she had never heard him make personal comments to anyone. His feelings about Nate's dependability and her happiness must run deep for him to discuss them with her.

She knew he'd had unhappiness in his life and came to Kincaid Springs from Austin because of it, but she didn't know the details. From overheard conversation, she knew it had something to do with cheating by his intended and that he hated lies of any sort. Yet he lied by omission for Nate.

What would she do to retain Nate's presence in town? A hard question, and she feared the answer.

She realized she loved Nate more than life itself. In his way, she believed he returned her love. He loved her three children, of that she was sure, and they returned his love.

When she first met him, she thought him a wolf in sheep's clothing. Now she knew the opposite was true. Nate Barton, no, Nate Bartholomew, was a sheep in wolf's clothing. He might fight it, but he had good instincts. Hadn't he helped all the children, saved Joe, helped Gabe and Grandpa? Helped her?

She remembered the stack of letters she'd saved from her mother. Hating Mama's business so much, she'd read only the parts about Mama herself, scanning or skipping the other sections of the letters. Suddenly she could hardly wait to retrieve them from the ranch and reread them to see what Mama had said about Nate.

The train pulled into the depot at Kincaid Springs on Friday morning. At their layover in Austin, Drake had wired the Judge their arrival date and success. Nate had sold the jewels while they waited in Austin. He'd received even more than he'd dreamed. Not only that, he coerced Monk to agree they would use it to open a business in Kincaid Springs that Monk could run while Nate worked with Gabe.

After they replaced what Hargrove had spent, they had enough for a good start in Kincaid Springs. If they were allowed to remain, that is, and not be hauled off to jail the minute they stepped off the train. Nate saw the crowd waiting on the platform and figured he and Monk were in big trouble.

He muttered to Monk, "Looks like the whole damn town turned out in anticipation of an event. Like lynching, maybe."

Drake peered out the window, "Never heard of a brass band at a hanging."

They stepped off the coach, Nate lagging behind. Tape bound his chest, restricted his breathing, limited his movement. And his ribs hurt like hell.

The band struck up a barely recognizable rendition of "When Johnny Comes Marching Home Again" while folks cheered. Excited well-wishers pressed in on all sides asking about Pinkerton's agents and how Nate and Monk had recovered the money. Before any of the four men could respond, the Judge stepped forward.

To the four who'd returned, the Judge muttered, "Don't say anything. Just smile and nod. Fill you in later."

He turned to the crowd and held up his hands, "Now folks, these men have had a hard trip. Give them a chance to rest up a bit. We'll have a big meeting tonight at the schoolhouse with refreshments. All those who invested, bring your certificates to get back your money."

Puzzled, Nate searched the crowd for Sarah. He wondered if she'd gone to her school or still had no desire to see him again—or both. Gabe waved from the crowd, but no Sarah.

"Grandpa, can we put this in your safe until tonight?" Drake asked and held up one of the satchels of money. Storm carried the other.

"Sure thing," the Judge said and led the way.

As the townspeople dispersed, Nate stopped the other four men. Gabe ambled over to join them.

"Reckon I'll go on to the hotel with Monk," Nate said. "We'll show up at six at the school to get ready."

Drake nodded, "We'll bring the money."

Nate asked, "Think you and Storm could hang around in case anyone else in town decides Grandpa's place would be easy pickings?"

"You don't sound very trusting, Nate," Storm said. His eyes had regained their mischievous sparkle, though he'd still vowed to pummel Nate into the ground if he found Nate had messed around with Sarah.

Nate replied, "Heard there were crooks hereabouts." He and Monk turned toward the hotel.

"I'm supposed to fill you both in on an odd development," Gabe said as he joined them. "Let's stop by the office so we can talk in private before you go anywhere else."

Sarah's stomach fluttered as if a flock of butterflies darted inside her. Her finger traced the bow on a ribbon-tied stack of Mama's letters. How could she have been so unfeeling as to skip part of them when she received each one? What a prissy snob she'd been.

Now she knew how much Mama had cared for Nate, how the man Sarah now knew to be Monk had helped her mama in lots of little ways. Bound by her desperate search for propriety, Sarah had overlooked much of the good in Mama's life.

She heard the creak of Joe's wheelchair before he got to her bedroom door.

"You still mad at Nate?" he asked. Luke and Cindy stood behind him.

"Yes, but not as much." What would she say to him, she wondered. She'd hurried home from school and learned that he went to the hotel instead of returning to Grandpa's. What did that mean? Did he hate her for the cruel things she'd said?

"Reckon he'll stay here and be part of our family?" Luke asked.

Evading a direct answer, she said, "We don't know he's ever wanted to."

Joe nodded and said, "Yes, he told me he wants to 'cause he loves us. He said he'd done some bad things and couldn't be in our family, but he wished he could."

Her heart skipped a beat. "When did he say that?"

"Lots of times," Joe said. He looked at the ceiling and counted on his fingers. "When I got scared about the letter and tried to run away, that time I had nightmares and got under the bed, then when we were in the cave. Oh, and just before he left to go after that mean man who stole the money."

"He—he said he loves us? All of us?" She held her breath until Joe answered.

He nodded. "Yes. And he likes livin' here, too. Why can't he stay? I don't care what he did before. He can't be as bad as he said. He saved me and I love him." Joe looked near tears.

"Yeah, why can't he stay?" Cindy said, her lower lip forming a pout. "I love him and want him to be my new papa."

"Me, too," Luke agreed. He put his arm around Cindy.

"You three be good while I go to the meeting. Maybe I'll find the answers to all your questions while I'm there."

She kissed each of them and hurried down the stairs to join Grandpa and Fiona for the walk to the meeting. Neither the cool air nor the stroll soothed her quaking emotions.

Grandpa reached for Fiona's hand and gave it a squeeze. Fiona pretended to be offended and snatched her hand away, but she flashed a smile meant only for Grandpa. Sarah decided things must be moving along there as she had hoped. She and her companions joined the crowd descending on the school.

Once again Kincaid Springs' citizens packed the build

ing and no vacant seats remained. She and Fiona jammed together against the wall. A couple of men on the back row responded to Grandpa's glare and gave up their seats to the women.

Fiona leaned toward her. "I can't see a thing, dearie, not even the refreshment table. Are my cinnamon oatmeal cookies set out? They're Himself's favorites, you know."

Sarah craned her neck this way and that. "Can't tell. There are too many people milling about."

She heard rapping and the room stilled. Now she saw Nate and Monk at the front. Monk sat at the teacher's desk with a ledger and an open satchel while Nate stood beside him. Drake and Storm stood nearby looking as if they dared anyone to make a grab for the money.

"Folks, if you'll give us your attention, we'll get this over with as soon as possible."

He stepped to the front of the desk and looked around the room. "Many of you have come to know me, but as Nate Barton. My real name is Nathaniel Bartholomew, and my friend here is Michael Magonagle, also known as Monk. We're sorry for our part in the deception, but the money has been recovered."

Sarah held her breath, but no one questioned what part they played in the deception. Apparently everyone believed they had merely acted a part as agents for Pinkerton's.

"If you'll present your certificates to Mr. Magonagle, he will refund your money in full. Don't worry, each of you will receive all the money you invested."

He motioned to his left. "Form a line here. After that, or while you're waiting for the line to thin out, you're invited to sample the delicious refreshments supplied by Mrs. Kincaid, Mrs. Kline, and Mrs. Galloway."

He gestured to a table laden with a large container of lemonade, cups, and platters heaped with cookies and small tarts. Pearl and Rhoda Kline stood behind the table ready to serve goodies to everyone.

Several of those standing at the side pushed forward to be first in line at the desk or the table. Peter Dorfmeyer stood from his seat near the front.

"What happened to Hargrove?" he asked.

"Mr. Hargrove was killed attempting an escape," Nate answered without elaborating.

Gasps rippled through the crowd.

Storm stepped forward and held up his hands. "Before he died, Hargrove tried to shoot me in the chest at close range. I surely would have died if Nate hadn't stepped in front of me and taken the bullet. He saved my life with no thought of his own."

A din of comments and more gasps broke out.

Sarah pressed a hand to her mouth. The room spun around her and she slid to the floor.

When she came to, Pearl bent over her as Sarah half lay in Fiona's lap. Nate knelt beside her, holding her hand in both of his. A sea of faces peered around them.

"Are you all right?" Nate asked.

She tried to speak but could only nod, tears threatening to overflow.

Pearl stood, "She'll be fine, folks." She motioned people aside. "She just needs some air. Please help yourself to refreshments and wait for your turn in line with Mr. Magonagle."

People stepped back a little, but still loitered close, staring at Sarah and Nate.

"Sarah, are you still not speaking to me?" Nate asked.

"You . . . You almost died. You and Storm. You stepped in front of him." She touched his chest. "You must have been shot."

"I'll tell you about it later, if you'll let me." For the first time since they'd met, he looked unsure of himself. But definitely alive for her to claim.

"You'd better tell me lots more," she said, struggling to her feet.

He helped her stand and kept a protective hand on her arm. "What do you mean?" he asked.

"Do you plan to stay in Kincaid Springs?"

"Maybe," he said. "I guess that's up to you."

She put her hands on her hips and glared at him. "I'd say you darned well better." She realized people stared, but it seemed unimportant. Only Nate mattered.

"Sarah—" he started.

Before her head could stop her, her heart made her say, "And you'd better ask me to marry you while you're at it."

"Sarah—"

She stepped closer, confronting him. "Did you or did you not tell Joe you love me?"

He nodded, and opened his mouth, but she cut him off.

"Why didn't you ever tell me?" she demanded.

"Maybe if you'd be quiet, he would," Pearl said.

Nate smiled at Pearl. "Thank you, Pearl." He took Sarah's hands in his. "I love you more than life itself. Will you marry me and let me live with you and our children here in Kincaid Springs?"

"Oh, Nate, I thought I'd never hear you say those words." She sniffed at the happy tears pooling in her eyes and clogging her throat. "Of course I'll marry you."

A loud cheer echoed through the room as he gathered her into his embrace. She leaned near his ear to whisper only for him, "The sooner, the better, Papa."

A riot of colorful flowers bloomed in Grandpa's garden this fine June day. Not a cloud dared show itself in the bright blue sky, and a soft breeze cooled the rays of the sun. Rows of folding chairs lined the lawn facing a white awning. Reverend Potter from the Presbyterian church that Grandpa attended and Father Ignacio from the Catholic mission where Fiona attended mass waited there to perform an unusual joint wedding ceremony. Grandpa and Drake stepped under the awning and faced the crowd. The piano had been moved to the terrace for the occasion, and Belle struck up the wedding march while Lex beamed at her.

Cousins Cindy, Katie, Rosie, and Beth looked like angelic confections in their frilly pink dresses and matching little hats. They strolled down the aisle tossing flower petals when they remembered, and waving at family and friends when they didn't. The boys had begged their mothers not to make them participate in sissy stuff, and they sat with family members.

Dressed in an adult version of the girls' dresses, Sarah walked behind them. Pleasure coiled through her with memories of her own wedding to Nate only three months ago in the Presbyterian church. Even more people attended that ceremony than were here today.

Her stomach fluttered with a new feeling. Only yesterday her babe quickened within her, and now she felt the movement again. Across the crowd her gaze met Nate's and she smiled. As if he understood, he returned her smile, pride glowing in his wonderful wolf's eyes. She hoped that from some corner in heaven her mama looked down and saw their happiness.

Behind her Fiona strolled in time to the music. Wearing tailored blue linen, she had looked perfect when Sarah helped her dress earlier. Sarah stepped aside and took Fiona's bouquet. Grandpa took Fiona's hand and the ceremony uniting them in marriage began.

From her place under the awning, Sarah looked across the crowd. Beside Joe, Monk appeared somewhat bedazzled by his new family. To her surprise, Monk and Nate had partnered with Grandpa and bought the bank. She smiled, remembering Peter's quick departure when he learned Monk was his new boss.

As the new partner in Kincaid, Kincaid, and Bartholomew Nate worked daily with Gabe. And as a hero twice over, Nate commanded the respect of the townspeople. He'd added hi name with hers to the adoption of their three children, who now officially shared the name Bartholomew.

Sarah's hand rested on her daughter's shoulder, and her gaze once again met Nate's. Seated between their sons, he looked even more handsome now than the first time she'd seen him in St. Louis. She knew he returned her love, and shared her joy in their growing family. As Reverend Potter spoke of love eternal, Sarah pondered the love reflected in Nate's eyes and gathered it into her heart.

Jo's Applesauce Cake

Josephine Jorgensen was Sarah Kincaid's grandmother

2 cups flour, sifted
1 teaspoon soda
1 teaspoon ground cloves
$^1/_2$ teaspoon ground nutmeg
$^1/_2$ cup butter (or shortening)
2 large eggs
1 cup sugar
2 $^1/_2$ cups applesauce
$^3/_4$ cup raisins (or chopped dates)
1 cup broken nuts (Sarah used Texas pecans)

Sift dry ingredients together and set aside. In large bowl mix butter, sugar, eggs and beat well until fluffy. Scrape bowl while mixing. Add applesauce, raisins, and nuts and mix well. Add dry ingredients and beat slowly until batter is mixed very well and there are no dry spots. Pour into a greased and floured tube pan and bake in a medium oven (350 degrees Farenheit) for 45 minutes. Let cool in pan. When cool, serve or frost with Caramel Frosting.

Rochelle's Caramel Frosting

Sarah's mother used this frosting for her applesauce cakes after someone who'd once worked in a Denver confectioner's taught her how to make caramel

2 cups sugar
1 cup cream
$1/4$ cup butter
1 teaspoon vanilla extract

Put 1 cup of the sugar into a heavy skillet and let it caramelize slowly, stirring often, being careful not to let it burn. Set aside. Into saucepan put cream and remaining 1 cup sugar and let come to a slow boil. Gradually add the caramelized sugar into this and cook to a soft ball stage. Remove from heat and add butter and vanilla. Beat to desired consistency and spread on the cake.

ABOUT THE AUTHOR

Caroline Clemmons is a city girl turned country girl. After moves from Southern California to a series of small towns across West Texas, her family settled in Lubbock. A fourth grade teacher opened her world to the joy of reading. An eighth grade journalism teacher encouraged her to transfer her dreams and ideas onto paper. In addition to being mom to two daughters, Caroline has worked as a newspaper reporter and featured columnist, assistant to the managing editor of a psychology journal, and bookkeeper. Caroline and her husband are living happily ever after on a small acreage in Parker County, Texas. She loves to hear from readers at *www.carolineclemmons.com*.